EARLY JOYS

EARLY JOYS

BY

Konstantin Fedin

TRANSLATED FROM THE RUSSIAN BY
Mrs. G. Kazanina

WITH AN INTRODUCTION BY
Ernest J. Simmons

New York

VINTAGE BOOKS

A DIVISION OF RANDOM HOUSE

VINTAGE BOOKS

are published by Alfred A. Knopf, Inc.
and Random House, Inc.

FIRST VINTAGE EDITION

Originally published in English by Foreign Languages Publishing House, Moscow, in 1950.

Nina Fedina

naturalism vs reality
(imagination in
conjunction with reality)

INTRODUCTION

DURING the "thaw" that followed Stalin's death in March 1953, many Soviet writers looked back with nostalgia to the early days of the Revolution when a literature developed that faithfully reflected the tragic turmoil of class struggle and the shattering social changes in Russian life. In those early years writers listened to the music of the Revolution and felt free to express its fierce tempo in poetry, fiction, and drama filled with a fury of blatant experimentation in form and content. The Communist Party, however, soon recognized the importance of literature as a propaganda instrument, and by the time of the enforced formation of the single Union of Soviet Writers in 1934, the exciting early period of revolutionary experimentation had been brought to an end, and literature was compelled to submit to rigid Party controls.

Many of these early writers who sought to express their reactions to the revolutionary present in a spirit of free and untrammeled creativity have vanished from the scene. Some of the best of them, like Blok, Yesenin, Gumilov, Mayakovsky, Zamyatin, Bulgakov, and Pilnyak, were victims of either premature death, suicide, imprisonment, exile, or political execution. Of those still living, Konstantin Fedin, Leonid Leonov, and Mikhail Sholokhov are among the most notable, three novelists who—as I have said elsewhere*—bear a curious resemblance respectively to Steinbeck, Faulk-

* "Prefatory Note," *Russian Fiction and Soviet Ideology. Introduction to Fedin, Leonov, and Sholokhov*, Columbia University Press, New York; 1958.

ner, and Hemingway in their relative reputations in their own country and in the strikingly contrasting artistic flavor of their works. The theme that concerned them most, especially in their early tales and novels, was the tragic struggle between the old and the new, the desperate choice that confronted men and women compelled by the Revolution to renounce a past life that often seemed dear to them and adjust to a new existence that aroused their doubts and fears.

Of these three writers, Fedin is the oldest, having been born in the Volga town of Saratov in 1892, and perhaps by virtue of this fact his creative roots are deeply imbedded in the prerevolutionary past and watered by the wellsprings of Russian nineteenth-century fiction. After a rather unhappy childhood in a lower middle-class family and education in the Moscow Commercial Institute, Fedin went to Germany to perfect his knowledge of the language. There he was caught by the First World War and interned as an enemy alien. The rich experiences and impressions of his four years in Germany contributed importantly to his later writing. Upon his return to Russia in 1918, he found a chaotic world of revolutionary enthusiasm and changed values. A glorious new dawn for Russia seemed imminent, and like so many of the young intellectuals of that time, Fedin plunged into the building of this new life with zeal. For a time he worked in the Commissariat of Education, joined the Communist Party, and was assigned to a multiplicity of tasks in the Volga town of Syzran. When the Yudenich offensive began in 1919, he was mobilized into the Red Army and served in its political section as assistant to the editor of a military newspaper.

Though Fedin proved to be adept at journalism, he had also been nurturing an ambition to be a literary artist ever since the publication of his first youthful efforts in 1913. Accordingly, when he arrived at Leningrad at the end of the civil war, he hopefully sent a short story to Gorky for his criticism, a contact that began a long and valuable literary friendship. In fact, Gorky introduced him, in 1921, to the "Serapion Brothers," a brilliant group of young Leningrad writers who were determined to translate revolution-

ary enthusiasm into an artistic faith free from Bolshevik
banality. They demanded freedom from all regimenta-
tion, scorned political unanimity, and found their
inspiration in Russian and Western European literature
of the past. Under the influence of this brotherhood of
bright spirits, Fedin brought out his first volume of
short stories, *The Wasteland* (1923). With one exception, the tales in this collection represent an escape
into the world of lonely, little people, the world of
the tales of Dostoevsky and Chekhov. Fedin's genuine compassion for their patient suffering, however,
is often lost in his varied patterns of self-conscious
experimentation in style. Party critics expressed amazement that a Soviet author, at a historic moment of
revolutionary upheaval, should be concerned with the
individual experiences of petty people in the Russian
past. But by the time Fedin had published *The Wasteland*, he had dropped his membership in the Communist Party.

Fedin's first novel, *Cities and Years* (1924), was an
ambitious attempt to dignify the tragedy of indi-
vidualism in an epoch of revolt, in which is revealed
a great deal of the author's personal philosophy at
that time. His elaborate symphonic structure of war
and revolution in several German and Russian cities
between 1914 and 1922 tends to subordinate plot and
characters to an extensive preoccupation with social,
political, and cultural material. The events which influence the cities and their inhabitants provide a key
to an understanding of the actions and individual psychology of the leading characters, and especially of
the hero, Andrei Startsov, a sensitive, idealistic young
Russian, a hater of violence, whose deep admiration
of Western art and culture, developed during his
lengthy stay in Germany, leaves him ill-equipped to
face the cruel realities of his own country when he
returns there. Like many intellectuals in the early
years of the Revolution, Andrei Startsov longed to
embrace the utopian ideals of the movement but rejected the bloody struggle carried on in their name.
He is one of Turgenev's "superfluous men" in a time
of action, unable to realize that there was no longer
any question of acceptance or nonacceptance of the
Revolution. In every sense he is a victim of the strug-

gle between the old and the new; his failure to understand that the debate had ended, results in his execution by his former close German friend, Kurt Wahn, who has become a fanatical Communist. There is not a little autobiography in the characterization of Andrei Startsov, and in killing his hero, Fedin seemed symbolically to announce the death of an outmoded aspect of his own personality.

Yet Fedin returned to the struggle between the old and the new in his next novel, *The Brothers* (1928), when he again draws upon his own biography. Though the central figure, Nikita Karev, a promising composer, spends his formative years, like Andrei Startsov, in Germany, and as an artist and an individualist dislikes politics and loathes violence, in the end he is not destroyed by the Revolution but learns to assimilate the old and the new through the medium of his music. Throughout the novel, however, Fedin seems unable to surrender his own individuality to the Soviet pattern of life. For the most effective depictions are those of the early, prerevolutionary existence of the Karev family and the merchant Sherstobitov, and of Nikita's prewar experiences in Dresden. In fact, an aura of nineteenth-century Russian realistic fiction clings to the work and becomes clearly identifiable in such Dostoevskian emanations as the "infernal woman" Varvara and the Smerdyakov-like Vitka, the family servitor.

After finishing *The Brothers*, Fedin spent the larger part of the next seven years (1928–34) traveling in Western Europe, and the impact of this experience on the development of his creative art, as well as on his hesitant political and social views, soon became apparent in his fiction. For one thing, his first-hand observations of the depression years in the West inspired the theme of his next novel, a huge, two-volume work, *The Rape of Europe* (1934–5). His intention was to compare, through the activities of a large group of characters, the deteriorating social and economic life of the West with the full employment and economic upsurge that resulted from the first two Five Year Plans in the Soviet Union. The Dutch family of Van Rossums, importers of lumber, operators of ocean transportation, and owners of a large timber concession in Russia, and their various wealthy connections, stand as the symbols of the material and spiritual decline of the West.

In the first volume of *The Rape of Europe* Fedin's satire and irony were never more effective than in his handling of the big scenes and situations of European life and in the creation of a number of memorable characterizations, such as Philip van Rossum and Klavdia, the beautiful Russian wife of his nephew. Though a Soviet emphasis is apparent in these contrasting scenes drawn from the life of the European rich and poor during the depression years, the total effect is not one of hopelessly biased propaganda. However, when the scene shifts to Russia in the second volume, the answer of Soviet socialism to the economic defeatism of Western capitalism is unconvincing both as a rationale and as an artistically embodied contrast of both ways of life. Somehow Fedin failed to grasp with imaginative power and artistic authenticity the transformed Soviet mentality of Five-Year-Planism, as though he himself were not entirely convinced of either its aims or its necessity. And particularly Ivan Rogov, the socialist ideological opponent of the cynical self-interest of Western capitalism, is hardly the captivating image of the new Soviet intellectual which Fedin obviously intended him to be.

After his return to Russia, the unusual fascination the West had for Fedin as subject matter for fiction reasserted itself in a short novel, *Arctur Sanatorium* (1940), the scene of which is located in the Swiss mountain valley of Davos, where he had gone for treatment of a severe tuberculous condition. It is an interesting psychological study of illness with several brilliant characterizations portrayed with mingled pathos and humor. In certain respects the work may be regarded as a polemical answer to Thomas Mann's *The Magic Mountain* with its emphasis on the tragic helplessness of man before the cruel and blind laws of biology.

The war years and those that immediately followed were among Fedin's most productive, a period in which he achieved full maturity as a writer and resolved certain artistic and ideological problems that had been troubling him since the beginning of his career. He spent much time at the front as a reporter, and witnessed the frightful carnage and destruction visited upon his native land by the invading Germans. The war exercised a powerful influence on him, as it did on a number of distinguished Soviet writers, and a feeling of deep patriotism and new convictions about the purpose and ultimate destiny of the Soviet regime grew out of these harrowing experiences. In this new spirit of acceptance of the order of things, Fedin conceived his masterpiece, a work that won him a First Stalin Prize.

Shortly after the appearance of *The Rape of Europe*, Fedin pointed out in a critical article what he believed was the central weakness of that novel—his inability to create a Soviet hero who would stand as an effective "counterbalance" to the thoroughly believable Philip van Rossum. He concluded: ". . . the creation of a Soviet hero, bearing, so to speak, an 'individual' impress, the impress of his Western European antipode, is still the problem of our literature." In his masterpiece Fedin set out to create such a Soviet hero, and in an autobiographical account in the 1952 edition of his writings, he tells us of the inception and purpose of the work:

> During the war years I began to work on a trilogy long since contemplated, and in the course of 1943–48 I completed two parts of it, *Early Joys* and *No Ordinary Summer*. My turning to pure Russian material—for all my previous novels had been more or less linked with the theme of the West—was not only dictated by a powerful desire, but it was also an expression of my search for a great contemporary hero. In those years when the fate of our country was being decided in the Great Fatherland War, the conviction had grown much more strong than formerly that the future of Russian life was inseparably joined with the Soviet regime, and that a truly great hero of contemporary times must and should be a Communist whose active will was synonymous with Victory. I have attempted to make the principal character of these two novels such a hero, show-

ing his development in prerevolutionary Russia and during the civil war.

Kirill Izvekov is the Communist hero of the trilogy, the first volume of which, *Early Joys*, began to appear serially in 1945. Its action is centered in Saratov, Fedin's own native city, during the peaceful year 1910, and the other two parts of the trilogy, designed as separate novels linked by leading characters and an inner unity of theme, will concentrate on the years 1919 and 1941. It is perhaps significant that Fedin identifies the formative years of his "great contemporary hero" with the Russian past when political idealism was ennobled by the simple virtues of sincerity and integrity. For these are the virtues of young Kirill Izvekov when he begins his revolutionary education as a future Bolshevik leader in the historic year 1910.

The love of Kirill and Lisa Meshkova—and hardly anywhere else in Soviet fiction has young love been treated with such charm and psychological insight— is quickly enmeshed in the web of political conspiracy. This is the novel's central action that touches the lives of nearly all the characters, who appear to have been selected by Fedin to represent a cross section of the social stratification of Saratov. The artistic and intellectual aspects are mainly represented by the cold, calculating, and witty playwright Pastukhov and his foil, the generous, ebullient actor Tsvetukhin. Through this pair Fedin returns to a discussion of art which had concerned him deeply in his earlier fiction, especially in *Cities and Years* and *The Brothers*. Pastukhov ridicules Tsvetukhin's conviction that art is an imitation of nature, for this ends in the blind alley of naturalism. For Pastukhov the creative instinct manifests itself independently of the artist's will, which can submit neither to man-made rules nor to political necessity. The life of the imagination, he insists, is the primary function of the creative mind. Tolstoy is his literary and intellectual idol, and the death of the great writer in 1910 seems to be the only event capable of arousing the dormant social consciousness of Pastukhov. In this absorbing characterization, in part possibly an intellectual self-portrait of the author, Fedin no doubt intends, in the later parts of his trilogy, to work out the important theme of ideological opposition to communism in the course of which Pastukhov will eventually find his way to a sincere acceptance of the Soviet regime.

Tsarist officialdom is another stratum of Saratov society vividly revealed in the novel. Both irony and humor are manifested in the activities of the town prosecutor Polotensev and his minions such as Oznobishin when the revolutionary conspiracy, headed by the worker Ragozin, is discovered. Fedin imparts an intense detective story element to this section of the novel, but at the same time he brings out that measure of human cruelty among the examining officers of the tsar's secret police which only served to cement the revolutionary brotherhood of those days.

Nearly all the principal characters, including that wonderful creation Parabukin, are swept into the police net and grilled. The Marmeladovs in *Crime and Punishment* seem to have suggested the representatives of the lower stratum of Saratov society, the Parabukin family—the shiftless, chronically drunk giant of a father; his compulsively chattering drudge of a wife, Olga; the baby, Pavlik; and that preternaturally wise little daughter, Annochka, who is obviously destined for an important role in the continuation of the novel. The possible nature of her future role is suggested in the fascinating scene where she steals into the empty playhouse to watch a rehearsal. A vague yearning to identify herself with the make-believe world of the theater as much as a desire to escape from her own world of drab reality motivates this escapade of little Annochka.

The early development of the personality of Kirill Izvekov, however, is the main concern of the novelist. The steel of the young conspirator's nature is first tempered by his arrest when revolutionary idealism and harsh reality collide. But this experience matures without embittering him. He evinces an independence of his mentor, Ragozin, and one observes that his dawning political quest is focused in an emergent philosophy that compels him to probe his relations to society in terms of the progressive movement of the time. Even his love for the charming Lisa takes on a more mature and manly aspect in the midst of his tribulations. Her freedom and independence, he writes Lisa from his place of exile in the north, are more precious to him than anything, and hence he will try to understand if she elects to give her affection to another, although he cannot refrain from expressing the hope that they will one day be together again. Lisa, however, lacked his fortitude and did not share his political vision. Though her love for Kirill remained constant, her sense of duty to the will of her parents soon led her to succumb to the dogged insistence of her rigidly righteous father that she marry Shubnikov, the spoiled and foppish nephew of a rich merchant woman. It is the intellectual Pastukhov, incapable of positive, heroic action, who begrudgingly senses the real potential of Kirill Izvekov. In a patent allusion to him in commenting to Tsvetukhin on their idle life, Pastukhov remarks: "And somewhere, hard by, someone is forging our future for us, and, through the wild untrodden woods, torn and bleeding, pushes on toward the goal. . . . I mean some good-for-nothing boy." Even in this necessarily adumbrated characterization of Kirill Izvekov, one suspects that Fedin is on the way to creating what he had failed to achieve in all his previous novels—a convincing positive Soviet hero whose purely human qualities and failings will set him apart from the dreary, gray parade of two-dimensional stereotypes of Party perfection.

Apart from its absorbing characters and effective action, *Early Joys* is full of the sights and sounds of the streets, the docks, the Volga, and the social existence of Saratov. Brightly constructed genre pictures —the picnic, the colorful carnival, the hauling and singing of the picturesque stevedores, scenes in the flophouse, the raid at Ragozin's, and the charity ball —suggest impending change and at the same time advance the action and illuminate the manners and customs of the town's social strata. Fedin now exhibits a consummate control over all the surface features of fiction, and to the philosophical discussions of art, history, and morality he brings learning, wisdom, and a degree of detachment rarely found in Soviet fiction. Further, in *Early Joys*, Fedin reasserts that special

AUTHOR'S PREFACE

THE UNITY which I strove to achieve while working on the novels *Early Joys* and *No Ordinary Summer* comprises the most diverse phenomena.

The novels contain over thirty characters, not to mention incidental personages. Perhaps not all of the thirty exert great influence on the development of the action as a whole, but all of them are essential to the separate scenes from which I hoped to build a general picture of the epoch.

I chose two periods sharply contrasted in morals, in the tempo of living, in the nature and significance of historical events. The first was 1910, a period of reaction in prewar tsarist Russia (*Early Joys*); the second was 1919, when the civil war was at its height and the revolution entrenched itself by conquering the White armies of Denikin and the interventionists headed by the French and the English (*No Ordinary Summer*).

Through the lives of individuals I have tried to portray two worlds: dying tsarist Russia and the rising Land of the Soviets, whose new and unprecedented social system vanquished the old.

The historical theme determined the role played by each of the characters and which of them should hold the center of the stage at any given moment. The historical theme further decided the question as to which of these two novels should predominate in the mind of the reader. *No Ordinary Summer* surpasses *Early Joys* both in depth and sweep.

In the first book, a picture of the morals and daily life of old Russia is presented against a background of provincial life which in almost every aspect is stultified by the century-old traditions of *petit bourgeois* society, with gendarmes and state officials jealously guarding tsarist laws. The life of provincial intellectuals is taken up by lazy dreaming, and obscure though pretentious discussions having little to do with the struggle to improve the life of the masses. But this struggle was being waged. It was being waged deep down under the surface, hidden from sight. It banked on the future. It prepared the way for the coming fight for the happiness of the laboring man.

In conceiving the canvas as a whole, I naturally conceded a relatively small place to the underground revolutionaries in tsarist Russia. The supremacy of the reactionary forces was almost complete at that time, and Russia's finest people either perished or were forced to conceal their activities. But two characters of the first novel introduce the reader to those forces which later were to play the leading role in history. One of these characters is the metalworker Pyotr Ragozin, who participated in the revolution of 1905 and served a term of exile. The other is the young boy Kirill Izvekov, son of a schoolteacher. It is he who represents the revolutionary thinking of the most progressive people, and it is he who embodies the basic idea of the entire literary work.

Then came another historical period. The October Revolution broke the chains binding the workers and peasants of Russia, and the revolutionaries moved up into the front ranks of history.

The novel *No Ordinary Summer* explains many details from the biographies of the main characters of *Early Joys* and further develops situations which could not have been fully unfolded in the first novel without violating the exactness of the perspective. In the second book I introduce a new character in the person of Dorogomilov, whose purpose it is to show the reader in retrospect the path trod by Ragozin in tsarist times and to show the sweep of the underground work carried on by that professional revolutionary—in a word, to reveal what earlier was hidden from the eye.

The old world was shaken to its foundations by the Great October Socialist Revolution. It was my desire to show the tremendousness of this historical event through the psychological changes it wrought in all my characters, both great and small. The same social circles which figured in the first novel are met with in *No Ordinary Summer*, but under entirely different circumstances.

It is as though the characters have changed places: those who were brought to trial by the tsarist court now bring to trial the enemies of the new life. Court officials of the old regime hide from the vengeance of the people; gendarmes seek refuge in dark corners; merchants try to hoard remnants of their former wealth; the *petite bourgeoisie* submit to the inevitable. Some people join the Red forces as a matter of principle, others out of fear. Some are overjoyed by the victories of the revolution, others tremble before them. And above the din and strife can be heard the firm, confident, powerful step of the victors—the armed workers and peasants of Soviet Russia with the Bolsheviks in the vanguard.

Of the various characters in this novel, through whose lives I have tried to draw a general picture of the year 1919, first place is accorded to the builders of the future, the creators of socialism and communism. The fact that the Communist Party played the main role in defeating counterrevolution is a great historical truth. It is in the light of this truth that the characters are depicted during those most difficult days of civil war. This historical truth tells us of the inestimable service to the people rendered by the heroes of that time, of the decisive importance of the Stalin plan for defeating Denikin, and of the great masterbuilder of our victory—Joseph Vissarionovich Stalin.

It is through Izvekov and Ragozin that the main theme is presented—the theme of history, the theme of the future which has become the present. But they are not alone in giving expression to the central idea of this work. It is likewise expressed by Annochka, whose love for Kirill leads her to join her life with his; it is expressed by Dibich, the former tsarist officer, who later contributed all of his knowledge and ability to the cause of the Red Army; it is expressed by Dorogomilov, and by the soldier Ipatiev, and the sailor

Strashnov. But perhaps it is expressed to an even greater extent by the youngest characters of *No Ordinary Summer*—the children to whose portrayal I devoted much love and effort.

In attempting to create a unity out of the innumerable phenomena comprising an epoch so great and so significant for the future of our Soviet Land, I drew my aim and my inspiration from the fulness of life itself, with its infinite diversity, its contradictions, its clash of emotions, its joy, and its suffering.

KONSTANTIN FEDIN

June 2, 1949

EARLY JOYS

CHAPTER

· I ·

A BAREFOOT GIRL of about nine was jogging an infant up and down in her lap, hugging it to her and trying to stop up its wide-open mouth with a sop of chewed bread wrapped in a rag. The baby squirmed, turned its head from side to side, and drew up its little bare legs to its stomach, sobbing convulsively.

"Oh, shut up!" the little girl burst out crossly at last. Laying the baby on the stone flags of the steps, she stood up, smoothed her crumpled print frock, leaned against the sun-warmed wall of the house with her hands behind her, and an air of saying: "Scream yourself sick, go on—I shan't even look at you!"

It was at the end of Easter Week, when the celebrations were over, but the street still had the jaded, weary charm of the spring holiday and something of regret that it was nearly all over, and a consoling thought that the very end had not yet come and there might still be a chance of a spree. From the bank of the Volga below, wafted through the crooked lanes of wooden houses, rose the wailing of a drunken song, now fading into silence, now bursting out afresh, and rising to such a pitch that all other sounds seemed trifling—the concertina with its timbrels far out over the water, the chaotic chiming of church bells, and the busy hum coming from the wharves.

The pavement was strewn with crushed shells of Easter eggs—raspberry red, azure, magenta, and the dull yellowish tan produced by boiling them in onion skins. It looked as though the public had freely indulged in the chewing of pumpkin and sunflower seeds, and in the munching of filberts and walnuts, and sucking of caramels: the wind blew the shells and papers from the bald, round cobblestones into pits in the roadway and finally swept them into the gutter along the brick sidewalk.

The little girl stared straight before her. The river was in spate, the sandy islets were covered already, the left meadow bank looked nearer and heavier, the turbid, chocolate-and-manure brown of the Volga was cleft in twain from bank to bank by a living path of sunlight, shimmering like broken glass. There was a smell of young poplar leaves, of the sweetish riverside silt and musty garbage pits. Flies buzzed as they rebounded off the walls, only to settle again. Everything was saturated with the warmth of springtime, its scents, its sounds, its brick-pavement dust, eddying with the litter of the holiday in little whirls raised by the ground wind.

Nature often undergoes significant changes, marked by a strange state of expectancy, pervading everything around and awakening human emotions. Springtime, when it has ousted winter, tarries awhile, as though savoring the victory. Having exulted, it resumes its course. But the momentary pause is in itself enchanting. Nature looks at herself and says: what a good thing it is that I repeat myself infinitely and renew myself again and again!

The little girl stood there, momentarily and unconsciously imbued with the spirit of vernal retrospection. Her eyes were a deep blue, somewhat out of harmony with her pale flaxen hair. They were large, but lacked the alertness that is usual in children of her age, and because of this her glance seemed too concentrated. Her pigtail, which was about a finger's length, was tied with red tape; her frock with its faded russet sprigs looked neat enough.

The baby was still screaming and drawing up its legs convulsively, and still the little girl could not tear her gaze from some invisible point, which contained nothing and very likely included everything— the song, the bells, the mighty river, and the sun shining on it, the fragrance of the budding trees and the buzzing of the flies.

Suddenly she turned her head.

The clip-clap of horses' hoofs and the spasmodic clank of iron on cobblestones broke the silence of the deserted street. A dapple-gray horse caparisoned in a blue tasseled net was coming along at a trot. The driver of the hollow-tired carriage was wearing a white summer kaftan and drove with his arms stretched out, shaking the quivering blue reins with pompons in the middle. The equipage drew up in front of the little girl on the steps, and two men alighted from it.

The first to alight wore a black cape fastened with a gilt chain with lions' heads as clasps, and a soft black felt hat that had the sheen of a raven's wing. He himself was dark-complexioned, with a clipped mustache as black as tar. The second was dressed in a careless easy fashion in a sand-colored summer coat with a light nap and a sand-colored felt hat with a lilac-tinged ribbon. His face, rather flabby and complacent but still young and well cared for, looked as though tinted with pastels and gave the same impression of lightness and showiness as his clothes.

"Well, here we are," the man in black said in a deep, unctuous tone. "This is the spot."

They looked up at the rusty tin sign COMMON LODGINGHOUSE over the door. Unhurriedly they took in the façade of the two-storied house, the stucco pock-marked from rain, the windowpanes with their oily gleam, patched here and there with putty, the overhanging eaves with the broken drainpipe.

"Why don't you look after that baby, nurse?" the man in the light coat admonished her with pretended severity. "He's going blue in the face—he'll hurt himself."

"Not he," the little girl replied. "He's a regular howler, my little brother is—always has been since the day he was born. They send me out with him because everybody's sick of him."

"Where is your mother?"

"In the rooming house."

The man in the coat blinked as though something pricked his eye, gave a playful little tug at the child's pigtail, and asked her: "Who gave you your hair ribbon?"

"Mamma. She has a lot of them. She collects bits

of stuff from house to house and makes all sorts of
ribbons."

"What for?"

"To make women's caps with. She makes caps and
sells them at the Peshka Market."

"What do they call you?"

"Me?—Annochka."

"What does your father do, Annochka?"

"He's a stevedore on the wharf. And you're gentlemen, aren't you?"

The gentlemen exchanged glances, and the dark one,
throwing back his cape, observed in his peculiarly
unctuous voice: "Nice little girl, isn't she? Charming,
really." And he patted her cheek with his finger tips.
"Where's your father just now, down on the wharf
or at home?"

"We haven't any home. He's here in the rooming
house. Sleeping off the drink, very likely."

"We might as well start with this one, Alexander,"
the man in the cape said. "Take us in to see your papa
and mama, Annochka, will you?"

And negotiating his billowing cape from side to
side, he led the way and entered the rooming house,
with Annochka running after him, carrying the baby,
and the well-groomed man in the light coat following.

The cabby shot them a sidelong look like a horse,
raised his rump, pulled out a short-handled fly whisk
from under the dickey seat, then jumped down,
folded back the skirts of his coat and tucked them
securely behind his belt, then set about flicking the
dust off the wings of the phaeton in a businesslike
fashion.

CHAPTER

· 2 ·

ALEXANDER PASTUKHOV, the young but already prominent playwright, came home to Saratov in the winter
of 1910 to claim his inheritance after his father's death,
stayed and struck up a friendship with Egor Pavlovich
Tsvetukhin, an actor in the local theater.

To come down to facts, there was no inheritance.
Pastukhov's father, a man of note in the town, had
led a somewhat senseless existence, running from pillar to post in search of a chance to earn some money,
now employed on the railway, then on the traction
service. He had a try at publishing a cheap newspaper and even stood as candidate for the Second
Duma as a Constitutional Democrat,* but came a
cropper in every case, knowing how to do only one
thing well—wear the cap with the red band that be-
tokened his gentle birth. He kept mortgaging and
pawning everything, even the old-fashioned study
furniture, once brought here from the country estate.
It was for the sake of this furniture that Alexander
Pastukhov had hurried back to the parental nest and
settled down in the old rooms from whence in former
years he had gone daily to school.

Now, when he had achieved prominence and one
of his plays was running in a Moscow theater and
another in St. Petersburg, he no longer saw himself
as the boy who so short a while ago had been courting

* The Constitutional Democratic Party was the main party
of the Russian liberal-monarchist *bourgeoisie*.

schoolgirls, but as a new, responsible, superior person. Therefore the reminiscences that crowded in upon him, as he went through the familiar streets or sat in the empty rooms of the house where his father had coughed and roared in his drink-sodden octave, touched him, and he felt all the time something resembling a wistful love. He redeemed the furniture, called in a cabinetmaker, who filled the house with the sour smell of burned glue and the all-pervading pungent odor of cheap tobacco, and went on living and living, in no hurry to go anywhere, wondering if he had not been sent into this world for some appointed end, and where the star would lead that beckoned him from inscrutable heights, at the very outset of the exacting life of an author.

It was not because he felt drawn to actors that Pastukhov took up with Tsvetukhin. He discerned in Egor Pavlovich a man of a peculiar turn of mind, though a born actor, a fact acknowledged by the public, which loved the stage as it is loved only in the provinces. Tsvetukhin retained the fervor of the seminarist who reads forbidden books behind the rector's back, and brought with him from the seminary to the stage life in which he had gained a footing his lasting friendship for a schoolmate named Mefody, who played rather dreary supernumerary parts at the theater. But, unlike the actors who were engrossed in the vanities and cares of theater life to the exclusion of all else, Tsvetukhin found escape from his fame in loftier spheres, little known to him, in invention, in the culture and mysteries of physical development, in psychology, and in music. These were naive interests and perhaps essentially theatrical, but this theater in no way resembled the daily routine of the stage, with its managers, newspaper reporters, conceited actresses, debts to the bartender, and the somnolent boredom of the district constable in the second row of the stalls. This was like a rehearsal, a permanent rehearsal of a terrifically interesting role in some future, unknown production. The part he was thus rehearsing emerged from musical, psychologically complex discoveries and took shape in bodily strength, in muscles able to overcome any will that got in the way. Often, in his fantasies, Tsvetukhin met someone who raised his hand against him, and he saw himself seize the hand of that villain, force him to his knees, or fling him on the ground, and pass by, calm, majestic, with his cape flung carelessly over one shoulder. Who this person might be and why he crossed his path Tsvetukhin did not know, and did not stop to think much about—he had won, had brought his enemy to his knees, so he went on his way, imagining something—wings perhaps, or practicing the violin.

The real theater, even to the "sold out" notices at the box office and the prompters, was viewed by Tsvetukhin after his own particular fashion. He considered that the public could feel only the emotions that had been experienced by the actors themselves. Veteran actors ridiculed him and said he had caught the Moscow vogue for Stanislavsky; what was suitable for Moscow was not, in the old actors' opinion, suitable for the provinces, where the theatergoer preferred passion to mild emotions.

Tsvetukhin had thought of this pilgrimage to the rooming house to study "types" because the theater was rehearsing Gorky's *The Lower Depths* and where could they be seen to better advantage than on the Volga—the real live vagabonds who had reigned for over a decade in Russian literature? But his notion was looked down upon at the theater.

"What do you want to make of the actor?" the tragedian demanded. "Have you ever seen me as King Lear? Well, there you are? Marius Mariusovich Petitpas himself kissed me after my performance of Lear. Do you mean to say that if I can play kings I can't play some ragamuffin or other? You're wrong there, Egor. Leave it to the newspaper reporters to go to Guzzlers' Row and study scenes from life. The actor has an altar within his soul, understand? Do not defile it with the filth of life. The Art Theatre craze gives you no peace. There you go—you don't even shave off your mustache, aping Stanislavsky. But did it ever occur to you why the Art Theatre crowd go to study the dregs in Khitrov Market? Because they get cold feet when they have to act for the highbrows. The highbrows, they know, might go and see whether the vagabonds were properly done or not. But my idea is to act in such a way that the riffraff will come to the theater to see whether they can get up to my standard. I play for the gallery, not for the highbrows, Egor."

"Yours is the old way," Tsvetukhin said. "Now we have to play in a different way."

"What for?"

The whole theater was asking this question—what for? Would there be bigger box-office receipts from it? Nobody knew. Would the actors become more popular? There was no certainty about this, either. Would it be easier to live? This was another big question mark. Then why do things nobody knew anything about?

"One must search," Tsvetukhin impressed upon them.

"That's wisdom," the tragedian would say. "But seek in your own soul. Everything's in there. Even the kingdom of Heaven, brother. And you—you can't even find a vagabond."

Then Tsvetukhin told Pastukhov of his intentions.

"A very good idea, too," said Pastukhov, without reflection, only giving his friend a closer scrutiny. "Let's go. And then we'll have lunch. With radishes and whatever goes with them."

"I'll put Mefody in the humor for it and he'll arrange it," Egor Pavlovich rejoined delightedly, "he lives near the rooming house. Let's be starting!"

CHAPTER

· 3 ·

WHEN THEY HAD MOUNTED to the second floor, the
visitors found themselves in a large room, fitted up
with close rows of bunks. Annochka ran on ahead
toward a pink print curtain that partitioned off the
far corner, and dived behind it. Tsvetukhin and
Pastukhov looked about them with interest.

The room was bright enough; the windows, which
had evidently been cleaned for the holidays, revealed
a vast expanse of sky with white clouds sailing across
it and the glassy path spanning the Volga from bank
to bank. Yet the daylight did not enliven these re-
treats of poverty but only exposed the more unspar-
ingly their squalor and that apparently deadened
slovenliness—the heap of rags, the pail with the dingy
sides, the basins stowed into corners. It was plain
that these chattels were despised, yet needed; they
could not be done without.

By the window a woman was sitting in her chemise,
giving her head a thorough combing, her oily, light-
brown hair hanging to her knees. Under the other
window a ragged figure sprawled, emitting piercing
snores, his bare feet and his palms, all in yellow
callosities, outspread. His head was covered—evidently
from the flies—by a tattered waistcoat.

"The Lord of Creation," Pastukhov observed,
measuring him with a leisurely glance.

"We've come at a bad time: it's empty," Tsvetukhin said.

A slit in the pink print curtain opened in alarm, an eye flashed for a second and vanished. Tsvetukhin stood before the curtain and, with a respectful smile on his face, tapped soundlessly at the billowing calico as though it were a door.

"May we come in?"

A short, large-eyed woman stood wiping her water-wrinkled, whitish-pink fingers on her wet apron in front of a washtub, filled at one end with soapsuds and at the other with a heap of scraps of material of different colors. Beside her, Annochka was vigorously rocking the cradle in which lay her baby brother, still screaming. A man resembling Samson, broad in the chest and shoulders but rather flabby, raised himself, leaning on his elbow, one leg dangling over the edge of the bunk, and lay frowning at the intruders. He was hairy; the fair wavy hair, the curling beard and mustache with the light from the window shining through them, looked tow-colored and fine, stirring with every heavy breath.

"Have you come to see us?" the woman asked.

"Yes. Permit me . . ." Tsvetukhin said, raising his hat and revealing thick hair of the same raven's-wing sheen as his hat, so that it looked as though he had merely exchanged one hat for another. "We—er—wanted to make your acquaintance. Dropped in to see how you're getting on."

"I'm afraid there's no room to ask you to sit down, sirs. Unless, maybe, you sit here, please," the woman fussed, wiping the edge of the bunk with her apron.

"Shift your leg, will you?" she said to the man.

Looking about the corner and suddenly puffing and blowing as if he was in a steam bath, Pastukhov remarked with a careless indifference of manner that suggested he had known this corner and these people all his life and was on the friendliest of terms with them: "The air here is pretty heavy, isn't it? Enough to kill anyone."

"Well, you see, everybody caught cold when they opened the windows to clean them and now they're frightened of drafts. The folks all have colds, every single one's ailing with something or other. Summer and winter we live in foul air."

"You've come to gratify your curiosity about poverty, have you?" the man suddenly demanded hoarsely.

"Yes, we want to see the state and conditions people live in," Tsvetukhin replied rather primly, trying to make it sound as delicate as he could.

"In that case, allow me to introduce the family of Tikhon Parabukin," the man croaked, without altering his pose except to swing the leg in the blue homespun trouser leg as wide as a skirt and the foot shod with a bast sandal, tied with string. "Madame Parabukina, Olga Ivanovna by name, a workingwoman, my daughter Anna, a self-willed girl, my son Pavlik, six months old, and myself, Tikhon Parabukin, a handsome fellow of forty years of age. With whom have I the honor? . . ."

Pastukhov blinked fast and studied Parabukin with a curious, veiled glance—his rather small eyes were greenish, his gaze fixed, clinging as glue. The silence became too much for Tsvetukhin.

"We want to get a better understanding of your situation. We do it in your interests, of course—the interests of the poorer class."

"Then you're showing your interest in the wrong place. We aren't the poor class. We're what you might call temporarily distressed, needy for the time being," Parabukin corrected him. "My daughter, who is put up to it by her mother, tells everyone her father's a stevedore."

"And that's what he is," Olga Ivanovna interposed. "If he isn't, then what's this?" and she gave a little kick to an object on the floor—the leather shoulder strap that all stevedores use.

"Still, this isn't true. Originally, I was a respectable official, and like all officials, I still live with my family in my own private apartment with a separate entrance. And if I should take it into my head, I could have a bell fixed up and a brass plate on the curtain, like a real front door, so that everyone could see who I was."

"Well, it's all very interesting, I'm sure, to hear you talk," Pastukhov said in an offhand way, seating himself on the edge of the bunk that had been dusted for him. "Now listen to me. You're a man of education and you'll understand what I have to say: we aren't the kind of people who go about doing charity work for want of something else to do. We're actors. Playing at the theater, see?"

"I see," Parabukin replied, cautiously lowering his other leg from the bunk.

"We're going to ask you to show us the notables of the rooming house. You know who I mean—the lions and so on, who are known all up and down the Volga. You must have some famous characters here, haven't you?"

"Lions, did you say? No, we've never seen any lions here. Plenty of dogs, though. You don't want any curs, by any chance, do you?" Parabukin enquired. For a moment he sat silent with bent head. "Tell me, will you be wanting any costumes—fancy dress? I mean, do you want to buy any for the theater?"

"Why, what are you selling?"

"I suppose you wouldn't care for these, would you?" he suggested, plucking his voluminous trousers between finger and thumb and flapping them on his stiffly outstretched legs.

"No, I don't think we need any fancy dress," Pastukhov answered gravely.

"Ah, you don't? Well, maybe you wouldn't mind making a trifling contribution toward the fund for the erection of an edifice to the sacred memory of St. Half-a-Bottle?" Parabukin suggested with a bow.

"We wouldn't mind doing that, of course. And what's it to be followed up with?"

"Our prayers for your health, may Christ save you!" Parabukin bowed again, this time so low that his curls dropped to his knees.

Pastukhov fumbled in the pockets of his light and showy garments while his hosts of the corner waited, following his languid, gracious movements patiently and wondering what he would find.

"I say, Egor," he said softly at last, evidently amazed, "it looks as though I haven't a kopek on me."

"Your papa all over! The very spit of him! I knew you right off," Parabukin burst out, with a triumphant chuckle.

"What do you mean? Whose papa?" Pastukhov demanded in a displeased tone.

"Yours, of course—the late lamented Vladimir

Alexandrovich, Mr. Pastukhov. Always forgot his money at home. All his life. You'd go up to him and ask him: 'Vladimir Alexandrovich, you couldn't help me out with a ruble for a physic, could you?' And he'd raise his finger to his cap, polite like this, and say: 'Sorry, brother, but I seem to have left my notecase at home.' "

"Ah," said Pastukhov absently, "so Vladimir Alexandrovich knew you personally, did he?"

"Didn't he, though! When he was on the railway I was under him, a railway inspector on the express trains, I was. Madame here can bear witness to it that the Parabukin family never traveled lower than second class. . . . I knew you as soon as I set eyes on you. You're the living image of your papa, and a very smoothly finished one, too. Yes. But it looks as though you'd fallen on evil days like myself—gone on the stage, have you?"

"Look, here's a small offering toward the building of that edifice you were talking about," Tsvetukhin said at this point, taking out a fifty-kopek piece and placing it on the ledge of the washtub.

Hardly had Parabukin time to stretch out his hand for it than Olga Ivanovna had snatched it up and clenched her fist on it.

The placid good nature was wiped from his face as though by magic. Springing down off the bunk, he strode over to his wife as silently as a tomcat.

"You stop it! Give me that money!"

"You ought to be ashamed before strangers!" Olga Ivanovna exclaimed, moving aside.

But Parabukin was not to be put off like this. "It was given to me, not you. It's my money. Hand it over!" His voice was thick now, and he spoke with a dull restraint that held no hope of his yielding.

Then suddenly, as though rushing ahead of things and striving to convince herself and everyone else that she would never give in, Olga Ivanovna screamed: "You've been boozing all Easter, you bloodsucker! While I have to go ragpicking on the rubbish heaps day after day to keep bread in your mouth! I suppose I must never get out of the rubbish heaps, never budge from the washtub, never lay down my needle of a night, is that it?"

"Hand it over, I'm telling you!" Parabukin interrupted her wail in a threatening tone.

He was about to catch her by the elbow when she slipped out of reach, thrust out a hand, and unclenched her fingers. At the same moment Annochka grabbed the coin from her palm and stowed it in her cheek.

The tipsiness seemed to get the better of Parabukin once more. He swayed where he stood, his big soft body sagged, he flung up his arms in a futile way and let them fall heavily to his sides. He shook his big shaggy head and muttered, half to himself: "So that's your game, you young monkey. . . . You just wait. . . ." Then suddenly he yelled: "Take that howler of yours out of here, quick now! Clear out! D'you hear? Get out of here!"

Meanwhile Pavlik was screaming with all his might in his cradle. Annochka picked him up with her usual deftness and darted out from behind the curtain.

Without another glance at the guest, Parabukin gave chase in a determined fashion.

"Where are you going?" Olga Ivanovna cried.

She planted herself in his way, but he pushed her aside and tore off part of the curtain.

"Stop him, gentlemen, stop him!" she implored. And flung herself after him.

Tsvetukhin and Pastukhov drew back the curtain and stared after the two in silence.

In the big room the woman with the long hair was still combing it out; she had not moved. The ragged figure still sprawled on the bunk, snoring under the old waistcoat.

Parabukin had vanished through the doorway. Olga Ivanovna was running between the bunks, screaming:

"Help, gentlemen! He'll beat her, he'll beat the poor little girl. . . . Run, Annochka, run!"

"Come on," Tsvetukhin said, "what are we standing staring at?"

"The show," Pastukhov retorted with a chuckle that was more like a scowl. "And we're watching it, Egor my dear, we're watching the passing show."

· 4 ·

When Annochka heard that her father was chasing her and her mother's warning cry, she promptly put back the coin she had taken out of her cheek, laid Pavlik down on the doorstep, and took to her heels. She turned the corner of the rooming house and dashed along the path, trailing her fingers along fences and walls as she ran, a trick that all children have.

Parabukin lumbered after her, his bast sandals slapping hollowly on the dry ground, his coarse blue hemp trousers flapping in the wind like signaler's flags, the dust rising in puffs behind him. He ran as if his life depended upon it. At every stride the distance between Annochka and her father grew shorter, and he was already reaching out to grab her, when she caught at the corner of a house and darted up another street.

The cab horse under its blue net, feeling the driver's firm hands on the reins and hearing the familiar click of his tongue, was rapidly overtaking Parabukin. Tsvetukhin, ready for goodness knew that, was riding on the step of the phaeton, leaning forward and clinging to the dickey seat. His friend, who had lost no vestige of his somewhat pictorial dignity, sat erect and easy, and only his eyes showed that he was gratifying his insatiable curiosity, with a kind of physical pleasure. Two or three passers-by gaped in wonderment at the stormy though wordless incident. A child running away from a tramp would not have attracted much attention, had it not been for the phaeton and its remarkable-looking occupants, a rare sight in this little-frequented quarter.

The house Annochka was running past now was the public school, a heavy-looking, whitewashed building surrounded by a low stone wall, above which rose three old pyramidal poplars, just bursting into leaf.

At the open wicket gate stood a youth wearing the double-breasted jacket of the Technical School students' uniform over a white sateen Russian blouse, fastened at the side with gilt buttons.

On seeing the little girl and the burly man chasing her, the youth stepped aside and pointed to the wicket. Annochka dashed straight through into the yard, whereupon he resumed his place, blocking the gateway with his body.

Parabukin was panting, his big head shook, his curls shone in the sunlight—a tangle of sun-faded hay, his full pale cheeks glistening with perspiration.

"Let me in here, you, technician," he gasped, putting out a hand to remove the unexpected obstacle from his path.

At this juncture indecision was out of the question, so hot was the chase, so high the pitch of the man's eagerness to seize the girl whom he was within an ace of catching.

"Hands off," the youth said quietly in a level tone.

"Who are you—giving orders here?"

"I live here."

"I don't care where the devil you live. . . . Get out of my way! That's my daughter. . . . What are you hiding her for?"

"I don't care who she is, I'm not going to let you into the yard."

Parabukin planted one foot firmly behind him, jerked up his sleeve, and swung his arm.

"Try it," the youth said, still quietly, but in a grimmer tone.

Grim lines showed now in his strong, manly, well-formed figure. He was not tall, in fact he was rather stocky—one of those people who are called square: his shoulders were angular, his jaw prominent, the locks of hair were straight and parallel on his forehead, his eyebrows, mouth, and chin might have been

put in with a drawing pen, and only the glance with
its warm brown glint looked as though touched with
an artist's brush. He did not stir, but stood with his
fists thrust into his belt, barring the wicket gate with
his elbows; the sturdy, wiry figure suggested that it
would not be easily thrust aside.

Parabukin lowered his arm. "Where d'you come
from, you young imp?"

The cabdriver reined in his prancing horse—it had
not had time to get heated—and Tsvetukhin sprang
down onto the pavement.

"How many are there of you against one?" Parabukin growled, shooting a contemptuous glance in the
actor's direction. Now he was pulling down his sleeve
with vicious tugs that suggested an unwilling capitula-
tion.

"The row has fizzed out," Tsvetukhin declared.
"It's a shame for a father to frighten his own child,
all the same. That's what I think, anyway."

"Allow me, Mr. Actor, to tell you that I don't
give a damn what you think," Parabukin retorted,
wiping his hot face with his sleeve and making
something like a curtsey at the same time. "You aren't
thinking of giving me another fifty kopeks, I suppose? Or are you? A fellow has to have a drop to
sober him down, hasn't he?"

"You see that blue house yonder?" Tsvetukhin asked
him suddenly. "See it—right on the corner, at the far
end of the block?"

"Meshkov's, you mean?"

"I don't know whose it is."

"Well, I know. It belongs to Meshkov, the man
who owns our rooming house."

"All right—beside it you see a little cottage with
two windows. Come around there and I'll give you a
drop of something to sober you."

"You mean it? . . . Or are you only joking?"

"We're going there now, you come along presently."

After all, there are times when Fortune smiles upon
a man, usually when he least of all expects a smile—
and innocent hope illuminated Parabukin's countenance. He glanced at the young fellow in the gateway
and dismissed the whole affair with a gesture—his
good humor restored.

"You've been lucky, technician—thank your God for it."

"This is what I have to thank," said the young man, jerking his fist out of his belt.

Tsvetukhin, throwing back his cape, stepped up to him. "I want to thank you for your plucky conduct. Allow me to introduce myself—Tsvetukhin."

"I'm Kirill Izvekov."

The handshake was a momentary contest of strength, each feeling the other's fingers gripping his own.

"Oho!" Tsvetukhin remarked with a smile. "You go in for gymnastics, I see."

"Well, yes, a bit. . . . I knew you at once," Kirill replied, reddening.

"Oh, you did?" Egor Pavlovich murmured with the transient and superficially sincere astonishment actors express about their own fame, an astonishment intended to suggest: what on earth can there be so unusual about us that everybody knows us?

"You'll look after the little girl while her father's still about, won't you?" he said, tactfully changing the conversation. "A nice child, isn't she?"

"Yes, I'll take her to my home. My mother's the schoolmistress here."

They took leave of each other with the same manly handshake. Kirill stood watching the phaeton with rapt attention until it drove up to the Meshkov house. Then he turned into the yard.

Annochka was sitting on the ground under the fence, in a clump of tough acacias. She was hugging her knees, on which her head rested, and watching Kirill steadily. The sadness and intent curiosity in her big eyes made her gaze still more grave.

"Well, did you get a fright?"

"No," she replied, "Papa doesn't hit me hard, ever. He's goodhearted, you know. He only tries to frighten me."

"So you ran away from fright?"

"No! I ran away so as he wouldn't take the money away from me." And, unclenching her fingers, she showed him the fifty-kopek piece.

"Then you can go home if you like?"

"No, I think I'll sit here a little while."

"Why?"

"I'm frightened to go yet."

Kirill laughed. "You can come in and stay with my mother a while if you want to."

Annochka rubbed the coin on her bare knee, admired its bold glitter in the sunlight, and assented after a few moments' thought. "I wouldn't mind—just for a while."

He took her by the hand, and, with the air of a conqueror, led her across the yard to a heavy old-fashioned, single-paneled door. She was momentarily struck by the ponderous wrought-iron hinges, fastened with screws that had big shining heads like her fifty-kopek piece; then she stepped into the dim passage with its cool brick floor.

PASTUKHOV AND TSVETUKHIN went to see Mefody, who lived in a simple frame bungalow consisting of one room and a kitchen, the type of habitation named by its owner a "cottage," after the fashion prevailing on the Volga.

"At long last you're visiting me in my cottage. Come in, come in, you're very welcome."

"Make an obeisance, can't you?" Tsvetukhin suggested.

"Here you are, then," Mefody said obligingly, bowing from the waist in the old Slavonic stage style and touching the stained and waxed floor with his finger-tips.

"Take this," said Tsvetukhin, flinging his cape over Mefody like a horsecloth.

Mefody gathered up the chain in a handful, jingled it, pawed and stamped like a horse, and whinnied gently. To complete the illusion he got down on all fours.

"Steady!" Tsvetukhin said, like a cabby.

With a condescending air Pastukhov threw his showy spring coat over Mefody's back and stuck his hat on top of the pile, which was then cautiously carried by Mefody, still on all fours, over to the bed in the corner.

When he came back, he took his place beside the friends, a smile on his thick lips, which far from

marring, were the best feature of his face, disfigured
by a mark just below the bridge of the nose. This
was the result and the punishment of his own curiosity:
as a child he had been watching a certain domestic
incident through a crack when he lost his grip, the
box on which he had been standing had overturned,
and, in falling, he had struck his nose on the key
sticking out of the keyhole. He mentioned, if he did
not recount, the occurrence all his life long.

The two guests and their host gazed in blissful
fascination at the table in the middle of the room,
whereon the radishes exposed the juicy redness of
their rounded sides, now hiding coyly, now protruding their white tails. Spring onions flourished their
aerial blue-green darts from the plates. So delicate
were the cucumbers that it seemed the hothouse green
of their skins showed white. The slices of pink ham
were touched at the edges with a faint blue mother-of-
pearl film, and their fat gleamed like white porcelain.
Two bottles of golden-yellow glass, plunged in a
bowl of slightly melted snow, were embellished with
curling sprigs of radish leaves. That the table had
been laid by a man's hand was plain at a glance. A
spicy aroma of hot meat stew was wafted from the
big Russian stove in the kitchen.

Pastukhov's nostrils dilated. In a voice that sounded
unlike his own, he gabbled, a little nasally: "Listen,
Mefody—you're a Flemish master."

With a hand poised over a bottle, he hesitated, and
marshaled the table with another glance.

"Butter? . . . Here. . . . Salt? . . . Here. . . . Mus-
tard? Aha! . . . Bread?"—raising his voice questioningly—"Mefody, where's the bread?"

Mefody served him a breadbasket laden with the
Moscow variety of rolls, and chanted: " 'There is
nothing better under the sun for a man than eat and
drink and be merry. . . . Go thy way, eat thy bread
with joy, and drink thy wine with a merry heart.'
Thus sayeth the Preacher."

Tsvetukhin, chiming in like a priest, continued
on a higher note. " 'Live joyfully with the wife
whom thou lovest all the days of the life of thy vanity,
which he hath given thee under the sun, all the days
of thy vanity: for that is thy portion in this life,

and in thy labour which thou takest under the sun.'
Thus spake Solomon."

"Of all the rotten priests. . . ." Pastukhov sighed
with a grimace of disgust, as, lifting a bottle out of
the snow, he wrapped it deftly in a napkin and
poured out the vodka.

They drank, first toasting each other in a speech
which consisted of the simple words: "Now we're
off!"—contemplated the viands gravely, for the last
time, as though hesitating to disturb the delightful still-
life arrangement, then started on the radishes. Pastukhov ate in an infectiously appetizing fashion, roughly
and simply and without affectation, as peasants or the
old gentry eat: crunching his radishes, smearing butter
on them, dipping them in the salt on his plate, breaking
the fresh rolls with his fingers and putting the morsels
in his mouth with determined but unhurried movements. His cheeks were pale; he was giving himself
wholly to eating, savoring it with all his fleshly ap-
petite.

"You're like a singer, Alexander," Tsvetukhin remarked with a laugh, admiring him.

"And why not?" Pastukhov rejoined, with a sweeping gesture that took in the whole table. "This is
life's own reward. I love people who treat you with
genuine hospitality." He cast an approving glance at
Mefody, and added after a pause: "There's a clever
chap! Mefody's health!"

They clinked glasses, with the same brief toast
—"Now we're off!" and just at that moment heard
the click of the latch on the outside door. Mefody
got up and went into the lobby and, returning at
once, announced that there was a sort of tramp out
there who said he had been told to come.

"A stevedore, a curly-headed fellow, is he?" Tsvetukhin asked. "Call him in."

"What the deuce do you want with him?" Pastukhov demanded, looking disgusted.

"Oh, let him come in."

Parabukin entered, stooping as though fearful of
striking his head against the lintel. His smile, as he
turned toward his new acquaintances, was at once
pleading and ironical. His gaze alighted immediately
on the principal objects—the bottles of vodka—and

he could no longer tear it away from them, as though from some axis of the universe, miraculously appearing before his eyes. It was obvious that no words were needed, and what followed took place in general silence: Mefody brought a large tumbler to the table, Tsvetukhin filled it to the brim with vodka, Pastukhov put a nice bit of ham on a roll of bread, Tikhon Parabukin quickly wiped his mouth with his fist and accepted the glass from Tsvetukhin's hand in prayerful silence. He ceased smiling the moment the vodka was being poured out; his countenance expressed dread and the highest pitch of concentration, suggestive of a man listening to his sentence after a protracted and painful trial. He swallowed slowly, mouthful by mouthful, closing his eyes and stiffening, so that only the rings of light hair stirred slightly on his head as it tilted back.

"Well done!" Pastukhov said approvingly, handing him the roll.

But Parabukin would not eat. He gave a start, shook his head violently, rubbed his face vigorously with his palm, and exclaimed in despair: "Lord! Lord Almighty!"

"Are you repenting or something?" Pastukhov asked.

"No. I'm thanking the gentlemen and my God for the granting of the light."

"Been drinking long?" Pastukhov went on.

"In general, or do you mean the last bout or cycle?"

"In general," said Pastukhov with a chuckle.

"Oh, in general—it's been going on for ten years now. In connection with my family life, see? Not that it started because of that. It wasn't my family drove me to it: I should say it was me drove my family."

"Ever tried to get over it?"

"You mean boozing? Never. That's more in Olga Ivanovna's line—fighting it, I mean. You saw how she confiscated that coin, didn't you? No, I don't fight against it. Why should I?"

"You go in for drinking consciously, then?"

"Well, and how do you do it?—unconsciously?"

"No, till we lose consciousness," Mefody said.

Parabukin smiled, fearlessly now. His face brightened, the Samson-like strength revived in him; he stood erect, a grown man. Pastukhov never took his gluey, clinging gaze from him, studied him unabashedly, as though he were a stone atlas.

Tsvetukhin laid his hand on Tikhon Parabukin's
chest. "A beauty, isn't he, Alexander?"

"That's true," Parabukin agreed, "Olga Ivanovna,
when she has forgiven me, always puts her head here"
—he slapped Tsvetukhin's hand lightly and pressed it
to his breast—"and says: 'Tisha, my Tisha, why do
you torment yourself, a handsome fellow like you?'
and then she cries." The tears started to his eyes, and
he heaved a sobbing sigh.

"Is the vodka having an effect?" Pastukhov asked
curiously.

" 'Why do you torment yourself?'—she says," Parabukin continued. " 'Stop it, Tisha,' Olga Ivanovna says,
'go back to the old times. How grand it'll be—you'll
be a railway inspector on a train again, and I'll starch
your collars for you, Annochka will go to school,
and I'll look after Pavlik. Stop it, I say.' "

"And what do you say?" Tsvetukhin asked.

"And I say: 'Aye, Olga Ivanovna, this is the mixed
train of life we're embarked on, how can you stop it?
And perhaps our train with you and me on it has
been shunted into a dead end, into Meshkov's rooming
house, and there's no way out for us.' And she says to
me: 'Maybe it isn't a dead end, but a station?' 'That
may be,' I say, 'only I have to carry bales as a stevedore
on this station.' 'No,' says Olga Ivanovna to this,
'those who think of our rooming house as a station,
they struggle for life, and you don't. Fight,' she says.
'Tisha, I'm begging you to fight.' "

Parabukin gave a sob again and stretched out a
hand toward the empty glass. "Just another mouthful."

Pastukhov took the glass away from him. "No," he
said, "that's enough."

He turned away abruptly from Parabukin, and an
expression of disgusted boredom came into his face
for an instant; he looked gloomily at the still orderly
table. "Well, can you recommend us some colorful
character from among the tenants of your house?"
Tsvetukhin said in a gentle tone.

"The house isn't mine, the house is Meshkov's,"
Parabukin replied surlily. "Speak to him about it. He
lives here, you're right in his yard."

"Good afternoon," Pastukhov said, turning sharply in his chair and almost pushing the ham sandwich Parabukin had not yet touched into his hand. "Mefody, see him out, will you?"

Parabukin stalked away, throwing out his chest and stamping so heavily across the threshold into the passage that the board walls of the house shook and creaked.

"An impudent fellow!" Pastukhov said.

When Mefody returned and sat down at the table, the repast was resumed in blissful silence. Cucumbers and radishes crunched in the teeth, the now disturbed onions emitted their all-pervading scent, the sound of the knives on ham was heard, the plop-plopping of vodka. "We're off!" said the friends, quietly the first time. "We're off!" they exclaimed in a louder tone for the second time. "We're off!" they chanted in chorus the third time. After this Pastukhov burst out laughing, threw himself back in his armchair, and launched into talk, crunching radishes like nuts meanwhile.

"You're a fool, Egor Tsvetukhin! A fool! All these vagabonds are just lazy good-for-nothings. But someone started the notion that they are romantic, and everybody took it as gospel truth, and they came into fashion. And you fell for it—hook, line, and sinker— and like the rest you put it into these tramps' heads they're a kind of poetic geniuses. Now you've seen that hairy lout? He's just a boor and a drunkard, nothing else. Can you say you found anything new in him? All alike, in my opinion."

"I'm not glamorizing them, I'm doing this for art's sake," Tsvetukhin explained, much more seriously than Pastukhov's condescending tone warranted.

"What do you mean? You are striving to reproduce this hairy drunkard on the stage? Is that it? Now what's the need for all this exactitude, anyhow? To create a second rooming house on the stage? What for? You can go to the Upper Bazaar and see a second rooming house if you want to. But what has the stage, the theater, art, to do with this?"

"Oh, I know, I know what you are going to say!" Tsvetukhin exclaimed. "You're thinking of the pug. Goethe said that if an artist were to draw a perfect copy of a pug, there would be two pugs instead of one and art would gain exactly nothing."

"See how educated you are! Twenty or thirty years ago Zola set an example through all his books of copying reality in fiction. He traveled on a locomotive so as to portray the engine driver in his books, went down the mines and visited brothels. And just a while ago, when I was looking through some old French magazines, I found a caricature that came out after his novel *Le Ventre de Paris* appeared. Poor Zola was lying in the middle of the street under the horse's hoofs, with his pince-nez on a cord, and without his top hat. The caption under the caricature said: 'M. Zola threw himself under a fiacre so as to give a correct description of the feelings of a man who had been knocked down by the vehicle.'"

"Very good indeed!" Mefody chanted blissfully, filling the glasses.

They laughed and drank and munched, but the sharp edge was off their appetites now. Pastukhov handed round his big leather cigarette case, and through the smoke that wreathed around them in languid gray tentacles, Tsvetukhin said in sincere amazement: "You're a reactionary, Alexander. You say things that the most old-fashioned of our stage people, the routine actors, say. How can you deny that an actor ought to study actual life? This is sheer obscurantism!"

"Don't try to frighten me with words, Egor. I'm an artist and I'm not afraid of words. Only newspapermen are afraid of words because they attribute greater significance to them than words can have."

Pastukhov took a little red notebook out of his breast pocket and flicked over the leaves, but, unable to find what he sought, he continued calmly and unhurriedly. "I have been told that Leo Tolstoy remarked to someone at the tea table, not so long ago, that if you want to be an artist of the written word, your spirit must have the faculty for rising very high and sinking very low. Then, Tolstoy says, all the intermediate stages will be known to you and the artist will be enabled to live, in his imagination, the life of people at various levels."

"How good that sounds!" Mefody cried, seizing

the vodka bottle again. "This is even better—better than the things you told us about Zola. It's stronger. It's very well said, isn't it, Egor?"

He was listening to the conversation in a kind of exaltation, his thick lips parted, his expression showing not only eagerness to miss nothing of what was said, but also the smile of one who sees more than he is shown.

Pastukhov searched through his book again, then, with a touch of triumph, smoothed down the page he had found. "And here's something I found in Balzac. 'One of the evils that eminent minds are subject to is that they involuntarily attain everything—not only the virtues but also the vices.'"

"What's the connection?" Tsvetukhin said with a shrug of his shoulders. "And what is there here that contradicts the study of life?"

"Don't you see the connection? Tolstoy says the artist should possess the faculty for rising to loftiest heights and sinking to the lowest depths. Balzac says that the eminent mind can attain virtue and vice involuntarily. The connection lies in these two words —the faculty and involuntarily: both speak of something inherent in the artist or the unusual mind, both say that the attainment of the low and the high is their natural quality, that good and evil are attained by them independently of their will. The life of the imagination—this is the essence of the artist or of the outstanding mind. And—mark this—Tolstoy says: to rise and to fall in spirit. In spirit, my dear Egor, that is to say, in that same imagination, and in no other way. Otherwise the result will be like that caricature of Zola. It would mean that in order to sink very low one would have to commit some abominable offense in real life, and to steal so as to gain an insight into the soul of the thief. Now Tolstoy and Balzac are a denial of this way of studying life."

"Why does Balzac call this involuntary attainment of virtue and vice by a great mind—an evil?"

"Why? I think . . ." Pastukhov gave an unexpected chuckle and blurted out frankly: "To tell the truth, I haven't thought about it. It just occurred to me this moment, for no particular reason. But one thing I am sure of: calling themselves realists, Balzac and

Tolstoy were deluding us. These, as a matter of fact, are the most fantastic artists of all that have ever been. They made up everything: all their work is sheer invention. They had nothing whatever to do with copying from life. Their books are the fruits of the most refined imagination. That is why they are far more convincing than life itself. And here is my profession of faith: my mind's eye is the Lord of Art. The mind's eye, the omnipresent thought, you understand? I can see any rooming house with my mind's eye, just as I can see the Pharaoh of Egypt, the peasant's mare, or a member of the Duma. I rise and fall, do good and evil, in omnipresent thought. In my imagination, in my fantasy, I am subject to both the beautiful and the repellent, for I am an artist."

He raised his glass. "Hail the artist! and down with the copyist! Hail Tolstoy! and down with Zola! Hail the Lord of Art—imagination!"

"We're off!" Mefody wound up.

They were growing tipsy. The food was spreading over the table, converted from tempting morsels to waste scraps; cigarette stubs had wandered and, finding no ash trays, had landed on the plates. Mefody brought the meat out of the oven; the tobacco smoke retreated before the steam of the stew, reeking of bay leaf and pepper; appetites revived, voices grew louder and noisier, phrases were clipped, meaningless remarks took on the quality of gay witticisms.

"You're just a drunken toastmaster, Mefody," Pastukhov said, "but you've got taste. I adore you."

"Me—a drunkard?" Mefody repeated, evidently flattered. "Never! A drunkard drinks for the sake of drinking. I drink for the sake of eating. I can carry my liquor, I've full control of my words. But has a drunkard a word?"

"Yes, he certainly has," Tsvetukhin said with a laugh. "He says: now it's all done with, I shan't have another drop! And for two days he won't take so much as a drop of poppy dew."

"Listen, you fellows, deaf as woodcocks," Pastukhov said. "Hark to the sound of it! What a language, eh? Poppy dew! If I had a distillery, I would make a vodka called 'Dewdrop.' And beneath this word on the label I would print in brackets, in tiny letters, 'poppy.'"

"You would be as rich as Croesus in no time!" Tsvetukhin cried. "What a sale it would have, 'Dewdrop'!"

"Would you care for a few more dewdrops? Shall I drop a few in your glass?" Mefody murmured, and, as he filled the glass, he recited in a persuasive tone: "Salt meat's too salt, and dear is the stew: what's cheap and good is our poppy dew! or words to that effect."

There was so much noise in the room now that they did not hear the tapping on the windowpane at first, insistent though it was. Mefody went out into the passage and stayed so long that his friends followed to see where he was.

At the door stood a well-dressed man in a bowler hat. He wore a handsomely cut jacket with all four buttons fastened, and carried a silver-headed walking stick grained to show innumerable bird's eyes or knots. His beard, which was parted and combed, his shaggy brows and the hard eyes that had been squeezed in under them, the solid bearing of his rounded figure, had the sternness and peculiar dignity of people who are convinced that they cannot err. He was something over forty, and the first two or three gray hairs had appeared in his brown beard.

"Merkul Avdeyevich Meshkov, our landlord," Mefody said by way of introduction.

Meshkov raised his hat. "Excuse me for disturbing you, gentlemen. But this fellow here says he was invited by you. He refuses to say for what purpose."

Parabukin was seated on the steps, his elbows resting on his knees, which were set wide apart. He was still holding the piece of roll and ham—nibbled at one edge—and kept chasing away the flies that swarmed around the tasty morsel. He raised his head. There was something guilty in that upward glance. "You wouldn't treat me to half a glass, I suppose?" he asked.

"Not one dewdrop," Pastukhov said bluntly.

"You hear that, my lad?" said Meshkov, with a light touch of his silver-topped cane on Tikhon's shoulder. "Now go along out of this yard, you've no business here, go along, I'm telling you."

Parabukin got heavily to his feet and eyed each of them in turn. Tsvetukhin must have seemed the

most sympathetic, for his glance lingered on him
and he smiled a pleading smile, but the actor shook his
head—no, there was no use expecting generous charity
from these heartless folk.

"Why don't you eat your sandwich, instead of
squashing it in your hands?" Tsvetukhin said.

"That's my own business—I can do as I like," Parabukin retorted as, with a stevedore's slightly rolling
gait, he slouched toward the gates.

Tsvetukhin turned to Pastukhov, shook his forefinger at him, and asked: "Now you understand?"

Pastukhov only blinked at him with eyes that
seemed to understand nothing.

Meshkov saw Tikhon to the gate, closed and latched
it behind him firmly, then took off his bowler and
said good-by to the party.

"Oh, no, no, you must come and join us now,"
Mefody began. "Come now, it won't hurt you to
visit your poor tenant once a year."

"Yes, come along, you'll be very welcome,"
Tsvetukhin chimed in, acting delighted hospitality
with ease.

"Don't refuse us, I beg. Taste some of the poppy
dew at least, to celebrate the passing holiday."

So, bowing and scraping, they led Merkuri Avdeyevich Meshkov, still protesting with great dignity, into
the room.

CHAPTER

· 6 ·

THERE ARE VARIOUS ways of living. But it is rare to find anyone who, in answer to the question asked by his conscience as to whether he lives rightly or not, can say that the way he lives is perfectly right. Even a man who is in the habit of fooling himself, scrutinizing the path of his life will observe on it some rugosity, left by a wrong step, a habitual vice, or an unrestrained passion. And people capable of speaking the truth in the privacy of their own thoughts see their own mistakes so clearly that in the interests of self-preservation they prefer to console themselves with the familiar saying that even the sun has spots.

Merkuri Avdeyevich was sincere in admitting that he was not faultless, inasmuch as all mortals are sinful. And he not only knew himself as sinful but repented of his transgressions most fervently every year, sometimes the first, sometimes the fourth Sunday in Lent, and—but this was more rarely—in Holy Week; at any rate, whichever could be fitted in conveniently with business. On the other hand, taking a sober view of things (and Merkuri Avdeyevich reasoned very soberly), he had nothing to repent of—not, of course, to God and his spiritual father, but to himself and people, in particular to people. For Merkuri Avdeyevich lived rightly, that is, according to the dictates of his conscience, resting upon the foundations on which all earthly existence rested.

He used to say that industry was the main pillar; he demanded industry from everyone, and he himself was fond of work, never, from his earliest years, letting a day pass without work, without adding another stone to those that had been laid the previous day. This mode of life had entered into his blood and was so much a part of it that any other appeared unnatural to him, as unnatural as it would be for a pigeon to try to live under water, and he could respect none but those who built stone by stone, progressively, and, as it were, mathematically striving in this occupation toward an appointed limit, which was the worldly end of man.

Merkuri Avdeyevich owned a store for paints, oils, varnishes, and household goods in the Upper Bazaar, and two lots of land within a short distance of each other and not far from the Volga. He called one the Small, and the other the Big Place. He occupied the Small Place, which was covered with wooden buildings painted blue with oil paint. His house was two-storied, the retreat of his small family—he had only one daughter, Lisa—and the young shopmen and clerks. Then there were two cottages, one a little house occupied by Mefody, and the second, somewhat larger, rented out to Pyotr Petrovich Ragozin, a fitter employed in the railway roundhouse; finally, there were the domestic offices—the cellars and the drying sheds where the shopmen and clerks took up their quarters in the summertime. Part of the Big Place remained wasteland, overgrown with nettles and weeds and pink hollyhocks; part was occupied by a large stone building, long since converted into a rooming house, and a big gloomy-looking warehouse acquired by Merkuri Avdeyevich along with a rope factory. On warm days the peculiarly titillating, humid, and tarry smell of a wooden barge floated from this building along with the songs of the women employed in picking old rope for tow.

Meshkov had accumulated his possessions slowly, little by little, and not without trouble and disappointment. He did not care much about the rooming house—it was an untidy and troublesome place, but its conversion for any other purpose would have required a disproportionately large outlay. The ware-

house hardly covered the ground rent, but the time
was not ripe to put up a new building on this site.
The greatest vexation of all was that though he
would have liked to extend his estate over the whole
quarter, and to acquire the plot of land at the back
of the rooming house, practically merging with the
waste ground overgrown with nettles and hollyhocks, unfortunately, on this plot the old elementary
school building stood. It was owned by the town,
which would on no account give up this wealth.
Consequently, Meshkov took a dislike to the school
with its noisy little boys always up to some mischief
or other, and its teachers who had, to his way of
thinking, a far too independent bearing, and this dislike surprised even himself, for he had always respected schooling and particularly learning.

He genuinely respected learning in every form and
spoke of doctors as medical men, officers of the law
courts as jurists, and teachers of natural history as
naturalists, pronouncing these words with awe. But,
nevertheless, secular education was inaccessibly alien
to him, and his respect for it was confined to this
outward diffidence, this inadvertent awestruck dropping of the voice. Far more profound was his respect
for religious learning; he had revered scholars well
read in church books and the Scriptures from those
early years when he began to put by the first kopeks
for some special purpose. While still an apprentice
at an oils, paints, and varnishes shop, sprinkling figure
eights on the floor in water from the kettle spout,
preparatory to sweeping up, Meshkov was fond of recalling the wise words of the sermons heard in church,
words that had become the fountainhead of his en-
lightenment. Now, in the years of maturity, he often
went of a winter's evening to the Coenobites, the
local monastic community, to listen to the denuncia-
tory argumentation of missionaries with dissenters of
all persuasions, whom Meshkov understood as well as
he did bank notes. In the pulpit or at the reading
desk in the middle of the low-vaulted church, lit by
the wavering flame of wax candles, the monks, wiping
the perspiration from their fat faces, shamed the Old
Believers standing in similar pulpits opposite them.
The whole evening would be spent in thundering

denunciations of the "perverters of Orthodoxy" and heavily bearded men with long hair loose about their shoulders would argue furiously that "the shaving of the beard and mustache is in no way contrary to Christianity, and in some instances even needful, particularly the clipping of the mustache." Facing them, men no less hairy, who considered themselves as the beard defenders, flourishing the books of the Old Believers, asserted that the "sin of shaving the beard was such that even the blood of martyrs" was powerless to redeem. Very painstakingly Meshkov laid away in the storehouse of his memory, where nothing went to waste, the arguments employed by the seminaries in these debates, the statement of the truth and its opposite, with repetitions of all its "whereas firstly" and "whereas secondly." Many of his favorite ratiocinations he remembered by heart and recounted with exactitude, on his reaching home, to his spouse, Valeria Ivanovna, mildest of women. For example, he would say:

"Listen, Valyusha, how the Hieromonach Zinovi put the argument for allowing the hair to grow to its natural length: 'Inasmuch as the hair is a natural growth and not an act of faith, it grows upon us like the rushes and reeds in damp places; therefore, in itself it has neither salvation nor holiness in it. A shaven man may have a good soul, while, on the contrary, there are impious persons and malefactors with beards and mustaches. What then is the objection that these should cut their hair and shave their beards?' He's hard to answer, isn't he, Valyusha? And the Old Believers equivocate: they don't want to submit to the truth. The image of God Himself is bearded, they say, and therefore it is unlawful to shave the beard. Then Father Zinovi finished them with his answer: 'Not so,' he says, 'for two reasons: a) God is a spirit without earthly flesh and therefore has neither beard nor mustache; and b) since babes and women have no beards, then are they not made after God's image?' That's very deep, Valyusha, very deep!"

And, delighted with the excellence of his memory, gloating over the fact that the "heretics" had been pinned down in argument, Merkuri Avdeyevich would stroke his beard, and chuckle and exclaim to himself: "Such is the absurd doctrine of these advocates of beards!"

Meshkov regarded religious learning as the senior, and secular science as the junior, branch of knowledge, and had he believed that some form of dependence comparable to the nature of family ties existed between them, the proportion of publications of the church Slavonic press would no doubt have been reduced on his bookshelves. But science was in his opinion a prodigal son who had no intention of returning under the parental roof. Therefore, Merkuri Avdeyevich's respect for educated people was tempered by caution: God only knew if these medical men and naturalists were not perhaps connected with sectarians? Better keep away from them—it would be safer.

And that was why Merkuri Avdeyevich accepted the invitation of his gay tenant, Mefody, with interest tempered with a certain caution, particularly as he had not only recognized Tsvetukhin, the actor, and not only discerned in Pastukhov a rare bird such as, perhaps, he had never come across before, but moreover he was disturbed by the invitation to have a drink, a ticklish business in which he had never attained perfect command of himself.

"Here you are," said Mefody, handing him a glass with a rounded bowl filled to the very brim so that the vodka trickled down his fingers.

"Oh, no, thanks," Meshkov said, the drop in his voice suggesting that he was making a bow. "I don't drink, at least, hardly at all."

And then his eyes met those of Pastukhov.

CHAPTER

· 7 ·

THE MAN sitting opposite Merkuri Avdeyevich was young, but his stoutness and obvious flabbiness made him look older than his years. In the plumpness and complacence of that face there was something of superiority, but his lips and cheeks were lifted by a polite plaster smile and the eyes were in complete contrast with the repose of the face or the conventionally set smile—they had the inquisitiveness of a pike— greedy, cold, fishy eyes. Meshkov, after a glance into them, was thrown into a state which might be described in the words "Now I'm done for!" Still, it was pleasant and almost flattering to think that the set, conventional smile might waver for a moment and the extraordinary person would address his enlightened conversation to him.

And, true enough, Pastukhov's face became animated, his glance associated itself with the rest of his features, and he held up his glass to clink with Meshkov's.

"Now, none of that nonsense, please!" he said tactfully and at the same time familiarly. "Who's going to believe that you never touch vodka? You aren't a Skopets,* are you, or an old lady from the Salvation Army?"

* Skopets—member of a religious sect in old Russia, practicing castration.—*Trans.*

Well, Meshkov had never heard anything like this before! This sort of talk wasn't at all what he had expected from an educated man, and yet it was full of unusual things. He was particularly struck by the word "Skopets," and laughed. "Then here's to a happy holiday," he said, dropping his ceremoniousness. Brushing his mustache aside from his lips, he tossed the vodka down in a gulp.

"Where'd you attend the Easter morning service?" Pastukhov asked, under the impression that this would be the best conversational opening with Meshkov.

"I am in the habit of attending Easter early service at the church of the old seminary," Merkuri Avdeyevich replied, deciding to his own great satisfaction that he had come across a very intelligent person, after all.

"Well, have the seminarists forgotten yet how to sing?"

"No, they keep up the old custom. They sang 'Christ is risen' trumpet style—'*Christos anesti ek necron,*' in Greek."

"Ah, in the trumpet style, did they?" Pastukhov smiled.

"That's an expression we used always at the seminary: 'with trumpet voice we call,'" Tsvetukhin said.

"I remember you used to sing the 'Malefactor on the cross' when you were at the seminary," Meshkov said respectfully.

"Really?—did you recognize me again?"

"Naturally I would recognize anyone so eminent. I don't go to the theater, but you drop in here occasionally and I've seen you in the church. I was told that you sang in the choir this Easter too."

"So I did."

"You don't say so, Egor?" Pastukhov exclaimed in surprise. "You mean you actually sang the hymns?"

"Exactly."

"What on earth for?"

"Don't forget, Alexander, we're seminarists. We feel drawn to it. Thoughts go back to our young days and when we broke up for the holidays at the seminary. At Easter time there used to be such excitement. We all dressed up, and put on neckties, packed our dress baskets, and rolled up our bedding: early morn-

ing service and liturgy—and that was all. You would
sing at it and then—off for the holiday, off home,
to the country, far from the seminary, home to freedom, to your own people—trembling all over with
joy."

"How true all that is, Egor!" Mefody said sentimentally. "That was just how one felt—all of a
tremble with joy. You'd be as worked up as on
the stage."

"You're never worked up about anything on the
stage," Pastukhov said with a sneer.

But Mefody went on without listening to him. "And
to this day, if I don't put on my dress coat as I used
to do at the seminary, Easter isn't Easter to me."

"Actor indeed!" Pastukhov persisted. "Gets worked
up on the stage! What could he get worked up about?
His dress coat? And I don't believe in your seminarist lyricism, either, Egor. It just happens to be the
fashion, that's all. All the great actors sing in the
choir nowadays. And read the acts of the Apostles,
and the Epistles. And you're following the fashion.
You keep hard on the heels of your Moscow Art
Theatre, never let it out of your sight. They go to a
rooming house, so you go to a rooming house. They
go to the choir—you follow them. They are handed
consecrated wafers on a salver, and you wait till
you're handed them. All this looks a bit too hypo-
critically homespun. You see what I mean?"

"No, I don't," Tsvetukhin replied soberly and evidently puzzled. "I can't for the life of me see what
you have to be so annoyed about."

"I'm annoyed because you try to follow the fashion
so slavishly. And because you pretend that you sing
hymns in the choir out of emotion. You sing them
out of sheer vanity."

He rubbed a root of a radish between his fingers,
sniffed at his fingers, and threw the radish on the table,
saying in a disgusted tone: "It has a funny smell."

Mefody filled the glasses again, with an angry air,
as though he was doing it to punish them. "An actor
has no need to be ashamed of vanity," he said in a
dictatorial tone, raising his glass very high and then
lowering it again. "What kind of actors are we if
we haven't any vanity?"

"And what kind of an actor are you?" Pastukhov repeated, tauntingly.

"I am only the shadow of an actor. The shadow of the great actor, Tsvetukhin."

Pastukhov said nothing for some time, studying Mefody with a fixed look. "The shadow of an actor? That may be, but there's nothing shadowy about your vanity."

Staring him out of countenance and speaking only after a lengthy pause as he did, Mefody replied: "You've got your share of it, too, if it comes to that, Alexander Vladimirovich."

"We ought to love glory as well as you," Pastukhov admitted. "Otherwise no good will come of us. Glory is our driving power."

"And what might you be, if you'll forgive my curiosity?" asked Meshkov, who had not missed a syllable of the conversation and was particularly fascinated by Pastukhov's domineering and scornful manner of speaking.

"I invent all sorts of nonsense for these boa constrictors"—he jerked his head in the direction of the actors—"who in return are trying to choke the life out of me."

At this everybody laughed and reached out to clink glasses, while Meshkov said in a voice that had sunk to a whisper: "So it appears I'm surrounded by talent. In that case, permit me to drink to—talent."

He tossed off this glass, too, at a gulp and felt at once a current that sent his blood racing merrily, yet warningly, over his ears to his head. "Still," he said, persistently now, "with whom have I the pleasure?"

"Ah, it worries you, does it? I'm Alexander Pastukhov. Does the name mean anything to you?"

Merkuri Avdeyevich gripped the table hard with both hands. How on earth had he failed to recognize in this condescending countenance the sole heir of Vladimir Alexandrovich Pastukhov? He had the identical shameless glance, the same offhand way of speaking, as his father. He even laughed like him: passing straight from gravity to laughter as though something burst within him. And his cheeks, those clean-shaven, well-groomed cheeks, were already, in spite of his youth, inclined to droop toward the chin. Yes, indeed, the son had inherited all his father's bad points and it was no wonder that Merkuri Avdeyevich felt the gnawing of an inconsolable wrong.

He remembered that this man's father, Vladimir Pastukhov, had died his debtor, refusing to acknowledge his debt, and that he could not be compelled to acknowledge his debt. The affair had begun while Pastukhov had been employed in the railway central offices. Pastukhov had ordered some hardware and similar goods from Meshkov for the railway, and had received from him a certain commission—on the quiet, of course. The goods had been delivered, but the auditing bureau of the railway refused to acknowledge the order to the full amount. Meshkov tried for a long time, but to no purpose, to obtain compensation for his losses from the railway. Since the affair was a failure, he suggested that Pastukhov should return the commission he had received, but, in the first place, Pastukhov had left the railway by that time, and in the second place, Meshkov had no proof that the commission had been accepted, a fact which Pastukhov calmly pointed out to him when they were alone. Meshkov's utter helplessness in the face of this meanness gave him no peace. He lived an honest, upright life, he thought, and he expected and worried others to do likewise. The acceptance of a commission on orders was a regular thing among railway employees, and the fact that the purveyor paid the commission and that the employee accepted it did not prevent them from considering each other decent, honest people. It was a gentlemanly arrangement made for mutual satisfaction and might be compared to the musical chimes of a clock which merely mark the passage of time, without interfering with time itself. Nevertheless, once the passage of time is suddenly arrested, what use is the musical accompaniment? Meshkov considered that since the bargain had not come off, the accompaniment should be canceled, too. A gentlemanly interpretation of the affair required this. But ideal understandings of this kind were entirely foreign to Pastukhov. He considered that business was a gamble and that it was the businessman's lot in life to sustain the possible risks. So he asked

Meshkov: "What do you want from me, Merkuri Avdeyevich? Are you trying to say that I took a bribe from you? But I would never dare to accuse you of bribing anyone, I respect your reputation as an honest man far too highly to do that!" And after this he never failed to greet Meshkov in the street with a smile, politely raising two fingers to the red band of his gentleman's cap in salute.

It was this smile that opened the old wound as soon as Merkuri Avdeyevich heard the name Alexander Pastukhov. Still gripping the edge of the table, he said: "Why, of course, Alexander Vladimirovich, your name is familiar to me. The late Vladimir Alexandrovich, your father, was my debtor."

"You don't say so?" Pastukhov said with a chuckle. "You're not thinking of collecting my father's debts from me, by any chance?"

"And what do you think, Alexander Vladimirovich? The responsibility for preserving the good name of the dead is laid upon the heirs."

"The best you can do for my father's memory is to leave it alone."

"I'm counting on you alone to do something for his good name, Alexander Vladimirovich."

"Are you? Well, may I inform you," Pastukhov explained, with a touch of malice, "all I inherited from my father was a cupboard afflicted by dry rot and an armchair that stands on three legs. I am not going to pay any of his debts, for I inherited nothing. We'll drink to the eternal repose of his soul and let things rest at that."

"No," Merkuri Avdeyevich said, setting aside his glass, "no, your father never gave a thought to my repose, and you can drink to his without me."

"Now, look here, this is downright un-Christian of you!" Pastukhov exclaimed, apparently delighted. He and his companions burst out laughing.

"It's un-Christian, is it?" Merkuri Avdeyevich said, frowning as he stood up and pushed back his chair with his feet. "You want to teach me Christianity, eh?"

It was evidently his turn to laugh, and a smile seemed about to appear on his face, but froze. The blood darkened his eyes, they started from their sockets, while at the same time the brows drew together like a heavy beetling shade over the bridge of the nose. Again he felt a rush of hot blood to the ears, as though he had taken a gulp of spirit, but this time there was nothing cheering in this flush. He knew that he had only to raise his voice and he would be unable to control the bellow that was struggling for an outlet, and if he tried to stop it, then fury, irrepressible, animate—the fury innermost in him—would break out. He kept himself in hand by a tension still more intoxicating than that current he had felt. He did not shout. He stifled the voice of wine. He allowed his tongue behind those clenched teeth to shape the scathing epithets, capable of destroying opponents: words like "educated gentlemen," "actors," "jurists." Yes, that was the thing—jurists! He strode across the small creaking room, eyeing those "jurists" —those unconventional gents, with their casual manner, glanced through the window into the street, turned, and said in a low voice, so as not to let himself shout: "No, gentlemen . . . when it comes to Christianity . . . I won't allow you . . ."

He took a second glance out of the window, trying to gain control of himself, and though his eyes were dimmed by wrath, he saw with a strange vividness his own daughter, Lisa, strolling leisurely along accompanied by a young man, yes, indeed, that young Kirill Izvekov, from the Technical School. Lisa was walking on the sunny side of the street, and she was in her best school uniform, a brown dress with a lilac bow on the chest, the uniform of the Mariinsky High School; she was actually walking with a young fellow, as though her parents' house did not exist, in full view of all its windows, its blue gates, and wicket gate. The fixed, frozen parental gaze of Merkuri Avdeyevich—Good God!—saw her, yes, indeed, saw plainly his own Lisa strolling in the company of a young man, the son of the schoolmistress, Izvekova, who was as casual as these gentry here, an independent and perhaps even subversive woman-naturalist— of course, she would be a naturalist! They were all naturalists. Or jurists. And Merkuri Avdeyevich's daughter was gallivanting with a young man! Yes, no other word came to the tip of his tongue at

that moment and could not have come, so he delivered this word with indignation.

"I won't allow you gentlemen, excuse me—but I
won't allow you to do any gallivanting that way!"

With this he flung out—he did not walk out or
run out, but flung out—of the house, seizing his bowler
hat and stick and giving a perfunctory bow as he
went.

"I must be going. . . . Good day, gentlemen!"

Pastukhov got up quickly and went over to the
window. He was in time to see Meshkov swing open
the gate and bang it behind him so that the iron
latch clicked sharply.

"Now that's the fellow one should write about!"
he said quickly, passing his hand roughly over his
face as though wiping himself after a cooling wash.

"Then this isn't just imagination, but real life!"
Tsvetukhin exclaimed.

Pastukhov struck a match, flung it away into the
corner without having lit his cigarette, cast a glance
up at the foggy dim ceiling and walls, seeing nothing
but seemingly retreating from the bounds of the low,
small room.

"It's all the same," he said resignedly. "The dust
of impressions has settled and solidified into stone.
The artist imagines he is free to carve whatever he
wishes from the stone. He will carve nothing but life.
Fantasy is the fruit of observation."

"So the tramps will come in for something, after
all, you agree?"

"Everything the public likes will come in useful."

"And what about art, Alexander?"

"The public comes first, then art."

"Alexander! Ah, Alexander!"

In the tone of an indulgent mentor, Pastukhov went
on. "Egor, my dear chap, I'm very fond of you!
You're a charming provincial! . . . But don't you
realize—one must pander to the public? And that is
what you, with your tramps are doing—pandering to
it. Understand?"

"We do indeed," tipsy Mefody replied. "Not a
doubt of it. Goes without saying, even . . ."

THE THICK, carpetlike tablecloth with its raised pattern was strewn with leaves and flowers, and its yielding surface reminded you of a sandy river bottom underfoot when you first step into the water. Annochka sat turning the pages of a large book, and when she came to a picture, she thrust her hand under the binding and stroked the cloth.

"Do you have a cloth on the table every day or only on Sundays?" she inquired.

"We have a different cloth on weekdays," Vera Nikandrovna answered with a smile. "Which do you like best—the cloth or the pictures?"

"I like pictures to think about and I like the tablecloth to feel."

"You didn't tell us why you don't go to school."

"No, because you asked me if I learned anything or not and I said I didn't."

"Oh, you like to be very exact, don't you?"

"It isn't because I like to be exact, but because I only answer what I'm asked."

"I daresay you would do well at school."

"How do you know?"

"I'm a teacher."

"Do teachers know everything beforehand?"

"No, of course not. But I can see that you would find it easy to learn your lessons."

"This last autumn that came before the winter, Mama put me to school. And then she wanted to have Pavlik and so she took me away from school again to mind him. You see, Papa doesn't work on the Volga in wintertime, and Mama has to do more sewing than ever. She makes bonnets, you know, and if they're with insertion, she sells them for twenty kopeks, and if they haven't any insertion, they're only ten kopeks. Mama taught me how to do the button-holes when it's a buttoned bonnet, and when it fastens with tapes, I can sew them on."

Annochka ceased speaking to look at a large full-page colored picture. Vera Nikandrovna and her son were standing on either side of her, watching her face, to which curiosity lent various expressions: her upper lip curled slightly; the heavy downcast lids of her eyes trembled.

She felt entirely at her ease and, with audible sighs of envy, examined in detail the Izvekov household after Kirill had brought her there. The basement apartment with its iron grilles on the windows, as in old churches, struck her as unusually interesting. In the big room she paused in front of the bookcase and then was astonished to find that the cabinet in the little room was piled with books, too.

"Are these books that you've read, or are they just left there?" she asked, and when she learned that there were all kinds of books and that some had been read and reread several times, she remarked: "Mama says that if she hadn't to work, she would do nothing but read all the time. I suppose you never work?"

In both rooms she studied the arrangement of the beds with their white coverlets, and then, in a tone suggesting that she had now settled something in her own mind, said: "You sleep there, very likely, and you—here, don't you? And we sleep like this: Papa and Mama and Pavlik here, and I sleep by myself on the trunk."

In Kirill's room she looked at the pictures on the walls, but did not care for them: they were mainly bearded grandfathers in one color, except for a huge drawing, all white lines on blue paper. "What's that?"

"A cross-section of a steamer—you know, as if you cut it in two," Kirill replied.

"Cut a steamer in two?—what do you mean?" she

demanded, looking from the drawing to Kirill and his mother in astonishment.

They laughed, and then Kirill asked: "You can't believe that a steamer can be cut in two?"

Annochka moved away from the steamer, glanced into the kitchen, and shook her head sadly with a sigh when she saw the broad Russian stove.

"We haven't any kitchen at the rooming house, but when we lived in rooms like these—it was when I was only a bit bigger than Pavlik, Mama told me—we had a kitchen. And after Pavlik was born, Mama brought a kerosene stove, and she heats up Pavlik's bread-and-milk or cooks his gruel on it. And when Papa buys liver pie at the market, we heat that up on the kerosene stove, too. Ours is the only one in the rooming house, and everybody wants to borrow it, but Mama doesn't lend it. She's right, after all, we'd never have a chance of using it if we lent it to everybody."

They offered her a book with pictures in it to look at. She settled herself promptly on the couch, smoothed her dress over her knees, showed Vera Nikandrovna each of her outspread hands in turn, changing the fifty-kopek piece from one to another.

"They're clean. I washed them only a little while ago." And, to make sure, she rubbed them again on the front of her dress.

A picture over which she lingered was of a street crowded with gaily dressed people waving their arms and dancing, while above them floated green and red balloons and long paper streamers coiled and curled, flung down by other people on the balconies of the tall houses.

"Are they playing blindman's buff?" Annochka wanted to know.

"No, it's a carnival," Kirill said.

"Then why have they all bandaged their eyes?"

"They haven't bandaged them. Those are masks they're wearing."

"Why?"

"So as they won't know each other."

"But they have slits cut in the masks—they can see each other."

"Yes, but still they can't tell who is who."

"Are they actors?"

"Why should they be actors?" Vera Nikandrovna asked in surprise. "How do you know what actors are?"

"I know. They're people who make believe," Annochka replied without stopping to think.

"Make believe? Have you ever seen them?"

"Yes, I have. Some came to see us just now. And there was one just like this man in the picture—the black one."

And she pointed to a man in a black mask, dancing in a cape that billowed and blew out with his movements; then suddenly she burst into giggles, covering her mouth with her hand like a schoolgirl over her lessons.

"He gave Papa fifty kopeks, and Mama and me—we took the money off Papa."

"He felt sorry for you, and now you laugh at him," said Kirill, laughing too.

"So you didn't see the actors in the theater?" Vera Nikandrovna persisted. "And you haven't been to the show at the fair, either?"

"I asked Mama to take me on the merry-go-round. She keeps promising and promising, but she never goes."

"Kirill, you were thinking of going to the merry-go-round—take her with you. When are you thinking of going?"

He did not answer at once, but stood tugging at the folds of his blouse, drawing them toward the back so that they stuck out in a pleated tail from under the tightly drawn belt, as was the fashion among schoolboys then. "I thought of going tomorrow. But I don't suppose I'll be going by myself."

He said this very simply, but Vera Nikandrovna imagined at once that he spoke with reluctance, too, and that perhaps she was meddling in his private life, which was drifting further from home, but where exactly she could not tell as yet. There was no doubt that Kirill avoided conversations that might afford an answer to her conjectures about his new interests, attachments, or fancies. In her heart she was proud of the fact that she had brought up her son on a basis of mutual respect; they not only loved but also respected each other; in particular, she was proud that she respected her son. In early childhood she had trained him to be self-reliant, had imperceptibly instilled into him the idea that in its very nature the son's will cannot interfere with the mother's freedom, that the wishes of parents and children naturally coincide. She herself was convinced that this adroit move would bring excellent results. And true enough, Kirill always acted as he thought fit, and because of this, had no need to hide anything. Falsehood goes with compulsion. It is the bitter fruit of violence. Vera Nikandrovna never compelled her son to do anything against his wishes. And Kirill repaid her for his independence with complete trust.

She considered this kind of upbringing manly and valued what she had achieved, especially since she had brought him up without a father's help (Kirill's father was drowned in the Volga, his boat capsizing in a storm).

Vera Nikandrovna understood that her son was growing to manhood: he had turned eighteen, and was going up into the top class. She understood, too, that maturity meant changes. She expected changes. But she never dreamt that these changes might involve the loss of that frankness, that the change would consist of the appearance of secretiveness. She could not speak to Kirill about his lack of frankness. It was perfectly plain to her that such an admission, once made, would strike a blow at the edifice she had built up so painstakingly all these years. She kept up appearances as though nothing had changed, but she was amazed that Kirill was capable of falsehood and secrecy. She discovered this in the following way.

There was something wrong with his eyes. The eyelids were inflamed and the redness had a gray, sometimes purple, tinge. The ailment alarmed his mother at first, then an explanation was found for it, after which it did not seem so frightening—the eyes must have got some dust in them. Experienced people advised cleansing them with tea in an eyebath. When this simple domestic remedy failed in efficacy, they went to a clinic. The doctor made the necessary inquiries and wanted to know, by the way, if the patient had anything to do with lead, with some compound of lead, or perhaps with lead dust. Kirill said no, he had not, but after a moment's thought, he remembered

that in the tool shop of the Technical School some
spare parts were made of zinc. The doctor submitted
his patient's statement to a close scrutiny and asked
what kind of spare parts were made of zinc in a tool
shop, he did not think he had ever heard of them—
what were they for? They weren't really for anything
in particular but experimental purposes, for testing
instruments on soft metal, Kirill explained with a
quick glance at his mother, who was in the oculist's
room with him. And from the way that he glanced
at her and then turned away abruptly, Vera Nikandrovna suddenly realized that he was lying. Her discovery alarmed her. She decided that she must have
been mistaken, but from the moment that she decided
she was mistaken, she began involuntarily to watch,
to see if her son always told the truth. The doctor
diagnosed the affection of the eyes as lead poisoning
and declared his intention of mentioning the matter
in the proper quarters so that the health of the students should be better looked after in the Technical
School. Vera Nikandrovna fancied that the doctor's
words embarrassed Kirill, but almost immediately
she decided that he was not at all embarrassed, but
worried about his eyes, and she herself suffered
great anxiety about his health. The affection of the
eyes was eventually cured, but the impression she
had received from the discovery made at the doctor's
remained with her. It was not that relations between
mother and son lost their warmth; this, of course, was
out of the question, but the new phase in that indis-
soluble friendship was marked by a hardly perceptible
shadow, as the close of summer is manifested by the
first yellow leaf, still hidden from sight among vivid
green foliage.

And now once again it seemed that the yellow leaf
had reappeared. It was whirling, a reminder that everything passes—was glimpsed, fluttered and vanished,
and once again, as always, Vera Nikandrovna looked
into her son's face with the same pure gaze that said:
I believe you as I have always believed you and I
am sure that you are keeping nothing from me.

"I think I'll go for a stroll," Kirill said now, throwing his jacket around his shoulders.

"Didn't you go for a stroll only a little while ago?"

"No, I was only standing at the gate."

Kirill went out of the room with his heavy stride—his gait was not yet fully formed. In general, he strove for an appearance of burliness, though he was light and his movements naturally quick and agile.

Before he had time to go out, the door was opened by an uncertain hand and Parabukin peered in from the dim passage. His soft mane of hair stirred in the draft, his voluminous trousers flapped like a skirt as he moved, and the vague figure was something like a giantess.

"Who's there? What do you want?" Vera Nikandrovna murmured.

"Papa!" Annochka called out, jumping down from the couch behind the table.

"So this is where you're hiding," he said in a mild tone, crossing the threshold. "Good evening, and excuse me bothering you—I've come for my daughter. What are you doing here?"

"They're showing me pictures."

"Pictures, eh? That's hospitality, too, thank you for it. Here, take this," and he handed Annochka the ham sandwich which had bits nibbled off the edges.

"Come along home. Say thank you for the hospitality."

"Maybe we won't let her go with you," Vera Nikandrovna said rather uncertainly.

"You won't let her? And who may you be that you won't let a child go to her parents?"

"You're cruel to her. How can you?"

"Let her say how I treat her. Ask her, eh? Why don't you ask her, eh?"

"Tell me, do you want to go with your father or not?" Vera Nikandrovna asked gently and kindly.

Annochka had just bitten off a morsel of white bread; her mouth was full. She nodded affirmatively and padded across the floor to her father. Standing beside him, she looked at Vera Nikandrovna as though seeing her for the first time and not particuularly interested in knowing her. Triumphant, Parabukin drew the child closer to him.

"Eat the ham—go on, take a bit of the ham," he urged, pointing insistently at the sandwich. "Why are you eating only the bread?"

He shook his mane and threw back his head, wordlessly asserting his parental authority, his superiority over these strangers.

"Say thank you for the hospitality," he insisted in a challenging tone.

Then Vera Nikandrovna's voice assumed its more severe schoolmistress's note. "You talk about parents' rights, but what do you do with them? You don't even send your girl to school. And she's a bright child, she ought to go to school."

"Thank you kindly. I have had some schooling myself, and if there's anything I do differently than others, it's not because I'm more stupid than they are."

"Then you ought to be ashamed."

"Whenever anyone wants to live after his own way of thinking, people are sure to try and shame him."

"You say this before your own child?" Vera Nikandrovna gasped. "Do you mean that according to your own way of thinking you decided to let her grow up untaught?"

"Well, if it worries you so much, take and teach her yourself."

"Yes, I will take and teach her!"

"Then teach her."

"I certainly will teach her."

Kirill suddenly burst out laughing, and his laughter was echoed by Annochka, who turned away and covered her mouth with her hand. The grownups saw themselves as fighting cocks and might, very likely have gone on to talk in a different tone had it not been for an unexpected interruption. A baby's wail was heard, and Olga Ivanovna, with Pavlik in her arms, darted in from the yard to the passage and from there into the room.

"Oh, please forgive us, I beg you will forgive us for annoying you like this," she exclaimed as she ran in, hardly able to get her breath, her trembling fingers tidying loose braids of hair, her great eyes almost starting from her head. "Please excuse Annochka. . . . I've been looking for her all the time—I couldn't imagine where she'd got to. . . . Excuse her, she's not dressed properly. . . . And I'm not dressed, either. . . . Hush, Pavlik, sh-sh-sh! Here, you take him, Annochka, you can keep him quiet. . . . Now, how could you run here and bother strangers, my dear, that wasn't right, was it? . . . My poor little girl. And it's all because of you, Tisha—now, aren't you ashamed of yourself? This is no way to behave, is it eh? . . . Excuse us, won't you, we're very much obliged to you! I see you've made peace between father and daughter. Oh, what a disgrace, Tisha!"

She could not restrain the torrent of words that broke from her, and she appealed to each in turn, startled and yet pleased that, when all was said and done, things had turned out better than she thought. And, dumbstruck and embarrassed by her outburst of feeling, they all stared at her.

"And you're giving her food, too, you're giving her sandwiches," she went on, bobbing a curtsey to them, "thank you, and please forgive us all for the trouble. Thank you very much and please excuse us all. Thank you, thank you again. Annochka, give Pavlik a bit of the white roll and perhaps he'll stop screaming. Come along now, come along. . . ."

She hustled her husband and little girl out of the room, glancing back and apologizing all the time.

Vera Nikandrovna cut short her apologetic entreaties. "I promised to take your little girl to the merry-go-round. Have you any objection? Then send her to us tomorrow, will you?"

"Oh, I'm very much obliged to you," Olga Ivanovna gushed.

The Izvekovs accompanied them to the door. As they were leaving, Parabukin, awkward and somewhat abashed, asked Kirill with childish curiosity: "Would you have tried to stand up to me when we were at the gate, just a while ago?"

"If you'd wanted to fight, of course I would."

"You're clean crazy, young fellow! Why, I carry bales of about four hundredweights on the wharves. I can carry a piano on my back.

"What if you do? Kirill said with a shrug. "At home even the walls help—I dare say I'd have managed somehow. . . ."

He laughed and watched the strange procession as it filed through the yard: the little girl with the screaming baby in her arms, the huge loose-knit figure of the Samson behind her, and, last of all, the small, brisk woman who kept talking, talking, talking.

"That's a curious family," Vera Nikandrovna remarked.

"Yes, really amazing," Kirill agreed. "Well, I think I'll go for a stroll."

"Yes, do."

And, just as a little while before the two of them had stood watching the Parabukin family go, so now she stood alone watching her son as he crossed the yard and lingered a few moments at the gate, his elbows sticking out; she watched him go down the street until he dwindled in the distance and was lost to sight.

Was it conceivable that he was hiding something from her?

CHAPTER

· 9 ·

THE TOWN HAD a big boulevard with two flower gardens and a parklike square in the English style with pavilions where one ate ice cream with silver-plated spoons, and a kind of cottage where one could sit and drink kumiss and yoghurt. The avenues, planted with lilac bushes and limes, elms and poplars, led to a wooden stage constructed in the form of a large shell. The regimental band used to play here on Sundays and the whole town, people of every calling and of all ages, came here to pass the time. Each calling and each age had its own particular time for visiting the boulevard and its own part of it. The boulevard itself was known as the Limes and under this name had its place in the biography of every townsman, great or small. From the new flower garden, which was exposed on every side to the sun, came the piercing incantations of children at play: "Burn, burn bright, let it not go out at night!" and the babble of unwearying tongues, in counting-out games and the like, such as 'Your lady's sent a fine new gown, a hundred rubles to weigh it down, buy left, buy right, take no black, take no white, don't say yes and don't say no. What would you buy?" After sundown, when the scent of the tobacco flowers hung heavy and intoxicating on the air, the English-style square was full of silent ladies with parasols and serious men who wore Shantung silk jackets and read the popular novels. In the morning the kumiss cottage attracted people with weak lungs, and the sunlight, breaking through the foliage, dappled the little tables, the half-empty glasses, and the pale, tapering hands lying motionless beside them. On Sundays and holidays the shop assistants and artisans stood in a crowd in front of the shell-shaped bandstand, listening to martial music, applauding loudly, and calling "encore" after "The Railway Train March" had been played. Through the avenues flowed in opposite directions two slow streams of couples, pressed close to one another, polishing the paths with the soles of their shoes and watching idly the bottles of lemonade being opened in the pavilions, and the swarms of gnats dancing under the gas lamps, and the powdery dust wreathing up from the ground like smoke.

No, this was not the place where Lisa and Kirill met. The town had another boulevard, a small square of green in a side street near the riverbank. Here, too, the clipped acacias grew close to the wooden fence—the interlacing of them with lilac bushes was reminiscent of exposed tendons—the elms grew, and the limes aged. But no ice cream was sold here, there were no pavilions, no band played, no one drank kumiss. There was only a caretaker's hut with a piano-shaped bin against which he leaned his broom and a pair of oars. And there were a few low green benches in the single line of green that crossed the boulevard from end to end like an aerial dart. This boulevard was known in the town as Dog's Limes, and only an occasional passer-by glanced into its shade to fan himself with cap or handkerchief, mop his bald patch, and rest a few minutes before going on in pursuit of his worldly cares.

Dogs' Limes acquired the same place in the life story of Lisa and Kirill, as the real Limes—in the life story of many young people—having become an unforgettable, almost fatal landmark in the most treasured of their emotional experiences on the threshold of their youth. Here, before either one of them had reached the age of sixteen, Kirill handed Lisa his first love letter, which he had written high up under the roof beams of the school, where the pigeons were, written by the light that came from the dormer window and with the beating of wings of those homing birds all around him. His innermost feelings throbbed in this letter, but if a teacher of literature had read it, he would have discovered another secret: before climbing up to the attic with his paper, pen, and ink, Kirill had just finished reading Lermontov's *A Hero of Our Time*, and his note to Lisa was no less tragically worded than Vera's farewell note to Pechorin, yet it was full of sunny, bright hopes. As he slipped it into Lisa's palm in parting, she asked with alarm:

"What's this?"

"A note," Kirill replied in a scarcely audible voice.

"Who is it to?"

"You."

"Why?"

"You'll read it at home," he said—he could hardly speak, he was so afraid that she might not take it.

But she blushed, slipped the note into her bosom under the school apron, and ran away, while he stood panting as if he had come up to the surface of the water with a great effort.

They did not see each other for a long time after this, and when they did meet, Lisa returned the note to him and said indignantly:

"How dare you? . . . How dare you write so familiarly to me—using 'thou' everywhere! Write it all over again, addressing me properly as 'you.' "

Now, after two years, he was so grown up that he could smile when he recalled the incident of the note, but at the time Lisa's annoyed demand awakened in him a sense of unusual responsibility and he painstakingly carried it out, and copied his confession of love, addressing her as "you" and not "thou."

That first summer of their meetings they had discovered in Dogs' Limes their own special walk, a narrow path between thickets of old lilacs and a wall of acacias, where they were hidden from the eyes of the caretaker. Here, for the first time, Kirill took Lisa's hand and she did not snatch it away, and they strolled along the path, moved by the first diffident touch, gladdened and happy. Here, at the end of the summer, Lisa uttered at last the word "thou" that had annoyed her in the spring, when she had seen it written on a scrap of paper. Here, the following summer,

Kirill plucked a plume of white lilac that was just
coming out and, laying it carefully against her breast
beside the bow of ribbon she wore, said that white
went very well with her brown dress. As Lisa took
the flower, she pressed his fingers lightly against her
small breast and they both stood for a second, stunned. Then she hid the white lilac under her apron
so that the caretaker would not see it.

They had their own favorite bench at the far end
of the avenue, behind the caretaker's hut. They used
to have long arguments on controversial questions,
such as: is conscience an absolute conception or are
there different kinds of consciences, let us say, beggars'
consciences, the consciences of young people at high
school and technical schools, and the consciences of
women and men.

"Perhaps all this conscience business is pure invention," Kirill said doubtfully. But Lisa protested in a
whisper:

"You're crazy! When anyone blushes, it means he is
conscience-stricken, doesn't it?"

"Yes, but I'm talking from a philosophical stand-
point."

"And so am I. If the blood rushes to your face
or you can't sleep because your conscience is troubling
you, then something must exist. And that something is
conscience."

"Well, if it's repentance—that's a function . . ." he
said thoughtfully, and then the conversation drifted
into abstractions as sails glide away into the sea fog.

Their talk turned most often on what they would
do when they would be together. That was the way
they spoke of it from year to year: when we're together. Each was free to interpret it as he or she liked,
but both thought that they understood each other
perfectly. In general it seemed to them that they
knew all there was to know about each other and
had been living for each other a very long time.
Both kept their meetings a secret from their people
at home; Kirill did so because he considered that his
mother did not require an account of his own private
affairs, and Lisa because she was afraid of her father.

But the third summer, or rather, with the advent of
the third spring, they raised the most important ques-

tion—had the time come to disclose their secret? Lisa was finishing high school; Kirill had still another year of school. They saw themselves as students, living in little rooms, or perhaps—could it be possible?—in one room, somewhere in Moscow. It was decided that Lisa should tell her mother first. There was nothing at all frightening in that: for one thing, Valeria Ivanovna already suspected something; for another thing, she was so very kind; and, for a third, she would break the news to Merkuri Avdeyevich. It would be no trouble for Kirill to inform Vera Nikandrovna of the whole thing.

"I shall simply let her know," he said rather carelessly.

"It's easy for you in any case," Lisa remarked. "You kept the secret so easily, too. And it's worried me all the time. When you come to think of it, it's just the same as telling a lie."

"No, there's a tremendous difference!" he objected in a very decided tone. "In one case, you tell a deliberate lie, in the other you are simply silent."

"In my opinion, it's just the same; to keep silent about the truth or to speak an untruth comes to the same thing. . . . Tell me, could you keep the truth from me?"

"W-well, if it was for the sake of some very important purpose, I suppose I could."

"And could you tell me an untruth?"

"Why do you ask?"

"No, tell me."

"Lie to you? Have I ever lied to you?"

"Never!" Lisa exclaimed in indignation. Then, in an ingratiating voice she asked: "And you won't?"

"Why do you ask?" he repeated, in an offended tone.

"Oh, I'm simply asking," she replied reluctantly. After a few moments' silence, she asked, as though she was speaking of something quite remote: "Do you happen to know Pyotr Petrovich?"

Kirill suddenly fell out of step, gave her a quick glance, then turned his eyes away and went at a slower pace.

This talk took place on the day they called Independence Day. Kirill had seen Lisa coming home from church in the morning and had gone up to her, and it was so unexpected, bold and lighthearted, that they took three decisions at once: to proclaim that day Independence Day, to walk past the Meshkovs' house together quite openly that day, and the next day to go to the fair together in honor of Independence. Lisa's heart beat fast as they walked, slowly on purpose, keeping in step, along the street where every brick in the pavement and every twig in the fence was familiar to her and where her own home stood. She was expecting every moment to hear her father's voice calling her, a relentless, stern voice, the sound of which might turn her destiny, and she was sure that her mother's kind eyes, full of tears, were watching her bitterly from the window. She felt afraid and abashed. But now they had passed the house and nothing had happened. And, proceeding in the same prim, dignified way down the street, Kirill told Lisa about the incident with Annochka, his acquaintance with Tsvetukhin, and then they discussed the best way to break the news at home and went on to speak of truth and untruth, and it was at this point that Kirill suddenly fell out of step.

"Which Pyotr Petrovich is that?" he asked, apparently calm.

"Ragozin," she said.

"Yes, I know him," he admitted indifferently, "as well as one knows all one's neighbors in the same block. A sort of nodding acquaintance."

"Don't you ever drop in to see him?"

"Why should I?"

"Now that's a lie for you!" Lisa cried triumphantly and yet stricken.

"No, it isn't," he retorted sharply, slackening his pace still more.

"I can see it by your face. You've gone pale! What are you keeping back? I know you've been to see him."

"How you do go on," he protested stubbornly. "Where did you get this idea?"

"You came into our yard once with a troop of boys. Do you remember, it was the day after Easter, when that Bulgarian with the barrel organ and the monkey came and brought a whole crowd of idlers after him, you remember, don't you?"

"Well, and supposing I did come into the yard? I had a look at the monkey and then went off. If you want to know, I came more for the sake of looking up at your windows, thinking perhaps I might see you. I didn't want to look at the monkey at all. What would I want with a monkey!"

"That's not true, either! It's just another falsehood. I was standing at the window looking out at the performance. I can tell you everything the monkey did, in the proper order. First it showed how a lady walks with her parasol, then—how a peasant woman goes out for water, then a drunken tramp sprawling under the fence. . . ."

"I can see that you watched the monkey all the time. It's no wonder you lost sight of me," Kirill retorted with a grin.

"I could see you perfectly plainly where you were standing at the back of the crowd. And you didn't look up once at the window. Not once! Otherwise you would have seen me. Someone in the house called me for a minute; I went away from the window and when I came back you were gone."

"I got sick of all that mopping and mowing and went away."

"Where?"

"Out into the street and home."

"I ran out to look for you in the street and you weren't there. You'd disappeared, but without leaving the yard. Where could you have gone? Only into Ragozin's."

"Oh, look here, Lisa, what has Ragozin to do with it?" Kirill demanded, brightening and looking at her with a smile. His gentleness softened her. Soothed a little, but with a shade of disappointment, she sighed:

"Still, now I'm convinced that you can hide the truth from me."

"I told you—there are truths that ought not to be told."

"What do you mean?" she cried, "you think there can be two truths? One to speak and one to hide?"

She turned toward him abruptly, and as they were just going into Dogs' Limes, a backward glance showed her the street open before her like a leaf turned in a book, the street empty save for one person whom she recognized instantly.

"My father!" she whispered, forgetting all she had been saying.

As she passed through the gate of the boulevard, she seemed lifeless and stiff in her school uniform, her body losing all its suppleness. She darted into the lilac bushes that enclosed the avenue in a shielded thicket.

"Steady there." Kirill said sternly, trying not to give way and run after her. "Don't run, Lisa. Remember—Independence Day."

He hitched up his uniform jacket which he had worn since spring thrown carelessly over his shoulders, a fashion that distinguished the manly grown-up Technical School boys from the High School, Real School and Commercial School, and followed her slowly, disappearing into the thicket where the foliage rustled in alarm as Lisa parted the branches.

By the time Merkuri Avdeyevich reached the boulevard, he found it deserted. He turned back at once. He went up the street with his inexorable stride, stamping heels and stick into the pavement as though he was ready at any moment to halt and stand firmly wherever the necessity dictated; he was listening intently in his furious imagination to the things he would say to his wife, Valeria Ivanovna, when he got home. He would say:

"Conniver! What are you doing with that daughter of yours? If she went gallivanting about with her young men in the Limes, in the big boulevard, it'd be misfortune enough, but it wouldn't be a disgrace! Everybody knows that even the Limes is the resort of frivolity and looseness, still it's a public place. They aren't all rakes that go there; you can see very respectable people in it sometimes. Even consumptives go there for their health, and not just the riffraff and that lot. But what sort of a place is Dogs' Limes? How could you utter such a word before any decent person? A lot of shrubs and bushes, that's all it is. Bushes and nothing else. And what does that shameless slut, your Elisaveta, do but hide in the bushes with a young lad? You've brought up a treasure, haven't you, with your indulgence and connivance? She has neither shame nor conscience—that daughter of yours!"

Yes, Merkuri Avdeyevich was going to say this: that girl of yours has neither shame nor conscience—not a sign of it!

GLEAMING GRAY, a huge cumulus cloud fell from heaven to earth and the whistling wind rose up from earth to sky to meet it. This was the cradle of the swing boats, tossed upward and descending with an o-oh! o-oh! Girls squealed, concertinas wailed, lads whooped.

> *"So up I sail and down I sail*
> *Past my girl's porch with the fancy rail."*

The drums urged on the supremely oblivious whirling of the merry-go-rounds, the organ-grinders had long since become deafened, the show-booth bells vied with each other, the fairground was in an uproar, rending the air and drawing the crowd into some distant world where everything was painted, and tawdry, fantastic, and pinchbeck, a world that had no real existence and yet existed the more firmly the less resemblance it bore to life itself.

The waxworks, in which lay an effigy of Cleopatra, with a living asp now falling on her sugarywhite heaving breast, now squirming away. The diorama showing a brave cruiser sinking into the watery chasm, and in the depths the notice: "All hands on deck, comrades, for the last parade is coming! Our proud ship, *Variag*, will never surrender to the enemy—no one wants mercy!" The show booths of the "Spider-Woman" and the "Fish-Woman." The show booth with the parrot, the strong man, and the dancer. The show booth where the Black Corsair was beheaded before the eyes of the public. The booth with the dancing poodles and lap dogs. The transformation theater where men were turned into women and vice versa. The Dwarf Theater. The performing Shetland pony. The Human Aquarium. The Chiromancer who revealed the past, present, and future. The American bioscope. The orangutan. The fakir. All these wonders were hidden in mysterious depths behind signboards, linen curtains, fresh plywood, but glimpses could be caught through windows, from platforms, from tops of the steps, to attract spectators, and the crowd was milling around the touts, drifting slowly from booth to booth, calculating for a long time the best way to get their money's worth and hesitating between Cleopatra, the cruiser, and the orangutan.

Here and there in the throng one saw peddlers carrying on their shoulders huge glass pitchers filled with rolling bright-yellow and orange-red drinks. Girded with wet towels, into which sticky mugs were thrust, they proclaimed their wares in high tenor voices: "Cooling, sweetening, lemon- and orange-flavored." Their cries were echoed from various corners by the sellers of kvass and ice cream, cakes and gingerbread; back and forth the voices shuttled, cutting through the cheerful uproar, floating high above caps, headkerchiefs, hats, and shawls. Seen through the peaceful pall of dust that spread over this aimless babel, the buildings in the square seemed wreathed in smoke, and glancing around, Kirill could barely distinguish through the smoke the barracks, the tobacco factory, the jail, and the university. He wanted to get away from the medley of impressions, so he led Lisa out of the crowd. They stopped in front of the ice-cream carts, and he asked:

"What are you going to have—wild strawberry or crème-brûlée?"

They took a "mixed" portion, and he went on talking as he pursued with a bone spoon the balls of ice cream slithering around the saucer.

"I remember the things that went on here when I was a little chap. The cabbies nearly sank here in the autumn, the horses had to be hauled out of the mud. And in the spring the dust was so thick you couldn't distinguish one booth from another. There were far more merry-go-rounds then than there are now. My father used to bring me here—how long ago is that now? Years and years ago. . . ."

"Don't you like crushing your ices?" Lisa asked. "It's nicer like this."

"No, I like it hard."

"Oh, why! It's so buttery when it melts a bit."

"It was the university that squeezed the booths into a corner," Kirill went on explaining. "Soon it'll squeeze the fair out of here altogether. Should we go on the last of the merry-go-rounds, you and I? Do you like the university building? You do? So do I. It looks so free. You know, the main body of the building will be extended until it crosses the streetcar line, squeezes first the merry-go-rounds, then the barracks and the jail out of the square. . . . "

"The jail?" Lisa exclaimed. "It'll never squeeze out the jail."

"Well, I think it will. Look how everything's moving ahead all the time. It's not so long since you and I used to go by horse-drawn streetcar and now we're used to the electric streetcar. And we don't even notice that it's five times quicker. And we're living in what is already a university town. And who knows if, before we have time to look around us, there may be neither barracks nor jails?"

"None at all?"

"None at all."

"No," she objected, "that's what they call Utopia."

"I know it's called Utopia," he said. "But I myself have heard people arguing that we'd never see a university in this town, but look how quickly it all happened. Didn't it? . . . Let's have another ice—chocolate and cream, shall we?"

"It'll be a pity if the booths are crowded out, choked out by the university," Lisa said.

"The university never chokes anything. It will disseminate freedom," Kirill declared, moving closer to her.

She looked up at the white prison walls; it was a long, mournful, and rather misty look, then, crushing her ice mechanically with the spoon, she asked: "Why are the windows in one part of the building barred and those in the other part have some kinds of blinds over them?"

Lowering his voice as much as he could without becoming inaudible, he told her: "The place with the blinds over the windows is the penal-servitude prison for political prisoners mostly. The light comes in, but they can't see anything except a bit of the sky and then only if they stand right under the window. The place with the barred windows is just a common jail for criminals. In 1905 I saw them waving red handkerchiefs through the bars. Do you know any political people?"

"No, I'd be afraid."

"Afraid?" he said in a tone that suggested he was either surprised or offended.

"I suppose I would seem too thoughtless to anyone like that."

"Why? You could talk of whatever you liked. Just as you do with me."

"What a comparison! I couldn't talk to anyone else as I talk to you. Have you any acquaintances like that?"

"Yes," he said, looking around cautiously. "I have."

"Is it Ragozin?" she asked quickly.

"Names aren't mentioned in those sort of conversations."

She fancied that he uttered these words with a certain impressiveness, and there was a silence during which she stared down at her plate. The ice cream was melting in the sun. "I don't want any more," she said.

"But you said you liked it all messed about this way."

"And now I don't want it."

They paid for their ices. Unnoticeably, the irresistible surging tide bore them on, ebbing and flowing from one booth to another, so, to avoid being parted in the press, they linked arms.

"Well, if there isn't to be any more holiday-making here, it'll be a pity," Lisa said at last.

"The chief thing's movement," he said at the very moment that their way was blocked by the crowd in front of the booth where the beheading of the Black Corsair by the king of Portugal was taking place.

They were pressed on every side by hot, soggy bodies which turned Lisa face to face with Kirill, jamming her so hard that she could not stir a finger. She could now see in startlingly close proximity his dark level brows and the beads of perspiration over them and the straight, bold upper lip. He looked very grave, and it somehow amused her.

"Yes, the chief thing is movement," she repeated after him, looking still more closely at his upper lip. "You've got a mustache. I haven't ever seen it till now."

He said almost sternly, unheeding her smile: "Everything moves. When the show booths disappear, the people will go to the theater."

"The theater—oh, that's quite another thing! I'm awfully fond of the theater. I'd give anything for it — I love it so much."

"Why?" Kirill asked still more severely.

"Just to be there in the theater."

"You mean—to go on the stage?"

"Yes."

"You've never said anything to me about it."

"Nothing will come of it anyhow, it's just a sort of fancy of mine," she said with a sigh, and he felt her light, hot breath fanning his face—it was faintly reminiscent of the smell of milk.

He scrutinized her closely, just as she looked at him. Every eyelash was plainly visible, the greenish blue of her eyes was pure and soft, her chin, which quivered slightly, was delicate, her hair was very fine, too fine, and was full of air. Her eyes were narrowed slightly from the glare and her head tilted back a little, so as to see him better, whereas he could see her easily and so clearly. She was trying to free her hands, but he held them fast and was pleased that the throng still pressed close, milling around them.

"You don't look much like an actress," he said.

"And what are actresses like?"

"Different. You're better."

She managed to turn and now they could both see the booth. Pulling aside the unbleached linen curtains at the entrance, the people, dazzled by the sunlight after the dimness, came out, pressing on the crowd. The beginning of the performance was announced by a bell, and on the high platform, as though on a scaffold, the figure of the king of Portugal appeared. Robed in a brocade caftan, with a crown on his tow-colored hair, braided in a queue, he ascended the throne directly beneath the bell. Throwing one leg over the other comfortably—he wore white cotton stockings and gilt slippers with the toes turned up in Tatar style—he blew his nose in a red handkerchief and began to mop his moist neck in a leisurely fashion. His cube-shaped beard had come unstuck at one side and his cheeks were rosy as crab apples.

Hardly had the bell ceased ringing when someone called out from the crowd: "Pa'l Zakharich, what was it like?"

Pavel Zakharovich, who wore a print shirt and a cap with a stiff, shiny peak, promptly picked out the person who had called to him, and did some rapid elbow work in an effort to swim out of the crowd that had already seen The Corsair's execution and reach the crowd that had not yet seen it.

"Took it off clean!" he exclaimed in a high-pitched singsong voice, with such obvious satisfaction that the people around him turned and listened. "Took it off as clean as a whistle! But the blood that gushed out!—Oh, my! The hangman was a dab hand at the game. He wound the fellow's wild curls around his hand and brought his pole ax down on the neck with such a whack, the head rolled right off. And he chucked it into a basket and it hit the bottom with a thud like a block of wood, and the body without the head crumpled up and didn't get up any more. A short life and a gay one, you see, and he'd come to a bad end at last. Then the executioner pulls off his gloves and—chucks 'em into the basket, after the head, and rubs his hands, as much as to say, it's nothing to do with me—I have my orders and I do as I'm bid. But the king. . . ."

At this point Pavel Zakharovich turned and shook an accusing finger at the Portuguese king, and the heads of the crowd turned in the direction indicated by his gesture.

"That one with the crown on his head—he never turned a hair: he'd given orders for the pirate's head to be cut off and he wasn't going back on his royal word. He watched, the snake, how the blood ran out

freely off the ax onto the ground, as if he didn't
care a hang about it. . . . Aye, brother, you ought to go
and see it, really you ought. You won't be sorry, I
warrant! . . ."

The bell sounded the alarm once more, and a
heavily mustached executioner in a red tunic to his
knees and a top hat appeared on the platform and
took up his station beside the king. The human tide
surged nearer.

At that moment Lisa espied Vera Nikandrovna
emerging from the show booth with the crowd. It
suddenly recalled to her mind her father and the fact
that he had not yet uttered a word about the previous
day and that the worst was yet to come, and she felt
a melancholy ache welling slowly to her heart. She
could say nothing and only pressed Kirill's hand
warningly, but he misunderstood and responded with
a grateful pressure. In the crush of people it was impossible to avoid the impending conversation that she
was trying not to think about. Without taking her gaze
from Vera Nikandrovna, she realized at last that the
woman could see them and was making in their
direction.

Suddenly Kirill exclaimed delightedly: "Look, there's
Mama. That's splendid! Come, I'll introduce you
now."

Vera Nikandrovna was not alone—Annochka, now
with tidy, smooth hair and a holiday look, was
beside her and she was trying to shield the child from
the crowd. Well before Kirill said, introducing them:
"This is Lisa," Vera Nikandrovna was looking at her
with that all-seeing, pitiless, and piercing glance of the
mother scrutinizing the girl who can upset and
muddle everything in her son's destiny. Lisa blushed,
looking all the prettier in her confusion, but it did not
last more than a minute, because the conversation that
started effaced the ideas that excited them all, with
the exception of Annochka. Her presence proved to
be very opportune, as she diverted attention to herself.

"Did you like it?" Kirill asked her.

She found no words to answer him: the gloom of
the place she had just quitted still darkened her eyes,
the gloom lit by flickering yellow candles, and in

the light she still fancied she saw the dreadful, sound-less men as though in a night vision. Their life in these flickering lights flew by so swiftly and at the same time so terribly slowly that Annochka could have repro-duced every step of the executioner's, every sigh of the Corsair's, every gesture of the king's. They were grand and terrible. What could she say to such a question as: did you like them? They had over-whelmed her.

"She even screamed when the pirate's head was cut off," Vera Nikandrovna told them. "I'm sorry now that I took her to that dreadful show. She was very frightened. But she was so anxious to see it, there was no gainsaying her."

"No, no, you mustn't be sorry you took me!" An-nochka cried, seizing Vera Nikandrovna's hand and pressing close to her. "I wasn't frightened—no, not a bit. I wasn't the tiniest bit frightened of anything."

She shuddered, her mouth was never still for a moment, she kept moistening and biting her lips in turns.

"No, of course not, Annochka, there's nothing to be afraid of," Kirill said. "After all, you know, it's just make-believe."

"No, it isn't, it's real," Annochka replied in a very decided tone.

"No, there's nothing true in it at all. Do you think the Corsair really had his head cut off? And the blood isn't real blood, it's only made of cranberry juice."

"It isn't!"

"What is it, then?"

"It's real blood."

"Oh, you're just a little girl still."

"No, I'm not just a little girl. And besides, there were grown-up folks sitting there and they believed every bit of it. Because it was true! And the actors were there, too, the men who came to see us yester-day."

"Yes, Tsvetukhin was sitting next to us," Vera Nikandrovna said, "and do you know, Kirill, he applauded loudly. I was surprised—do you think he could have liked it so much?"

"Look, he's coming out now," her son interrupted

her, straightening himself as though afraid he might
not be noticed in the crowd.

Tsvetukhin was walking arm-in-arm with Pastukhov,
who was laughing heartily and smoothing down his
white suit—they were both dressed in white from head
to foot, and were thus very noticeable in the crowd,
especially as they wore panamas, one with a yellow,
the other with an orange band. They were the last to
emerge and they were not with the public, but came out
by the curtained exit through which the actors appeared on the stage. The crowd had dispersed, except
for the knots of people around the king and the
executioner, examining their robes and the ax with the
clotted traces of something red on the curved blade.
Pressed back by the crowd of idlers, Tsvetukhin and
Pastukhov paused before the Izvekovs. Kirill took off
his cap. Tsvetukhin shook hands with him, and
recognizing Annochka, clapped her on the shoulder.

"Here's your acquaintance of yesterday, Alexander,
did you know her again? I see you've made friends
with her," he said to Kirill.

"Yes. And this is my mother, allow me to introduce
you. This is Lisa Meshkova. I don't need to mention
your name because you're known to everyone."

"Meshkova?   Merkuri   Avdeyevich's   daughter?"
Tsvetukhin asked.

"Yes," Lisa's reply was a hardly audible sigh.
"Alexander, this is the daughter of that Meshkov we
met," Tsvetukhin explained.

Pastukhov held out his hand, at the same time continuing brushing and examining his suit. He addressed
everyone as though they were old friends to whom
one might talk without paying much attention.

"We've just been to see the scaffold. It's a monstrous
affair. A very devil of a machine! I got all messed
up with cranberry juice. There isn't a clean spot
left on me. This is terrible, really!"

"Do you hear that, Annochka? I told you there
wasn't any blood. It was only colored with cran-
berries," Kirill said.

Annochka shot Pastukhov a somewhat unfriendly
glance. He blinked at her, glanced at Kirill, and in
the tone of a mentor exhorted him:

"There's no such thing as cranberry in that spot,

young man, as you should know. It's all real pirate blood, shed by His Majesty's own personal executioner. You're right, little girl. They only call the blood cranberry juice so as it won't frighten people too much." He chucked her under the chin. "Look, Egor, she's a real siren. A mermaid, eh?"

"We saw the mermaid, too," Annochka informed him, conscious of her own superiority, and confident that no one would get the chance to make fun of her.

"Well, do you want to turn into a fish?" Pastukhov asked.

"Now you're contradicting yourself," Kirill remarked dryly. "If the blood is real, then the siren must be real. How can Annochka be turned into a siren?"

"That's what you think, is it?" Pastukhov asked quite seriously.

Then Kirill continued with dignity: "Of course. But everyone knows that these tricks are done with mirrors."

"Are they, though?" Pastukhov returned in a still more serious tone, then, after a few moments' silence, burst out laughing at his own peculiar pitch, wiped his hot face with his hands, and spoke in an off-hand tone, through his teeth. "I'd advise you, young man, to give up all this corrosive skepticism. It's just overdone rationalism, that's all—speaking scientifically. I believe that women may be turned into fish or anything you like. Would you want to be a fish—a mermaid?" he said, turning to Lisa with a sudden smile.

"In temperament—no," she replied, blushing.

They all looked at her. The color spread over her face, she saw that Kirill was blushing, too, and she hastened to recover herself.

"I just remember that a friend of mine, in the same class at school, was called after a fish, Crucian, because she had such a phlegmatic temperament. I'm not a bit phlegmatic, am I, Kirill? So if I'm to be transformed into anything, it shouldn't be a fish, but something else."

"What about a spider?" Pastukhov asked in a businesslike tone.

Everyone was amused. Vera Nikandrovna felt a flush of pride in her son and a sense of goodwill toward Lisa, as though Kirill had passed an important examination and Lisa had helped him to pass it.

"Did you really like all that pantomime?" Vera Nikandrovna asked Tsvetukhin with a smile.

"Awfully. I was crazy about that Corsair, especially when he refused to ask for mercy as he was mounting the scaffold. How he acted! He's a marvel!"

Tsvetukhin thumped his chest, pointed down at his feet and the ground, wagging his forefinger right under Pastukhov's nose defiantly, as much as to say: "So Your Portuguese Majesty wants me to go down on my knees to him, does he?—not on your life, I won't."

From his place on the boards the king watched Tsvetukhin's pantomime, glanced at the executioner, and they both burst out laughing. A voice in the crowd cried: "Look, those are players, too!"

"And which booth are you playing in?" Annochka asked innocently.

"I?" Tsvetukhin exclaimed, amid general laughter. "I'm at the biggest show booth of all. When you're a bit older, you'll come and see me."

"Are you a pirate, too?"

"Yes, I'm a terrible robber. Everybody's frightened of me."

"I'm not afraid," Annochka said, raising her head.

Tsvetukhin hugged her. While he was speaking to her, he kept looking at Lisa, and fancied he saw something in common in the way they both listened to him. Only there was more mistrust in Annochka, and tremulous curiosity in Lisa.

"Are you fond of the theater?" he asked her suddenly.

"Very," she said in a scarcely audible voice, and was glad that the bell, jingling its desperate alarm, almost drowned her answer. Tsvetukhin took a step toward her, as though expecting her to repeat it and said aloud, but in a tone that probably no one else could hear:

"When you go to the theater, come round by the stage door and see me."

She made no reply.

Pastukhov touched his elbow. "Come along. Let's be going. We decided to see all the shows together," he added as the good-bys were beginning.

When they had gone a little way, Tsvetukhin asked: "Did you notice the way she cast down her eyes, Alexander?"

"Who? The little girl, you mean?"

"No, not the little girl, the big girl."

Pastukhov said nothing. After they had gone a few yards, Tsvetukhin turned around, but he could not see either Lisa or the Izvekovs.

"A wonderful girl!" Tsvetukhin remarked.

Pastukhov pretended he did not hear.

"Wonderful girl, that of Meshkov's, isn't she?"

Pastukhov blinked at the kvass-sellers who were coming toward them, the stall-keepers, and the showbooth touts. Suddenly he stopped Tsvetukhin and without a word pointed at the signboard. It showed a black poodle standing on his hind legs, holding a cane, a pair of white gloves in his teeth. "Can you see it?"

"What?"

"You understand what it is?"

"Well, what is it? A dog with a cane."

"It's exactly what you are," Pastukhov said with conviction.

They shot sideways glances at each other and both smiled, but Tsvetukhin was slightly ruffled.

· II ·

During the Jewish pogrom of October 1905, Pyotr Ragozin was arrested by the police along with some members of a fighting squad that was firing at the pillagers. No arms were found on him, but a witness fawning on the police testified that Ragozin shot and wounded a carter in the crowd. Still, no proof that the prisoner belonged to a fighting squad could be produced. Ragozin was kept a year in prison, and thereafter banished for three years on a charge of disturbing the peace.

The day he was starting on his journey to the place of banishment, his two-year-old son died of scarlatina, but the news reached Ragozin much later. His wife, Ksenia Afanasyevna, Ksana for short, a small, pale, fair woman, with perpetually raised brows and a small chiseled nose, sharp elbows, and tapering arms, might have passed for Pyotr's daughter when seen beside him. He was lean and big-boned. His heavy, clumsy body was set on long, slightly bowed legs with a marked inclination forward, giving the impression of being ready to topple any moment. At the time of his arrest he was thirty, but his big face with its close bristling brown beard and curling mustache wore a good-natured, understanding smile such as may be observed on the faces of those who have seen a great deal in their time and grown wise with the years,

and for this reason many took him for a man of forty
and more. As he lumbered along at the side of his
Ksana, the very stoop of his figure had a paternal
protectiveness, and she accepted this shielding attitude
naturally, as a weaker and more delicate creature. The
street was fond of watching them, and laughing at
them, calling Ragozin by his nickname, "The Wheel of
Babel," or just "Babylon." This joke lost its sting and
became more a mark of affection after the baby was
born, and on Sundays, Pyotr, bent even more than
usual, would be seen carrying the bundle wrapped in
a patchwork quilt, with a corner of a lace-edged
sheet indicating the place where the infant's head
should be.

"There's Babylon taking his family out for a walk,"
the neighbors would chuckle. They regarded the
Ragozins as a happy and even an affectionate couple.
And it was true—the only roughness Ksana could ever
remember experiencing from her husband was on that
unhappy morning of the pogrom.

She was standing with some of her neighbors at
the gate, holding an icon, so that the ruffians who
were carrying on the pogrom would not think the
house she lived in was tenanted by Jews. The black
gang, flourishing their knobkerries, whistling and
howling like wolves, rushed through the streets. Some
of the more bloodthirsty among them dashed into
yards, hot on the scent of Jews who had hidden, or in
search of their abandoned homes, and the mob would
fling itself upon the prey, crushing everything in its
path—human bones, window frames, screaming children, stands of crockery, setting fire to everything and
leaving in its wake the creeping stench of smoke.
Suddenly a different group of men ran out from
around the corner, and stretched out in a line across
the road. "Fire point-blank!" came the order in a low
voice. Ksana did not notice when Pyotr, who had
been standing beside her at the gate, had slipped into
the house. She saw him when he reappeared suddenly,
the outside man in the file, and moved ahead briskly
with the rest, never glancing back. Ksana thrust the
icon into someone's hands and ran after him. She caught
at him, but he went steadily on, without taking his
hands out of his pockets, or turning, at his heavy, lum-

bering gait. She clung to his jacket. He still went on.
She hung on, screaming: "Petya, Petenka! My own
dear Petya!" He was dragging her along now, seemingly unheeding of her weight. She wailed: "Think of
the child!" He turned then, tore his jacket from her
clutch, pushed her angrily away on to the road, and
went on. From where she lay on the ground she could
hear pistol shots, and, covering her face with both
hands, she burst into tears.

Pyotr Ragozin never returned home. It was an
unexpected turn in affairs, of course, but Ksana understood it as something inevitable, led up to by other
unexpected things: the fact that he had left her without saying a word, that he had pushed her away with
unaccountable roughness, that he had fired at people,
that he had never mentioned the possession of his
revolver to her. Every Sunday for a year she went to
the prison, to the iron armored gates painted a dull
green, and through the square barred window she
would thrust in a bundle to the guard to be handed to
Pyotr Petrovich Ragozin, who was "in detention pend-
ing his trial." Her elbows grew sharper, her fingers
thinner, but her own endurance astonished her, and she
used to say that she seemed to have two lives. She got a
job in a stocking factory and moved to other rooms—a
tiny little house in Meshkov's yard. When she learned
that her husband was to be given a sentence of banishment, she grew still more grim and resolute in her
efforts to overcome her fate.

Early one leaden autumn, after a wearing illness,
the little child died. It was at night, and the next
morning Ksana went out to see her husband off.

The party of prisoners was leaving from the railway depot, and Pyotr Ragozin saw once more the
smoke-grimed roundhouse and the shop where he
had worked as a fitter. An old man who had worked
alongside him came to say good-by and give him some
tobacco for the journey. Two prison cars were
coupled to a freight train; one was for the convicts
going to penal servitude. They were in irons, and as
they were crossing the tracks, raising their feet with
an effort over the rails, the clank of the metal was
heard above all other sounds on the station, though
it could not drown them; the shrill whistle of the

shunting engine could still be heard, the buffers clattered, the bugles of the assemblers sounded like a hunting call, the waste steam in the roundhouse issued with a threatening hiss. It made a queer kind of dialogue: "Life's gone by, gone by," the prisoners' irons clanked. "Life goes on, goes on," the railway iron clamored and sang. The argument nagged and worried Ksana, who thought of but one thing: how to go through it all, how to keep on her feet, and not crumple upon the ground as she had done that dreadful morning of the pogrom.

"I daresay he can talk by now, pretty well, too?" Pyotr Petrovich asked her about their little boy.

"Yes, he can talk all right," she replied.

"And does he ask where I am?"

"Yes, he often asks me."

"Always in mischief now, is he?"

"O, yes, you can be sure of that."

"And how does he sleep—is he quiet?"

"Yes, he's a very quiet sleeper."

"He doesn't bother you as he used to do?"

"No, not a bit."

"Give him a kiss from me, will you?"

"Yes, he shall have a kiss."

"Must have cut all his teeth now, eh? Well, you give him a good kiss from me, Ksana."

"Oh, you can be sure I'll give him a good kiss."

So they parted. The train with the prison cars was soon lost; it disappeared among the other trains which stood motionless or puffed out very slowly. The old man who had been Pyotr's comrade was about to say good-by to Ksana before going back to the shop to work, but when he glanced into her dry eyes, he was dumbfounded: one might have thought that it was she and not her husband who had been in prison a year. Suddenly she appealed to him to help her bury the child.

"What child?" he asked.

"My dead son."

"Your son? But weren't you talking about him to Petya just now and promising to kiss him?"

"Yes. When I go home I'll kiss him. He's laid out on the table."

At this the old man's tongue seemed to cleave to the roof of his mouth.

Good people helped her in her sorrow. It was through her sorrow that they came to know her, and her good repute was not left unnoticed, though, as the old saying assures us, that is the way of things; she was spoken of and reports of her passed on secretly from mouth to mouth until they must have reached some wise people.

The third winter that Ksana had been leading her solitary life, she had a visit from the tall, elderly workman who had come to see her husband off and later helped her to bury her little boy. He started in a roundabout way but finally led up to the point, which was that he needed a trustworthy person for a certain job.

"In what way must he be trustworthy?"

"He should be able to hold his tongue."

"Well, I can do that."

"Well, I know. I saw it. That's why I've come."

Next day two tubs were brought to her on sleighs. Wrapped in old blankets, they were let down into the cellar and set on birch logs, like tubs of winter pickles. The wrapping was not removed, and Ksana remembered the tubs only when she went down there for pickled cabbage. The entrance to the cellar was from inside the house, and led straight from the passage.

One evening as dusk was falling—it was near the end of winter—a Technical School boy came up to her in the street and asked her when it would be convenient to drop in; he had a package he had been asked to pass on to her. He could not say what was in the package: he had only been asked to take it to her because he lived near by. Ksana hardly had time to notice that his voice broke and that he kept clearing his throat as though he was trying to pull himself together. Late that evening he brought something that looked like a postal package. He unbuttoned his jacket and, taking off his cap, wiped his damp forehead with a handkerchief rolled into a ball. He said nothing.

"It doesn't look as if the package was a light one,

if it's taken so much out of you," Ksenia Afanasyevna said with a smile.

"If it's too heavy for you to put away, I'll help
you," the boy suggested.

Ksenia Afanasyevna tried to raise the package from
the floor, but found she could hardly shift it.

"What's this? It must weigh about three stone."

"I don't know," the boy said, "they only asked me
to say that you would know where to put the package."

Alert and concentrated, with every feature in his
face expressing an aloofness that discouraged questions,
he started to fasten his overcoat. The woman smiled
again.

"Have you been doing this sort of thing for long?"

"What?"

"Gymnastics," she said, with a jerk of her head
toward the package.

"I've been fond of gymnastics for a long while—
since I was a child."

"You've been carrying around secret packages since
you were a child, have you?"

"What is there secret about it? I was asked to do it,
and as I know you, I brought it and handed it to you,
and that's all."

"Well, and suppose I don't take it? After all, I
don't know who it's from."

Instead of answering, he held out his hand to say
good-by and at the same time indicate that he declined
to joke about things that were far too serious for that.
In the doorway he paused, thought for a moment, and
asked in an undertone: "Is it true that your husband
will be home in the autumn?"

"Yes, he ought to be. His time's up in the autumn."

Ksana's first acquaintance with Kirill went no further
than this. He came again with another package, and
after that she saw him no more for several months.
During these visits he avoided confidential conversation
as before, and she decided that perhaps he really did
not know what he was asking her to keep. At all events
she accepted the packages quietly, since she had been
told that she should take them in and keep them with
the tubs in the cellar.

When Pyotr came back, that especial period began
of mutual recognition, such as is usual between people

who are very close to each other but have been forced
apart and have lived far from each other for a long
while. Traits of character, habits of life, and even
physiological points and marks that once seemed so
important had lapsed into insignificance during the
years of separation, while those that once seemed
trifling had now come to acquire a significant place.
To the recognition of alterations, of those things
easily discernible by the eye, touch, and instinct, had
been added long narratives of all that had been lived
through, in its most unexpected, trifling, and—to the
eye of the outsider—unnecessary details. By degrees
it became clear and comprehensible why it was no
longer possible to take Ksenia Afanasyevna for Ragozin's daughter, why she had lost her fragility and
become supple, almost adroit, and why Pyotr Ragozin's
whole figure seemed to have undergone a change: the
forward stoop or inclination of his body was less
marked, the step was firmer and his gait had almost lost
its roll.

They understood that their love had not passed
but had grown richer with time, and that the fear
that it would be dimmed was entirely out of place
in the feeling with which they awaited each other.
They acknowledged and were infinitely glad that
in their sorrow as mother and father they saw not
only the lost son but also the child they both wanted
and grieved for with a grief that merged with the
passion, now finding free outlet at last. Added to this
joy of feeling was a new appreciation of all that had
happened to them, as something of great value. Ksenia
Afanasyevna never once told her husband that if he
had not belonged to the fighting squad and had not
gone out with them into the street and fired, there need
have been no prison, or banishment, and, possibly, their
son need not have died and they could have lived
peacefully. And Pyotr Ragozin never once reproached
his wife for keeping the child's death from him so
long. It did not alarm her at all that her husband would
have to live under police surveillance, and she took it
for granted that he returned from banishment a member of the Workers' Party. All she said when he told
her this, was:

"And you're perfectly right, too."

She had no very clear idea about political parties, but she felt an unabating personal enmity toward that green gate, toward the little wicket through which she had delivered bundles to her husband in jail. She had a melancholy recollection of the chapel at the green gate, where candles were set before an icon of Christ wearing a crown of thorns, and an iron collection box hung in a bracket fastened with a lock as ponderous as that of a warehouse. The legend above the box said in church Slavonic letters: "Contributions for the improvement of the prisoners' food." Once, as she was waiting on the steps of the chapel for the opening of the wicket to deliver her bundle, Ksenia realized that if there had been no prisoners, there would have been no need to collect money for their food. But, glancing into the chapel, she saw, in the humble glimmer of the candles, the Christ's hands bound with cords, and suddenly she fumbled in her purse and took out some coppers and dropped them into the box, and all day long the sense of injury and pain would not leave her—she wanted to weep, but the tears would not come and never came all the years that she lived alone. In place of the tears she felt a distinct certainty that her husband had wanted to do right and that he was a just man and for this reason he was being tormented. The habit of thinking that it was natural to him to do only what was right and just, grew on her. She was worried that she might have done him harm by consenting to keep those mysterious and dangerous things without his knowledge, but he said she did right. This mutual approval became the starting point of a new existence which at the same time was a continuation of the former old existence and yet such as they desired for themselves.

All the little things of a life that resembled everybody else's life Ksenia Afanasyevna employed to cover that second existence now led by Pyotr Ragozin whenever a convenient opportunity permitted.

Kirill Izvekov soon entered this life. The visionary expectations that had led him here found embodiment and were transformed into practical tasks, the most important of which became the necessity to conceal this second secret life from the whole world.

Perhaps it was not the second, but a fourth or even a
fifth life. But it was a very special life, and when he
discovered it, Kirill felt that other lives followed
their course apart, as though afraid of it, and made
way for it. It was hardest of all to keep it from Lisa,
because Lisa herself was a mystery arisen out of a
dream. Both mysteries were akin to each other in some
way, and it sometimes seemed to Kirill that they were
ready to merge in one. He was greatly struck by the
fact that Lisa had got on the track of his association
with Ragozin, but little by little grew more at ease
and saw in this the first promise of the future, when
everything would be merged in one for them and Lisa
would undoubtedly come to see things as he did.

Since the greatest trial of all was to hide things from
Lisa and then from his mother, he came to believe
that what was hidden from them was well hidden from
everyone. These two knew him too well; they could
read his thoughts. What stranger would devote enough
of his busy attention to one of the Technical School
boys, with his gilt buttons in the neckband of his
shirt, his blue pipings, his simple little badge on his
capband—with the crossed hammer and spanner?
What could there be in a young fellow like this to
attract the attention of, say, Merkuri Avdeyevich
Meshkov? Nevertheless, after Merkuri Avdeyevich
had encountered Kirill in the streets with his Lisa, the
crossed hammer and spanner ceased to be merely a
school badge to him, and the blue pipings on the
buttonholes and cap acquired a certain magnetic
property.

The day that Lisa went to the merry-go-round,
Merkuri Avdeyevich, on his way home from the shop,
caught a glimpse in the gathering twilight of a familiar
squarish figure in a short jacket above which a white
collar showed. Kirill Izvekov was going toward the
Meshkovs' house. Without looking around, he opened
the gate quietly and, latching it behind him without a
sound, disappeared into the yard.

Merkuri Avdeyevich stood stock-still. Could things
have gone so far? Could the talking-to that the
girl's mother had received from him only the day
before have had no effect? Was she still conniving?
He rushed to the gate. The yard was deserted. He

looked in every nook and corner, but there was no sign of anyone. He entered the house on tiptoe, holding his breath and hearing the alarmed beating of his own heart.

He went straight to his daughter's room. Lisa was lying on the bed, leaning on her elbows. She was wearing the dress she usually wore about the house, one with light blue stripes on a dark blue ground. Books were spread out all around her and she was nibbling the top of her pencil and waiting for the newly lit lamp on the chair at the bed head to warm to a glow under its colored paper shade.

"So you're at home, child?" Merkuri Avdeyevich asked.

"Yes," she replied. "Why are you breathing so hard?"

"I've been hurrying. When is your first school examination?"

"In two days' time."

He patted her shoulder lightly and smiled. "Well, you'd better come and have your tea now."

When he closed the door behind him, he gave a sigh of relief. "Thank God." Still, it surely could not have all been fancy or his failing sight? He went out into the corridor and, pacing the glassed-in gallery, looked out into the yard.

Mefody's windows were dark. A faint light appeared behind Ragozin's windows, over which Ksenia Afanasyevna immediately drew a brown curtain that scarcely let any rays through. Everything was quiet. Slowly the night leveled earth with roofs, roofs with sky. Where could that Kirill Izvekov have dodged into? Nowhere but one of the two little houses. What was the use of those "cottages," mere board shanties they were, which brought in very little profit and a lot of trouble? One tenant drank vodka—he could not say why; the other did not drink vodka—he could not say why, either. Those houses should be pulled down and a profitable warehouse built in their place. Or still better—they should be pulled down and nothing built on the site, except a good strong fence and the gates kept locked day and night. Then one would have peace instead of always bothering about the tenants.

These were the thoughts that occurred to Merkuri Avdeyevich as he stood on his gallery that dark spring evening. As for Kirill Izvekov, well, maybe it was all fancy that the young fellow had come into the yard? Everything looked quiet, everything was decent and respectable in Meshkov's yard. God was merciful.

CHAPTER

· 12 ·

In Low Week, after Easter, people went for picnics in the country around the town. Family parties, with all the children and kindred, came with their samovars, big iron pots, and frying pans and camped in the groves, gulleys, hillocks, and glades, boiling dumplings, roasting mutton. The smoke of their campfires wreathed along the slopes of the surrounding hills, and the smell of scorching leaves, embers extinguished with water, and burned pork fat was carried on the wind. They drank vodka, bawled songs, played concertinas and guitars.

The Ragozins set out early in the morning for their holiday picnic. Ksenia Afanasyevna carried the samovar, Pyotr Petrovich—the basket of crockery. On the way they fell in with a family they knew, loaded down with provisions. They climbed the hill along a straight street of wooden houses, which crawled almost to its crest, diminishing steadily in size, as though the bigger ones had no strength to climb higher, while the little ones had clambered on somehow. At the very end of the street stood tiny cottages with only one window, then came dugouts, lower than a man's height, and these burrows terminated the street. Higher up, the clayey, bare part of the hill was belted by ledges dug out to hold the moisture, and they were planted with neat rows of young saplings. They let down their roots, and grew—some into long spindly shafts, others into thick bushes. On the slopes over the other side the trees grew closer and the wind whispered in their foliage, a man could be lost sight of among them, the tops of some trees shot up over the coppice—a promise of the woods of the future. Here one happened on gulleys with steep, craggy sides, and springs of water on the sandy bottom.

Ragozin chose the place where they were to pitch camp. He quoted Pushkin: "From hence the Swede we'll threaten," and sat down on the brink of a gulley, with his legs dangling. From this spot nothing could be seen but young green trees swaying in the breeze. They fetched water, lit the samovars, fanned the embers to a glow, and the whole company set to work to peel potatoes for the soup.

Just as the water in the pot was coming to a boil, Kirill turned up. First he whistled from the bushes, Ragozin answered, and, as soon as he saw the boy's face between the parted branches, asked: "Did you find us easily?"

"Yes, by the samovar."

"But there are plenty of samovars."

"Yours has a whistle, though."

They smiled. "Are you going to share our soup, young gallivanter?"

"You bet I am."

"Well, here's a knife for you, peel a few potatoes."

He spoke in a patronizing but good-natured tone; Kirill tried to copy him in this as he did in his heavy, rolling gait, and it looked as though they were making fun of each other.

"Whoever peels potatoes like that? You'd think you were sharpening a pencil. If you were to do it like that in banishment, you'd be laughed at."

"Why should I ever be in banishment?"

"Why? So as you'll learn how to peel potatoes. See how I do it—I get one ribbon of peel from a whole potato. A thin skin, too, look!—you can see the light through it. You can even see Ksana pouring out the vodka for us."

He taught Kirill to chip the potatoes into the big pot and mix into it a thickening of flour and sunflower oil, and to flavor it with pepper and salt and spring onions. Out-of-doors every kind of food delights the heart, and there is none tastier than that prepared on a tripod and smelling of the smoke of brushwood. The senses are sharpened and alive in a man as soon as he squats down before a fire and sniffs the steam of a boiling pot. Air becomes sweeter, the distances attractive, people are kinder, and life is somehow easier. And all that is needed is a boiling iron pot.

Kirill, lying on his back on the grass after the meal and gazing up at the sky, glimpsed through the green of boughs dancing in the wind, was recollecting aloud:

"We were each given a bucket, a little spade, and wooden dibbles. A bunch of seedlings—short, miserable little twigs they looked—were stuck in each bucket. The whole school started up the hill. Everything had been marked out on the ground, and when we arrived, the rest of the schools were here, and there seemed no end to them. The planting was easy enough. We bored a hole in the ground with the dibble, set the seedling in it, and filled in the earth with our spades. Then we fetched water and each of us watered the seedlings he'd planted. Mine were only up to my knee. They were all so dry and puny, no one in the town believed they would thrive. And the idea that there would ever be a wood here was just scoffed at. When we went back to school, a photo was taken of us, just as we were, with our buckets and dibbles and spades. I have the picture still. I'm sitting cross-legged, Tatar fashion, on the ground, at the feet of our drawing master, and under the photo it says: 'The Tree-Planting Holiday.' Seems queer when you think of it—it was nine years ago. What'll we see here in another nine years' time!"

"I know."

"Well, what?"

"I'll be forty-four."

"I know that, too. But tell me, will everything be better then?"

"Yes, it's going to be all right."

"And what exactly will be all right?" Kirill persisted, lowering his voice. "Is there going to be a revolution?"

"You're a sly one!" Ragozin laughed. "If I say no, there won't be any, you'll give up straight away, I suppose?"

For a long time Kirill did not reply but lay chewing
a twig of Tatar maple. His jaw stuck out at an acute
angle on his upturned face. His gaze was fixed, the
green of the floating spots of foliage reflected in the
yellow of his pupils. His knitted brows straightened
slowly, wrinkling the young lines on his forehead. He
said very softly:

"I've chosen my road and I won't turn from it.
It makes no difference how long I have to go—nine
years or twenty-nine."

Ragozin raised himself on his elbow. The sprinkling
of freckles on Kirill's nose and cheeks made him look
younger than ever in Ragozin's eyes. He took the
boy's hand and squeezed it in his harsh, knobbly
fingers.

"Chuck it," Kirill said, trying to free his fingers.

Ragozin would not let go.

"Let go! I know you're stronger than me."

Ragozin went on squeezing Kirill's strong, resisting
wrist, feeling it give way, and smiling.

"All right, it hurts. Chuck it—what d'you want?"
He wrenched his hand away, wrung it in pain, and
chafed the crushed fingers.

"Time," Ragozin uttered, "time, my dear lad, is a
big thing. If it hurts for a day—that's one thing. But
if it hurts for a hundred days—that's quite another
thing. The people suffer. It makes a difference to them
whether the suffering lasts nine or twenty-nine
years." He turned, without getting up from the
ground, toward the fire and said aloud: "Ksana, why
don't you all go for a stroll?"

Ksenia Afanasyevna took their friends to see the
spring. Their voices and laughter could be heard for
some time as they slid and scrambled down the steep
crumbling clay bank of the gulley.

When the two were alone, Ragozin asked: "Have
you brought it?"

Kirill pulled a roll of proclamations out of his
trouser pocket. They smoothed them out and put
them with the batch that Ragozin drew out of the
basket with the crockery.

"Count them out in tens."

The leaves of thin pink newsprint were folded in
four and replaced in the basket under the towel.
The work went on easily, noiselessly, and soon the

last folded batch—the size of half of the palm of a hand—had been hidden away. Ragozin put the basket back in the bushes.

"Formerly, round about the first of May we could always contrive to hold a meeting in the woods," he said. "But nowadays you have to live like a snail— and drag your whole household, kitchen cabinet, and all on your back. Drink your tea, play your concertina, but as to having a good talk with folks— not a chance! You may spoil the whole show."

"If it comes to that, of course, you might wait twenty years drinking your tea and playing your concertina," Kirill remarked.

"I see you liked the way my samovar whistled, didn't you?"

Ragozin smiled and repeated very distinctly the whistle with which he had greeted Kirill.

They listened. There was no reply. Only the fragrant saplings, swept by the breeze and gleaming in the sunshine, kept rustling, and the hawk circled in endless curves over the young wood, occasionally piercing the emptiness of the sky with its keen note, like a diamond cutting into glass.

"I got to know Tsvetukhin a few days ago," Kirill said. "Do you know him?"

"I've heard of him. Flying high, aren't you?"

"I'm not flying anywhere. It was just an accidental meeting."

"Don't get vexed with me."

"I'm not vexed. Pastukhov was with him. The playwright. He's well known."

"Is that so?"

"It would be interesting to know their way of thinking."

"Did you talk to them at all?"

"Yes, but not much. We talked about art. Or I should say—fair exhibitions, really. We met at the fair."

"Well, go on."

"Oh, there's nothing much to tell. They seem to have no very clear idea of the scientific basis on which all these illusions and the like are based. I mean the spider woman and tricks of that sort. I noticed a certain muddleheadedness."

"Uneducated folks, eh?" Ragozin prompted with a derisive chuckle.

"I expect they're rather hazy about questions of physics."

"A-ah, I see. . . ."

"It would be interesting to give them one of the proclamations. . . ."

Ragozin sat up suddenly, and, tossing back his hair, pressed it down with his big palm, the better to observe Kirill. "Did you give them a proclamation?"

"No, it only came into my head this minute."

"They may be decent people," Ragozin said, in a quieter tone, "of course, I don't know but what they might be. But in a case like this you've got to look well before you leap. What interest could they have in us? Mere curiosity? You see, the worker comes to revolution like a man coming home to his own—there's nowhere else for him to go. But they—they may think better of it."

"The idea simply crossed my mind—I wondered what their attitude would be!" Kirill explained.

"You need to be very circumspect here. You wouldn't say you couldn't trust your own mother, would you? And yet you keep quiet about this and you don't even tell her, do you?"

A low whistle was heard close at hand, and Ragozin nodded. "There it is, my samovar."

He gave an answering whistle. A minute later a tall, thin, elderly man with a wedge-shaped beard emerged from the grove onto the edge of the gulley. He wore a suit of Sunday black, and he looked about him.

"Hey! Have you lost your way?" Ragozin called out.

The old man strolled over to where they were sitting, greeted them, raising a well-worn black shiny peaked cap with a narrow crown. "You picked a nice spot for your tea drinking, Pyotr Petrovich."

"We'll be glad if you'll join us."

"Thanks, I've had my tea."

"It's more cheerful to have it in the open air. Sit down, won't you?"

"No, I've been sitting down a good while."

"Well, then, stand—if your legs will hold you."

"They're used to that, standing in the work shop for twenty years and measuring the ground for sixty." He looked about him once more. The bushes were on a level with his cap. "It's getting greener every year— the woods are coming on fine," he remarked approvingly.

"The young folks did their best, they planted the trees, it seems, and watered them," Ragozin said.

"That's it, is it?" the old man said, his eyes narrowing as he scrutinized Kirill. "In the old days the old folks planted for the youngsters. Looks as though it's the other way about now, eh?"

"There are young people who think of something besides themselves," Kirill spoke up suddenly looking straight into the quizzical narrowed eyes of the old man.

"Ah . . . So they're thinking of planting along with us?"

"Exactly," Kirill replied.

"Well, well," the old man said, looking at Ragozin. "What are we going to plant with these young folks, Pyotr Petrovich, what kind of orchard will it be?"

"Hand us that basket there," Ragozin asked Kirill.

He got out from under the towel a folded batch of papers and handed it to the old man, who took it, fingered it as though feeling the strength and weight of the paper, bent down, hitched up one leg of his trousers to the knee, slipped the wad down into his high, rough, rusty-looking boot, and then straightened the trouser leg as neatly.

"Maybe that won't be enough for you?" Ragozin said.

The old man was silent a moment, then said, with his head on one side: "Yes, indeed, I might limp, you know."

"Here, then, have another, so as you won't be taken for a drunken man rolling from side to side," Ragozin said, handing him another batch.

The old man hid it in the other boot. "Now thank you for your welcome. What the eye don't see, the heart don't grieve for," he remarked with a knowing wink at Kirill, then suddenly smiled kindly. "Now you and I are going to know each other. And as to our names, Pyotr Petrovich will tell you, I expect."

"That's right," Ragozin agreed. "Is there anything to talk over?"

"Yes, plenty."

"Sit down, then, and you, Kirill, you ought to slip away, but don't draw attention to yourself."

"I'll go down to the Volga," Kirill said, holding out his hand to the old man.

"Good day, dear comrade," the old man said with an unexpectedly gentle smile that had a touch of mockery in it.

"Good day, comrade," Kirill muttered, feeling the sudden flush rising from his breast to his cheeks, temples, ears, and head.

He plunged into the grove, flinging aside the tangle of clinging boughs. He felt like a strong swimmer in a murmuring green sea and kept hearing in its rebellious ebb and flow the echo of the booming word: *comrade, comrade!* For the first time in his life he, Kirill Izvekov, had been called by that name— comrade, and for the first time in his life he himself had called someone comrade— that old man, who came from the people among whom his life was to be spent in the future. So he strode—or rather, swam —on and on until the cool green rustling waves had borne him out to the bare island of a hilltop from which he could view the large town encircled by hills, a town which was wooden at the sides and brick in the middle, like a pie, cut into fairly equal slices by the streets. Below him lay this great as yet untouched wooden pie with its brick filling, above— the scud of cloud, driven across the blue by the wind, and at his feet the crest of the hummocks, curved like a mane, and this he followed until he came to the Volga.

He ran down one slope and climbed another and so went on running and climbing. This again was like his swimming a few moments since through the young greenwood, only this time the waves of the hills were longer, and instead of foliage he had to plunge through the bittersweet fragrance of fresh wormwood, all-pervading, drugging the hills with its spiciness. In this way he reached the cliff that overlooked the Volga and sat down on it, unfastening his collar and throwing off his cap and belt.

His heart throbbed insistently in his breast, and he laughed, and because he did not know why he laughed, he could not stop laughing. So there he sat, with his feet dangling over the edge of the cliff, rocking himself to and fro, and laughing, and his laughter seemed to him like both the talk and the songs that are sung in the East, the songs of things he had seen and heard.

He looked out over the boundless valley through which the turbid river flowed. He saw the Green Isle, overgrown with willows, standing in water up to half their height, and bending their silvery-white tops meekly before the gust. He saw the orange barge becalmed in midstream, looking like a house made of matchstalks, and somewhere far, far away, one behind the other, two caravans of barges, like the parting stitches of a ripped seam. The slow-gliding cloud shadows stained the rippled surface of the river, the clumps of willows on the islet, the crowding vessels at the town wharves. Everything was on the move, filled with the distant hum of work and traffic, a hum that was borne on the wind and in no way disturbed the all-embracing stillness.

After having rested awhile, Kirill sat up, hugging his knees, his chin pressed hard between the kneecaps, and tried to concentrate and bring some sort of order into his thoughts. He put questions severely to himself: what do I want? What am I going to be? What is the chief thing in life? But each time, as soon as he was on the point of putting into words the answer he had guessed fairly accurately, the words would slip from reality into a half-dream and become transformed into pleasantly colorful, constantly changing patterns. He fancied that he was moving and rearranging extraordinarily large masses of material: the river itself was raised by his hands and flowed through the sky; the snowdrift clouds filled a fathomless, now deserted watercourse; black oaks grew along the banks in an avenue; a barge sailed along this avenue, unrolling herself thunderously as she went like a huge ball of yarn, leaving in her wake a pathway of evenly laid amber logs. Kirill was standing before the blackboard, doing sums with his hands, which had suddenly grown very big, and the teacher kept nodding approvingly and flinging a multitude of pince-nez off his fleshy nose, first one pair, then another, then a third, faster and faster, until soon thousands of eyeglasses strewed the distant waters with a glittering ripple. "Very well," the draftsman was saying, "if you want to pass the examination, you must do a cross-section of the town in which you want to live." Kirill's drawing grew and grew until it was far too big for the board, and the board spread endlessly, and innumerable rooms like the cells of a honeycomb appeared on it, and over them sped the cloud shadows, and Lisa was standing in one of the rooms. "I have passed all my examinations," she said. "Turn away." "Why?" Kirill asked. "Turn away, I'm telling you." "But you're my wife," he said. "It makes no difference, turn away," she repeated, and turned away herself. Her dress was fastened at the back with innumerable hooks and eyes, and when she raised her arms over her head to unfasten them, her long braid caught in the hooks and he went up to her and freed the hair from the hooks and unbraided it. The hair had the fragrance of wormwood and was overpoweringly strong; it grew steadily stronger and warmer. Lisa turned around very slowly, and when she did, Kirill saw the sweet face of his own mother with the faint pockmarks on the upper lip and brow, and she said: "Only give me your word that you'll never go out to Green Isle in your boat. Remember that's where your father lost his life, Kirill!" Her voice had altered strangely and she pronounced his name in a rough manner, like a man.

"Having a nap, eh?" someone quite close to him said in the same rough tone. "Kirill, are you asleep?"

He opened his eyes, and, without getting up, with his head still resting on his hands, he saw Ragozin a few paces away, looking out over the Volga.

"Don't get up and don't come near me," said Ragozin. "See you don't drag anyone after you. There's a young chap roaming these hills—high boots, trousers inside. Keep an eye on him—he's a plain-clothes policeman." Ragozin looked lazily around the horizon and then, as he turned to go, said: "There's going to be a shower. Mind you aren't caught in it and get cold."

Only then did Kirill notice that the sky had clouded

over. He raised himself on his elbow. Over the hilly bank and the islet the warm yellow-green color still shone, but the further he looked on the lower meadow side, the colder the tones became; the river looked blue, the white crests of the breakers took on a steely tinge, and there was a long, gloomy, purplish-black strip by the shore itself, as though thick ink had been mixed and shaken up on the bottom and it had floated to the surface. Over the opposite bank sailed a low gray cloud with silvery edges. The barge drifted far downstream and was no longer orange but drab, as though begrimed with smoke. Caravans of barges were hastening townward in apparent anxiety. The first faintly audible mutterings of springtime thunder seemed to Kirill fraught with a threatening and solemn exultation.

He glanced around. A smart young fellow in a red Russian blouse and a short, fancy-weave, well-pressed jacket was striding toward the edge of the cliff with a careless, swaggering gait. His wide corduroy trousers were worn inside high boots and had the fullness eased over the tops of the shining boots, which were creased in concertina folds above the ankle. His thick, fair hair was neatly cut, and on his snub nose he wore smoked glasses on a black cord. He looked like a shop assistant who would attend night school. He paused on the brink and stood admiring the view.

"So there you are, my lad!" Kirill said to himself feeling a thrill of pride that he had been followed and that he was aware of it and saw through this young bounder in the high boots and eyeglasses.

Kirill lay down on his back and stretched himself to his heart's content. Covering his face with his cap, he muttered with satisfaction into its stifling satin lining: "To hell with you! What do I care for the rain? But what will you look in it, you slick, dandified ass!"

· 13 ·

IT IS NOT so easy to prepare for examinations, especially when you have passed nine and three still remain. Would there ever be just one left, and then
nothing? There were still three to pass, a whole three!

This was the third pencil that had been chewed,
and how many exercise books had been filled, how
many ticks made beside questions on examination
papers? How many times had Lisa's mother, Valeria
Ivanovna, said: "Lisa, that's enough, it's time you
were in bed, you'd better get up a bit earlier in the
morning."

Suddenly her thoughts stood stock-still and—would
go no further. Her head was stuffed as full as a sack
of flour; it wouldn't hold any more. And somewhere
deep in that flour lurked, motionless, a fragment of
a phrase—"three elements." But which three elements,
why three elements was more than she could understand. Perhaps it was the three examinations that were
on her mind? Or three chewed pencils?—or three
questions not yet crossed out on the examination paper? No. Just three elements, do what you like about
it! Perhaps three worlds? No, there was only one
world, one and the same world before our eyes,
the one that was familiar through and through: the
glassed-in gallery of the corridor, and below the yard
with the little blue "cottages," the cellars and the drying sheds. The summer hardly begun, the motionless

sun, the stillness, Then, the trilling of the balalaika. That was the young shop assistants who had moved out to the drying sheds for the summer and were practicing their rural repertoire: "The Moon Shining Brightly," the waltz "The Hills of Manchuria," and a plaintive song:

> *In the city of Kuznay*
> *There's the hostelry Cathay,*
> *Waiter, waiter, waiter mine,*
> *Fetch me quick a draught of wine.*
> *Bring me vodka, bring me beer,*
> *Give me back my darling dear!*

The gate banged as a Bulgarian beggar in a rusty-looking ragged cloak passed through to Ragozin's house. He tapped at the window with upraised bony hand, and Ksenia Afanasyevna came to the door and gave him a piece of bread. He threw open his cloak, exposing the coppery-brown body under the tattered clothing. He uttered pitifully inarticulate sounds, opening his mouth wide and pointing to his mutilated tongue. The whole street knew that his tongue had been cut out by the Turks, in some vague bygone day known as the "times of the Turkish atrocities"; everybody knew that this Bulgarian was not the only one, and that a whole lot of them went about in unbelted cloaks, begging for old linen. Lisa could hear him mumbling first at one door, then at another, in the yard, until at last the banging of the gate denoted that the beggar had gone, and the next turn in the program came on, the cracked, three-voiced hurdy-gurdy filled the street. Memory prompted the words, familiar from childhood, to each stage of the melancholy tune:

> *The apple of my mother's eye,*
> *Her darling daughter once was I,*
> *Till one autumn night I slipped from bed*
> *And with my love from home I fled.*

From the end window of the gallery she could see the corner of the schoolhouse, the whitewashed brick wall, and above it the three poplars with their pyramidal tops pointing toward the sky. The hurdy gurdy passed from song to song with a click like that of a rifle lock, while Lisa sat gazing at the poplars. The green stood out in sharp contrast to the encircling blue, but if you stared fixedly, without blinking, the blue of the sky turned greenish and the leaves were touched with blue, and then you were in a whole world of bluish-green, and the white school and white wall around it were slowly immersed in this world, and Lisa began to see in it things that were hidden from the eye by the neighboring roofs and trees in the street.

She was seeing in imagination the basement windows of the schoolhouse with their heavy bars, the rooms, as Kirill had described them to her—his room with the blueprint on the wall above the bed and the portraits of great men. Once he told her: "When I'm thinking and looking at them, I imagine that they might open their mouths and talk to me, especially if I'm just falling asleep. Don't you love great people?" She had replied that very likely everybody loved great people but that this love was only in their minds because great people were out of reach. "Why out of reach?" he demurred. "People go to Yasnaya Polyana to see Tolstoy and he talks to anyone who wants to see him." "And would you go and see him?" "No. I don't agree with his views. He considers that good should be implanted in man and I consider that evil should be rooted out." "Isn't it just the same?" "No, it isn't. The main thing is the order in which it's done. First comes the destruction of evil." "Have you a portrait of Tolstoy in your room?" "I used to have, but now I've moved it into Mother's room."

Lisa could see in her mind's eye his mother seated under the picture of Tolstoy. She looked into her face very closely as she had done that day on the fairground, and the face seemed kind, and the faint pockmarks above the upper lip and on the brow— unusually attractive. Lisa was thinking that she might become very fond of Kirill's mother and would be sure to love her as soon as she and Kirill were together. Of course, she would still love her own mother better than anyone else in the world.

Lisa's mother was a plain, simple woman. One

could not imagine a portrait of Tolstoy hanging over her bed. It made Lisa smile—it was so incongruous: Mama and that bearded, lined face with the shaggy eyebrows. Although, very likely, Mama had, deep down in her soul, just the thing Tolstoy advocated: she would implant only good everywhere. She obeyed one law that she never mentioned and that needed no words to express it, though Lisa could express it with confidence: love is beautiful, malice is hideous—this was what Lisa felt about her mother.

Then she remembered Valeria Ivanovna's account of the conversation with Merkuri Avdeyevich, and his sermon, as he called his interminable reprimands.

"You're answerable for Lisa, you're her mother," he said. "Is this the way you've brought her up? She's hanging about that place, Dogs' Limes, with one young scamp today, and she'll be with another tomorrow, and a third next day!"

"Why should you insult the girl—talking about a second and a third?" Valeria Ivanovna protested.

"You want to say—she's keeping company with one all the time? What's the meaning of this—is it a settled thing, a love affair?"

"Oh, who's talking about a love affair!"

"What do you suppose it is, then, if she's with him day in, day out?"

"Well, ask her yourself what it is."

"I'm ashamed to talk to my daughter about love affairs."

"Well, Merkusha, what do you think you can do if the girl falls in love? You can't forbid her, can you?"

"Nobody's going to forbid her. When the proper time comes, she'll meet some decent, respectable man who will marry her, and for all I care, then, let her love him as much as she likes. Would I be the one to stand in the way of her happiness? But you've got to get all that nonsense about love affairs out of her head."

"She hasn't got any nonsense about love affairs in her head. All she wants is to go on with her schooling."

"Oh, so that's the case, is it? You want to make one of those new-fangled college girls out of her for me? Like those that sit in the Limes, with their hair cut short? Not for me, thank you! The high school isn't enough for her—she must go to the Women's College! And which, I'd like to know? What is she going to study? Medicine, or maybe, jurisprudence? And she'll have to go up to Moscow or St. Petersburg for that, eh? Allow me to ask you—for what purpose? So as to leave her parents' house and go to live in furnished rooms? What's the idea? What exactly would be the use of it to her?"

He had gone on like this all the evening, pacing to and fro, from corner to corner, occasionally thumping the table or the backs of the chairs, raising his voice to a yell, then lowering it to a whisper fraught with sinister warning, and threats—"I won't stand it!" "I won't allow it!"—until at last Valeria Ivanovna had relapsed into silence and wept.

As she recounted all this to Lisa, she wept again and, clasping Lisa's head to her bosom, breathed with a sob into her ear: "And what if you have fallen in love, Lord have mercy on you!"

And, throwing her arms around her, Lisa whispered her thoughts—and wept, too. And they both sat down on Lisa's bed, crying with their arms around each other, and wiping away their tears with the corners of the same handkerchief until it was soaking wet and the tears came to an end. Then her mother questioned her about Kirill, and what he was like, and how they had contrived to keep out of sight for three years, what they thought of doing now, and how was she to tell all this to the father so that it would not bring down anything worse than a sermon on their heads.

Now, as she sat listening to the mournful crooning of the hurdy-gurdy, and staring through the glass of the gallery at the hazy greenish-blue world—the world of Kirill—Lisa's thoughts went over that conversation with her mother, on the bed, when all her thoughts had begun and ended in vague, sweet fears for the future and all her feelings had dissolved without a trace in her mother's caresses. Suddenly Lisa tore herself away from the window and ran to her mother.

Valeria Ivanovna was showing the servant how

to iron men's shirts: first the back and sides, then
the sleeves, cuffs, shoulders, and last of all the starched
front, and heaven forbid there should be a crease, a
wrinkle, or a ridge on that. And before starting on
the front, the charcoal in the iron must be blown
on so that the embers would glow, but it must be
done away from the table to prevent the ashes from
settling on the ironing board, otherwise it would all
be labor in vain.

"Blow it like this, see!" Lisa cried as, running to
her mother, she plumped down beside her, hugged
her knees, and started to blow on the hot iron with
all her might.

"Stop that now, do you hear! Look what you're
doing!" Valeria Ivanovna cried, trying to move the
iron out of Lisa's reach, and blowing and fanning
away the flying ashes that were settling on the ironing board and rising to the ceiling. "Take away the
linen, roll it up quick!" she called out to the maid.
"Throw it into the basket—the basket, I'm telling
you!"

Jumping up, Lisa embraced Valeria Ivanovna, set
a wooden stool for her, and made her sit down, then
sat on her mother's lap.

"My dear, you're overdoing this learning of yours,"
Valeria Ivanovna said with real anxiety.

"That's true, Mama, it does seem as if something's
stuck in my head. I thought if I blew hard on that
iron it might clear it."

"I know what's stuck in your head. You'd better
go out for some fresh air, I think. . . ."

When she was outside the gate, Lisa looked up
as she always did at the austere walls and the school
fence. The poplars stood sentinel over the unpeopled
quiet of the place. They were guarding Kirill's world,
his room with the portraits of great men. A stunted
little peasant appeared at the crossroads with a wooden
grinding machine over his shoulder and called out
in a ringing voice: "Any knives or scissors to sharpen!"
stood awhile looking about him at the silent houses,
then went reluctantly on his way. A brisk woman
came round the corner with a small girl. They were
carrying bundles. The child nodded to Lisa from a
distance and she recognized Annochka.

"Good morning, Miss, how are you?" the woman said in an effusively sociable manner as she came up to Lisa. "Annochka, shake hands and say how d'you do. She told me she met you at the fair. I'm her mother, Olga Ivanovna. Very pleased to meet you."

"You know where we're going?" Annochka volunteered. "We're going to the theater."

"Yes, indeed," Olga Ivanovna broke in. "We're taking clothes there for the people, we were asked to do it."

"Clothes?" Lisa repeated softly.

"Costumes for the play," Annochka explained.

"All sorts of rags, you know," the woman added almost apologetically. "This is the second time we're going there. At first I collected things that looked fairly decent, from people I knew. I thought things that weren't too worn or shabby would be wanted. When I brought them there, they said: 'Whatever's this? Take them back. What we want is the oldest stuff.' To put it plainly, they want rags and tatters."

"That's so as they can show the life of poor people," Annochka said very seriously.

"I've just come out for a walk—so may I see you a little way?" Lisa offered rather shyly.

"That'll be very nice indeed." Olga Ivanovna went on garrulously. "Weather like this makes you want to go out for a walk. Annochka, you'd better change hands or you'll get tired. Here, take this bundle, it's lighter. Well, as I was saying, an actor there, an elderly man, but very nice-looking, said to me: 'We want to play true to life and so we need the sort of rags that the poorest tramp would scorn to wear.' I've collected such rubbish this time that I'm half ashamed to take it there. And can you imagine, as soon as ever they heard in the rooming house that ragged clothes were needed, they put up the price—why, you couldn't get near them! To tell you the truth, I can't make out why the theater should show poverty. After all, it's not beautiful, is it? I remember when I used to go to the theater—in the days when we were quite well-to-do, my husband and I—I would always choose the most beautiful show. It was something to look at and to remember afterward for a

long time, and you'd think that though you yourself
may never have a beautiful life like that, still you
have seen real beauty in your time. That's true, isn't
it?"

Lisa listened with interest to her new acquaintance.
Her irresistible flow of words was engaging enough,
but behind this talk she fancied she sensed something other than what Olga Ivanovna was saying.

Lisa rarely went to the theater because Merkuri
Avdeyevich allowed her to see only those plays that
the high school approved of, plays that were instructive. Her memories of plays she had seen were festive
and she adored the town theater. Her head swam a
little whenever, tense and silent, she mounted the
slippery painted asphalt stairs from circle to circle,
passed the ushers, and entered the low box. The
program trembled in her hand; her opera glasses
grew hot in her palm. She was no longer in the
theater, but in another sphere, beyond the rim of life.
The world of home and even of Kirill retreated before
a third world, inaccessible and aloof as a divinity.
When the curtain went up, it was as though the
divinity permitted mortals to look upon his countenance. Then one ceased to breathe, the heart stood
still, and the miracle happened. For a few fleeting
moments Lisa felt that she might be not just herself
but anyone—more beautiful or more malicious, better
or worse, older, nobler, sadder, smaller, or gayer.
She might give herself to everyone and yet have
everyone within her power. In all her imaginary
transformations she gave herself to people and they
submitted to her. She became that very miracle at
which she was looking. She became an actress.

No one else knew of these states of mind, nor did
Lisa care to speak of them to anyone. Alone with
her own heart she acknowledged that for her a stage
career was as inconceivable as a flight across the ocean
with wild swans. She was pleased that the conversation
which had arisen unexpectedly with Kirill at the fairground had concluded with that true word—phantasm.
But the other subsequent conversation arising still
more unexpectedly with Tsvetukhin recurred restlessly in her mind, expressing itself again in the con-
cluding words of this conversation: "Drop in and see

me—come around to the stage door." For some reason a very clear impression remained that the words
had been spoken in a whisper. At any rate, he had
bent so close to her that it must have attracted
everyone's attention, and she herself had been struck
by the gleam of his raven-black hair on the right
temple, revealed by the panama, and also by his clipped black mustache, seen as closely as she had seen
the youthful, hardly perceptible growth on Kirill's
lip a few moments before.

And now she looked at Annochka with a wistful
envy. This little girl was able to go to the theater
now, though the doors were, with the exception of
the mysterious side entrance near the garden, still
closed to the public, while she, Lisa, would have to
turn back and go home. . . . Suddenly she felt Annochka's thin hand squeeze her fingers as the little
girl murmured: "Come on in with us and let's have
a look at everything! There are all sorts of things to
see!"

"Yes, do come. If you'd care to see it, let's go to
the costumier's room—it's very interesting," Olga
Ivanovna chimed in.

"But what shall I say?" Lisa asked her, making up
her mind at once and startled by her own determination.

"We'll say we've come together."

Various objections arose and subsided rapidly in
her mind, but meanwhile the door opened and a damp
smell, as of freshly washed linen, was wafted into the
street.

Here everything was in twilight or else in complete darkness—the passages, the corridors, the steps,
the stair landings, veiled in a sleepy pollen-like light
from the electric lamps. Then a bright room opened
where, on two rows of wooden stands, were hung
as though frozen, the outward envelopes of some
strange human lives, brocade, satin, cloth, silk islands
in an abyss of braid, lace, beads, jet, and ribbons.
The draft created by Olga Ivanovna as she made
her way with the bundles through this cosmos of
clothing occasionally stirred one of the stiff integu-
ments, which now reminded Lisa of a dying boyar,
now a spirited Spaniard, now a mocking French

marquise. Annochka paused before a rich caftan swaying slightly on its hanger, touched the brocade, whispering to Lisa: "This is gold."

"Yes, it's for Tsar Fyodor," Lisa told her in a whisper.

They entered the costumier's workshop. The bespectacled tailors, surrounded by scraps of material of many colors, sat on the tables, plying their needles silently. Olga Ivanovna undid her bundles. Two men in their waistcoats rummaged in the things she had brought.

"I'm downright ashamed of the stuff, I really can't tell you how ashamed," Olga murmured apologetically.

"That'll do for the Baron," said the costumier, spreading out a dirty torn jacket by its sleeves.

"Not for a Baron, surely!" Olga Ivanovna gasped in horror.

Meanwhile Annochka was winking hard at Lisa to induce her to bend down and listen to a secret.

"Let's go out there."

"Where?"

"Where they're playing."

Lisa shook her head, but Annochka was drawing her away by the elbow and she found that they were near the door.

"I've been up here before," the little girl confided when they were in a narrow passage redolent of glue and a barbershop.

They went down some steps, climbed others, and from there entered a shadowy ravine of extraordinary depth. They were at the very bottom of the ravine; above them, where the daylight filtered in diffidently, vast folds of canvas daubed with color hung at the ends of motionless ropes. Lisa found herself in front now; she seemed to have changed places with Annochka, who lingered to look curiously at every object.

Suddenly she heard slow steps. A man's figure emerged from the twilight. He was coming straight toward her, and this was a very narrow place. She kept close to the wall on her right hand. He moved in the same direction. She dodged to the left. Now he wanted to step aside and let her pass and so made the same movement. Immediately they both decided to correct themselves, moved at the same moment, and instantly collided with each other. Then he said in a low, unctuous voice: "Well, let's stand still a minute."

She recognized Tsvetukhin's voice. Then she recognized his face—as it had looked in her mind's eye a few minutes before, on her way to the theater, only now he wore no panama and his black hair gleamed.

"So it's you?" he said softly, then, after a pause: "You? Lisa Meshkova? How did you get here?"

All this time she had been thinking of what she would say if she were asked how she happened to be behind the scenes and she had decided she would tell the truth. But now she stood transfixed looking into Tsvetukhin's eyes. He smiled, took her arm, turned and led her along with him.

"Come along to my room," he said.

They emerged at last from the hangings, mounted an iron staircase, then he opened the nearest door.

Lisa paused on the threshold. The sun was shining in at the window, reflected in the glass and playing on the frames of the photographs arranged on the wall around the large mirror. The reflections played everywhere, multiplying the innumerable small objects scattered about on the long table. Playbills with Tsvetukhin's name in startling letters covered the walls to the ceiling and were garlanded with ribbons that repeated his name in gilt letters. A sword with a bronze hilt lay on an armchair covered with a gray cloak. Tsvetukhin picked up the sword, threw the cloak onto another chair, and said, pointing to the armchair: "Won't you sit down?"

Lisa did not move.

"How did you get in here at this time of day? Have you friends in the theater?"

She looked at him almost imploringly.

He smiled again and asked, as he stood with one foot advanced, tapping his boot with the sword: "Did you want to see me? Is that it?"

She turned her eyes away.

He repeated in a still lower tone: "You thought you'd meet me? Why don't you admit it?"

"No."

"You're not speaking the truth."

"Now you're being discourteous," she said quickly.

"Forgive me," he said, smiling more broadly. "But I can see that you are hiding the truth from me."

"Then why do you try to make me speak?"

"Oh, but I'm not making you do anything. I'm begging you to do it. What brought you here at this time of day?"

"It's a—coincidence."

"Ah, a coincidence, was it?" he gave a pleased laugh. "Well, it's a very lucky coincidence! For me, at any rate. And what about you?"

Lisa, surprisingly enough, sat down in the armchair. Gripping one arm of it tightly, she raised her other hand, palm outward, as though to ward off Tsvetukhin.

"You're talking to me as though I'm a little girl," she said. "You're mistaken. A little girl would hardly be able to understand that you're a very spoiled person. But I can see you are. Seems as though I knew that before. I thought it likely . . . and natural enough in an actor. But I didn't think you were unkind. You seemed quite different then. If I was mistaken, it's a great pity." She was very pale, her lips still trembled when she had ceased speaking.

Tsvetukhin looked at her with surprise. He waited a few moments, then bent over her and said anxiously: "I didn't mean to offend you. You must be tired. Are you? Your school examinations are going on just now, aren't they?"

"Yes."

"Have you many left?"

"Three."

"And then that will be the end?"

"Yes, that will be the end."

"The very end?"

"The very end!" she answered with a faint sigh.

"And then liberty, eh? What are you thinking of doing? Going to college? Or perhaps you're thinking of the stage? Is that it?"

She shook her head.

"It frightens you?" he asked inquisitively and, without waiting for her answer, bent the sword in a bow, let it go with a swish, and walked over to the window. "Yes, of course, it does," he answered in the affirmative. "I understand you perfectly. Beware of the theater, beware of art. It is a beast that knows no mercy. It either devours a man, or rejects him. It demands everything and yet stands in need of none but itself. If it swallows you whole, you may be thankful. But woe betide you if it casts you out!"

This was not the Tsvetukhin who had smiled at Lisa only a brief moment ago. The sun blazing through the window outlined with its radiance the motionless black silhouette with the outflung hand leaning on the sword, its point resting on the floor.

"Keep away, keep as far away as you can from that beast," he said, admiring the insinuating shades of meaning in his own voice. "Better to live the simple life of unobtrusive labor than stand here in front of this mirror, with all this color and these cloaks. A woman, particularly a woman, needs ordinary, unembellished happiness. And if you were to ask me what I would wish you, a young girl, on the threshold of freedom, I would say—love, the most ordinary love a woman feels."

He went up to Lisa and said, in a very low voice: "But perhaps you possess this already—this that I'm wishing you? Perhaps you love someone?"

"What kind of a sword is that?" Lisa asked loudly, in an effort, apparently, to throw off the spell of his voice by the force of sound.

"You haven't seen me in Hamlet, have you? No? I'd like you to see me in that."

He stood *en garde*, made a lunge with the sword, and declaimed in a somewhat disillusioned and derisive tone: "This sword pierces the triviality and insignificance that hide under the cloak of nobility."

"Aren't you afraid it might pierce you?" Lisa asked, glancing at him from under her brows.

"O-oh, I see you're going to be a dangerous woman!" Tsvetukhin said with a laugh.

He bent toward Lisa, but at that moment there was a knock at the door; it opened and a man in a waistcoat sidled into the room.

"Egor Pavl'ch, will you come for a trying on?"

"What is it now?"

"Clothes for the Baron—it would turn you dizzy

to see the gorgeous rags they've brought! Just the kind you were wanting."

"I'll have to be going," said Lisa, rising.

"Oh, don't be in such a hurry, please," Tsve-tukhin said to her, waving away the man in the waistcoat and shutting the door in his face. "I want you to come and see me. . . . You're fond of the country, aren't you? Come out and see me—I'm staying at a cottage in Kumiss Field with a man you know, Pastukhov. Will you come?"

"How could I possibly do that?"

"Oh, but why not? You could perhaps drop in . . . by accident? By a lucky coincidence, let's say." He smiled without a trace of slyness, almost apologetically.

"Oh, no, it's quite out of the question. Good-by!"

"Wait, you'll lose your way here, I'll see you out."

"No, please don't trouble, I'm not alone."

"So you'll come, won't you?" he called after her, and, pausing in the doorway, listened to the tap of her heels hastening along the asphalted corridor and then ringing on the iron stairway.

Around one of the corners she suddenly came upon Annochka, who darted up to her with: "What happened? Did the black man scold you?" and she dropped her voice to a hasty choking whisper.

"Oh, no, the black man didn't scold me," Lisa assured her without slackening her pace as she pressed Annochka's untidy head to her side. "But now you go back to your mama and I'll go on alone. No, don't come with me. I'm going out by myself."

And now she was in the street again, in the singing sunlight of the day. And what a day! She was going straight across the square with its uneven clumsy cobbles, but the bumpy bluish stones slid as easily from under her feet as the stained asphalt of the theater corridors had done, and the sun shone solely, it seemed, to keep before her mind's eye the black silhouette of the man against the shining window, and she could still see the contour of the outstretched hand resting so magically on the bronze sword hilt. The third world, the world of wonders, was suddenly filled with flesh and blood, and Lisa felt and bore it within her to those other two worlds into which she was returning with a heart that was tranquil and, strangely, grown-up.

As she stumbled over a crooked cobblestone, she laughed: three more examinations—what a trifle! One step, only one gaily taken step, and then—a life as free and transparent as air, infinite vistas would open before her! And Kirill, dear Kirill, he did not even suspect how right he had been when he said that great people were perhaps more accessible than ordinary mortals!

· 14 ·

WHITSUNDAY was spent at the Meshkovs' according
to the custom of their forefathers. A cartload of young
birches and herbs of various kinds was brought from
the market. The birches were placed in the corners
of the rooms, and over the doorways; all the floors
in the house were spread with the grasses and herbs.
On the window sills wild thyme was strewn and pot-
ted plants and flowers in glasses were set. The fresh
earthy breath of the woods and meadows filled the
house from the day before, and by morning it had
the languorously sweet and savory smell of spiced
honey biscuits.

But more than on any other holiday one wanted
to escape from these indoor groves and meadows to the
growing trees and flowers. Lisa felt the call of the
out-of-doors still more strongly now. She had passed
her examinations and all that remained was the gradua-
tion-day ceremony. So Whitsunday was the first day
that she awoke no longer a schoolgirl. Kirill presented
her with a notebook bound in red silk, with a gilt
monogram in the corner, "E" and "K" interlaced,
which, of course, meant Elisaveta and Kirill. On the
first page he had written with India ink in script such
as he used on his plans, two words: "Liberty, Independence."

They had agreed to go out to the country. Lisa
suggested the Kumiss Field. She said at home that

she was going out with her school friends—but the pretext was obvious even to her father.

They took a streetcar as far as the last suburban stop and then climbed the hill through the thick coppice of young oak trees, Tatar maple, and hawthorn. They did not talk. The moment was not to be compared with previous emotional experience; now one could speak only of significant things, of summaries or plans, or even of unalterable feeling, and only in very special words. The wild rutless woodland path, its sides overgrown with fresh turf, and the foliage that like a grotto shut out the sky, held such suggestion of suspense that one was reluctant to disturb it with talking. Another vast, unbounded grotto of warm rain clouds was descending lower and lower over the woods, and all living things seemed to wait, scarcely breathing, anticipating the coming change. It grew very dark, and when they emerged into the sparser birch grove, the tree trunks stood out as white as strips of paper molded on the purple dusk and the first early dog daisies shone with the same papery whiteness in the grass.

Kirill plucked a flower, moved a few paces aside to pluck another, then another, and this gathering of the flowers became the trivial occupation that relieved the mind of all thoughts. Kirill went farther and farther into the grove, and when he returned, he had a rather clumsy-looking bunch of dog daisies in his hand, and he himself looked to Lisa so clumsy with his nosegay, so much more boyish than ever, that he reminded her of a sturdy, pleasant young oak tree. She was waiting for him where he had left her when he went to gather the dog daisies, and, for some reason, while waiting for him she saw herself as a grownup and Kirill as a little boy, and this made him all the dearer. He gave her the flowers; she pressed them with his fingers to her breast and asked:

"Do you remember?"

"Yes, I remember," he said. "Only that time it was lilac."

"Yes," she said. "and the dress was my brown school uniform. And now I shall never put it on again."

"Not even for graduation day?"

"No, I'm going to wear this blue one."

She was still holding his fingers in hers. At that moment they realized that they were both expecting that this day would bring them something inevitable.

"It's going to rain," Kirill said presently. "Don't you find it awfully close?"

"I don't care," she replied in a hardly audible tone, so that he did not so much hear but could only guess at the word and the meaning behind it—the readiness not merely for the absurd inconvenience caused by the rain, but for anything that might happen.

The woods were now at the tensest pitch of expectancy, all movement was stilled, every leaf seemed to have found its place in the universe forever. Then, from afar, a shudder of alarm ran through the tops of the birches, a masterful gust burst between the tree trunks, and everything was driven into movement, tossed into confusion. "We were watchful, watchful," moaned the boughs, swaying their quivering leaves, "we waited and waited and now it has come, it has come, the storm is upon us." The purple dusk was suddenly swallowed up in a seeming collapse of the sun, the birch trunks went black for an instant, then all was plunged in darkness, the woods trembled, and a series of gay and reckless thunderclaps like a succession of salvos came hurrying one after another.

"That was very close," Kirill said. "We'll be drenched in a minute—let's run for it."

He seized Lisa's hand that held the nosegay and they ran to the gulley overgrown with stunted oaks. Stooping, they crept under the thick foliage and, settling in the close and warm leafy cave, listened to the drumming of the first heavy drops overhead.

They sat close together, and Kirill embraced her. "This is our first home," he said. "Rather an unexpected one, isn't it?"

"Will there ever be a second?" she asked. "Everything happens so unexpectedly in this world."

"Will your father let you go to Moscow?"

"I fancy he will. He always minds what people think. You know, he wouldn't even let me go to high school. And then, after a while he began to feel awkward about it—and think, well, are the Meshkovs any worse than other folks? Still, he's so inflexible."

"If he doesn't let you go," Kirill continued with concentration, "wait a year, and I'll have finished the Technical School by then. I'll have a trade and I'll be able to start work. And then you'll leave home and come to me. Will you?"

Lisa was thinking. The downpour was crushing and threshing the wood; soaked through, the trees hung heavily under the downpour in the swishing and splashing of the torrent. To make themselves heard above the storm, the two had to talk very loudly in their cocoon of leaves with the water running over it, and so, instead of answering, Lisa lowered her head. Kirill repeated his question, his lips just touching her ear, covered by a strand of soft fine hair.

"Will you leave home?"

"Yes," she replied.

He kissed her on the cheek, very lightly; then, after a minute, he kissed her again, a stronger and more lingering kiss this time. Neither noticed that the earth was picked out of the darkness by flashes of white flame and then slid back into darkness, only to reappear in the flame; nor did they hear the joyous peals that reveled in this rocking back and forth from light to darkness—they were motionless.

They returned to the realization of their surroundings only when silence fell and sunshine dappled everything with gleaming spots, and slow, fragrant drops plopped heavily from the trees.

"Is it all over?" Lisa asked in wonder. She was the first to creep out from under the shelter, shivering a little as the drops trickled down her collar.

"Everything looks quite different now," she said, glancing about for the best spot to jump across the stream racing toward the gulley.

The grass laid low by the rain was straightening slowly and vapor rose from it, drawing a milky film over the pools. The silver birches looked spotless and newborn.

The path soon led out from the wood to a clearing, where they could hear the hoofs and neighing of horses. A drove of mares with their foals was galloping across the ground toward the path, but the sudden appearance of strangers startled the leading mares.

They stood still an instant, then turned and dashed across the clearing at an uneven, random gallop. The others tore after them, and as they turned their well-fed, agile bodies, their sides and haunches caught the sunlight and reflected it in their wet, sleek hides.

"You'd think they'd won a victory," Kirill said.

Then out of the wood a Tatar with a cataract over his eye appeared on a nag, rose in his stirrups, rode athwart the drove, cut it off, and turned it toward the road. Kirill inquired of him where kumiss was sold. The Tatar pointed with his knout at the birch grove, gave a wild, ruthless whistle, and galloped away.

Outside a cabin, blue from the rain, close by the paddock where the mares were milked, a table and a bench had been fixed into the ground. A Tatar boy in a loose coat nodded his freshly shaven bluish-pink head, crowned with a raspberry-red skullcap, swished the water off the table with the tail of his coat, and ran down to the cellar. The glasses dimmed at once with the cold kumiss; its sourness had a heady flavor and tingled in the throat. As though by silent agreement, Kirill and Lisa paused at the half-glass, clinked glasses, and drank.

"Someday," said Lisa, "someday you and I will be drinking real wine together."

"Soon," he replied, "very soon, I believe."

CHAPTER

· 15 ·

As THEY WERE finishing their second bottle of kumiss, the Tatar boy counted out the change and jingled his purse delightedly. "The players are coming here for kumiss," he said, and showed his small teeth in a grin of satisfaction.

"That must be Tsvetukhin and Pastukhov," Kirill said.

Lisa was finishing the last of her kumiss, tilting her glass awkwardly as though she were trying to shield her face with her elbow.

As Tsvetukhin drew nearer and saw her, he beamed and was about to take off his hat when Pastukhov stopped him and, standing stock-still, intoned:

"Look there, Egor, at that charming couple—the youth and the girl! How pathetic to think of their mournful fate! That sweet creature, the girl, still hopes she will live to come here and drink kumiss, but already the sinister, unsparing blight of sickness is upon her, dragging her down irresistibly into the yawning chasm of oblivion. Nature sparkles with all the colors of the rainbow, but her face is pale, her fingers tremble, she is doomed. Poor girl! Poor youth! Ah, this poor pair! And poor you and me!"

Tsvetukhin waved him away, and they both came up laughing, holding out their hands across the table, and Lisa and Kirill laughed in response, and the Tatar boy again displayed all his teeth, and was evidently under the impression that merriment accompanied these amazing people wherever they went.

"And what if I really were ill?" Lisa asked with a playfulness unexpected in her.

"Good heavens, do I look such a fool?" Pastukhov exclaimed seriously. "You are the flat denial of illness. I was merely chanting a dirge over nature, which pales before your vivid color. Now, do stop blushing, don't do it any more—really, it's becoming positively unnatural! Ahmet, why do you stand there staring?—bring us three bottles of champagne, and the older the better!"

"There you are, then, the lucky coincidence again," Tsvetukhin was saying. "Where did you shelter until the rain was over? Why didn't you come to our cottage?"

"You seem to think everyone knows you have a cottage here," Kirill said.

"I told Lisa about it."

"Did you?" she said in surprise. "Yes, you did mention it in passing, but it slipped my memory, somehow. . . . We were sheltering under the trees. . . ." She paused a second and added: "It was a good place to shelter. We came out quite dry."

"Dry out of the water, as the saying goes," Pastukhov remarked. His curiously clinging scrutiny was turned languidly on each in turn. He gave the impression of being perfectly sure that nothing was concealed from him, and that if he were asked, he could tell the future as a fortuneteller does by the cards. He saw that this nice young fellow was about to suffer the first hurt to his feelings. Oh, of course the blow would not be dealt in ill will: how could there be ill will in this gentle and rather ardent girl? But the pen in the hands of fate is capricious. What will it draw? Its favorite sport is making fools of people. Tsvetukhin—this was the man destined to try the still diffident attachment of the young people. And would it stand the test of his experienced trifling? He had already entered into his part and he would act it even if only out of sheer boredom, and were he to drop it when he got halfway, Lisa would still prefer unhappiness with him to any other state of bliss. Anyhow, what kind of bliss awaited

her with this youth who would get a post as a draftsman on the railway and demand his fish cakes on
Sundays? True, he was evidently a strong-willed
young fellow. But Lisa would hardly be likely to find
amusement in the obstinacy with which he would insist on his hot Sunday cakes. Her dreamy disposition
required larger joys, sweeter torments; she sensed
them in Tsvetukhin; she could no longer look calmly
at him. Fate was seducing her and mocking her young
friend. It was all perfectly plain to Pastukhov in the
cards of the future, relentless and sorrowful in their
penetrating combination.

"Why do you look like that?" Kirill asked.

"I was thinking what a serious person you were."

"You find me serious—in what way?"

"Well, by your curt manner of speaking—if by
nothing else."

"No, no," Lisa broke in, "he's shy, that's all . . . and
so am I. And it seems to me that you and not Kirill
are speaking very harshly."

"Oh, but you don't know Alexander!" Tsvetukhin
chimed in. "He is an exceptionally gentle character."

"I wouldn't say gentle, but certainly a man of goodwill," Pastukhov corrected him. "I feel the greatest
goodwill toward you," he said pointedly to Kirill,
with a slight inclination of the head.

"Thank you."

"Not at all."

There was a silence. Pastukhov drank his glass of
kumiss and wiped his lips with a dissatisfied air. "I
think," he began in a tone that called for undivided
attention, "I think that—"

He stopped short and filled his glass again.

"Let us speak plainly," he began again, seeing that
they were all waiting to hear what he had to say. "I
like you all very much. I am about ten years older
than you. That is so, isn't it? But I am young, and the
spiritual life of young people is still very dear to
me. You are at the stage now when you are mistrust-
ful of everything. Particularly everything that comes
from your seniors. Every word uttered by your seniors sounds to you like sermonizing and is offensive."

"No, I wouldn't say every word," retorted Kirill,

"nor every senior. If that was so, we could never have learned anything."

Pastukhov made a pause that might have been taken to suggest that he ought not to be interrupted. "You're at the age when every attempt by outsiders at frank conversation is taken as an encroachment on your inner liberty. Shyness becomes secretiveness. I remember that at your age I was rather surly, aloof, and unsociable. I could not carry on a conversation, I imagined nobody would understand me, that everyone was inimical to my tastes and hated my convictions."

"But Kirill isn't in the least like that!" Lisa protested, offended.

"And besides," Kirill said, "you cannot say who of us is frank and who is not, because we hardly know each other."

"I'm speaking of myself."

"Yes, you're speaking of yourself, but what you want to say is that I am just like you were. But I am not like you: I do not consider that everyone must necessarily hate my convictions for some reason or other."

"And what are your convictions?" Pastukhov asked, quickly settling himself with his elbows on the table as though he was prepared to listen for a long time.

Even in the bright sunlight it was plain to see the color flooding Kirill's cheeks, and he went hard all at once.

"There you are—lost the power of speech straightaway," Pastukhov said, smiling.

"Not a bit of it. But I don't understand. . . . What exactly are you interested in?" Kirill retorted in an unexpectedly challenging tone.

"I'm interested in youth," Pastukhov replied quietly. "I would like to know whether it hopes for anything big, or is it just doing the usual things, exercising with dumbbells, reading *Training the Will* by Jules Peillot, and roaming through the Limes with young ladies. At least, that's what I did in my time. And when 1905 came around, I positively didn't know what to do with myself—whether to go out with girls or punch heads with a dumbbell. That is to say—what I wanted was to be on the barricades. But I didn't know the way there. Is it possible that the same thing will happen to you?"

"You mean, to me personally?"

"Yes, my friend, to you personally."

"No. It will be different with me."

"That is to say, you will know the way to the barricades?" Pastukhov asked, making each word distinct by significant pauses.

Kirill glanced at Lisa—she had half risen, astonished, as though scarcely able to believe that this was the Kirill with whom she had sheltered in the gulley from the rain. Very distinctly he answered: "I know it."

"Well, congratulations," Pastukhov said without any affectation.

"Enviable assurance," Tsvetukhin observed. "Sounds well, too. The road to the barricades. The road to the scaffold. It might be staged quite nicely."

"I'm not an actor," Kirill retorted, flaring up. "I'm not attracted by effects. And as for the scaffold—a good soldier doesn't think of death when he goes out against the enemy. That's one thing. For another, I know you want to quote the hackneyed truth about history repeating itself. I don't know that. And nobody can say yet who is going to the scaffold."

"Good heavens!" Pastukhov gasped.

Kirill gulped down the last of his kumiss as though to cool his ardor.

Tsvetukhin never took his eyes off Lisa. Her face reflected not only the phases in the conversation but the fullness of her feelings—something resembling fear for Kirill, and pride, and happy perplexity, almost bewilderment, at his boldness. Her glowing face and the pose of her slim figure expressed the pleasure of excitement, even bliss. Tsvetukhin might of course have attributed this excitement to his own account for the simple reason that Lisa was trying not to look in his direction. But it was unlikely that either he or Pastukhov could have guessed that she was enjoying her part in something bookishly highbrow, this meeting in the glade, the unusual conversation which disclosed the divergence in views and might lead to a quarrel. Not a vulgar squabble, not a row, but a bookish difference, such as Turgenev might have described, when disputatious people argued with each other about something abstract but very essential, and left each other with increased respect for themselves. It turned out that such people were possible not only in books, and Lisa was here among them. Tsvetukhin could account for her state of mind by his presence if he so wished. He purposely avoided reacting to Kirill's audacity: Pastukhov had started the argument—let him carry on with it, but he, Tsvetukhin, found Lisa's naïve emotions far more engaging. Of course, he was interested in the argument, too, and was following it, particularly as the talk had turned on his favorite subjects, but he had been nettled by the disrespectful reference to actors who were alleged to be forever striving after effect. And how had this reference been made? With truly boyish harshness, just as one might read in Turgenev. From the lips of a boy like Kirill it would have been strange to look for profound thoughts. He did not even suspect that Pastukhov was toying with him—a cat-and-mouse game. Still, Tsvetukhin and Lisa did not miss a word of the conversation that was going on.

Musing awhile, Pastukhov came to the conclusion that Kirill was even more serious than he had supposed. The recognition of this aroused Kirill's youthful curiosity and he wanted to know why exactly Pastukhov was making fun all the time—no, no, not of his vis-à-vis (Kirill didn't suffer from hypertrophy of his self-love: he actually used the word *hypertrophy*), not of his vis-à-vis, but of the very subject of the conversation, as though he were far above all this sort of thing. Then Pastukhov asked if Kirill had taken offense, perhaps, at his mention of the dumbbells, or had he wanted to take up the cudgels in defense of will training? It then appeared that Kirill went in very seriously for dumbbells and saw nothing funny in this, particularly since Egor Pavlovich Tsvetukhin himself went in for morning exercises on the Muller system. And as to will training, that might be funny only in a case where the purpose of training the will was unknown. At this point the temptation was too great for Pastukhov, and with a quizzical glance through his narrowed eyes at Lisa, he said:

"So you do exercises with dumbbells and read about

will training. But you don't go to the Limes with young ladies, do you?"

Kirill threw his leg over the bench, sprang to his feet, and took the threatening pose that best of all, very likely, defends the right to personal life, but getting himself in hand, he said, even managing a laugh: "If it comes to that, the pleasantest of all these occupations is just the Limes."

They all laughed, but Kirill was not comforted by the cold shower he had given himself, and added, scowling like a neglected husband: "It's time for us to be going, Lisa."

He would not hear of the invitations to Tsvetu-khin's cottage; the more Lisa hesitated, the more obstinate he became in his assertions that it was time for them to go. The kumiss had been drunk long ago, the Tatar boy had been paid, and they set out across the glade, Tsvetukhin and Lisa leading the way.

Pastukhov, as he walked along, plucking and rubbing between his fingers the plumes of last year's sorrel, talked, more for himself than to them.

"The thing I used to call will power now seems to me only the despair of youth. It is courage born of yearning for an inaccessible, better life, when everything around repels you with its falseness, and you want either to throw up the whole business and run away without a single backward look, or to smash it all. The actions performed at such moments have the appearance of being strong-willed. But actually they are prompted by despair. They are irresponsible as regards yourself and other people as well. And in our young days it is this irresponsibility that makes them so good. It is remembered with wistful regret by the grown man overburdened by responsibility and enslaved by duty."

"I disagree. I think that youth has its responsibility, too," Kirill said. "When all is said and done, the origin of will power — whether it's despair or daring—is not of such great importance. The important thing is the application of the will. The important thing is the result of the effort. Excuse me, but didn't you say you were only ten years older than me? Yet you are somehow far—"

"Older?" Pastukhov took him up, seemingly pleased.

"That's because I try to understand youth. It ages one."

He plucked a dog daisy and put it in the button-hole of his light blue jacket, which hung on him as loosely as a blouse.

"I like the way you talk. You're all bristles and thorns."

He was about to take Kirill's arm, but the boy abruptly quickened his pace. They overtook the others, and as they walked four abreast, Pastukhov complained with a rueful smile:

"Can you imagine, Egor, we argued to the point of my being called an old man. And you know, it doesn't seem so far from the truth? There are times when I find myself full of veneration for traditions. The last time I went to see my father's country home, it had already been auctioned off. I strolled through alien, sad-looking avenues, glanced into the old hollows of the trunks familiar to me from childhood and thought: the lime tree planted by Grandfather Pastukhov is not simply a lime, but Madame Lime. And I daresay I was too careful as regards the springs which with us are liable to be filled up with rubbish and treated without the slightest care. . . ."

"You're from the Atkarsk district, aren't you?" Tsvetukhin asked.

"No, we are not connected with those Pastukhovs," Alexander Vladimirovich said with a fleeting touch of hauteur. "We're the Khvalynsk Pastukhovs. We come from the same neighborhood as the Radishchevs."

He looked superciliously at Kirill and Lisa and suddenly became aware that they had heard nothing of what he was saying about either limes or springs. Lisa's eyes were filmed with sudden alarm as though the clear childish tears were about to gather in them, the sense of alarm seemed to have communicated itself to Kirill, and a disapproving look, such as one might see on the face of a judge, clouded his brow, harshly outlined by the dark hair. At that moment they were absorbed in each other, so Pastukhov, altering his tone with his usual facility, remarked to Tsvetukhin:

"Come along, old man, let's go back to our cottage. Our friends" (throwing his arm around Kirill's shoulders for a moment) "have come here because they want to be alone. They are bored with our melancholy and all that sort of nonsense."

"I thought they liked being with us," Tsvetukhin protested, appealing to Lisa with an apparently naïve look.

But she did not heed him because she still could not take her eyes from Kirill.

When at last they had said good-by to the two men and were alone, she said hurriedly: "I'm going back."

"Why?" Kirill asked in a low voice.

"I won't be a minute, I left my bunch of dog daisies there on the table."

"I can see that. But why go back for them?"

They walked on a few paces, slowly and tensely, holding themselves very straight, as though afraid of touching each other.

"It was so unexpected—the way you spoke today. . . . And I've become rather absent-minded, you know? Well, and how am I to blame if you are quite different?"

"Yes, but you are different, too, Lisa!"

Then they fell silent and walked on at a quicker pace. The clearing was hidden from them by the slender columns of the birches which seemed to circle —the near ones lagging behind, the distant running far ahead. In the depths of the grove horses were roaming, or standing almost motionless with heads bent to the ground. The vapor left by the rain had vanished; only here and there among the taller broad-fronded ferns and grasses the great drops sparkled an instant like gems and went out. In the gulley, where Kirill and Lisa had sheltered from the rain, long, peaceful shadows were spreading, and the treetops, rinsed clean by the downpour, brimmed over with shining green foliage.

Only a short while ago, when Kirill had been gathering the dog daisies between the trees, he had seemed a boy to Lisa, and now when she looked sideways at him, she felt his incredible superiority: he was grown-up, while she was still a little girl. He could ask her questions like a father, but she could not answer them. Wordlessly, they walked amid the stupefying radiance of the well-watered, well-nourished satiated foliage, remembering how perfectly at their ease they had felt in their silence an hour ago, on this same neglected, grass-grown path, under the canopy of this same grotto of maple, hawthorn, and oak.

When at last they were in sight of the streetcar stop, Kirill broke the unbearable silence. "Have you been seeing Tsvetukhin?"

And Lisa said hurriedly again: "Quite by accident, you know. It was a rather funny coincidence, too. Only once. We haven't seen each other since then and I was going to tell you. But it was so nice with you today, Kirill . . . I forgot everything, everything. You understand? You were somehow altogether new to-day!"

He did not reply. They got on the streetcar, a light-green car, clean-washed like the leaves, with a Whitsuntide birch bough on the roof, and Lisa suggested going inside and sitting down. But at this the young bull-spouse butted her away.

"Sit down by all means," he said, "I'll stand out here."

CHAPTER

· 16 ·

MEFODY, dressed as a Tatar,* was seated by Tsvetukhin, watching him making up, and as he talked, his
protruding lips made an aggrieved, smacking sound,
"In dry summers a tiny little maggot settles on currant bushes and weaves a sticky kind of web all over the
bushes—you can't touch them. And nothing remains of
the berries but dry rot and still the maggot goes on
weaving and weaving. That is the way we are—we're
all messed up with this sticky cobwebby stuff and
can't free ourselves of it."

"You want me to come a cropper this evening?"
Tsvetukhin demanded, never taking his eyes from
the mirror.

"You're quite another story. The web won't cling
to you. You, as you pass through our backyards, look
around at once to see if any burs have stuck to you,
and then back you go to your realm. You're sheer
talent, Egor!"

"That's right. Keep it up, old man, another rub
with the rosin and the violin will sing out."

"But what am I?" Mefody went on. "I've been
given the role of the Tatar: all I have to do is go out
on the stage with my hand bound, pray and moo like
a cow—and that's the lot. You can't imagine what

* The Tatar—a character in Maxim Gorky's play *The
Lower Depths*.

I've had to stand all because of this very mooing, from my friend here: why am I any better than they are, they'd like to know, that I should be on the program? The role of the Tatar is a very big one, you see—leading artists play it at the Moscow Art Theatre, and when they moo, the whole audience bursts into sobs. You have to know how to moo, see? I'd never have got anywhere near such a part if I hadn't hung on to Tsvetukhin's coattails. 'You're a fawning slave,' they tell me. The fools! Tsvetukhin and I sat on the same school bench until our pants shone, we've eaten a barrel of salt together. He's a friend of mine and he doesn't give a hang for the lot of you, I tell them."

"You haven't had a drop too much, by any chance, have you?" Tsvetukhin inquired.

"I'm not drinking, I'm reading nowadays. Since the time Pastukhov spoke to us of Leo Tolstoy, I can't get Tolstoy out of my head. I've got hold of some books and it seems as though my eyes were opened. It makes me feel still sorrier for myself: the currant maggot, the sticky web that I am! He scrapes the bark off me with his life-giving finger, seeks out what is noble in me that I may soar higher. But, shivering with fear, I see myself so deep, so very deep at the bottom of the gulley, and despondency comes down over me, and I'm powerless to climb out of it. Or I am overwhelmed by despair, or else conscience-stricken to the point of tears, and I can feel my legs twitch of themselves, wanting to be off somewhere, and the path winds upward out of the gulley, far above me, I fancy, beckoning me on—to be bold and take it. Mefody, I think, you're going to rebel, watch out now, that's what you're going to do. And it frightens me, you know, it gives me the creeps."

"Read 'drinking' for rebelling, and I should think you'll just about hit the nail on the head," Tsvetukhin remarked, powdering his mustache. Then, turning abruptly to face his friend, he demanded in a mock drunken voice: "Dear tippler, do I resemble you at all?"

His bleary dim eyes stared straight before him. His jowls had sunk, the mouth hung loose, the head trembled, but the sparse grizzled hair which quivered on it had a quirk about it, something that suggested

scorn of the squalid countenance that it adorned and
the wounded pride of the unfortunate.

"They may say I'm a fawning slave, if they want
to," Mefody declared piously, "but you, Egor, you
are perhaps a genius."

Tsvetukhin drew himself up before the mirror with
an air of haughty elegance and said in a low tone:
"Sh-sh, Lady!"*

"Genius!" Mefody breathed softly and left the
dressing room, pulling his long Tatar tunic close about
him and bowing his head meekly.

Tsvetukhin did not even notice that he had gone.
While he was altering his looks, his talk with Mefody
had amused him, but afterward it only bothered him:
he finished the work of transformation before the
glass, and the glass began to work its spell on him.
His altered countenance convinced him that he no
longer existed, and he gradually began to lose his
distinguishing characteristics, one after the other—
gait, build, height—until the man who rose before the
glass was the enfeebled Baron, the boastful habitué of
the rooming house and—who knew?—perhaps the
onetime owner of a gilded coach with footmen.

"Sh-sh, Lady," the Baron said again, and laughed, a
thin, crumbly sort of snigger.

Each time he walked onto the stage he was haunted
by an awareness of the audience, like the awareness of
an imminent change in nature—the diffident rise of a
planet, a relentless storm, or the first light flurry of
snow. Curiosity, sweetness, dread of the unknown—
none of these was adequate to express that foreknowl-
edge of the public, that wistful tension, with which
he awaited his cue, his emergence before the public.
As a matter of fact, he did not even see the public,
but perhaps, in the black chasm, eyes, someone's
eyes, would be devouring him steadily, and he would
act for them alone, act to the utmost, to sheer re-
incarnation, and the eyes would justify and release
his awareness of the change. He fancied that the eyes
in the crowd this time were, unexpectedly enough,
those of the little girl who had run errands for the
actors, behind the scenes—for cigarettes, or to the bar,

* "Sh-sh, Lady"—says the Baron, a character in Gorky's
play *The Lower Depths*.

or the post office for a stamp—the lingering blue glance, uncommonly thoughtful for her years—Annochka's glance. True, he had only a fleeting awareness of these eyes; then they gave place to others—the soft, rather frightened, greenish-blue eyes of Lisa Meshkova, and, with this momentary awareness of the audience as the eyes of Lisa, Tsvetukhin came out on the stage.

Lisa was in the crowd, somewhere up in the circle, but she felt singled out from the crowd because she was sure that she was waiting for Tsvetukhin's appearance more tensely than anyone else. The festive air of the audience at this first night of the play did not satisfy her, and she explained this by the fact that the members of the audience did not know Tsvetukhin as well as she did. Kirill was sitting beside her. This was the first time they had been to the theater together, and her parents knew of it. Merkuri Avdeyevich had worked for a long time on his beard with the palm of his hand before he had answered:

"It's more than I can understand why they show such things as *The Lower Depths* on the stage. I've been told that they had to go to St. Petersburg to get special permission to show it. It shouldn't have been permitted."

"But you haven't read the play, Papa, have you?"

"Why should I read it? People try their hardest to keep their heads above water, and here's the theater dragging them down to the depths. They write about goodness only knows what these days. All those Pastukhovs and the like. They don't know what life is."

Lisa knew that the best way to win her point was by silence; yielding to him disposed him favorably, obstinacy drove him to frenzy.

"You ought to be able to judge for yourself, of course, you're grown-up now," he began cautiously, as though half afraid that he was giving his daughter too much rope by admitting her to be grown-up. Then he asked with a quizzical expression: "Are you thinking of going with . . . your young man?"

Taking a deep breath, she replied: "Yes."

"So that's it," he remarked after a long pause.

He was beginning to give way: today he had reconciled himself to Kirill, tomorrow he would recon-

cile himself to Moscow. This was a triumph: Lisa was
sitting in the theater, afraid of no one and nothing:
she felt as fearless as an infant. From that hour she was
free to enjoy herself as she wished and she wondered
at herself that she could sit through act after act,
perfectly motionless, while within her such a turmoil
was going on, and her eyes smarted from the hot
throbbing blood.

When the play was over, and they were pushing
nearer to the stage through the storm of applause
and the crowd that was reluctant to disperse, Lisa said:
"But I've seen the people from our rooming house
hundreds of times. Why did I never know that they
were like these? I never felt the least bit sorry for
them, they even repelled me. And here the very rags
they're wearing seem enviable, don't they?"

"So you liked Tsvetukhin?" Kirill said.

"But you'll agree that his Baron is the most unfortunate of them all and that one pities him most.
And the principal thing is that one feels sorry for all
of them."

"No, the principal thing is that they arouse your
indignation."

"Yes, they do arouse one's indignation against . . .
against everything. Just because one feels sorry for
them. And for the Baron most of all. Listen, they're
calling for Tsvetukhin all the time."

"They're calling for him because he's the favorite.
That's always the case with the public. They may be
applauding him because they liked him last year."

"No, it's because of his Baron."

"Or perhaps because he walks about in a cape."

"But you can hear them all calling—Baron! Everyone
was moved by his playing and everyone has seen that
tramps are as unfortunate as the rest."

"I see all this quite differently," Kirill said coldly.

Then Lisa called out with the rest in an insistent
voice: "Tsvetu-ukhin!" and clapped her hands, purposely holding them as close as she could to Kirill.
At almost the same instant someone took Lisa by the
elbow, a touch that controlled her ardor. She turned.
Pastukhov was beaming at her good-naturedly.

"That's right, that's the way: Tsvetukhin was
good!"

Lisa, delighted to find this unexpected ally, blurted out: "But I can't convince Kirill that Tsvetukhin as the Baron is a revelation."

"It's the author who made the revelation by looking beneath the surface of life," Kirill retorted in a sententious tone, so startlingly like Merkuri Avdeyevich's that Lisa's eyebrows went up: where did this come from?

"It's pleasant to hear such an opinion," Pastukhov said, laughing. "After all, I'm a playwright, too. But a good actor shares the credit with the dramatist."

"Not every dramatist sees what's hidden beneath the surface," Kirill persisted as sententiously and as angrily as before, addressing Pastukhov. "It's not enough to be even a poet, for that you have to be . . ." (he moved closer to Pastukhov) "a revolutionary!"

"Still on the same tack!" Pastukhov said, laughing again. "Let's go and congratulate Egor Pavlovich Tsvetukhin."

"Oh, yes, let's go and see him!" Lisa almost cried.

"I don't want to," Kirill said flatly.

"Leave the profound thoughts for a while, my friend," Pastukhov advised in a fatherly tone, taking an arm of each. "You enjoyed a good show and never mind the rest."

The curtain went up no more. Shouts were still hailing down with unabating energy from the audience in the gallery, but the stalls were deserted, and the theater seemed still more splendid: with the crushed red plush of the seats and tier upon tier of circles glowing like embers in the light of as yet unextinguished chandeliers. Then suddenly the lights dimmed, and it looked as though a crowded ball was just over, and only the smell of finest dust and perfumed dresses hung about the silent dusk.

Carpenters ran about the stage, dodging under scenes that slid upward magically. Nails were pulled out of the floor with a swish. The firemen unbuckled their belts—their brass helmets were already hanging up on the wall.

The tragedian who had played the Actor in the play was going down the corridor past the open doors of the dressing rooms, mopping his face with a napkin that looked marbled with streaks of make-up, and repeating the words of his part in stentorian tones.

"The theater creaked and shook with the enthusiasm of the public!"

He dropped in at Tsvetukhin's room, kissed him thrice on the cheeks, thrusting his fingers into his tousled hair.

"That was acting, old man, that was acting! I congratulate you. But don't imagine that your going to the rooming house has done it. I acted well, too, and I have never been inside a rooming house. It was the divine spark that helped you—that was it, old man! Understand? And the same with me."

Pastukhov embraced Tsvetukhin, too, and stood silent for a minute, gripping his hand. Then he moved aside and indicated Lisa and Kirill, who had paused in the doorway.

"Here's a delegation from the public."

Tsvetukhin opened his arms to them with an irresistible welcome that suggested he did not doubt that everyone was ready to fall into his embrace. And although Lisa recoiled, he clasped her to his breast, in the Baron's tatters, and seemed very touched and kept murmuring grandly: "Thank you! Thank you!" Then he opened his arms wide again to clasp Kirill in them, but the boy stepped outside the door and held out his hand from the corridor.

"It's bad luck to shake hands across the threshold!" Tsvetukhin exclaimed, drawing him into the dressing room. "Well, what was it like?"

"Amazing, simply amazing!" Lisa replied, her eyes shining and moist.

"Was it really, though?"

"Wonderful," Lisa repeated.

"Thank you very much indeed! And what about you? Did you like it?" he asked Kirill.

"Yes, on the whole I did," Kirill replied quietly which made them all prick up their ears and look sharply at the critic who struck a discordant note in the general laudatory tone.

"What was it you didn't care for, in particular?" Tsvetukhin asked curiously, rather in the encouraging tone one uses to children.

"I didn't like you."

"There you are!—how do you like that from a delegation!" the tragedian exclaimed in his deep bass.

"Me? But why?" Tsvetukhin wondered.

"You acted the part much too sentimentally and aroused everyone's pity. I happen to have read the play and I know it isn't a bit like that."

"It would be interesting to know what you got out of it," Tsvetukhin remarked with a touch of mockery.

"In the play all these tatterdemalions are defiant, they don't give a hang for anyone. And you think they're just poor wretched drunkards."

The tragedian shook his marble-streaked napkin as though flapping away flies. "An actor must stir the public. Didn't you see the public weeping? You didn't? Well, since we've managed that, we've won. Bravo, Egor, bravo! Why rationalize overmuch?"

Suddenly a new voice chimed in—it was Mefody's. Still dressed as the Tatar, he had been sitting quietly in the corner. Now, straightening himself and advancing slowly on Kirill with the big drops of perspiration starting through his weird make-up, he said wrathfully: "Aren't you taking a great deal upon yourself, young man? You've come to a great actor at a moment of triumph when the public has just given him an ovation, and you dare to teach him! Don't you know that perhaps tomorrow it will be the talk of the town? And that the capital will hear of it? And that this is a social event? Do you know that the inspector came behind the scenes to us and forbade us to play the guard in police uniform because it evoked ridicule of the police among the public?"

Hereupon they all gasped, exchanged glances, and threw back their heads as though at a flash of lightning in a clear sky, and Mefody, rolling his eyes belligerently, whispered:

"Why, after this there'll be prayers offered up for us. This production will go down in history—yes, history, young man."

"I'm not saying anything against the production," Kirill said steadily, returning the Tatar's formidable stare with quiet persistence.

"But you take it upon yourself to teach actors?"

Tsvetukhin strolled over to the looking glass and said with a shrug of his shoulders: "Drop it, Mefody. Everybody has the right to express his own convictions."

The hurt in his voice roused Mefody still more; he moved forward, ready to vent his indignation on Kirill, but at this moment Pastukhov stepped between them.

"I'm going to defend the public from the actors."

"I can defend myself if I'm given a chance to speak," Kirill declared, emerging from behind Pastukhov's back, so that his eyes met his opponent's again.

"Oh-oh, unbending pride!" Pastukhov said, turning to him.

"He simply loves to argue," Lisa gabbled in fright. "Oh, I'm so ashamed, I must ask you. . . ." She turned swiftly toward Tsvetukhin. Pale, with one trembling hand outstretched, she stood still before him as though she had lost the power of speech for a moment. Her cheeks were smeared with tears like a child's. She managed to stammer out the words: "Forgive me . . . forgive us both!" and then ran from the room.

They called after her—Pastukhov, Tsvetukhin, and someone else. She heard footsteps overtaking her and did not turn once, but hurried blindly through dim corridors and staircases, overtaking people, until she was out under the coal-black sky with its milky-blue trail of star dust.

She went across the deserted square, and as she slipped and stumbled over the round, bald cobblestones, she recalled returning across the square that sunny day after the first meeting with Tsvetukhin, and suddenly saw with agonizing clarity that the sunny day had gone forever.

When she reached home, she undressed quickly and went to bed; then, creeping under the bedclothes, she cried bitterly.

"Everything's ruined," she confided to her pillows. "I thought I was free, and find I'm mistaken. Kirill is going to torment me all my life. Such a dreadful, dreadful person!"

She fancied people were moving about in the house.

Something stirred in the passage downstairs; something fell.

"I'm raving. I'm so unhappy," she whispered, and, pulling up the blankets closer about her ears, fell asleep.

CHAPTER

· 17 ·

THE NIGHT ALARM in the Meshkov household started with Glasha the cook, who, trembling with excitement, announced that an officer was asking to see Merkuri Avdeyevich. Throwing on a few clothes, he went down to the kitchen, where, in the flickering light of the newly lit wick, he saw the bright buttons and silver shoulder straps of a huge black-clothed figure. The visitor said he was a gendarme officer and that he had come to search the premises where one Pyotr Ragozin lived, and that the landlord, Meshkov, was invited to be present as a witness. He asked him to dress without delay and accompany him to the little house in the yard. The night air struck chill to Meshkov's bones, though he had felt it very stuffy up to then and had slept covered only by a sheet. Valeria Ivanovna had a sudden lapse of memory: where Merkuri Avdeyevich's coat had got to she could not imagine, and while she was pottering, flustered and aimless, from the wardrobe in the hall to the cubbyhole under the stairs and back again to the wardrobe, the gendarme officer had called out "Please be quick!" twice from belowstairs, after which Merkuri Avdeyevich's bowler hat that had fallen down on the floor during the fuss and had rolled under the table, disappeared. At last Valeria Ivanovna made the sign of the cross at her husband's back as he was going downstairs, and recited from the prayer book: "Open the door of mercy to us." Standing at the head of the stairs, she listened for any sound of her daughter awakening, then went out into the gallery to watch the yard.

Merkuri Avdeyevich could not distinguish at first the shadows of the gendarmes, which merged with the night. They were ranged along the walls and he could not count them because they were in twos and threes as far as the porch steps of the wing, where they were grouped thickly. He heard the thin clink of spurs, the metallic click of the ends of the shoulder knots, the whistling snuffles; it was very quiet. Suddenly Glasha's protesting voice said:

"But, Your Honor, I'm only an ignorant woman."

"You don't need to be anything else!" the officer said curtly. "You just say what I tell you and that's all."

She was pushed on ahead. She knocked at the door. Ksenia Afanasyevna came out at once into the passage (she must have been sitting up) and asked: "Petya, is that you?"

"No, it's me," Glasha replied.

"You? Whatever's the matter?" Ksenia Afanasyevna asked.

"Well, it's like this. . . . They delivered it to us, but it's for you. I was told to bring it to you."

"Bring what?"

"Well, this. . . ."

The gendarme officer had to prompt her in a whisper. "A telegram."

"The telegram," Glasha gasped tearfully.

No one breathed, and Merkuri Avdeyevich fancied that the stars were growing larger in the heavens and that the whole yard with its buildings had mounted silently to meet the stars. Then suddenly the yard fell away underground with a terrific row, and only then did he realize that it was the sleepy rooster flapping his wings and crowing in the neighbor's henhouse. "Before the cock crow, thou shalt deny me thrice," came into his mind, and thereupon he heard Ksenia Afanasyevna saying in a different voice, low and despairing:

"Just a minute—I'll dress myself," and she must have run back out of the passage into the room.

"Now, then, Paschenko! Put your shoulder to that door!" the officer ordered in a louder tone.

Two gendarmes, crouching slightly, then straightening at once and setting their shoulder against the door from below, forced the bolt. The whole company rushed into the room through the passage, and matches were struck. Merkuri Avdeyevich could see the varigated shadows of caps and mustached profiles, shifting to and fro against the Russian stove—he was standing at the back, behind them all, against the door post, and found he could not cross the threshold: his feet had a dull heaviness, as though they had grown to ten times their usual weight.

"Where's Ragozin?" the officer demanded.

"He's at work," Ksenia Afanasyevna told him.

"Has he been gone a long time?"

"Since morning."

"Did he say when you might expect him home?"

"No."

"Are you his wife?"

"Yes."

Her voice had changed again. Merkuri Avdeyevich fancied he heard a note of dislike and defiance in it. That wasn't the way for a guilty person to talk—and after all, no innocent person's house was searched at dead of night. An innocent person would have pleaded: "Your Honor, it's all a mistake, a slander." That was what Merkuri Avdeyevich—innocent though he was of anything—would have done. He was ready to throw himself on his knees and wail: Have mercy! And now—the disgrace would be laid at his door! It would be all over the street tomorrow: a regular den that house of Meshkov's had turned out to be, a sink of iniquity and impiety! Meshkov had given shelter to crime, to rebels. Meshkov's houses had to be searched at night; they were looking for traces of subversive activities. In a case like this you wouldn't stop at going down on your knees, you wouldn't grudge any sum of money, only to lighten your fate.

And here was Ksenia Afanasyevna flatly refusing to answer any questions. She was sitting with her elbows on the kitchen table, her arched brows knitted; Merkuri Avdeyevich looked at her from the doorway with alert eyes that reflected the orange light of the lanterns lit by the gendarmes. Had it not been for this little woman sitting at the table with her braids of straight fair hair tucked behind her ears, and with her chin propped on her fist as though to keep her mouth more tightly shut—had it not been for her, Merkuri Avdeyevich might have been snoring away comfortably in his bedroom, under his sheet, instead of cringing on a stranger's threshold like a beggar or an outcast. Authority had forgotten him—what did it want with Merkuri Avdeyevich? He had been ordered to stand in the passage, so he had to stand there. And were he ordered to clear out, he would have to clear out. Yes, he ought to have given up this business of letting houses long ago. What good did he get out of a fellow like Pyotr Ragozin? You couldn't call nine rubles a month money, could you? Of course, he ought to have raised the rent: it wasn't such a bad little place— a kitchen, two rooms, and outhouses. If he had charged about twelve a month or even eleven, he might have let it to a clerk or a widow living on a pension. But nine rubles! What respectable person would rent a house at nine rubles? Now he was getting the interest off his one hundred and eight rubles a year: he, Meshkov, was to be talked about, disgraced, his good name ruined. The name he had taken such care of all these years! Never getting enough sleep, enough to eat, grudging a penny on the horse-drawn streetcars, tramping everywhere and picking his steps over the cobbles so as not to wear out his shoe leather too soon.

"To think of this happening!" he sighed. "It looks as though I've just lived for Ragozin's convenience."

His feet were beginning to swell, and there was no place to sit down except on the threshold, as the rooms had been ransacked by the gendarmes who were standing over the jumble of things, their stout bodies bent as though they were reaping. Merkuri Avdeyevich was growing tired of watching them bob up and down, and the shadows of bodies, heads, and arms creeping up the walls and slipping over the ceiling and suddenly falling from there to scurry after the moving lanterns and be swallowed up by the light. His eyelids were closing, lulled by the dancing shadows, when suddenly nocturnal reality substituted its dread meaning for the unreality of the dream.

"Witness, come this way!" the officer called out.

Ksenia Afanasyevna was no longer sitting at the kitchen table, but was huddled in a corner, with her face covered with her hands. The board of the table was raised and beneath it, fitting the table top exactly, lay a shallow case, partitioned into cells of equal size, each a little larger than a matchbox.

"A type case," the officer informed Merkuri Avdeyevich. "This is type. See?" He picked a lead letter out of one of the cells, passed his finger over it, and, showing them all the black trace made by the ink, said: "It's still fresh. They've been using it just lately."

The shadows danced toward the cellar now and, growing livelier, leaped up the board walls. Empty barrels rolled with a hollow sound from corner to corner. The noise, which gave the impression that a scuffle was approaching its decisive moment, kept growing louder. Now they were hauling up the heavy trap, covered with floor matting, that had filled the entrance to the cellar, the lanterns vanished below ground, and the waxen yellow light streamed up through the opening, picking out the beams.

Merkuri Avdeyevich was called in again. The gendarmes made way for him to pass through to the bright square of the cellar hatch, and his trembling foot groped for the rickety ladder. In the middle of the cellar stood a low machine with a soiled patchwork quilt made of three-cornered scraps thrown off it and trailing on the ground. The officer pressed the lever with his foot, and it sprang into life, the well-oiled transmissions creaking obediently.

"Nice sort of things go on in this yard of yours," the gendarme officer remarked playfully.

"The compositors' shop up above and the printing press down below."

Making a terrific effort to awaken, Merkuri Avdeyevich realized to his horror that he was not dreaming: he put out a hand to touch the machine, felt the sting of cold metal, and gave a convulsive start. The ladder shook beneath him as he climbed out of the cellar.

The cock crowed again and flapped his wings triumphantly. It was growing light as Ksenia Afanasyevna, carrying a small bundle, was escorted across the yard by two gendarmes.

When they reached the gate, she looked back at the deserted house and gave a hardly perceptible nod to Merkuri Avdeyevich, most likely because there was no one else she knew to whom to say good-by. He made no response. He was not thinking of her. Going up closer to the gendarme officer, he gently flicked something off his tunic just below the shoulder strap.

"You've got your uniform soiled, Your Honor," he said, "it looks dusty in several places. Perhaps you'll come across to my place for a brush up?"

"It might be as well," the officer agreed.

Standing in the middle of the kitchen and turning slowly in front of the window so that he could see where to brush his uniform, the gendarme officer said in a weary but not ungracious tone: "How did it come about, old man? In your yard?"

"It's beyond believing," Meshkov said in a dejected voice.

"It's a nasty business, you know."

"Yes, a blow for me!"

"You'll never hear the end of it!"

"What am I to do now, what am I to do, Your Honor?"

"Mm—yes. That's the question."

"Would you care for a cup of tea? I'll order them to put on the samovar."

"Oh, no! There's no time for that now. I've got to do a whole lot of writing. This is a special case. It has to be reported to the colonel at once. And then it'll go higher and higher. The colonel will write to the governor, the governor to the Ministry. This is a case of particular importance, I tell you. It'll end in imprisonment in the fortress. . . ."

"Good Lord! For whose sins! . . . Maybe, after all, you'd like something to warm you, Your Honor?"

"What exactly?"

"Well, something in the way of a drop of brandy or vodka with rowanberries. After a night like this, eh?"

"Rowanberry, eh? . . . No. Better not. I have to draw up my report. Pity we didn't haul in that Ragozin. Must have cleared out. What do you think of him?"

"I couldn't say. He didn't arouse any suspicions. The only thing was—he never drank. That was the only thing you could call a bit suspicious. As for the rest, he seemed a decent enough fellow. It would never come into my head to doubt him."

"But you knew he was under police surveillance!" the other exclaimed reproachfully.

"So I'd heard. Still, I thought he was going straight."

"Going straight, indeed?" the gendarme rejoined with official brusqueness. "I've never heard of such a thing. Never. The idea! That out-and-out, experienced old birds like this ever went straight! . . . Well, am I all right now?"

"Yes. . . . Just let me give this cuff a touch. That's all, your coat's quite clean now."

"Now, let me tell you: not a word of this must leak out. . . . Understand? Not a word!"

"Yes, of course, I understand that! Only . . . what about me?"

"You'll be called as a witness."

"I suppose I couldn't sign as a witness here and now, Your Honor, so as I wouldn't have to go there?"

"Not a chance, old man. You can't get out of going there when you're sent for. Your business is to keep your mouth shut, as I'm telling you. And then there's that cook of yours—what do you call her? Glasha. Make her hold her tongue. She hasn't seen or heard anything at all. Understand? Or else. . . ."

He raised a threatening finger, then touched his cap, turned on his heel smartly in military style, and marched out, leaving an echo of the heavy crystal-clear clank of spurs.

Merkuri Avdeyevich went upstairs. His gait was drooping, much heavier than usual, his shoulders were stooped. Valeria Ivanovna glanced at him in alarm. He looked as though he had been toiling all night as a longshoreman on the wharf. He passed into the bedroom, said a prayer, bowing to the ground and striking his head three times on the floor, then sat down in an armchair. After a few moments' silence such as is kept before starting on a long journey, he said in a melancholy voice: "Trouble's come upon us, Valyusha."

"Mother of Heaven!" she murmured. "Are they thieves or what?"

"Ah, if they were nothing worse than thieves!"

"Merciful God! You don't mean they've done murder?"

"Maybe, for all we know, they have done that, too. But that they were printing false money I saw for myself."

They both crossed themselves and sat in stunned silence a minute. Then Merkuri Avdeyevich said: "They took Ksenia away."

"But she's in the family way!" Valeria Ivanovna exclaimed in a shocked tone.

"Well, it makes no difference what way you're in if you're in jail. . . . Lisa didn't wake up, did she?"

"No, but she kept turning and tossing in her sleep."

"Not a word to her about the search, for God's sake!" Merkuri Avdeyevich warned threateningly.

And again they sat, petrified.

CHAPTER

· 18 ·

IT HAD BEEN light for some time now, but the lamp was still burning with a feeble smoky flame. Vera Nikandrovna was seated on a disordered bed, her hands, palms upward, on her lap. From time to time she looked around the room with astonishment that, flaring up for an instant, died out slowly. All the objects in the room looked at her from their wrong side, an unfamiliar side, and seemed to have just appeared in it. The pictures hung askew, the blueprint of the cross-section of the steamer held by one drawing pin. The mattress was ripped open and its striped cover trailed from the bed onto the floor, which was strewn with tow and rubbish and bore the footprints of large boots. School books and exercise books were scattered in the corners. The greenish-black "Judith" had been pulled off its nail and was leaning against the post upside-down. An overturned chair lay in the middle of the room.

Once these things had belonged to Kirill. Once he had written on the pages of these exercise books. Once his textbooks had stood on the shelves, the blueprint had been neatly pinned on the wall, the mattress had been hidden beneath a white coverlet. Once. . . . Only a few minutes ago Kirill had been sitting on that chair in the middle of the room, had just overturned it, stepping back from Vera Nikandronva, when she had said good-by, raising her

hands to his face, and he had winced, aging by years
in one instant. Only just now she had pressed his
head to her shoulder, and he had torn himself from
her embrace, while he crushed her fingers painfully
and stroked them. The noise of the falling chair was in
her ears still, all else had slipped away somewhere
to a day fifteen years ago, when they had come to
tell her that her husband had been cast up by the
Volga on a sandbank, and she had to go and identify
his body. She had sat the whole night long then, as
now, her arms hanging loosely, afraid to stir. But
then four-year-old Kirill slept under the white coverlet beside her, and though death had mutilated the
past, life had left Vera Nikandrovna an isle where
bees hummed around the honey-laden trees, larks
soared into the skies, and springs of clear water flowed
in cool groves. The isle grew and flourished, covering
the earth, embracing the world, and now it had sunk,
and was swallowed up in a fathomless bog. The
white coverlet was flung on the floor, the house was
empty, Vera Nikandrovna was alone.

She reviewed as in a vision all that had happened,
in its insistent, petrified obviousness.

Hardly had the gendarmes begun the search when
Kirill came home from the theater. They opened the
door to him and closed in on him at once. Vera
Nikandrovna had time to glance into his face and
see the instant darkening of his brows, eyes, and temples, and the sudden appearance of a straight dark
patch over his upper lip, as if his mustache had just
grown. They turned out his pockets and felt him
all over from head to foot. They crumpled all the
seams of his jacket, rubbing them in their hands.
Then they sat him on a chair in the middle of the
room. They rummaged in his bed and his linen, tapped with their knuckles on the drawers and legs of the
table, and on the door posts. They raked the ashes
out of the stove and dug over the rubbish heap. Then
they started on the books, and as they were flicking
over the leaves of a bulky and much-read volume
on "Mechanics," seven small pink wall notices, about
the size of a man's hand, slipped out and fluttered
to the floor, and the old gendarme with the debonair-
looking whiskers picked them up unhurriedly and

said with a kind of good-humored gratification: "Aha!"

Kirill was sitting there very straight, his legs twisted boyishly around the chair legs, his hands deep in his pockets.

"Where did you get these, young man?" the gendarme asked in a sociable tone, showing him a pink notice.

"I found them," Kirill replied.

"You don't happen to remember whereabouts, do you?"

"Somewhere in the street."

"In which street would that be?"

"Oh, a long way off."

"A long way from where?"

"Not far from the Technical School."

"A long way off and yet not so far, I see. And so they were lying all together, were they?"

"No, they'd been thrown away."

"You mean the whole wad of seven was lying where it had been thrown down?"

"That's it."

"And so you picked them up?"

"Yes, I picked them up."

"Off the ground?"

"Yes, of course, off the ground."

"And there they were, as clean and fresh as this, without a spot on them, lying on the ground?"

Kirill said nothing.

"Ah, you poor young greenhorn, why didn't you think first of what you were going to say, eh?"

"I needn't answer you at all. I'm not obliged to."

"Now that's something you've been put up to by other people—they've told you that you needn't answer," the gendarme said reproachfully, returning to his search through the books.

He had carried on the whole conversation in the insinuatingly kind tone of a mentor who is sure that the schoolboy is going to tell a lie. Vera Nikandrovna wanted to forbid him to speak in that tone to her son, who never lied. But the stubborn calm of Kirill's replies made her keep silence. She had a feeling that he was directing her and she had better suit her conduct to his. She imagined that he was wordlessly inviting her to join the conspiracy against the thieves who were rummaging among his things. Her pain and fear for him retreated before her admiration. He knew how to conduct himself at a moment of abominable and undeserved humiliation. Now she could see plainly the change that had taken place in him. Oh, yes—he had changed, and it was a change that made her prouder of him than before. All this that was going on in their home was, of course, a sad mistake, which had to be endured as her son was enduring it. He was teaching his mother to behave with the dignity she had dreamed of seeing in him, not rudely, but in a hard, unbending way, a man's way. God, how he had grown up, how manly he was! And why had she only understood this now, at this stark, pitiless instant?

"Now, isn't this funny, young man?" the gendarme said, taking down a portrait of Przhevalsky from the wall. "You play at revolution and here you have a picture of an officer over your bed."

"That officer had nothing in common with officers like you, Mr. Gendarme," Kirill informed him. "He brought Russia glory."

The gendarme tore down the picture and threw it on the floor.

"I'd advise you to consider your mother, even if you don't care a hang about yourself," he said weightily, and they noticed how he controlled his voice so as not to shout.

Kirill ought to consider his mother—they were cold words, uttered by a stranger, but they scalded her heart with despair. It was true, after all: Kirill was not thinking of her. He was killing her with his unfeeling attitude; he did not sense her pain. He had brought a terrible unhappiness upon her, he had ruined himself, cruel boy, poor dear, dear boy!

"Kirill," she called out to him timidly, helplessly, "why don't you explain? It's all a frightful mistake."

"Say good-by to him," the gendarme advised her. "We're going now."

"What? You're going to take him away? You want to take him . . . from me? But . . ." She rose to her feet and took a short step forward. "I'm his mother. . . . And how can you do such a thing? Without going into the question properly?"

"Don't you want to say good-by?" the gendarme repeated.

Two of the gendarmes went up to Kirill. Then, with a little cry, she darted forward with outstretched arms.

And now she could not tell whether much or little time had passed since she had embraced his burning head. She was sitting on his bed, surrounded by scattered things that had once belonged to Kirill. And he was not there. He was no longer there. . . .

The rectangle of sunlight, cut up by the shadow of the bars of the basement window, shortening and growing brighter, was moving along the floor, brightening the leaden film of ashes, the tangles and wisps of tow. The flies, happy in the warmth, buzzed more loudly. The old poplars sighed reposefully outside the windows, the sparrows chirruped noisily, squabbling over who should perch on which bush, and promptly made peace again.

Accustomed to these morning sounds, which for her denoted complete quiet, Vera Nikandrovna suddenly became aware of something disturbing this quiet. She fancied that someone was stealing through the adjoining room, coughing nervously. She came to herself.

Annochka was standing in the doorway, gaping, her eyes staring.

"What is it? What do you want?" Vera Nikandrovna asked in a whisper.

"I don't want anything," Annochka replied hastily, shaking her head vigorously. "Who were you talking to?"

"Talking? I wasn't talking to anyone."

"Oh, well, then. . . . Oh, I just . . . I thought you were talking to someone."

"But how did you get in?"

"The door's open."

"The door? Open?"

"Yes, wide open like this. I came in and heard you talking very quietly to someone."

"Ah, yes, I must have forgotten. That was it."

"And why is the lamp burning?"

"The lamp? Oh, yes, yes, indeed," Vera Nikandrovna said, starting up.

Annochka darted to the table, turned down the lampwick, and blew on the glass, from which a reddish globe of soot shot up. She made a grimace and glanced guiltily at Vera Nikandrovna, then went over to her impulsively and touched her drooping shoulder. "Was it the soldiers who made all this mess here?" she demanded in an indignant and at the same time condoling tone.

"Which soldiers?"

"The soldiers who came to take him away."

Vera Nikandrovna seized the little girl's hands and, without letting go of them, pushed the small, light body away from her. "How do you know? Who told you? Tell me, who told you?" she demanded, squeezing and rubbing Annochka's hands.

"Mama was told."

"But who could have told her? Do you know who?"

"There's a man who comes to sleep in our rooming house and he told Mama that when he was on his way home last night—it was just getting light, he said—he saw the soldiers taking a schoolboy along with them not far from the school. Mama asked him: 'What boy was that?' and he said: 'How the devil should I know? I only saw he had a school cap.' Then Mama said: 'Maybe it's the schoolmistress's son?' She was thinking of you. And he swore again and said: 'Maybe it was, for all I know.' And I thought so, too."

"My God, my God!" the woman sighed, releasing the child's hands.

"Our Pavlik wouldn't go to sleep last night, and when at last I got him off to sleep this morning, I laid him down and ran to see you."

"So everybody knows about it already? So soon?"

Vera Nikandrovna drew Annochka toward her again and made her sit down on the bed beside her and clasped her close, stroking the roughened braids of hair. "No, no, nobody can have heard it yet except you and your Mama. That's right isn't it? And don't you tell anyone—you mustn't. You understand that, don't you? It's all an accident. They'll let him go. He'll soon come back. He will come back, you understand, don't you?"

"Yes, of course, I understand. He's very good, I know."

"Yes, he's very, very good!" Vera Nikandrovna cried, kissing little Annochka on her cheek with all her heart. Suddenly, her talk became impressive, and almost calm. "You know what, little girl? You remember Lisa Meshkova, don't you? Well, now, you go to her house and tell her that I want her to come and see me. Only don't say anything about Kirill, mind. You understand that, don't you? And she should come here as soon as ever she can. Now run off, and meanwhile I'll tidy the room and sweep up."

"No, don't bother to sweep up," Annochka told her. "I won't be long, and then I'll come back and sweep up for you properly."

Vera Nikandrovna kissed her once more, locked the door behind her, and started to tidy up. Her movements were as quick and purposeful as though she was making up for her long and tormenting immobility. The thoughts which had been crowding in upon her that night and seemed to have frozen in the subconscious now thawed, melted, and, returning to life, burst all bounds. Now she had a plan of action ready and felt certain that everything would turn out as she intended.

But a setback awaited her at the first step: Annochka returned with the news that she had been met by Merkuri Avdeyevich, who had questioned her as to her business there, and had told her to say that if Madame the schoolmistress wished to speak to any of the Meshkov family, she might come herself and see them, but he saw no reason for Lisa to go there. Annochka selected and memorized the gist of what he had said.

"He said you should come to them, he won't let Lisa come here—not for anything, he won't."

Vera Nikandrovna thought for a minute, went over to the mirror, smoothed her hair, which was parted neatly in the middle, rubbed her face with a dry towel, and looked about her: no, she could not forget anything—all that she needed was with her, her plan of action, her will, the idea that was sharpened to a fine point. She saw Annochka, and with a stinging suddenness the tears started to her eyes for the first time in those hard hours. Annochka had rolled up her narrow sleeves and was shuffling and bobbing up and down jerkily at every step, swishing away with the broom, industriously sweeping the tow out of the mattress into a little heap, while the dust that arose whirled merrily around her from head to foot and played in a beam of glowing orange sunlight.

"Little girl, my dear girl," Vera Nikandrovna said in a low voice.

"I'll stay here and mind the house while you go there," Annochka said. "You mustn't worry—I know how to do everything."

Vera Nikandrovna almost ran out of the house.

She traversed the distance that divided her house from the Meshkovs as quickly as though she was passing from one room to another. The blue yard lay steeped in the morning sunshine like a vessel safe in harbor and ready to be loaded; there was even a flagpole over the gate; the sun-dappled windows winked blithely, the steps were washed clean.

The Meshkovs' reception of Vera Nikandrovna was respectfully stiff. Merkuri Avdeyevich presented her to his spouse. Valerie Ivanovna was a little embarrassed that she was only in her plain house dress, because she had not been warned.

"You must excuse me," Meshkov said, "for seeming to have obliged you to come here: I don't know, of course, how your messenger gave you the message. But I considered that though our young people have cultivated an acquaintance without their parents' knowledge, that is no reason for us to follow our children's example. We have nothing to hide."

"But are they hiding anything? I know your Lisa."

"Do you? Then it seems she isn't such a secretive person as your son," Meshkov rejoined with a chuckle. "I was thinking it might look a deal better if this secret acquaintanceship of theirs was carried on in the open."

"That's quite true," Valeria Ivanovna said, "our Lisa never keeps anything from us. She's been brought up like that ever since she was a little thing. . . . Well, the samovar's ready, won't you come and sit down? Only you mustn't mind our having nothing better to offer you. If I'd only been told beforehand. . . . I'm afraid there's nothing but plain tea, as they call it."

They were seated at the table when Lisa came down to breakfast. Sleep—though it had been none too sound that night—and a wash, and the triumphant strength of girlhood seemed to have created her, inimitably, just to match the morning. The shyness that came over her at sight of their guest added to her attraction, and while she was greeting her, and seating herself, touching her cup and saucer and serviette, and taking a slice of bread, as though searching for an object which might help her to preserve her equanimity, the three grownups sat silent under the spell of her charm.

"I haven't seen you, Lisa, since you left school," said Vera Nikandrovna, breaking the silence at last.

"No," Lisa acquiesced.

"Have you decided to go on with your education and enter the Women's College?"

"She is waiting for me to decide that question first," Merkuri Avdeyevich declared, "as in every other important question."

"Of course," Vera Nikandrovna agreed, "important things like this cannot be decided without one's parents."

"Exactly: these sort of decisions rest with the parents," Meshkov repeated emphatically in the tone of a mentor.

"Did you like the theater yesterday, Lisa?"

"Oh, ever so much."

"Whom did you like best of the actors?"

"Tsvetukhin."

"A celebrity," said Merkuri Avdeyevich.

"And did Kirill like him?" Vera Nikandrovna asked.

Lisa was about to blurt out no, when she caught herself in time and coughed.

So Vera Nikandrovna must know already all that happened yesterday in the theater. She must have come to speak about that awful scene in Tsvetukhin's dressing room, and Lisa's flight home alone through the town at night—or perhaps of something else? Of something Lisa did not yet know and that was of the utmost importance to her—of Kirill? Lisa had left him alone with people he had annoyed. Something irrevocable must have happened, very likely. What a misfortune their acquaintance with Tsvetukhin had been! Why on earth had she ever promised to go and see him behind the scenes? Had it not been for the quarrel with Kirill, everything would have been so much easier now. Of course, it would still have been terrifying, but not as bad as all this. After all, Lisa had long been preparing for the inevitable meeting between her father and Vera Nikandrovna. She had had a presentiment that it would be a decisive, perhaps fatal meeting. But could she ever have imagined that it would be at the moment of a rift—had they really come to a break?—with Kirill and that she would not know what had become of him?

"Now, see what a cough you've got!" Valeria Ivanovna remarked. "That comes of going to the theater, I suppose, it's always very drafty."

"Well, take that theater, now," Merkuri Avdeyevich said, stirring his tea. "The things it goes in for! Impersonating the sort of characters that haunt common lodginghouses."

"Yes, it shows every side of life," Vera Nikandrovna assented, as though she had not understood him.

"But where's the sense in showing all sides of life? People should be shown good examples so that they'll know what to emulate. That's what the Christian church teaches. And here they start exhibiting all manner of baseness as much as to say—here, have a good look and see how abominable men can be."

"Yes. Of course, the church and theater are two very different things," Vera Nikandrovna observed.

Merkuri Avdeyevich pursed his lips under his mustache with a touch of condescending reproach as much as to say: the lengths people go to!

"Different things—I should think so!" he said with a smile. "I suppose your son holds the same views as you do? It would be interesting to hear what he told you about the play."

"He could not tell me anything about it yesterday evening," Vera Nikandrovna said in a low voice.

"You haven't had a talk to him about it, then?"

"No," she replied, and, with downcast eyes, asked: "Could I speak to Lisa alone?"

There was silence a moment, then Merkuri Avdeyevich, leaning cautiously back in his armchair,
protested: "But what for? I was under the impression that we had met for the purpose of doing away
with all these mysteries. And you—it turns out that
you are on the side of secrecy in the young people's
behavior. Is that it?"

"Very well, then," Vera Nikandrovna said in a
still lower tone, and, taking up a serviette, unfolded
it slowly, then folded it again neatly in the ironed
creases. "I wanted to let you know, Lisa, that a terrible mistake has happened about Kirill. For some
reason or other . . . he was . . . arrested last night."

Lisa stiffened and stood up, holding on to the edge
of the table with the tips of her fingers.

"I want to ask you," Vera Nikandrovna went on,
her tone never changing, her monotonous voice seemingly devoid of feeling. "You know Tsvetukhin
well. If you were to ask him . . . you needn't go
alone, but with me, perhaps. Of course, he would
do it for you. If you were to ask him to use his
influence to help Kirill, I'm sure . . . he's so influential. And then everything would be cleared up
very soon. You know Kirill. . . . And this is a stupid
accident and of course it'll be obvious that Kirill
. . . And then Tsvetukhin—there's his friendship with
Pastukhov, who is very well known, too. . . . And
I'm sure . . ."

Lisa was slipping down slowly, as though she wanted
to pick up something off the floor. Her head drooped
slowly till it lay on the table, jolting the cup of tea.
A lock of fine soft hair adhered to the tablecloth,
darkening from the spilled tea, and her face turned
as white as ivory.

"Lisanka!" Valeria Ivanovna shrieked, darting to
her daughter's side.

Merkuri Avdeyevich, with instant presence of mind,
seized his daughter under the arms, lifted her—apparently without an effort—and carried her to her
room. The whole house was thrown into a commo-
tion. Valeria Ivanovna called for Glasha, ran to the
stairhead, and thumped on the banisters: the decanter that usually had drinking water in it proved to
be in the kitchen, the medicine chest was locked, and

the keys had disappeared. Lisa was attended to, her dress was unfastened, her temples moistened with Eau de Cologne. She soon came to, but her mother kept on fanning her with a calendar that happened to be handy and had a picture of the Tsar's family on the front.

Meshkov closed the door of Lisa's room and went back to Vera Nikandrovna. She was leaning against the wall between the two windows. Her shoulder had touched a philodendron, reaching as high as the ceiling, and its heavy leaves quivered, the patterned reflection of them playing on her face and the hands pressed against her breast. Her eyes were full of anxiety as she looked at Meshkov, but the reflections of the quivering leaves gave them a pensive, faraway look.

Meshkov stood opposite her, his feet planted firmly on the floor, and he twitched at the watch key attached to his watch chain. His breath came with a whistling sound through his bristling mustache; his beard was brushed askew.

"Allow me to inform you, Madame," he began on the low, muffled note his voice took when he wanted to keep himself in hand, "that my daughter had no connection whatsoever, and never could have had any, with your son. And I'll allow no one to impose on her. You've come to the wrong spot about your affairs. No one in my house takes criminals under his wing. And I think it only my duty to protect my girl from suspects. You must reap what you sowed yourself. You'll get no help from us. I have the honor to wish you a good day."

He stood aside, making way for her to go out.

"Well, then, there's nothing to be done," she said, bowing her head. "Only I am very sorry for your Lisa."

"As to that—you can suit yourself, of course. She has parents who are sorry for her in their own way, not your way. And now there's my door and I'll trouble you not to darken it again . . ." and he pointed to the stairs.

She descended the stairs, never raising her head, and went out into the yard. Meshkov followed her. He felt inclined to see her out to the wicket gate,

to make sure she had quitted the precincts of his
fortress.

But hardly had he crossed the threshold when
he was suddenly brought to a stop: no, it seemed
that the cup of misfortunes of the night was not
yet full. Across the yard toward him, with a self-
assured and threatening step, came a policeman,
round and ruddy as an orange, with an impressive
mustache to match, in a white summer uniform with
orange piping on the collar and cuffs, orange shoulder
straps, a glitter in the new metal number on his
cap and the polished sword hilt. Were the dreadful
visions of the night to haunt Merkuri Avdeyevich
in the daytime, too? Was he never to know any
peace and quietness again? Would he have to go about
all the time with either gendarme or police uniforms
at his heels? And wasn't it his bad luck that it should
so happen that this pest with the metal number on
his cap should bump into this nasty, mischief-mak-
ing visitor whom he didn't know and cared nothing
about!

But no—apparently the policeman had not noticed
Vera Nikandrovna. He did not even glance in her
direction. He was making straight for Meshkov, and
the shorter the distance grew between them, the nearer
the ends of that orange mustache crept to the eye,
the deeper sank the sharp dots of the pupils in the
puffy slits between the eyelids.

"How do you do, Merkuri Avdeyevich," the policeman rumbled, and Meshkov recognized him as the
officer in his ward.

"Good morning, I'm glad to see you," he returned
with satisfaction and even that touch of obsequious
respect which was heard in his voice only in conversation with very exceptional people. "How is it I
didn't recognize you at once?"

"You haven't seen me a long while, Merkuri Avdeyevich. I haven't been around since Shrovetide.
I've been home to the country—on leave."

"A-ah, so that's it? Very nice. What's it like in
the village these days?"

"First rate, thank you kindly. My family's very
well satisfied with everything. The peasantry is law-
abiding and orderly."

CHAPTER

· 19 ·

Egor Pavlovich Tsvetukhin had arranged to have lunch with Pastukhov on a streamer. About eleven in the morning the passenger boat *Samolet* used to arrive from somewhere upriver and stand a long time for loading, and people who understood something about cuisine liked to spend an hour or two in the restaurant on deck.

The weather was depressing and foggy. Even by midday the Volga could not free itself from the dank mist it dragged, wreathing over its sleepy waters. The air mingled in a dull quivering of sandy-white smoke in which the sirens of the steamers were stranded, the whole town seemed muffled. Hoofs that had lost their ring thudded hollowly up the cart roads.

Tsvetukhin was walking along in a state of mind that might be called vacuous: his thoughts spread like boughs on every side. He raised his head and, seeing the high intricate network of cables over the roof of the telephone exchange, recalled his old interest in inventions. He had never invented anything and could not have worked anything out, but from time to time various technical brainstorms whirled in his head, such as, for instance, an electric accumulator that would be small, light, and powerful. Had he hit on some unknown kind of insulation, of course, the whole thing would have been perfectly simple and straightforward. Chance often came to one's aid in research of this nature, as in all manner of discoveries, but for some reason chance failed to come up to the scratch in the present case.

While he was walking along the wooden pavement near the Volga quay, a girl passed Tsvetukhin, the heels of her new shoes clacking on the slats. As he looked at the dark blue bow on the end of the long pigtail flapping against her fashionable wasp waist, he fell to thinking of Lisa. Her excitement had pleased him: the scene in the dressing room the previous evening looked promising. Lisa had been mortally offended on his account and had run away in such embarrassment that she was not likely ever to make it up with Kirill, who had caused her so much suffering. Who knew but she might be thinking of Egor Pavlovich this disconsolate yellow day, and a feeling might grow in her and awaken a response in him, and then they would find that they were meant for each other, and Egor Pavlovich would marry and be happy.

No doubt, the general impression was that Egor Pavlovich Tsvetukhin, the actor, must be a success in his private life. Very likely people thought that being a celebrity in a way he never lacked for affection and caresses; that love and joy followed hard on the heels of fame. Only Tsvetukhin himself, and perhaps Mefody, knew how very far this was from reality.

Tsvetukhin was married to an actress, Agnia Lvovna Perevoshchikova, but they had been separated for over two years now, and she toured alone with a theater. A venomous woman, without any talent to speak of, she had a small mind and had reckoned on Tsvetukhin's bearing her out like a sail into the open sea of success, but the sail had proved inadequate; indeed, it is doubtful if a gang of bargees could have towed her out. She blamed him for his indifference, but when he wanted to help her, took offense, since she was capable only of faultfinding, not learning. All through his short married life with her, Tsvetukhin found that he was constantly accused of something. It was less a marriage than a lawsuit, and not until he had left her did the culprit feel that he was cleared.

When a man is getting near thirty, even the best of friends are but poor comfort in his loneliness. Now and again Egor Pavlovich's thoughts would turn back to the days when he was in the position of the prisoner in the dock, and laugh, and ask himself: had it all been as bad as he had imagined? And if things had turned out badly once, might they not turn out better the second time? And so, as he descended to the riverside, he found himself listening involuntarily to the clacking of new heels on the wooden steps, and could not take his eyes from the blue bow flapping against the wasp waist, and kept watching it until it vanished suddenly behind the piles of matting in a shed on the quay. Yes, he ought to be starting divorce proceedings, but so many other things hindered him.

His work at the theater, with crowded human contacts and bittersweet delights, now filled his days, now left him desolate. He had grown accustomed to this fever and was a little afraid that, perhaps, the play in which he played the Baron so well might be banned and that would mean the end of the season, already protracted, and then he would be left to himself until October.

Thinking of this and that, Egor Pavlovich reached the quay and went up the shaking gangplank, keeping out of the way of the stevedores who were moving along rhythmically in two lines: one in which they were bending under their loads, the other in which they were returning, erect, with their hooks over their shoulders, to the bank. As he went aboard on the lower deck, Tsvetukhin stopped.

On his left the hatches of the hold in the bows were open, and the cargo shot down into it along smooth polished boards; below decks lit by electric lamps, the bosun was roaring in a bored way at the stevedores. He had taken off his cap and was scratching the back of his head. On the right, in front of the engine room, towered an extraordinarily clumsy and at the same time aerial construction of huge flat shapes, planes, cables, and ties. Tsvetukhin guessed at once that they were the parts of a biplane, and, on making inquiries, learned that the aviator Vasilyev was transporting his flying machine. It took up a fearful lot of space, but in such a way that it did not seem to take any at all: you could pass through it everywhere and see the whole contraption—from below, and above, and the sides, and it was all plain and simple, but in its very simplicity, in its every wire, lay an enigma; the canvas of its wings—tight as a drum and varnished—was mysterious. Gathering his cloak close about him, Tsvetukhin walked around the biplane, looking at it from every side, peering under the wings, feeling them, flicking at the canvas, sniffing at their varnish, measuring, carpenter fashion, with outspread fingers like a pair of dividers their length and breadth. His heart began to thump for some reason — he could hear it. His panama fell off and he stepped on it accidentally, then picked it up, hastily rolled it up, and kept on walking around the plane, bobbing up and down, rising on tiptoes to look down the spine of the apparatus. He got in the way of the line of stevedores in front of the hatches, and they all shouted at him: "Gangway! Gangway there!"

At last one of the men gave him a hard knock on the shoulder with a bale, shouting: "What the hell! Out o' the way, sir, or I may knock you off your feet!"

Tsvetukhin moved slowly away from the biplane and climbed the steep trap with its brightly polished plates to the passenger deck.

Pastukhov was already there, seated at a little table, facing the river, drinking Zhiguli beer and eating crayfish. "I was beginning to think you weren't coming," he said, ringing for the waiter.

"Do you happen to have a sheet of notepaper about you?" Tsvetukhin asked impatiently. "Or perhaps you'll tear one out of your notebook."

Pastukhov wiped his fingers very thoroughly on his serviette, fumbled in his pockets, then threw a worn-looking letter on the table. Egor Pavlovich picked it up and started to fold the sheet of paper into some mysterious shape, carefully creasing the corners, measuring and tearing off the sides. Pastukhov watched him, sucking at the crayfish necks meanwhile. The waiter came up.

"Another dozen crayfish," Pastukhov ordered, "and a nice sterlet."

"Steamed?" the waiter asked, bending toward him.

"Yes, steamed."

"Rolled?"

"Yes, rolled."

Tsvetukhin finished the paper model he was making, folded it, got up, and said to Pastukhov: "Come here and look at this."

They stood by the rail, and Tsvetukhin let the paper fly. It flew further and further from the steamer with a slow, even movement and alighted on the water, spreading its wings. Pastukhov watched it awhile as it was caught by the current and drifted away, then he glanced indifferently at his friend, returned to the table, and tucked his serviette into his waistcoat.

"Interesting sort of bird," he remarked as he pulled off a claw of a crayfish and bit into it.

"Doesn't it suggest anything to you?"

"No, nothing whatever."

"That's a pity."

"I'm thickheaded."

"You are lazy. And this isn't a thing that requires a laborious effort of mind. The bird's flight followed the hypotenuse of a triangle which is three times the length of its height. Therefore, if I were to leap on wings like these from the height of a verst, I would fly three versts."

"If you were to leap from that height, you would be mashed up with a crunch like the crayfish in my teeth."

"And observe," Tsvetukhin went on in a serious tone, "the bird flies without a motor. If it was fitted with a motor, with a light, powerful accumulator, the distance it flies might be multiplied a great number of times."

"Have you been looking at the biplane down below?"

"Yes, but it seems to me, Alexander, that our fliers are on the wrong track. They think the bird requires to push off from the earth in order to take flight. This isn't true. A bird will fly anyhow even if it is held by the feet. It needs neither pushing off nor a run to gather speed. It can break the thread that binds it to the earth: it can raise its weight in the air solely by the strength of its wings. Two things have to be invented: how to rise in the air without taking a run, and how to make the lightest possible motor."

"Here, cool off a little, Thinker," Pastukhov advised, pouring out the beer. "Do you want me to tell you what I think of your inventions? You acted magnificently last night. That's your job. Do it. Leonardo de Vinci invented wings. But we know him only as an artist."

"That's our fault."

"No, it isn't. Read his Codici. When he writes about his 'Flood' his language makes you tremble. He says: *'may the dark air be seen.'* This is the Lord of the Days of Creation speaking: let there be Light. But his drawings of his machines are—venerated relics and nothing more."

"Would you like to fly?" Tsvetukhin interrupted him.

"I fly all the time."

"But you've never even seen an aeroplane in flight."

"Yes, I have. A cricket contraption rose into the air over the racecourse, circled once over the roofs and alighted on the telegraph wires. The aviator dislocated his jaw."

"The fledgling falls out of the nest first time, Alexander."

"I understand that. The fledgling becomes a bird. But I shall always take flight in a better way. I sit here, eating crayfish and I see your bird getting wet in the river, and then cling like a bit of slimy rubbish to the boatman's oar. The boatman merely gapes at the shore. But I see the shore swelling with the huge humps of cargo, and people swarming in the trenches between them. Yonder, two have stopped by a pile of dried fish, flung back a corner of the tarpaulin, picked out one of the bigger fish, knocked it on a packing case to make it softer, and now tear off the head and clean it. Can't you hear the skin crackling as they rip it off the back? Can't you see the silvery scales flying off the skin. But here under my nose is the same crayfish."

"It isn't that you're afraid of alighting on the telegraph wires by any chance?" Tsvetukhin asked.

"Very possibly—or even of falling face downwards in the puddle. But flights like this are in the line of my profession, and I don't want any other."

Tsvetukhin said nothing. He still saw with his mind's eye the paper model, and followed its flight in thought, while his physical eyes seemed to traverse again the route by which Pastukhov had led him: through the yellow fog he saw the riverside, all in hills and hollows of cargoes, shrouded in sailcloth.

Just then the stevedores were changing shifts—one gang going off work, the other getting ready to start and having a meal first. On the ground between the piles supporting a huge warehouse, from beneath which the spring waters had only recently subsided, the men knelt in a circle around a big pot, eating a hot mess. The ganger, Tikhon Parabukin, had stripped off his shirt, and his great body with the golden hair growing crosswise on his chest gleamed in that dim place. He dipped his spoon into the pot along with the rest and carried it carefully to his mouth, holding a chunk of bread beneath it to catch the drops.

Leaning against a log closer to the light, with her bare legs stretched out, sat Annochka, sewing the buttons on her father's shirt. Olga Ivanovna had sent the child to the wharf with the pie and a needle and waxed thread because she herself was angry with her husband. Tikhon had been drinking all the week and loafing about the riverbank. Whenever he showed up at the rooming house, he was rowdy, thumped his breast, and shouted: "Don't rouse the beast in me!" and seized the bottle that stuck out of his pocket. Once she had found him in a tavern, another time under a derelict upturned rowboat. His clothes were hanging in rags these days, he had sold his stevedore's shoulder strap for drink, and when he went back to work again, he was ashamed to show himself to Olga Ivanovna, so he asked his fellow lodgers to tell Annochka he needed a bit of mending done. She came and brought her father his favorite liver pie and sat down to her sewing. She sewed the buttons on most conscientiously, after a man's fashion, as her father showed her: she did not draw the thread tight, but wound it around several times to form a stem, and, in putting on a patch, left extra material around the hole. Her face wore the serious businesslike expression of all the women who sewed for the stevedores on the riverbank.

Parabukin glanced into the pot, rapped the spoon on the brim, and called out: "Scoop up all of it!"

The men sharing the meal started to scoop out with their spoons the bits of meat, watching that no one took more than his share. Soon they had reached the bottom, scraped it clean, then, making the sign of the cross, they got up from the ground. As they moved off they settled their shoulder straps and pads and, flourishing their hooks, emerged from under the warehouse into the light, walking with their dignified, slightly rolling gait. Parabukin pulled on the mended shirt and stroked Annochka's hair lightly, as though unsure of himself. She trotted along beside him, delighted that she had pleased him and could stay on the bank awhile—it was a welcome change from minding Pavlik.

The gang had to load a bower anchor of nearly two tons. Parabukin walked around it, while his men stood waiting. They all knew how to tackle this by no means easy job, but they had to wait for the word from their leader.

"Heave it," said Tikhon quietly.

Five men raised one barb of the anchor, slipped the end of a rope under it, and, moving over to the opposite side, did the same with the other barb. Then they knotted the rope on the heel and the whole gang spread out in a line on each side of the anchor.

"Take hold," said Parabukin.

They picked up the rope.

"It's no go, it's no go!" Parabukin chanted in his hoarse voice, and the deep voices repeated the words in a languid, tuneless chant, as though addressing the anchor that lay, a dead weight pressed into the ground. The deep voices were promptly echoed by high, the mingled sound united the gang, they leaned forward as one man, stretching out the rope and taking a firm grip of the ground with their feet shod in bast sandals.

"And now it'll go, now it'll go," the high voices chanted.

"It's no go, it's no go!" the low voices responded.

"And now it's off, and now it's off!" the high voices sang out as the anchor shifted, heaved itself reluctantly out of the hollow, the heel squeezing the sandy-yellow moisture out of the earth. Then all the voices blended into a ripple of a wondrous harmony. A song was borne out over the waters, such as delights and comforts the heart of the Volga riverman, a song with a simple pattern of words which now argue, now defy, a refrain which leads the men in unison year after year, generation after generation.

The anchor dragged, stumbling at every unevenness in the ground and then, with reluctant obedience, shifting as though the cast-iron bulk itself was becoming animated by the all-powerful song.

Pastukhov and Tsvetukhin, having finished their lunch, sat still for a long time listening to the song that floated out over the water from the bank on one and then another side of the steamer, now gathering strength and ringing out, now dying away in the mist far out over the river.

"Let's go and watch them," Pastukhov said, with sudden eagerness.

They went through the saloon and came out on the opposite side of the deck, which overlooked the gangplank leading from the steamer to the wharf. Leaning on the rail, they watched the stevedores at the head of the group set foot on the gangplank and the whole gang clinging to the rope like fir branches to the trunk grow, as it were, into the body of the streamer and disappear below decks.

"Look," Tsvetukhin exclaimed. "Do you recognize him?"

Parabukin, bent forward, was at the back of the group. For the look of the thing he held the rope in one hand and was watching tensely the movement of an anchor spread across the entire width of the gangplank. His tousled curls hid his face and neck, which quivered with the ponderous jerks of his body.

"Magnificent!" Pastukhov said, with a laugh. "Imagine—if a fellow like that got you by the throat!"

"Why should he get you by the throat?"

"For no particular reason. If he was sick of life, perhaps."

"I doubt if he's sick of it yet. See, his little girl is down there, too. . . . Annochka!" Tsvetukhin called out.

Annochka was mincing along behind the head of the anchor, in a crowd of small boys, barefoot like herself, who had run up to watch the loading and were as fascinated and swept away by it as though it were a military band playing a march. The song broke off at that very moment. The most critical point of the job had been reached: the anchor now had to be placed heel upward and dragged by its shank along the deckside toward the bows. Annochka glanced up, saw Tsvetukhin, and nodded to him as to an old friend. Then, taking advantage of the momentary delay, she slipped aboard the steamer. It took her some time to reach the upper corridors, darting in and out of cabin doors which all looked alike, and was somewhat bewildered by the luxury of the gleaming polish everywhere, the brass rails, chandeliers, and glass. But she greeted Tsvetukhin in a simple and easy manner: she had already come into contact with him as well as with the other actors at the theater. She had dropped in there several times during rehearsals, and they were getting used to seeing her around. And so now, as she expected to be sent on an errand, she asked without stopping to think: "Do you want me to go for something for you?"

"No, we don't want anything. Have you come to help your father?" Tsvetukhin asked, thinking of the loading.

"Yes," said Annochka with perfect gravity.

Pastukhov pulled her hair playfully, smiling. Moving out of his way, she added in an independent tone, pointing to the needle with the thread wound around it, stuck into her dress: "I've sewn on every one of his buttons. And soon I'll be able to do all the sewing for him, Mama says. She's promised to show me how to make a shirt. She'll cut it out for me, and I'll make it."

"Perhaps you'll make one for me, too?" Tsvetukhin asked her.

"I don't know about that. I'll have to help Mother first and then Vera Nikandrovna. She's going to teach me to read and write, and I'll help her with the house-work."

Annochka cast a sharp glance at each of the men in turn, stretched up toward them on her tiptoes, and breathed in a loud whisper that both could hear: "They've taken away Vera Nikandrovna's boy."

"Who is Vera Nikandrovna?" Tsvetukhin asked. Then, turning abruptly toward him: "Alexander, who's that? It's Kirill, isn't it?" He turned back again to Annochka. "You mean Kirill Izvekov from the Technical School, don't you?"

"Yes, of course," Annochka retorted. "Vera Ni-kandrovna hasn't any more sons, has she?"

"What's all this nonsense? Who took him away?"

"It isn't nonsense. I was at Vera Nikandrovna's yes-terday, I stayed all day. And the night before that, a man from our house said he'd seen them taking him away."

"But who was taking him away? And where were they taking him?" Tsvetukhin persisted, then, suddenly realizing that the child was telling the truth, he stop-ped speaking, and with raised eyebrows looked at Pastukhov again.

Pastukhov was standing motionless. The lower part of his big face looked heavier, his eyes narrowed and blinked jerkily. Every feature expressed disillu-sionment in its own fashion. He seemed to have re-treated somewhere far away and returned, to depart once more on some uncertain errand. Tsvetukhin fancied that Pastukhov had caught himself in some unpleasant error and was unable to believe that he had erred.

"What's all this, Egor? Are they hauling schoolboys off to jail now?" he said at last.

He took Annochka's small chin in his hand and turned her face up to his, looking steadily and curi-ously into her bold, wide-open eyes.

Down below, the chanted argument arose again, "And now it's off and now it's off!"

But all of a sudden the part song broke off, interrupted by the command: "Stop!" then: "Hold on!" then a medley of voices, cursing and grumbling, reached them, and Annochka, uttering a pitiful squeal, cleared the rail, slipped over the baluster of the wharf, then darted, quick and agile as a mouse, between the legs of the men on the gangplank.

"Must be an accident!" Tsvetukhin exclaimed, leaning over the rail and trying to make out what was going on below.

"Parabukin's had an accident," he said quickly, and rushed away, catching his cloak around him with one hand.

Parabukin was lying on his back, his eyes closed, drawing short, sobbing breaths as though keeping back his weeping. Beads of perspiration glistened on his forehead. The stevedores crowded around, arguing as to whether he had fallen on his back or his side.

"How did it happen?" Tsvetukhin kept asking as he pushed his way through the crowd and appealing to everyone who made way for him.

"Got hit with the shank," one of them said.

"What shank?"

"Knocked down by the anchor. They were in too much of a hurry to heave at it," a second man explained. "There's no room here."

"We'd have turned," said a third, "if it wasn't for this blasted thing straddling all over the place," and he struck his fist on the wing of the biplane, which answered with a humming of wires.

"Get a doctor. You must send for a doctor or an ambulance man. He must be brought round," Tsvetukhin babbled stooping down beside Annochka, who was squatting by her father's head.

"It'll be all right, these folks can stand a lot," the wharf clerk said calmly, settling his pencil behind his ear.

"Medicine—there should be medicines on board the steamer," Tsvetukhin persisted.

"Ah, don't meddle, sir. He isn't the first to get hurt," said an emaciated-looking stevedore with a bristling piebald beard. "Come on, lads, let's take and lay him on the bench in the stern."

The stevedores stooped down and lifted Tikhon.

"Gone all limp, our ganger has," someone sighed.

Moving unevenly and often changing step awkwardly they bore him to the stern. Annochka hurried after them, striking her small clenched fists together in agitation. Tsvetukhin followed.

They laid him down in the stern with his stevedore's strap and shoulder pad under his head. The man with the piebald beard took down a fire bucket from its nail, tied it to a hawser, dropped it overboard, drew it up full.

"Now, then, young one!" he commanded, "keep out of the way!" and doused Tikhon with the bucket of water.

Tikhon's curly hair suddenly darkened and lay close to his head, making it look small and throwing the big lumpy white forehead into relief like that of a corpse. Then a shudder passed through his purple lids as they opened a little; between them the still blind pupils showed dully; the big chest heaved. Parabukin uttered a groan. Drawing back his elbow beneath him, and leaning hard on it, he made an attempt to rise, but could not.

"Station . . ." he croaked hoarsely.

Annochka seized his hand. "Where does it hurt, Papa?" she cried in a choking voice, and clenched her little fists impatiently again.

He turned his eyes, which brightened faintly, toward her, and his cheeks twitched. "Your mother . . . you mustn't tell her." He forced the words out and for the first time took a big, noisy breath.

The lean man with the patchy beard emptied the rest of the water in the bucket overboard, hung it on its nail beside the rest, each of which bore a letter of the word *Samolet*, and waved his hand as much as to say—that's that.

"Come on, let's go, lads! He's got over it now— got his wind back."

They dispersed slowly, taking out and unrolling their tobacco pouches.

Tsvetukhin looked up. In the stern of the steamer, apart from the throng of passengers who were watching what was going on down below them, stood Pastukhov. He was smoking a cigarette, nervously and frequently blowing out rings of greenish smoke.

Tsvetukhin pressed his handkerchief to his temples, forehead, and chin cautiously, as though afraid of removing make-up. Then he looked at the handkerchief. It was wet. He was perfectly still for a moment, then he turned suddenly and went up to Annochka.

"Here, wipe his face."

She pushed away the handkerchief, apparently not understanding him, suddenly took to drying her father's head and face tenderly and painstakingly with the narrow, patched sleeve of her print frock.

CHAPTER

· 20 ·

AT ABOUT MIDNIGHT on Saturday a small card party was going on at the home of the prosecutor of the law courts. There were only two tables. Between the rubbers the men went out on the veranda to stretch their legs and smoke. The veranda was overgrown with the motionless foliage of the wild vine, gilded by the light from the electric lamps, around which the owl moths danced. The frenzied quiver of their wings, now illumined, now extinguished, seemed to emphasize the soundless serenity of the night.

The host paced beneath the canopy of vine leaves, pausing at the turnings and watching the moths with curiosity. The man who paced and paused beside him was a frequent guest, the youngest of his subordinates, a minor office holder in the law courts, Anatoli Mikhailovich Oznobishin. There was something of the kangaroo in his build—his short arms with their slender, unmasculine wrists, his long legs, a torso that thickened downward and stuck out slightly when he walked. Good-natured and considerate in his manner, he was liked not only by the prosecutor but by his spouse in particular, and the female members of the household in general—the aunts and the young niece—who were inclined to be dreamy about him. The men he worked among found him insinuating and were certain that his meekness would not hinder him from getting ahead of even some of the sharper ones in the service.

"It's a very strange thing!" the Prosecutor remarked,

"the dancing of these moths always has a soothing effect on me. Even more soothing than cards."

"On the contrary, cards are exciting," one of the guests said.

"To the player who loses one rubber after another, they would be," the host retorted with a chuckle. "But I take no risks and so it's a rest for me."

"Well, we'll see what the next pool will show us," the guest said, leaving the veranda and going back into the room.

"It's perfectly true, Your Excellency," Oznobishin said when he was left alone with his chief. "It's as hard to tear one's gaze from these moths as from a bonfire."

"Sparks that die as they fly," the Prosecutor mused, repeating a line from a well-known song.

"They do resemble sparks, indeed they do. And they put one in a contemplative mood."

"And set you thinking of the vanity of human existence," the elder man sighed. "Have you heard anything new?"

"No, nothing much. The town's still talking about those leaflets."

"Oh, yes, the case of those youngsters, you mean? How's the inquiry going on?"

"I can't say exactly. You know, of course, Your Excellency, that the Assistant Prosecutor is none too well disposed toward me. I asked him twice if he would permit me to be present at the investigation. He promises, but—"

"Hmph . . . Perhaps you would like me to mention the matter to him?"

"If it wouldn't be too much trouble, Excellency, I would be very grateful. It would be very instructive, and perhaps I might prove of some slight service. The case promises to be unusually interesting. They say, for instance, that Tsvetukhin is mixed up in the affair."

"Who? The actor?"

"Yes, indeed."

"It's scandalous! What did he do?—scatter leaflets in the theater boxes?"

"No, he's supposed to be mixed up with the other case—the printing press."

"Both are connected, I'm sure."

"So far, Excellency, no connection can be proved.
. . . They have failed to link them up. . . . The two
cases are separate, they say."

"Who has failed to link them up, my dear chap?
The Lieutenant-Colonel? The Lieutenant-Colonel can
link up anything! He's like a chef—he mixes oil
and vinegar and there you have French dressing!"

Oznobishin laughed at that and his laugh lasted,
at a restrained, well-modulated ebb, while the smile
lingered on His Excellency's lips. Then he remarked
in an extremely confidential manner: "Pastukhov's
name is mentioned, too."

"Pastukhov?"

"Yes, they say Pastukhov was in it as well."

They stood silent. The minute shadows of the
owl moths flitted over their faces, suggesting the
rapid succession of their thoughts. A burst of laughter
reached them from within the room.

"And you said you hadn't heard anything new?"
the Prosecutor said reproachfully, listening to the
laughter.

"Oh, but I've no really authentic information, Excellency. If I say something and then it turns out
that there's no confirmation for it—it will look as
though I, Oznobishin, was spreading rumors. After
all, I haven't been able to see the charge sheets to
this day."

"Yes, you're right. I'll tell them to report to me
tomorrow."

The older man shook his head reproachfully, and
with a sideways glance at the open door of the room
where people were laughing and talking, he said:
"And they must certainly allow you to familiarize
yourself with the information bearing on the case.
It will give you a chance to gain some experience.
I understand you. You will look into the thing and
then keep me posted on it. Since I've been ordered
by my doctor to wear spectacles, my dear fellow, I
find reading much more trying. As soon as I put on
my glasses, I feel drowsy, just imagine. If I take
them off, I can't see a thing."

"The eyesight, Excellency," Oznobishin said with an
air of great penetration.

"That's it," the Prosecutor agreed. "And then, he's one of these modernists, isn't he?"

"Pastukhov?" Oznobishin said, guessing at once. "Oh, of course, he's one of the modernists."

"They praise him in the newspapers. But his father was such a good-for-nothing fellow. You know, always full of some project, or other. Got into debt, too. . . . If the son took after him, it's natural enough that he should go wrong. And then, it's only what you might expect from a writer. I suppose you read these modernists, do you?"

"I've tried, Excellency. All their stuff is . . . built on—ambiguities. Even to the point of indecency sometimes."

"Yes, they certainly take liberties. . . . Still, some are rather entertaining and colorful in a way, you know. . . . I happened to read a novel. . . . I can't remember the author for the life of me. . . . It was before I got those spectacles. One of these new writers, anyway. But I remember the title:: *Virginity*—it was, you know. Very daring. Oh, very. Reads well and holds the interest. There was a young girl in it, you see. . . ."

At that moment the niece, who was obviously enjoying herself, came out on the veranda to invite them in to supper, so the Prosecutor went back with her into the room, asking her what had amused them all so much.

Seated as he usually was between the ladies, to whom he obligingly but rather awkwardly passed dishes with his small hands, and exchanging suitable and noncommittal remarks, Oznobishin felt a pleasant excitement. He hoped that after the very gratifying conversation on the veranda his relations with the Assistant Prosecutor, whose province was political affairs, would assume that confidential footing which so far he had been unable to establish. The young official's zeal did not appeal to the Assistant Prosecutor; he often snubbed him, thus endeavoring to teach him that if a man was to advance successfully in his career, restraint should take precedence of inquisitiveness, and he gave him nothing better to do than the compilation of files of very minor importance. Now,

when the Prosecutor was to have the handling of a
case that had created a sensation in the town, Oznobishin hoped to push himself forward, both through
acquaintance with the procedure of the investigation,
and by assisting in drawing up the indictment. His
part in the affair he envisioned as an important beginning to what might prove a decisive advancement
in his career; he regretted that he had found no
opportunity of talking to the Prosecutor previously,
and was delighted that he had secured it at last. Like
most young people, he was troubled by an unsatisfied
desire to bring about a change, to improve, and he
thought that he would astonish everyone when it was
discovered that he had revealed so much that had
hitherto passed unnoticed. He had not the slightest
desire to disturb the machinery of the law; on the
contrary, he imagined that when he was allowed
to handle it, he would make it present such a cunning
play of all its minutiae that even old officials would
gasp and revere it still more. The chief thing he
dreamed of was to see the accused in the flesh, and
it was extremely vexatious that the Assistant Prosecutor failed to observe his interest in the inquiry.

The interrogation had been going on for over a
month. A fair number of people had passed through
the hands of Lieutenant-Colonel Polotentsev of the
gendarmes, and details were collecting on the case
like shells on the keel of a ship.

Among those summoned to the headquarters of
the Gendarme Police Force was Merkuri Avdeyevich
Meshkov.

Well dressed and well turned out, he looked as
though he were going to church. The questions put
to him at first, concerning himself and establishing
his identity, were not hard to answer. He replied
with promptitude; the arrangement and convenience
of the form dispelled his dread, particularly as Polotentsev kept almost excusing himself all the time for
the trouble he was causing him.

Polotentsev was a man with a longish head, shaved
clean and shining, and with a well-developed mathematical bump at the back. His short yellow eyelashes
seemed to repeat the thin gold rims of the glasses.

He wore his nails long, and they were very white, and while he wrote, his little finger, on which the nail was especially long and white, pressed into the paper. At work he put on a tunic without shoulder straps, which gave him a look of being on his travels, as though the Lieutenant-Colonel were in a first-class railway carriage and there were no need to stand on ceremony—it was to be a long journey, the places were very comfortable, the traveling companions pleasant enough, and he was about to open his light portmanteau and say: "And now, let's see what the best of wives has packed for her husband on the journey."

It was in a similar good-humored, kindly disposed tone that Polotentsev informed Meshkov that witnesses guilty of giving false evidence would be liable to punishment under the law should they be detected in premeditated suppression of facts or of libel.

"I understand, I quite understand," Meshkov assented, which was true, because he had understood at once that the convenient questions were over and done with now.

Polotentsev then asked what Meshkov knew about his tenant Ragozin, after Ragozin's disappearance.

"What could I know about him, if he has disappeared?" Meshkov countered with rising agitation.

"In the future I am going to ask the questions and you are going to answer me," Polotentsev corrected him in the tone of a mentor.

From that point onward he proceeded unwearyingly, it seemed to Meshkov, to ask the same question put in different ways. Who had gone to Ragozin's, whom had Meshkov seen at Ragozin's, who visited Ragozin's, and then, who had gone to see Ragozin's wife, where was she in the habit of going, whom did Meshkov meet at the Ragozin's?

Merkuri Avdeyevich made prodigiously tiring efforts of memory to say something other than "I don't know," which would have arrested the persistent repetition of a perfectly senseless question; a frightening and melancholy sense of guilt was growing on him that he had not used his life on an affair of such great importance as watching his tenants the Ragozins, but had been busy with goodness only knew what, and now, because of this unforgivable error, he had brought misfortune on Lieutenant-Colonel Polotentsev and was doomed like him to torment himself over unanswerable questions. Merkuri Avdeyevich had only to say something to Ragozin's credit, such as that he paid the rent very regularly, for Polotentsev to start to wring a statement from him as to whether he had noticed that Ragozin spent his money very freely, how much the man lived on in general, had Ragozin some hidden bent toward luxuries, or was he, on the contrary, avaricious and saved money?

It began to look as if Meshkov was stubborn, as if he denied things, and he kept secrets known to himself alone, and of course would have only himself to thank if Lieutenant-Colonel Polotentsev ceased to trust him and feel well-disposed toward him.

"Is this how I am to understand you, then, that you have no desire to help the inquiry about the state criminal to whom you leased a private cottage and an outhouse where a secret printing press was found?" Polotentsev asked, pressing the nail of his little finger into the clean sheet of paper, on which he was about to take down the reply.

"But—excuse me, Your Honor," Merkuri Avdeyevich protested, quite startled, stretching out a hand toward the officer as though imploring him not to write down anything yet, and wiping his perspiring brow with the other hand. "I'd be only too glad to aid in the legal procedure, but what if it is beyond my power?"

"Now, can you really mean that it's beyond your power?" Polotentsev exclaimed with kindly reproach, moving the paper away from him. "Well, tell me what you know about your other tenants."

"Which other tenants? The only other one is that actor."

"Oh, yes, yes, that's it—tell me about that actor," Polotentsev said, delighted. "What's his name—this actor fellow?"

"Mefody," Merkuri Avdeyevich informed him, with a sense of pleasant relief that his thoughts were at last out of the blind alley into which the questions about Ragozin had driven him. "Excuse me, but Mefody's surname completely escapes me. . . ."

"You'll remember it later on," Polotentsev said soothingly. "Tell us what you know about this actor's contact with Ragozin."

"I only wanted to say—"

"What did you want to say about Ragozin's association with the actor whose surname you can't remember?"

"It wasn't about Ragozin," Meshkov replied in a meek, hopeless tone, "not about Ragozin, it wasn't. . . ."

"Yes, you're right," Polotentsev took him up hastily, pushing up his spectacles on to his shining head and rubbing his screwed-up eyes with his knuckles. "I've got this Ragozin on the brain—it's nothing but Ragozin here, day in, day out! Then it's not about Ragozin but about his association—with whom, were you going to say?"

"You mean about Mefody?" Meshkov ventured.

"That's the one, yes. So he was associated with whom, did you say?"

"He has an old friend, they used to be at the seminary together—Tsvetukhin, an actor like himself."

"Tsvetukhin," Polotentsev repeated in an affirmative tone, drawing the paper toward him in a businesslike way. "Tsvetukhin, the great lover, the hero. Well, well!"

"You're going to write it down?" Merkuri Avdeyevich asked.

"No, no, please go on, go on by all means. Plenty of time to write it down afterward: the writing can wait. Only just a few pencil notes. So you say that Tsvetukhin used to drop in at his friend's, at Mefody's, where he would meet Ragozin—is that what you give me to understand?"

"No," Meshkov protested, endeavoring to give his reply finality. "I can't state what I don't know. The actor Tsvetukhin used to go and see Mefody. Once, at Eastertime, I saw Pastukhov there, too. The late Vladimir Alexandrovich Pastukhov's son, if you remember."

"That's it, that's it. So there were gatherings of people at Mefody's. . . . Gatherings . . . And so who are you prepared to give evidence about?"

"That's not quite what I'm saying, Your Honor. My tenant invited me in at Eastertime to have a drink, as it was the occasion of the holiday. And while I was there I met Tsvetukhin and Pastukhov."

"Tsvetukhin. Pastukhov . . ." Polotentsev repeated, drawing ovals around the two names he had written. "And who else was present during your visit at your tenant's?"

"Well—he wasn't exactly present at the meeting, but he came up to the steps, a tramp it was—he just glanced into the yard, a fellow from the rooming house."

"You mean from your rooming house?"

"Yes, he rents a corner there, a family man, a drunkard."

"Whose name you've forgotten, no doubt," Polotentsev said affirmatively.

"His name's Rubakin, or . . . no, excuse me, the other way about—Burakin."

"Oh, never mind, you'll have plenty of time to remember it yet. Now, let's see, your tenants were in the habit of meeting . . ." the Lieutenant-Colonel continued unhurriedly, drawing ovals and enclosing question marks in them.

"Parabukin!" Meshkov blurted out, bobbing up on his chair and suddenly breaking free into fluent narrative.

When all was said and done, why should Merkuri Avdeyevich jib at recounting the conversation that had annoyed him with people of loose morals, scribblers, and mummers? He was only going to tell what had actually taken place, without adding or suppressing a word. To be sure, nothing very good could be said of either Mefody or his friend Tsvetukhin: men who had forsaken a theological seminary for the stage and entertainment. That was nothing to be proud of, was it? And who was this Pastukhov? What was it that he was inventing for the theaters? An ungodly man, who scoffed at his own friends for their fondness for the Easter hymns. A son who refused to pay his father's debts and, judging by all one could see, was hiding the fact of having inherited something. And what good could one say of that tramp and tippler, Parabukin? Merkuri Avdeyevich regarded them all with pity and sorrow: let God be their judge!

"Yes," was Polotentsev's response, made with sympathy and even pained fellow feeling, to this sad story. "Just think, Merkuri Avdeyevich, just consider what misfortunes you have brought on yourself by letting your rooms to suspicious persons. You say—let God be their judge: God helps only those who help themselves. We are appointed to judge people here below. In Heaven judgment will be meted out to them without us. And you did not even ask yourself: for what purpose do these suspicious persons congregate together, as you say, on your premises and draw characters like Parabukin into contact with them?"

"I'm not saying they're suspicious, except in regard to their morality, so to speak," Meshkov cautiously corrected him. "The people in question seem to me to be immoral."

"Yes, as you, a religious man, would express it, they're immoral, and as we, in legal parlance, put it, they're politically unreliable. So what do we find? That three of your tenants: one—Ragozin, under police surveillance, another, Parabukin—a tramp—"

"But what sort of a tenant of mine is he?" Meshkov pleaded.

"He lives in your rooming house, not mine, doesn't he?" The Lieutenant-Colonel struck his palms on the table and got up suddenly, pushing back his heavy armchair with his heels. "No, no, Mr. Meshkov, there's something very funny about your . . ."

He paced up and down the room, obviously steadying his nerves with an effort. Then he came closer to Meshkov, looked at him tensely, took off his glasses, and once more rubbed his eyes with his knuckles as though driving away the drowsiness that threatened to overcome him.

"I must admit one thing: that it's a bitter disappointment when one finds quite unexpectedly that one has been mistaken in a witness. When the witness in question proves to be an accessory. M-yes-s." He turned away.

"Your Honor," Meshkov said submissively, "may I ask for a glass of water?"

"Ah, a glass of water!" Polotentsev echoed. "I'll tell them to bring it at once," and, with a cheerful ringing of spurs, he went out.

Leaning back in his chair, Meshkov covered his face with both hands. He tried to keep his heels pressed hard on the ground, but they slackened and beat a feeble tattoo on the boards.

Suddenly the door was flung open. The black-clothed gendarme officer who appeared suddenly in the room brought with him the chill of the night and the sinister shadows of gendarmes shifting over walls and ceiling in Ragozin's house, when Merkuri Avdeyevich had stood leaning against the door post like a beggar.

"Has the Lieutenant-Colonel gone out?" the officer asked.

"Yes, that's right," Meshkov answered loudly, giving a start.

"A-ah!" the other drawled pleasantly. "An old acquaintance!" He advanced a couple of steps impulsively as though he was about to shake hands with Meshkov, but just as he started from his seat, the gendarme paused halfway and said in a disappointed tone: "You're here in connection with that case, eh? A bad business, old man, now you're in for it!"

"Look here, Your Honor—" Meshkov began.

"Oh, no, don't, what's the use?' the gendarme officer said, hastily dismissing the matter. "How do you like our Lieutenant-Colonel? Penetrating mind. But, you know, not fond of trifling. Oh, no. Anything but that." He wheeled and vanished as quickly as he had appeared.

Left alone, Meshkov sat down, feeling the trembling in his legs and almost asleep with the heavy lassitude that had come over his whole body.

The Lieutenant-Colonel seemed in no hurry to return. When he did, he arranged with grim energy the papers in blue folders that he had brought with him, then ripped open a new pad of paper with his nail, and drew the inkstand nearer to him.

"I asked . . . for a drink of water," Meshkov said.

"Didn't they bring it to you? I gave orders," Polotentsev said, picking up his pen. "And now, let's
draw up the statement. We'll begin with your valuable
deposition about Ragozin. . . ."

Meshkov could never understand where he found
strength to sit on the chair and speak of the thing
that kept continually eluding him, as water escapes
from a leaking vat, while Polotentsev refilled the
vat again and again. Whether a long time had passed
since that early hour when he had left home to come
here, Meshkov had no idea. It seemed to him that
the lamp in the green-folder shade had been burning
for ages and that the white fingernail, moving un-
feelingly over the paper, had yellowed with age.
He visualized the glass of tea with a lazy tongue
of steam rising from it which Valeria Ivanovna poured
out for him in the morning. He could hear her persuasive voice begging him to take just a mouthful; he
drove the mirage away from him, recalled it again
with longing. Words lost their sense for him, and
when the interrogation was over, he was still mumbling
something.

He tottered along the corridors, swaying slightly,
reached the glassed-in vestibule, and had his hand on
the door when a stentorian shout reached him. "Defendant Meshkov!"

A gendarme noncommissioned officer was running
down the corridor after him. "Are you Meshkov?"

"Yes, I'm Meshkov, but I'm not a defendant, I'm
a witness," Merkuri Avdeyevich muttered.

"The Lieutenant-Colonel says you're to come
back!"

Keeping close to the wall, Merkuri Avdeyevich
went back. Polotentsev got up from his place at the
desk to meet him.

"Excuse me for delaying you a minute," he said
with a look of anxiety and perfectly sincere regret.
"A question of rather minor importance has arisen.
It seems that your daughter, as far as I know, is
a great friend of a young man called Kirill Izvekov. I'm right, am I not? I just wanted to know—
has this young man often been to your house, or
not?"

Merkuri Avdeyevich saw, with startling clearness, a glimpse of a white rim of color above a short square back in a Technical School uniform jacket— just a glimpse before it vanished through the wicket gate. And at the same instant that he saw the white rim of collar, the blue stripes of Lisa's house dress swam through his inward vision. And then—the brown hanging that let the lamp light through in the window of Ragozin's house, and he, Merkuri Avdeyevich himself, peering speculatively down at the quiet yard, from the upper gallery of his house.

He stared fixedly at the Lieutenant-Colonel.

Polotentsev said nothing. Then suddenly he raised himself and said in a sympathetic tone: "I can see you're frightfully tired, and so please kindly excuse my persistence. And anyhow my question may be postponed till next time. I only wanted to tell you that your daughter's young friend is also charged with a crime against the state. So I must ask you to remember without fail for next time, whether he was ever in your house. So as to be able to clear up this business about him and your daughter once and for all. And now—I'll wish you good evening. Really you seem quite worn out! I am sorry, very sorry, but it is an official matter, my duty requires it of me."

When he got out into the street, Merkuri Avdeyevich moved like a drunken man who had just been brought around. No trace of the morning's smartness and neatness remained. His jacket hung on him loosely, his trousers bulged at the knees. Under the matted mustache that did not feel like his own he was aware of his parched, cracked lips. For a long while he could not understand what sort of a fog it was that wavered before his eyes. It was only when he had gone a few blocks that he was able to make out a cloud of gnats that was following him steadily and took on a bronze glow whenever he passed a street lamp. He tried to wave away the cloud, but it whirled about him and danced ahead like a mocking mirage.

Suddenly Merkuri Avdeyevich stopped dead. For the first time that day a comforting thought impressed itself upon his mind.

· 21 ·

IN THE COURSE of one of the conversations that Lisa called philosophic, in Dogs' Limes, the talk had turned on what fate was. Kirill said that a person's dependence on events was very likely what was meant by fate or destiny. Lisa did not care for this definition.

"And supposing there aren't any events?" she objected. "If nothing happens, but things just go on in the ordinary, humdrum way, or don't even go on, but stand still and—it's all endless boredom and nothing else? Then what?—does fate disappear?"

Kirill denied that there was any such thing as entirely uneventful times. He considered that boredom and dullness were also events.

"Very well," said Lisa, "have any events you like. But don't you see, they go on and on, following their own course. Man gets used to them and perhaps feels happy. And then, all of a sudden, everything in his life collapses. What do you call that?"

"But what are you talking about exactly?" Kirill asked. "Personal happiness? Surely you know the saying—'In your own smithy forge ye your own happiness.'"

Lisa would not agree with this. "Then what would you call it when the smith forges in his smithy and thinks everything is going on quite satisfactorily and all of a sudden the smithy burns down and nothing is left of it?"

"That's a fire," Kirill said with a laugh. He was rather fond of laughing things off if he could not explain them. And then he always saw good times ahead. But Lisa often had strange premonitions. Now she was convinced that they had not deceived her, that in the conversation so long ago about destiny she had been right; everything had seemed as usual, and she had been happy, and all of a sudden Kirill had been snatched out of her life. Everything had seemed as usual, and she had been happy, when into her home floated a name she had never even dreamed of: Victor Semyonovich Shubnikov. This was destiny itself. . . .

The town knew two shop signs whereon in gold letters on black was inscribed the name *Shubnikov.* One was on the store opposite the Upper Bazaar, the other—on a big shop in the very heart of the market. In both of them fabrics were sold; the store kept the higher quality goods—cloth, velvet, and silk; the market shop—cotton prints, ginghams, and sateen. The business was carried on by Shubnikov's widow, Daria Antonovna, assisted by her nephew, Victor, whom she had spoiled from his early childhood and intended to make her successor.

A man of twenty, fond of dressing smartly, lounging at the barber's while his flaxen hair was marcelled with curling irons, and of ordering from Warsaw some fancy device advertised in the papers, for keeping his mustache neat, or a gutta-percha apparatus invented by a Lodz hygienic firm for face massage, Victor Semyonovich had gained a name for himself among the younger set who never overtired themselves with work. He was the sporting type, impatient by nature, and for this reason never succeeded in completing his education, though he sought to acquire learning with great gusto, several times changing from one high school to another, trying the Commercial and Real Schools, in each case ordering for himself a new uniform of excellent cloth from the family store and finally abandoning the various school caps in favor of the cyclist's headgear fashionable at the time.

He was a first-rate cyclist, riding like a professional—leaning forward from a high saddle over low
handle bars curved like the horns of an ox, with
rubber tips. He even trained for the race track, and
was thinking of carrying off a prize, but fell off as he
was veering and injured his knee cap, and then seemed
to take his rivals' success as a personal slight.

But no one could compete with him on a horse.
He brought from the steppe a pacer from Bokhara,
nothing much to look at, red and rough-coated, with
a light mane. At Shrovetide Shubnikov showed off
before the local amateur judges of horseflesh, with
the nag harnessed to a very small featherweight
sleigh, into which only one person could squeeze himself. In Kostrizhnaya Street, where people in family
sleighs driven by a pair or a troika of dignified
horses were cautious of turning, and where only
thoroughbreds tore along, Victor Semyonovich Shubnikov and his little devil performed miracles that
made people catch their breath. To say nothing of the
beauty and buoyancy of the animal, which raced as
though wrought up to the point of playful madness,
the dashing skill of the driver evoked general enthusiasm. He neither rode, sped along, nor flew, but
soared somewhere beyond earthly spaces, away from
the smooth rolled road, all in snow dust, and it
seemed as though he was not sitting in a sleigh, but
stood, aimed by the taut reins like a stone from a
sling into the frosty air. Leaning sideways so that the
sleigh ran on one runner, his eyes screwed up, dodging
the fiery, long-haired tail and the icy clots of snow
cast up by the hoofs, Shubnikov sped by like a
meteor now and again urging his steed with: "Hey!
Hey! Hey!"

"Stick it, Vityusha! Stick it!" his friends yelled
from the sidewalks.

And he did, overtaking, one after the other, the
trotters of the fast Orel breed, hearing nothing save
the whistling of the wind and the drumming of the
snow clots on the front of the little sleigh.

But, like every other passion, racing of this kind
demanded sacrifices, and Victor Semyonovich nearly
got into serious trouble over his indulgence of it. A

worthy representative of the law, the Assistant Prosecutor, was crossing the street at Shrovetide during the traditional sleighdrives that took place, when he fell and hurt his leg at the very moment that Shubnikov was racing past at full speed. Had it been an official of any other administration, no ill consequences would have followed, but a justiciary found no difficulty in presenting the matter as though the driver had blown the passer-by off his feet and only narrowly missed killing him. The case dragged out for a year. Daria Antonovna became familiar with the lowest and the highest of the law offices before she finally extricated her nephew out of the mess, and the case ended with her having to pay the costs of the complainant's medical treatment. After this, Vitenka's name as daredevil acquired a still brighter luster, and he ordered a coat of buff serge to render himself more easily identifiable and conspicuous as the hero of the sensational adventure.

Daria Antonovna kept her nephew in comfort. He never knew what it was to want for anything; she refused him nothing, and required very little work from him—He will have plenty to do, she used to say, 'when I am dead.' He had his own part of the house. Here he kept his collections of books on horses, on skating, cycling, and sailing, his catalogues of coins and medals, arranged his many suits on wooden hangers in the wardrobes, put on the gramophone with a horn that shone like a trombone, hummed an accompaniment to Vialtseva's and Varya Panina's singing, pottered with photography, developing negatives in the bathroom, and massaged his face to get rid of his pimples.

That summer he was getting his half of the house redecorated, and Daria Antonovna went with him to Meshkov's shop to choose the wallpaper. Merkuri Avdeyevich himself set chairs for them and showed them his stock, hanging up the rolls of paper that were brought down from the shelves and unrolled by the shop assistant as fast as he could. His customers were hard to please, but that only made him all the keener—he knew the Shubnikovs' value, they had the right to be exacting—and he preened himself on his salesmanship as a peacock spreads its tail.

"Here's another thing, a sample of a stamped design suitable for a gentleman's study," he said, admiring it. "If you were to combine it with that mat surface panel in a darker tone, and divide it with a narrow stripe of a lighter tone, it would look very dignified. You think it's a shade too dark? Well, of course, we can find something that would lighten it up. But it's always advisable to have a bit of variety in colors in rooms. Take this design—one of the latest things—a crushed satin effect. If the room is luxuriously furnished in, say, the Moderne style. . . . What style are your furnishings in the drawing room? Moderne?"

"Viennese bentwood," Victor Semyonovich said.

"Then this would go very well with it. Now look at the effect if you frame a rich tone like this with a broad cornice stripe."

"And what do you think about a ceiling?" the customer asked.

"I was just going to suggest it to you. Are you thinking of painting the moldings? No? Then the plafond needs a frame. You get a fine contrast if you have a space of plain white ceiling divided from the wallpaper by a landscape ceiling—like this. Or still better. . . . Petya, get down the plant ornament—all the numbers."

When the inspired show was at its height, when the customers' heads were beginning to swim with the paper rainbows dancing before their eyes, Lisa came into the shop. She had been sent by her mother with some message for her father. He told her to wait while he attended to the customers. She went up toward the cashdesk and unfolded the newspaper lying on the counter. She did not really take in what she read—a description of the questionable dealings of the owners of the fishing industries, the debates in the town hall, shipping news—all words were equally meaningless for her. No matter what they spoke of, she read into them nothing but her own misery. Her hand was already turning the page before her gaze had detached itself from the end of it, and later turned back to what she had read as though it was something new.

From the moment of her appearance there was a

second person in the shop who was not thinking of what he was doing. The rolls of paper still rustled and unfurled, the assistant shifted his stepladder to reach down more paper from the shelves, Merkuri Avdeyevich admired his own powers as an orator, but for Victor Semyonovich panels, ceilings, and cornices had ceased to exist: of all the conceivable varieties of paper, he was attracted solely by the newspaper turned by a slim leisurely hand on the counter. He got up so as to be able to see her better, and his answers to Merkuri Avdeyevich were all wrong. Twisting his mustache (which grew in little white curls at the corners of his lips, while under the nose the lip was still bare), pulling his jacket down, and shifting his feet slightly, he waited patiently until Lisa raised her eyes, into which he had had time to look deeply while she was talking to her father. But she did not raise her eyes from the paper, and later, when Victor Semyonovich recalled this unexpected meeting, he remarked that he was struck by the contrast between this specimen of charming girlhood that he saw in Lisa at once, and her unnatural interest in the masculine occupation of reading a newspaper. Could he have said so at the time, he would have wanted to know, of course, what she found so remarkable in the paper. And had she heard the question, she would very likely have said in amazement: "But was I reading the paper?" If Lisa had been in the place of the eloquent Merkuri Avdeyevich, it would have sufficed for her to murmur: "Oh, that's a nice wallpaper!" and Victor Semyonovich would have had all his rooms papered with the one she chose. But she did not even glance at the customers, and, bored with waiting, drifted out of sight somewhere at the other end of the counter.

Victor Semyonovich was by nature very impatient. In his childhood his nurses had nicknamed him "Give-it-me-quick," for if anything took his fancy, it gave him no peace; he could not sleep until his wish was granted. The first words he lisped were not "Mama" and "Papa" or "Baba" but a demand to be let go. He kept pushing away the nurses and other children, and, with his baby hands, pushing ahead to wherever he wanted to go, and lisped: "Let go, let go." His aunt Daria Antonovna only nodded her head understandingly when he suddenly lost interest in the repapering of his rooms, when he grew melancholy and flashier than ever in his clothes, and disappeared for long intervals, and then let the cat out of the bag by entrusting a certain Nastenka to obtain for him a photograph of Lisa Meshkova. Everything became as clear as daylight.

Nastenka regarded herself as one of the family and turned up at rare intervals, staying for a week or two, after an absence at other friends' houses or a pilgrimage to a convent for prayer. She had a faculty for making herself pleasant—through her conversation, and through her sympathy, through her obliging ways, especially if the service was no trouble to her. Her face had something reminiscent of a plum in it—glistening with satisfaction; and sheer joy of life gleamed in her youthful black gaze, though she was regarded as a woman of austere character and piety, devoted to prayer and even to fasting, yet withal fonder than anyone of tasty things to eat. She had brought the art of taking, accepting, and acknowledging gifts to such a point of refinement that those who gave were invariably left with the impression that it was she who had made the gift and they who had received it from her as from their benefactress.

It required no particular effort on her part to obtain access to the photographer who had taken photographs of the girls who had finished school that spring. He received from Nastenka all possible assurances that the picture was needed for perfectly legitimate purposes, and was, actually, pleased by the success of his firm.

In this picture Lisa looked rather wistful; the oval of her face merged elusively into the slightly fluffed, cloudy hair that framed it. Something pensive emanated not only from her gaze but pervaded the whole picture as one picked it up for closer inspection. After Victor Semyonovich had possessed himself of the picture, he felt that all his former life had been no more than the backstairs to that fragrant dwelling through the windows of which he had glanced timidly and which he longed to enter. He waxed sentimental,

wept and fell into a lethargy for days on end, lounging on the couch, now demanding that his fortune
should be told, now wanting prayers to be said
for him, now clamoring for the doctor to cure his
insomnia, or the tailor to take his measure for a
new suit.

The sapper work was undertaken with great
thoroughness by Nastenka and Daria Antonovna; this
necessarily evoked increasingly louder and more insistent mention of the Shubnikovs from the Meshkovs, until this deep sapping ended in Merkuri Avdeyevich's announcing one day that Daria Antonovna
intended coming to tea.

"Why on earth has she taken such a fancy to our
tea?" Lisa asked, staring at her father queerly.

"Well, we've been neighbors in trade for so many
years, and the families don't know each other," Merkuri
Avdeyevich replied.

"Why—have things changed all of a sudden?"

"Yes, one or two things have changed, my love.
I was in the bank yesterday, redeeming bills. I was
standing by the teller's window, waiting. The manager
happened to pass by, and as he saw me, he stopped
to speak. 'Don't trouble yourself waiting here, Mr.
Meshkov,' says he, 'come straight into my office,
please. I'll tell them what you require and everything
will be done without delay!' and he shakes hands with
me. Well, you know, there was a time when the bank
manager wouldn't have known that Meshkov
existed. . . ."

So it happened that one sultry August day, after
church, the Shubnikovs, accompanied by Nastenka,
dropped in at the Meshkovs to sample their Sunday
pie.

CHAPTER

· 22 ·

VICTOR SEMYONOVICH attired himself in a suit of coffee-
and-cream color, with a piqué waistcoat that buttoned
high. From the lower pocket of the waistcoat hung
a short black ribbon instead of a watch chain, with
a thin gold charm in the form of an envelope with
one corner turned down and glowing with a ruby.

The weather was very close and his jacket was
open. The trinket lay against the waistcoat, glittering at every breath the wearer took. He was breathing hard and fast. He had made several attempts
to start the conversation, but Lisa was unresponsive.
She liked it better when he stumbled over every
phrase and broke off feebly, directing at her bewildered and imploring looks. At last she took pity
on him.

"There's something written on that charm of
yours, isn't there?"

"Yes," he said, taking out his watch hastily. "It's
a souvenir. Please look at it if you want to."

She read the inscription, engraved with many
flourishes: "To Victor Semyonovich Shubnikov with
kindest regards from his friends." And on the other
side: "Stick it, Vityusha, stick it!"

"What does that refer to?"

"It's a reminder of a race. Last winter. Driving."

"So it's a prize?"

"Yes, it is in a way. From my pals. My horse came in first."

"And what does 'stick it' mean?"

"Oh, nothing much. Just the sort of expression common among racing fans."

"How long is it since you've taken up racing?"

"I haven't really taken it up. I'm only an amateur."

Throwing the weight of her small agile body toward Lisa as though hastening to the rescue, Nastenka said in one breath: "Vitenka rides a bicycle and skates, as well."

"Oh, this is hardly the time to talk of skates," Victor Semyonovich said apologetically. "This is the weather for yachting."

"Vitenka's a member of the yacht club," Nastenka put in, "and his yacht—you should just see it! It's a gem."

She had to supplement the things the others could not say in order to fill in the pauses, and bent now to the left, now to the right, because she was prevented from seeing them all at once by the big china lamp in the middle of the round table at which they were seated.

If one did not count Victor Semyonovich, perhaps Valeria Ivanovna suffered more than anyone else from the consciousness of her own dullness in conversation. Daria Antonovna sat majestic and gracious in a purple gown, the gleaming folds of which seemed to stand erect, rising from floor to knee and waist and enshrouding the whole armchair, and making its wearer resemble a memorial.

Her talk, though dealing with the most commonplace topics, was conducted on a high note, with a certain trend toward national production or economics. This could only scare Valeria Ivanovna, whose conception of economics amounted to ascertaining whether goods had been plentiful or not at the market, but as to the why and wherefore of this plenty— who could ever understand it exactly! Of course, the supply did depend on certain pillars—those on which the rest of the world stood. It depended, for example, on the frosts, or on Holy Cross Day, or the first thaw, or the winter or spring Feasts of St. Nicholas. But all these things were too far removed from

practical things. Having dealt with the problem of
the market supply, Daria Antonovna passed over to
the busy season in the field work and to country
life in general, and then to what she called the Peasant
Question.

"Although we're townspeople by rights," she observed, "we're dependent to a very great extent on
the Peasant Question. Take our business, for instance,
textiles: the peasant may not want to buy even
the commonest gingham, and then all of a sudden
he'll demand the best prints you've got in stock. Just
now the country people are the best customers."

Discussions on this theme were within the com-
petence of Merkuri Avdeyevich alone, but he could
not permit himself to be drawn by their theoretic
charms and talk with complete freedom.

"Yes," he replied, after a moment's thought, "the
village is looking up these days. But it isn't every trade
can profit by it. Our paints and varnishes never were
much in demand in former years, and they don't
go well now."

"Why, how's that?" Nastenka put in. "You don't
mean it, surely? When I go about I'm always surprised at all the houses going up in every street. And
very handsome houses indeed! At the front staircase
there are lifts worked by machinery to take you
right to the top, you don't even need to use your
legs. Instead of floors there's concrete parquet, more
like a cathedral than an ordinary building. The banks
alone—you see them wherever you turn—bank after
bank. There must be people who put in their money
in them. Buildings without end."

Yes," Daria Antonovna agreed, "whether a building
is big or little, it can't get on without you, Merkuri
Avdeyevich. It'll fetch you customers one way or
the other."

"Well, but that's the town and we were talking about
the country villages."

"Money's the same, Merkuri Avdeyevich, whether
it's town or country."

"Oh, no, it isn't, Daria Antonovna. The peasant
holds on to his money a good deal more tightly
than the townsfolk."

"No matter how tightfisted he is, he has to have

the window frames painted sometime and now and
again paper the best room. And then a tavern may
be opened, a rural school built, a church done up
and they all come to you, and to no one else."

"I don't supply the rural board, so what interest
have I in their schools?" Meshkov replied. "And as
for the new churches, they have to deal wherever the
diocesan administration tells them to deal. And as
for the peasant, he'd sooner buy his wife an extra
dress length than linseed oil for painting the window
frames. So it looks as though the village money box
was shaken out oftener for you, Daria Antonovna
than for me.'

"M-m, I can see you're pretty tightfisted," Daria
Shubnikova's sober and mocking eyes said. She had
noticed as soon as she entered the room that the
wallpaper was of the cheaper kind, the floors had
not been stained for some time. "He grudges his
own wares on himself," she said to herself.

"I don't deny," she said, her eyes on the ground,
"that we do fairly good business. But your business
is a profitable one, too, and you do a brisk trade,
Merkuri Avdeyevich."

"The goods sell well, but the buyer wants a lot
for his money."

"The better off they get, the more they expect,
Merkuri Avdeyevich. As you say yourself, the peasant is getting much more reliable nowadays."

The conversation demanded skillful handling. Nastenka's smiles were becoming far too knowing, as
much as to say: it's easy to see that Merkuri Avdeyevich is anxious to make himself out much poorer
than he is, so as to avoid promising anything as his
daughter's marriage portion, while Daria Antonovna
makes herself out richer than she is so as to let
them feel that her young falcon is soaring over golden mountains.

"Yes," Merkuri Avdeyevich agreed, fidgeting on
the chair, "the peasants have been taken down a peg
and they've seen that you get more by hard work
than setting fire to gentlemen's houses. What the folks
need is a firm hand."

"It's easier to manage the village than the town,"

Daria Antonovna said, continuing her own line. "The peasants are more timorous than the townfolk."

"That's true enough," Merkuri Avdeyevich agreed cautiously.

"No matter where you turn in the town—there's nothing but malice and envy," Daria Antonovna complained.

"A wide field for envy," Merkuri Avdeyevich assented rather reluctantly.

"And then . . . there is so much malice in people. You may live with a person, show decent fellow feeling for him, help him in his troubles, and then . . ." Daria Antonovna paused and leaned closer to Meshkov. "And then you find you've been warming a viper in your bosom, so to speak. . . ."

"Who do you mean by a viper?" Meshkov demanded mistrustfully.

"Well, take that unpleasantness you had, for instance. I felt so sorry for you, Merkuri Avdeyevich, I declare I couldn't sleep the whole night for thinking of it. Just imagine, I said to myself, here's a God-fearing man, respected by everyone, with a daughter at home of marriageable age—and that such a thing should happen—oh, it's terrible!"

"You're thinking of . . . what exactly?" Meshkov began, determined to flatly deny any vague hints, but with growing anxiety.

"I'm talking about your underground political worker," she rejoined with apparent simplicity.

She made a gesture of heartfelt sympathy, spreading out her palms toward Meshkov and sitting with her head a little on one side, motionless, as though posing for a picture of deeply-moved sympathy. Nastenka was alert, gathered into a ball with impatience, her face ready to assume any grimace or expression, according to what she might hear. Lisa and her mother and Victor Semyonovich watched Merkuri Avdeyevich closely and with something like dread.

His face darkened with the rush of blood to the head, and for a few seconds he neither moved nor even blinked. Then he smoothed the mustache from his lips with his thumb and spread his beard, which gave him a more reasonable and somehow more holiday look at once.

"*My* underground political worker?" he repeated with emphasis, lowering his voice. "I've never had any underground workers here—it's unthinkable!"

"Well—the one who was caught in your house," Daria Antonovna explained, with a still wider gesture.

"The Lord has preserved my house from people who ought to be apprehended. What are you thinking of?"

"Oh, it was in your grounds, anyway—all the town is talking about it."

"There's always plenty of gossip going about. The wife of some agitator or other was arrested in a neighboring house. Am I supposed to be answerable for her?"

"Who's wanting you to be answerable for her, Merkuri Avdeyevich? I'm only saying—how very unpleasant it must have been for you."

"But why should it be unpleasant if it doesn't concern me?" said Meshkov with dignity—he had already got a foothold and was feeling his way out.

"Well, it must be unpleasant to have people talking about you, I should think."

"But you, as a good friend of mine, and since today, of my whole unblemished family—you, Daria Antonovna, shouldn't repeat what's been said to you. You should instead put down once and for all the rumors that are going about."

"Whatever do you mean, Merkuri Avdeyevich?" Daria Antonovna exclaimed, suddenly taking a commanding tone and briskly smoothing the folds of her rustling gown. "As though I would allow anyone to so much as hint at anything suspicious or cast aspersions on you! I only think how worried and upset you must have been when they came for that mischiefmaker's wife."

"Why should I worry when I had nothing on my conscience I need be ashamed of before either God or my neighbors?"

"Oh, if you were alone, it would be quite a different thing. But you have a daughter. Valeria Ivanovna has a mother's heart, and I'm sure it was aching for fear

that Lisanka might have come into contact with
dangerous persons."

"Ah, don't let's think about it!" Valeria Ivanovna
cried from the depths of her heart.

"Why should my daughter have come into contact
with dangerous persons?" Meshkov demanded, his
brows knitted in a threatening frown.

"But you yourself say, Merkuri Avdeyevich, that
the rebel's wife was arrested in your yard," Daria
Shubnikova said again in the tone of an innocent
inquiry.

"Well, and supposing it did happen in my yard,"
he retorted angrily, "my daughter doesn't live in the
yard, thank God, but at home and moreover with her
mother and father, Daria Antonovna."

"Allow me to tell you how it all came about,"
Victor Semyonovich burst out all at once in alarm,
evidently anxious to make things agreeable and having
collected by now, during the silence which had tormented him, sufficient determination. "My aunt was
most upset when she heard that this underground
business had been discovered in your yard. I mean to
say, in that sense, as you put it, Merkuri Avdeyevich,
she wanted to put an end to these rumors once and
for all. And she said: "Hold your tongue. . . . If,' she
says, 'you don't know for certain, then better not let
your tongue wag. . . .' I mean to say it was I who
told her about this. And to tell the truth, I had only
heard talk. It was just that our shopmen were talking
and gabbing, saying that some revolutionary had been
found hiding at the Meshkovs' and that he was mixed
up in some big case—well, you know what they call it
nowadays—distinguished himself in 1905. I mean to say,
these aren't my words: what kind of distinction could
you have if you were a rebel? And so he was run
in. And that was all. What could Lisa have to do with
this?" (He turned toward her. "If you could only have
been—excuse me for mentioning it—suspected, it could
only have been for being associated . . . Well, I mean
you're supposed to have been associated with young
people. But in that case anyone . . . I mean I could be
suspected myself." He made a movement intended to
show that if it was necessary he was ready to take

nobly, any guilt upon himself if only he could by this
means relieve Lisa of it.

"What are you talking about, Vitenka!" Nastenka
broke in, deploying her forces instantly. "Anybody
might think that the talk, as you call it, included
Lisanka."

"Nothing of the kind!" Victor Semyonovich protested, bouncing up again.

"No, of course, there could be nothing of the kind,"
Nastenka chanted with a penetrating glance at Lisa,
who turned away abruptly. "As if it would enter
anyone's head to associate a character as pure as an
angel's with earthly troubles. Vitenka happened to
be talking to his aunt while I was there—you remember, Daria Antonovna, it was when you were giving me
coffee in your rooms? And Vitenka had hardly time
to so much as mention these rumors about the underground rebel when Daria Antonovna said: 'That'll
do!' "

"I only mentioned the matter now so as to hear
the denial from your own lips, Merkuri Avdeyevich,"
Daria Antonovna added in an aggrieved tone.

"Well," he said quietly, "I'm telling you the facts."

"That's the thing—everything's cleared up that way,"
Nastenka swept on irresistibly. "At the same time
Vitenka told us that some boys from the High School
and Technical School had been arrested and that
even in the Theological Seminary some had been
found who had distributed around the town leaflets
against the tsarist government. To cut a long story
short, all those mischievous young people. Daria Antonovna crossed herself then and said: 'Thank the
Lord, Vitenka, you're not that kind. But for goodness'
sake,' she says, 'be careful and see there isn't anyone
among your friends who has anything to do with those
arrested boys.' That was the sum and substance of the
whole conversation, Merkuri Avdeyevich. No gossip
about you was encouraged at all, and Lisa's name was
never so much as mentioned."

Her chatter broke off suddenly. Her glance, hover-
ing hither and thither, rested tenderly on Lisa as, in a
totally different, confidential, and insinuating voice,
she went on, conning a well-learned lesson. "I have
to be quite frank: the darling name was mentioned,

of course, only in a quite, quite different connection. But let anyone else who likes tell her about it, I won't!

Victor Semyonovich rocked, as though seeking the equilibrium he had suddenly lost, and was about to say something when at that moment Valeria Ivanovna moved up quickly to Lisa and asked in a whisper that everyone could hear:

"Are you feeling faint?"

Lisa was very pale. She strove with all her might to preserve the immobility that she had bound herself with, then suddenly overcame the strain and rose with relief. "Perhaps you'll ask everybody to the table, Mama?" she said.

"Yes, do, Valeria Ivanovna," Merkuri Avdeyevich agreed, pulling himself together, and his sigh was the signal for mutual exchange of courtesies. With bows and thanks they all rose and moved toward the table.

But by this time neither the titillating fragrance of hot pies and cakes, nor the aroma of jams, nor the mirrorlike brilliance of the samovar, which reflected starrily the glitter of knives and forks, could disperse the stiffness and depression of the conversation; it began with Valeria Ivanovna's urgings to "Do try some of this, please," and ended with Nastenka's praises, such as "What a splendid cook you are!" or Daria Antonovna's "I don't remember ever tasting such short crust as this puff pastry."

Victor Semyonovich clinked glasses of Nezhin rowan-flavored vodka with Merkuri Avdeyevich, and emboldened, tried to ascertain from Lisa if she would care to drink from the life-giving source, but encountered such a glance that his shyness returned with redoubled force.

He kept silence throughout the lunch, except to squeeze out an occasional "thank you," and when he got up from the table, shuffled, kept making way for everyone, and recoiling with apologetic delicacy and a frozen smile. Lisa could not repress a giggle. Then he was overcome with confusion, turned, knocked against the round table on which the lamp stood, tried to rescue it, but instead pressed harder against the table and overturned the lamp. The globular glass shade slid down onto the carpet and, with a sound like a sigh, split in two as cleanly as a watermelon.

Victor Semyonovich pressed his hand to his fevered brow. Some word or other—perhaps it was "I'll pay for it," or "I'll mend it"—nearly escaped his lips, but stuck inarticulately in his throat; all he could do was scrape his feet and bow stiffly like a puppet to Merkuri Avdeyevich and Valeria Ivanovna in turn. He did not dare to turn his head toward Lisa.

"That's a good omen, it means good luck!" Nastenka cried ecstatically, rushing to pick up the pieces, while the host and hostess were murmuring something, laughing over it and trying to set the unfortunate man at his ease.

Daria Antonovna took Lisa by the hand and said, without a trace of embarrassment, even with a touch of real condescension: "You might think, my dear, that Vitenka behaves like a bull in a china shop, but it's only because you made him feel shy."

"He's anything but awkward, anything but awkward as a rule!" cried Nastenka, who, having glanced around at all of them, was ready to smooth everything over and console everyone.

The accident unexpectedly refreshed the company (with the exception of Victor Semyonovich) as a pun may enliven a bored party, so the farewells were very cordial.

But no sooner were the Meshkovs left to themselves than a dismal gloom descended upon them. Lisa went over to the window, feeling her father's and mother's expectant gaze fixed on her back. The empty cups on the table, the petrified philodendron in its pot, the disarranged furniture, the broken lamp shade on the tablecloth—seemed awaiting the inevitable conclusion of all that had taken place.

And Lisa, clasping her hands tightly at her breast, turned slowly toward her mother. "Did they come here to view the bride, Mama?"

Valeria Ivanovna drew her handkerchief out of her sleeve.

Merkuri Avdeyevich demanded in a challenging tone: "And what if they did—what's wrong with that? We didn't invent these things. Our fathers before us kept to the custom. And the church doesn't look with disfavor on it. Are we heathens or what?"

"I was simply asking."

"No, you weren't simply asking. You were asking defiantly. It's not for you to be defiant, I can tell you. You've heard the talk that's going about the town?"

"The talk?"

"Yes, the talk about you and—associating you with these underground rebels."

"Papa!"

"You may well say Papa! What were the Shubnikovs quizzing us about, do you think? Did you imagine we were the only people who knew you went about with a young man who has been put behind prison bars? You have to be saved now, before it is too late—saved! Do you understand me?"

"Yes, I understand you," Lisa replied. "I'm beginning to understand, anyway."

"You've forgotten how you should speak to your father, I suppose? You're educated now, are you? And what has your education broght you to? When I was asked at Gendarmerie Headquarters: 'Tell us what is your daughter interested in?' what could I say? That you were interested in rebels. You and your mother— you're like two moles, you don't understand a thing. And what if they come some night and grab you? What then?"

"What would they do that for?" Valeria Ivanovna exclaimed in alarm.

"You went to theaters with Kirill, didn't you? So there you are! They won't go into the why and the wherefore of the thing. She's in danger of her very life, and I'm telling you, Lisa has to be saved somehow."

"And you intend Shubnikov to be my savior, is that it?" Lisa asked, trying to grasp the idea.

Then Meshkov shouted: "I'll take it upon myself who's to be your savior!"

He marched up and down the room with his hands behind his back, doing a fancy step or two at the turning. This heralded one of the sermons which were the pillars of family life; Meshkov, thank God, was still at the helm!

"Only your obedience, nothing else, can save you now. How have I brought you up? In implicit obedience. If you had ever had words with your father, you'd have seen nothing but unhappiness in your life. And what is obedience? How does the church under-

stand obedience? One of the holy fathers who wanted
to test a novice ordered him to plant a stake in the
ground on a high mountain and to water it every day,
bringing the water from the foot of the mountain.
The novice did as he was bid, obeying the father's
orders implicitly and with such humility that it never
occurred to him that watering a stake was a senseless
thing. And inasmuch as he did this in all humility, he
had his reward: after five years of patient watering
the stake took root and put out shoots. . . . It goes
without saying that this was obedience of the monastic
kind and it's not what I require of you. But I have
the right to expect a daughter's obedience from you.
You've never denied me this and I value you for it.
You've always known that everything was done for
your own good. Do you think that a chance like the
Shubnikovs is likely to come again? Never. You should
have heard what they told me at the bank about Daria
Antonovna. Why!—I could never even dream of credit
like hers! And she has but the one heir. Would I be
likely to put you into bad hands? You're my own
daughter. I think of your happiness day and night. . . ."

Suddenly, without hearing him to the end, Lisa
turned and left the room. There was something in her
abrupt departure that not only cut short Merkuri
Avdeyevich's endless flow of words but even prevented
him from trying to detain her by word or gesture.

She went downstairs and out into the street. It was
a day of languorous clearness; the heat had not yet
reached its zenith, but all life was stilled, wrapped in
the breath of the red-hot earth. On days like this a
moment comes when time seems to pause, waiting
for some sharp, saving change; one expects that now,
just now, a sudden shriek, a shout, an explosion,
might come from somewhere, restoring to life the
stifled and almost immolated nature.

The whitewashed schoolhouse was pasted like a
patch of lime against the green-tinged sky, and the
poplars looked like black planed-down props. The soil,
hard and seamed with cracks, rang responsively under
the heel. Lisa did not hasten her steps, but neither
did she dawdle—hesitation was a thing of the past.

For the first time she found herself before the door

that led to the world where she had spent in thought some of the best moments of her dreams. And she paused before that single-paneled door, with the nail-heads, the scrolls of the heavy hinges, the ponderous, rusty latch. Here, in the dim brick-floored passage the heat abated, and the thin breath of coolness brought a sudden poignant remembrance of the frowning auster-ity of old buildings, where the stones were silent witnesses of men's destinies; she fancied for a moment that she was standing not before a door but a gate, and if she entered it, the past would retreat from her forever.

For a long time she stood without moving. Then she lifted the latch cautiously. The door was opened to her by Annochka.

"How did you come here?"

"Oh, I come here regularly to tidy up for Vera Nikandrovna," Annochka replied, smoothing down her dress. "Have you come to see her?"

"Is she at home?"

"Yes, come along, I'll take you in to see her."

Vera Nikandrovna came out to meet Lisa on the threshold of Kirill's room. They stood silent, trying to read each other's thoughts. Very different in outward appearance—in their general build and height, in their complexions and hair, in their slightest feature—they were apparently seeking in each other some sig-nificant, intimate resemblance, and the passionate desire to find it illuminated them with an identical feeling of anguish. Putting out her suddenly weakened arms, Lisa darted toward the woman, crying: "How is Kirill?" and would have fallen if Vera Nikandrovna had not caught her in her arms.

With their arms twined about each other, they went over to the bed and sank down heavily upon it. Lisa's face was distorted with pain as her head drooped and rested upon the older woman's lap. Softly at first, then more frequently and violently, her shoulders and her body began to shake with sobs.

Vera Nikandrovna stroked her tousled hair, her back, and the hands wet with tears, and sat rocking herself to and fro with closed eyes.

When the sobbing had subsided, she raised Lisa,

set her a little away from her, and dried her face with her handkerchief. Clasping the girl to her breast, she made her rise to her feet.

"Come," she said in a low voice. "Come at once." Then for a second she paused and looked sternly into Lisa's eyes. "You knew?" she asked in a low voice.

"Knew what?"

"That Kirill had the leaflets."

"He never said a word to me about it."

"That's what I thought," Vera Nikandrovna said quickly.

She took Lisa firmly by the arm and led her from the house. And Lisa walked in step with her, submissive to her calm and convincing power.

Annochka poked her head out of the door and watched them steadily with her wide-eyed, luminous gaze.

CHAPTER

· 23 ·

Kirill's count of time began with the moment that an unnoticeable wicket gate opened in the big green gates of the jail. It was the changing of the guard—at four in the morning—and there was a slight delay at the sentry post while the outgoing guard handed over the keys to the new watch and talked about some cart or other.

A lonely black poplar grew near the post. Its lower boughs were richly leafy, its upper boughs, broken by the wind, were withered and sparrows hopped about on them, fussily polishing their beaks and chirruping noisily about the urgent affairs of the morning. The sun had just risen above the flattened roof of the jail and it was growing warmer. The yard was bare, the earth worn smooth by boot soles and cartwheels, and only at the foot of the wall was its arid baldness touched with a faint green.

Kirill was led across the ground, hardened by years of treading, to an inner yard, where the fading breath of cool morning was mingled with the stench of a cesspool. Some prisoners wearing short thick jackets and round army cloth caps were busy about carts loaded with barrels. Kirill noticed that the man nearest him wore fetters: from a metal belt a chain hung down between his legs, forked at the knees, and ended in iron shackles. The man was rubbing the horse's withers, and the animal jerked its head—it had a large pink patch on the nose—and the clink of the bridle echoed the duller sound of the iron fetters.

Kirill slackened his pace, but his escort urged him on with a shove on the shoulder and said in the deep muffled voice of a carter: "Get along! Don't go to sleep." The boy turned and noticed the wall past which he was being led: it was about four times the height of a man, and through its plaster, big old bricks, red in the sun, showed like sores. He suddenly remembered the blind wall very similar to it in the settings for the third act of the play he had seen at the theater, and then the whole play came back to him, and Lisa, and how she had taken offense on Tsvetukhin's behalf and run away, crying for some reason or other "Forgive us!"

It was hard to understand why she had apologized —he had merely expressed his opinion, nothing more, to Tsvetukhin. The queer, incredible thing was that he had just seen a wall like this in the play and now it had followed him into the prison yard and he was no longer a member of the audience but a character. Still more extraordinary was the fact that only four hours had passed (actually, a few minutes) since the end of the play, and so many things had happened in that time, and they had evoked such a rapid sequence, such a tide of feelings, that Kirill and Lisa seemed to have been in the theater a long, long time ago, in an altogether different life, already screened by the veil of the past.

He began his count of time from those four hours, and marked it at first by the number of separate nights and days, then the number of whole days, then of weeks. The higher the count became, the more alert he grew, listening to the advance of time, and how occasionally it paused in the slightest fractions, and thus he learned to calculate the time of day or night as exactly as though he heard the chiming of the clock.

The first chime was the distant thud of horses' hoofs on a highway deep in soft dust. The thudding filtered in through the tiny half-open barred window and the funnel-shaped iron shield that covered it outside. All sounds from outside filtered through this black, rusty funnel that hid the light of day, and so were muffled. Nevertheless, as time dragged on, Kirill distinguished them in increasing number and soon understood which way the windows were facing. He learned to distinguish the winds, their direction and force, by sounds. The West wind bore to his ears the measured sigh of the earth under the tread of platoons of soldiers; the North—the singing and humming of transmission belts in factories. The harbinger of the torrid South wafted to his ears the bells of the streetcars and sometimes the panicky tooting of a cyclist's horn. Hearing replaced sight, as in the case of the blind. He saw with his ears: the barracks were opposite his window, on the right stretched the buildings of the tobacco factory, to the left the new university was being built. Outside the small window, beneath the black funnel, lay the dusty square where he had once gone around the booths of the fairground with his father and the last time—with Lisa. They had eaten ice cream with bone spoons, and, standing in the thick of the holiday crowd, had looked up at the prison, at the windows hidden from the light of day by black funnels, and had spoken of that far-off day when there would be no more prisons. From time to time birds flew past the window. They were mostly flocks of sparrows. The rapid beat and flutter of their wings made his own heart beat faster. He remembered the sparrows he had seen on the black poplar that first morning. Sometimes he recognized a pigeon by the strong swish of the wings.

At night the sounds from the free world outside died down and the prison sounds grew louder. Prison sound were footsteps in the corridor and wall conversations. Lying on his cot, Kirill heard his neighbor tapping on the wall; he understood nothing, only knew that someone was trying to send a message to him. His own answers made no sense. Then after a while he guessed that his neighbor was teaching him to talk, but he could not understand how it should be done. It was a big day for him, a holiday, when he suddenly realized that this was the alphabet that they were teaching him. He had to pretend to be asleep, and, afraid to stir, he almost cried with joy.

The next night he mastered the divison of the alphabet into sets of letters, the cunning pauses, frequent and infrequent taps, the science of the captives who lived by hearing alone. Hardly had the steps in the corridor receded than, with the blanket pulled well over his head, he began his tapping. From that hour he was no longer alone in his stone casket—he could talk to someone. And the first thing that he said was: "I understand!"

In the daytime he paced up and down, describing a figure eight—turning the right shoulder at one corner and the left at the other. The cell was five paces on the diagonal, and he counted up to hundreds and thousands of paces. Then he made interruptions—long and short—in his pacing. It was like counting the small, medium, and large series of beads on a rosary. He did exercises several times a day, for he had made up his mind to look after himself and keep fit like a piece of well-tended machinery. While he told the rosary of those paces, he trained his memory to go over all that he had ever learned. He taught himself to draw plans in imagination, demonstrate formulas in physics in his head, prove theorems, and draw maps of travel routes.

About eight years earlier, when only a small boy, he had seen the first film at his school. The apparatus had crackled on a tripod in the middle of the classroom, casting a ray of gaslight on the screen. The gas came from a balloon which lay under an eighty-pound weight. One picture was called a "comic": a workman was painting a park bench, then he put a notice on it—"Wet paint"—and went away. A fat man reading a paper strolled into the park and sat down on the bench, engrossed in an interesting article he was reading. The audience rocked with laughter when the fat man got up again, still reading, and they saw his back striped with paint. But this was only the beginning of the fun. Another picture showed a swimming contest: the swimmers dived from a board at an immense height. The splashing and waves were exactly as in real life, and the swimmers swam, gasping and blowing. Then the film was shown the other way about—from end to beginning. And the audience saw a most extraordinary thing: the people bounced out of

the water and flew into the air feet foremost, ran
along the jumping-off place backward—everything
was the other way around. And the laughter seemed
to shake even the heavy water-splashed screen.

Kirill called to mind this gay picture show, for he
was recalling his whole life and in particular trying to
remember the most amusing bits of it. He was surprised to find how very few amusing passages there
had been in his life and how very little he had enjoyed himself. Had a gloomy youth been his lot? He
did not want to admit that. He was sure he had had a
great deal of pleasure and entertainment, and that
boredom was out of the question. True, he was more
attracted by serious things, and did not notice the
amusing so much. But in the serious he sensed a joy
like the vivid tremor of dappled sunlight in the
woods.

Reviewing the past, Kirill saw himself at the prison
gates and from there retraced his steps, unwinding
the film of memory backward. Its course he learned
more exactly than the sounds of the prison, than the
cell, than the fingernails that had to be trimmed down
with the teeth, for there was no means of cutting
them. His mind was made up on one score as firmly
as the sheet anchor is fixed at the shore; Ragozin was
a stranger to him and therefore he knew nothing that
could have even the remotest connection with that
name. He had sworn to himself to believe nothing and
to deny everything.

At the first very brief interrogation which took place
in the cell soon after his arrest and was more like the
sort of talk that takes place during the regular rounds
of the prison, Kirill repeated what he had said during
the search: that he had found the leaflets in the street
where they had been lying in a wad, all together, and
he had slipped them into the book, in which they had
been discovered. Had he read them?—he was asked.
Yes, he had. Why had he not destroyed them? He had
thought of burning them when the stove was heated,
but it was summertime, and so they did not heat it,
and he had been in no particular hurry, as he did
not think them of any great importance. But they
spoke insultingly of the person of His Imperial
Majesty—he must have understood that? Yes, he had

understood that, but he thought they were old leaflets such, as he had heard, were distributed in great numbers in 1905, and perhaps someone might have lost them. That was all. The interrogation was conducted by a gendarme officer, who announced, on entering the cell, that he was Lieutenant-Colonel Polotentsev, and that he was conducting the investigation, adding that if Kirill should have any complaints to make, he should address them to the Assistant Prosecutor, indicating with a glance his companion, who kept a forbidding silence all the time. Following the interrogation, he informed Kirill that he was permitted to go to the steam baths regularly and receive fresh linen from home, and that if he wished for something to read, he could have the New Testament.

Time after time Kirill went over, very carefully, every word the gendarme had said, considering every slightest shade of meaning in the questions and convincing himself that if he held fast to his anchor of denial, the secret could not be discovered. He waited, with growing impatience, for the next interrogation, which he fancied must decide the whole thing. But the weeks dragged by, and no one came to his cell except the guard, who, dully and silently, brought his bread, boiled water, and thin broth.

If, with the pale beam of light that filtered through the tiny window, its vital force broken by the iron funnel, a human gaze could have penetrated into the cell, it would have lighted upon a boy with a thin neck, exposed by the wide crumpled neckband of the shirt. The boy wore no belt; his shoulders looked angular. With measured, even tread like an animal's, he moved from corner to corner of his cage or, standing in the middle of the floor, stretched his arms above his head in regular movements that, because of his emaciation, were robbed of any elasticity. His hair had grown long and was much darker, framing his forehead in straight lines, and his brows rose over the bridge of the nose, as though expressing by their arch his continual surprise. His face was the color of raw potato; the freckles had faded, leaving no trace; his cheeks looked flabby. The yellow tinge in the eyes had grown deeper, but they had not warmed, they had the dry smolder of embers. Kirill himself noticed one thing, that his lips were uncomfortably parched and scaly—that, and his thinness. It was a job to keep his clothes from falling off him these days.

At last the interrogation took place. It was the seventy-first day of his imprisonment.

He was led through the yard to the unimpressive office of the prison chief. The dazzling light started a roaring in his ears, and though he only had to go straight across, he involuntarily kept swerving either to the right or the left.

Then he was left alone in a little room with barred door and window, facing Polotentsev, who looked at him with stern sympathy.

"Well, now, young Izvekov. Your case is being cleared. Your mother is interceding with the Prosecutor for leniency toward you during detention—on account of your health. You certainly look far from healthy. You understand what leniency in the manner of detention means, don't you? You don't? There you are—you don't even understand ordinary things like this. And you were intending to shake the realm or something of the sort, weren't you? Well, let's see now, if there's medical evidence of your ill-health. . . . . Did anything ail you formerly?"

"No."

"Your mother says that you suffered from scrofula."

"Perhaps I did, in childhood," Kirill said.

"Ah, yes, in childhood. Not so long ago, either, I should think. . . . Humph. It can't be so very long ago, I'm saying. Your eyes look as though they ailed you at some time, and your mother confirms it. That's true, isn't it?"

"Yes, I had something wrong with my eyes once."

"Zinc poisoning, wasn't it?"

"That was a mistaken diagnosis."

"Ah, a mistaken diagnosis! Still, you underwent some treatment for them. And it helped. So it can hardly have been such a crude mistake on the doctor's part, can it?"

Kirill said nothing. He was separated from Polotentsev by a narrow table. A cheap marble writing set stood on it and there were some finely sharpened pencils in a bronze holder. Kirill took out one of vari-colored wood—it was long since he had had the pleasure of feeling this simple everyday thing in his fingers.

"And then you yourself explained to the doctor that you had been making some zinc parts, I believe. Something like that is mentioned in the medical report. You don't happen to remember what kind of parts they were? They wouldn't be type by any chance."

"What has that to do with it?" Kirill asked with a faint smile.

"I'm very ignorant of technical things," the Lieutenant-Colonel was smiling, too. "So you hold all the trumps. That's why I'm asking you—what did you mean by the zinc parts you mentioned to the doctor?"

"I don't remember. It was a long time ago."

"In your childhood, eh? The time you and your comrades used to play with your toys. Do you remember you had a school friend in your class— Ruderbach? You couldn't tell me, I suppose, the kind of toys the two of you used to play with?"

Kirill twirled and twisted the pencil in his fingers, never taking his eyes from the gleaming rainbow of its polished surface.

"All right, I can tell you the things you and your comrade Ruderbach used to amuse yourselves with," the Lieutenant-Colonel went on with an air of exasperated dignity. "You used to go to the printing works that belonged to his father and he taught you the compositor's work on the quiet. We know everything. Ruderbach has been arrested and confessed the whole thing. There is no point in denying it any longer. It will only be the worse for you. What did you need to learn typesetting for?"

Kirill gave a shrug. "Once in our class we decided to print our essays and at first we thought of hectographing them and then Ruderbach said that if we did the compositor's job ourselves, we could print them there. But it did not come off."

"And what did come off?" Polotentsev demanded unhurriedly. He settled his pince-nez, as though taking a better aim at Kirill, and untied, as daintily as a woman might, the bow of the tape on the cardboard folder. He threw back the leaf and flicked open with his nail the light card flaps. "This was what actually came off, wasn't it?"

Picking out a few of the leaflets found during the search at Kirill's, he shoved them toward the boy. "Recognize this?"

"It's one of those that I found in the street," Kirill remarked, skimming the text.

"As to where you found them, that's another question. For the present we find that on your evidence you learned printing in Ruderbach's printing shop."

"I didn't learn it."

"On the basis of the facts and your admission, it is established that in working at the press, you infected your eyes with zinc dust, through inexperience."

"I never said so."

"It only remains to answer the question," Polotentsev continued inexorably, "of how you came to infect your eyes more than a year after you had learned the business. It appears that you must have had something to do with other type than Ruderbach's. And this is proved beyond a doubt in the following manner."

Hereupon Polotentsev laid neatly at the side of the leaflets the impression of a page from the press. "Compare this type with the printing on the leaflets."

"But I'm not an expert," Kirill said, "and besides, it doesn't concern me."

"Oh, I quite agree. But you're not being asked to give an expert opinion. The experts have already established that these leaflets were printed in the very same press from which the impression was taken. And the impression was made. . . ."

Unhurriedly, Polotentsev laid the leaflets away again in the folder, tied the tape daintily in a bow, and once more straightened his glasses, focusing them on Kirill.

"The impression was made in Ragozin's clandestine printing press," he said very quietly.

Kirill dropped the pencil and stooped to pick it up. It rolled under the table. Polotentsev waited patiently, watching as Kirill, on one knee, groped under the table, then got up, and, taking his place at the desk again, put back the pencil point downward in the holder and thrust his hands into his pockets.

"Answer me," Polotentsev said in the same quiet

voice, after a pause. "What originals did you print the leaflets from in Ragozin's press?"

"I don't understand your questions," Kirill said, "I've never printed anything and I don't know how. And I haven't the least idea who Ragozin is."

Polotentsev looked him straight in the eye. Then he reached out slowly across the desk and picked out of the holder the pencil Kirill had been twirling in his fingers two or three minutes before this. The lead was broken.

"The pencil point broke, did it?" Polotentsev asked, his eyes narrowing as he watched Kirill.

"Excuse me, I dropped it and I'm afraid it broke."

"Show me your hand!" the man shouted suddenly. Kirill drew his hand out of his pocket.

"No, the other hand! You picked up the pencil with your right!" Polotentsev sprang up from his place and ran around the desk. Grabbing Kirill's hand and jerking it toward him, he looked closely at the fingers. The forefinger and the thumb were smudged with the gleaming black lead crumbs.

"You broke off the point and hid it in your pocket. Give it here! Or else I'll make them tan the hide off you, boy! Get up! Get up!" Polotentsev shouted. "Turn out your pockets, quick now!"

He himself thrust his five fingers into Kirill's pockets, turned them inside out, and shook them, slapping his thighs as viciously as he could. The perspiration started out of his shaven head, his glasses slipped. As though he had found relief after protracted constraint, his whole body twitched while he gave vent to explosive orders.

"You thought you'd send word to someone outside, did you? You thought you'd get the better of us, eh? There's no getting the better of jail. Jail's broken bigger men than you milksops! Thinks he's a giant, does he? The impudence of a little runt like you! You haven't had a good hiding often enough, that's what's wrong with you. Well, you'll get plenty here. You'll sing out. They'll make you dance!"

Kirill stood without moving, biting his white lower lip. His head was a little on one side, as if he was listening to some scarcely audible sound, like a hunter waiting for the flight of a bird in the distance. The broad collar of his shirt, open at the breast, rose and fell slightly, and from time to time his hands, which were hanging loosely by his sides, twitched.

The Lieutenant-Colonel's shouts broke off abruptly, he returned to his armchair, and smoked a cigarette. The pause lasted a few minutes. Outside, the ground was being dug, and Kirill could hear the spades swish as they drove into the soil and the heavy clods drop with a sigh. Someone was filing iron with a plaintive sound.

"Now look here, Izvekov," Polotentsev began again in the voice of a man burdened with vain earthly cares, "you'll be given paper, and you'll give your evidence in writing about Ragozin and the part you both took in this underground organization. It'll be much easier for you if you make a full confession of your guilt."

"I don't know anyone called Ragozin, or anything about an organization."

"Stop, stop!" Polotentsev broke in. Darting to the door, he spoke through the grating to the guard and told him to call the assistant superintendent of the prison. Meanwhile he puffed at his cigarette and paced up and down by the door until an extraordinarily lean, withered, freckled man appeared who looked as though he had been specially cured in the sun, like a kipper. He wore a prison official's faded uniform with a sword that looked far too stubby for his size.

"This young fellow's tongue seems to have swollen," Polotentsev said without turning to Kirill, but indicating him with a long-nailed little finger. "He needs proper treatment. . . . Put him in the cooler!" he ordered in a thin, whistling voice, suddenly fixing his dull, smoke-filmed eyes, with their yellow eyelashes, on Kirill.

Raising his sword, the superintendent pointed it at the door and then followed on Kirill's heels.

When Kirill crossed the threshold of his new abode, he felt an irritation in his throat as though he had swallowed something sharp. In pitch darkness he groped for the wall and, holding on to it, slid down onto the floor. With astonishing clearness he saw in his mind's eye his former cell with the black funnel over the high window through which the dear pale light of day filtered in and the winds sang, bringing so much of life into his cell—and now that cell seemed to him a Promised Land, lost forever.

CHAPTER

· 24 ·

THE IDEA of seeking influential help and support in her efforts for her son had never been given up by Vera Nikandrovna. But hardly had the idea taken shape—the morning after Kirill's arrest—than she saw plainly that she was all alone: there was nowhere to go, no one she could turn to in her trouble. Kirill had filled her life, her consciousness, and while she had had him with her, she never suspected that in the whole town, in the whole world, there was none to whom she might go in time of need. It looked to her as though she had been thrown into the water and then everyone had turned away from her. She seized eagerly on the hope of getting some help from Tsvetukhin or Pastukhov. And strangely enough, while she had built up and lit this hope, she was almost certain that nothing would be left of her phantasmal plan as soon as she attempted to put it into practice: her expectations would evaporate and there would be nothing to substitute for them. The fear of losing her hope grew stronger than the hope itself.

"What do you think?—will he respond?" Vera Nikandrovna asked Lisa thoughtfully as they went arm in arm to Tsvetukhin's.

"I imagine he is responsive," Lisa replied.

"I think the same, for some reason," Vera Nikandrovna said rather uncertainly.

The determination with which she had set out,

drawing Lisa with her, was weakening as they were approaching their goal.

Tsvetukhin lived near the Limes in a hotel. Its whitewashed, one-storied buildings were scattered without much formality in a courtyard with lawns and asphalted paths. Beside it rose the roof, crowned by queer-looking cowls, of the music school, from which came the mildly argumentative sounds of instruments that seemed to chaff the military band in the boulevard. Unlike the big hotels, this one attracted people with an inclination toward a settled life, and its atmosphere was pleasantly reposeful.

As Izvekova and Lisa were crossing the yard by a path lined with slender trees, they heard a cultivated voice asking: "Are you looking for me, I wonder?"

Lisa stood still. A radiant Tsvetukhin was looking down at her from an open window. He was wearing a starched shirt with a turned-down collar of the style known as "Robespierre" among the fops of the Limes, and its whiteness made him look swarthier than usual. He was holding an open book in his outstretched hand, and he waved a welcome with it.

"So I guessed right, didn't I? Do come in—I'm coming out to meet you."

Their visit undoubtedly gave Tsvetukhin sincere pleasure. His speeches, smiles, and compliments were most attractively gentle. He made up his mind that he simply must treat his guests to ice cream, and so, although they refused vehemently, he insisted on sending a waiter to the Limes, giving him a china soup bowl, and scribbling the kinds he wanted on a scrap of paper.

"But we've come to you on business, very important business," Vera Nikandrovna began, with rising agitation.

"And we won't stay long," Lisa chimed in, "only a few minutes."

"Now, please don't justify and excuse yourselves," Tsvetukhin said. "Don't you see what I have come to? I was actually reading verse, and I would have died of boredom if you hadn't come. You've saved me, honestly!"

"Yes, but I'm afraid our business will seem too . . . well, you may be still more bored," Izvekova continued impatiently and at the same time rather timidly.

"Oh, come now," Egor Pavlovich expostulated, apparently touched and amazed, as though prepared by the very essence of his nature to serve his neighbor in every way. "I think I can guess what it's about: you've heard something about your son, is that it? Well, how is he?"

"It's true," Vera Nikandrovna said in a very low voice and her eyes brightened. "You must have read my thoughts at once. What else could I be thinking about? Unfortunately, there's no change in the case. I don't even know if there is a case. That is to say, I'm sure there isn't."

"Yes, of course, of course!" Tsvetukhin agreed warmly.

"And you understand the state that Kirill must be in? What are they keeping him there for? Is it possible that just because the boy was found in possession of some papers that might have come from goodness knows where, he has to be kept week after week under these conditions?"

"But what's happening to him?" Tsvetukhin asked. "Is he really being kept in prison? I mean to say—is there no change all this time?"

"No, that's just it! They're dragging out the investigation as though it was heaven knows what dreadful crime."

"This is the very devil!" Tsvetukhin said, glancing at Lisa with an expression of startled sympathy.

"It is really," Lisa said in a scarcely audible voice, with a shy little shrug.

"And then, you know," Izvekova went on, "the indifference of those officials can drive one crazy. It's nearly six weeks now since I sent in an application to the Prosecutor, and I haven't had an answer except: 'Call again next week.'"

"What sort of an application?" Tsvetukhin asked, trying to get a grasp of the affair.

"I want to get Kirill out on surety."

"Ah, yes, of course," he said approvingly, then added: "Only you see, nothing has changed very much as far as the officials are concerned since the time of Gogol's *Inspector-General*, alas! You remember? Khlestakov asks Rastakovsky: 'And how long is it

since you sent in your application?' and the other says:
'Well, to tell the truth, it isn't so long ago—in 1801, as a
matter of fact, but for thirty years it hasn't been considered!'"

Tsvetukhin told the story like an actor, in two different voices, smiling with satisfaction because it
turned out well. Lisa smiled, too, and lowered her eyes
so as not to see his face and laugh. But Vera Nikandrovna was silent, and catching her glance of sad reproach, Egor Pavlovich said hastily:

"I think they ought to let him out on surety."

"I'm sure they will," she rejoined eagerly, "but only
if I can get some influential support for my request.
That's why Lisa and I have come to ask you not to refuse us, please."

"With the greatest . . . I mean I should consider it
my duty. . . . But I must confess I can't imagine how I
could be of assistance."

"Your name would be sufficient if you appealed to
the Prosecutor. . . . "

"My name!" Tsvetukhin sighed softly with profound self-pity and, apparently, long-accumulated
weariness.

"Why, of course!" Izvekova said, surprised. "Your
name!"

"Your name!" Lisa repeated, leaning forward and
suddenly checking herself.

"But—believe me, my dear friends," Tsvetukhin protested, highly flattered. "It is sheer nonsense that an
actor's name possesses any kind of magic. While we're
on the stage, I agree, our road is open for us to any
heart. But if we were to go next day to the very person whom we had moved to tears and ask him to do
us a favor—good heavens, what a fright we would give
him! We're admired in art. But people beware of us in
everyday life. We are doubtful characters, unreliable,
hysterical, always mixed up in some nasty affair, quar-
rels, lawsuits, and scandals."

"You're slandering yourself," Lisa declared,
wounded. "It isn't true, it isn't true. . . . "

"My dear friend! You think better of us than we
deserve. That is natural to youth. But just think for a
moment: supposing I was to go to the Prosecutor, and
they would announce: 'An actor to see you, sir.' An

actor?' he would ask, raising his eyebrow a trifle. 'What can an actor want with me?'"

"It wouldn't be simply an actor, it would be Tsvetukhin," Lisa said with reverence.

"Oh," said Egor Pavlovich modestly. "Little as you know about actors, I can see you know still less about prosecutors."

"The chief thing they should understand is that public opinion is informed about the boy's fate," Vera Nikandrovna said, pressing her twitching fingers to her breast. "And if only you wouldn't refuse us . . . "

"But wait a minute . . . " Tsvetukhin exclaimed. "Public opinion! Who could be better than Pastukhov in that case? Pastukhov—there you have public opinion. Pastukhov should be asked to do it. . . . "

"I am thinking of him, too. Of you and of him."

"Oh, never mind about me! Imagine what an impression it would make if Alexander Pastukhov appealed to the authorities! He's well known in St. Petersburg, he gets into the newspapers. That's no mere actor, that's quite another thing!"

"But I'm afraid he won't agree."

"Of course he will! He's what you might call a public figure by profession, and he would be only too glad of the chance to show what he can do. I'm certain of it. And what a coincidence!—I'm just waiting for him, he promised to come, and we'll ask him straightaway. . . . "

Growing thoughtful, Egor Pavlovich looked at Lisa a moment.

"Only—I'm thinking what would be the best way to do it? Pastukhov didn't say when he would be here. If you go and see him, you may miss him. You know what," he said with a pleased air, "we'll do it this way. You, Vera Nikandrovna, should go to Pastukhov's and Lisa can stay here, in case you miss him. So that one way or another, he won't slip through our fingers."

Lisa was startled by the aged look that came into Vera Nikandrovna's eyes, and she did not venture to object. They came to an agreement that if Izvekova found Pastukhov at home (he lived nearby), she would not come back. Tsvetukhin saw her out with encouraging words of kindness.

The ice creams were brought in, and, a few minutes

later, saucers and spoons, and while Tsvetukhin bus-
tled about hospitably, rattling them and removing
from the table anything that might be in the way,
Lisa looked out of the window.

Stifling heat still emanated from the earth, and from
the look of the thin dusty branches of young trees,
motionless as though in prayer, it was plain how
languorously nature was waiting for movement,
change. Lazy holiday voices drifted in an unharmoni-
ous jumble through the open windows—a burst of interrupted laughter, the sound of a kitchen knife, a
child's scream. The heat seemed to bite off and swallow up sounds before they could blend with the general noise.

"Everything is ready, have some, please," Tsvetukhin said.

"Have we troubled you a great deal by asking this
favor?" Lisa asked suddenly.

She turned her back to the window, and now she
could get a good view of Tsvetukhin in his dazzling
white shirt, and a leather belt as broad as his palm,
with a patterned buckle and watch pocket. She seemed
to see again the shining trinket with the inscription:
"Stick it, Vityusha, stick it!" and she smiled.

"You're laughing?" Tsvetukhin exclaimed in alarm.
"I must have seemed insincere to you, is that it?"

"It looks as though you hadn't refused us . . . and
yet, perhaps you need not do anything. That's true,
isn't it?"

"You're mistaken, I assure you! Pastukhov can be
much more useful in this case. It's his field."

"Don't be angry," Lisa said, moving toward him.
"May I ask you something else?"

"Why, of course, Lisa."

"Promise me to do all you can to persuade Pastukhov to help Kirill. I know he offended you that
time at the theater. He behaved very badly, terribly.
But he isn't like that at all—no, not at all."

Tsvetukhin took her hand, led her to the table,
and, making her sit down, took his place beside her.
"Are you suffering a great deal on his account?" he
asked, leaning forward and looking into her eyes.

She spread the melting ice cream in the saucer. As
she did so, a sudden vivid memory returned to her of

a white sateen school shirt with brass buttons, tightly belted—schoolboy fashion, and a splash of light on the belt buckle. Then again she was reminded of the watch charm with "Stick it, Vityusha, stick it!" and she glanced at the belt with the watch pocket.

"Is he your fiancé?" Egor Pavlovich asked.

"Who?" she returned quickly. "I have never called him that." Blushing suddenly, she moved slightly away from Tsvetukhin. "I have quite a different fiancé," she blurted out with a short laugh.

"You don't say so? Who can it be? Is it a secret?"

"He's an athlete."

"An athlete? What does he do?—wrestle at the circus? Or is he an acrobat? Or a trick rider? You must be joking."

"Why should I be joking?"

"But it all sounds so queer! What's his name?"

"Shubnikov."

"Shubnikov . . . " Egor Pavlovich repeated. "Shubnikov . . . But wait . . . Isn't that the draper?"

"Yes."

"Good Lord!"

He jumped up, went over to the window, then came back and stood awhile by Lisa, looking into her face, which was bent over her ice cream, and then asked: "Matchmaking's going on—is that it?"

She said nothing. He sat down beside her again, ruffling his hair and coughing a short, spasmodic cough, as though punctuating his own thoughts.

"Look here, Lisa: I think I'm beginning to understand. It's a fairly common fate for a young girl—to love one man and marry another, isn't it? But you shouldn't do that. You mustn't do that. You mustn't go against yourself, it will tell on you afterward. It will tell on you all your life. Better to shoulder something now, something hard and risky, to endure any ordeal, than to be always under constraint, to repent endlessly, when it's all too late. You're being driven into this marriage, aren't you?"

"I don't know," she said. "It's called something different."

"Yes, it's called—everything's being done for your own good. I'm right, am I not? The highly respected Merkuri Avdeyevich is doing his best for the happiness

of his child. That's the line, isn't it? Oh"—he gave a bitter little laugh—"Oh, how plainly I can see your parent
in the role of the builder of his darling daughter's
happiness. Unhappiness—the greatest unhappiness!" he
cried, seizing Lisa's hand in both of his. "Consider, my
dear girl! This mustn't happen."

"It won't happen, either," Lisa said, freeing her hand,
"if you help Kirill. Help him, do help him!"

And, resting her elbows on the table, she covered
her face with her hands.

"I give you my word," Tsvetukhin said, sincerely
and with a touch of exaltation. "I give you my word
that Pastukhov and I will do everything in our power.
But you must give me your word that you won't
throw away your life so foolishly."

She smoothed her hair and straightened herself. "You
say one ought not to go against one's self. Does that
mean one may go against one's father?"

"And what help would Kirill be to you?" was
Tsvetukhin's very sober question.

He stood up once more and paced the room in silence, glanced into his open book, turned over a few
leaves, and shrugged his shoulders.

"Kirill is still only a child, a schoolboy. You noticed
how jealous he was of me with you?" Tsvetukhin said,
laughing.

Lisa hung her head.

"Do you want me to tell you what sort of a fellow
Shubnikov is? He's a spoiled merchant's son, a lover
of—"

"No, no, don't tell me," said Lisa, "I don't know him
and I don't want to know him."

The actor turned another page. "Are you fond of
verse?"

She did not reply.

In a rich, silken voice, leaning against the window
frame, he recited:

> "*To see form in the formless eddy of feeling,*
> *That in the pallid glow of art*
> *Men might know life's despoiling fire. . .*"

"Good, isn't it?" he asked, coming up to her soundlessly.

"I'm afraid of verses," she said.

"Why?"

"I don't understand them and . . . I . . . love them."

He studied her closely. "You know what?" he said at last, evidently satisfied with his examination and arriving at the conclusion he needed. "Will you have me as an ally against your father?"

She was afraid to raise her head.

"If you refuse to marry Shubnikov, you will have to leave home. I want you to have my support. I'll arrange everything for you."

She stood up and, without looking at him, replied: "That would mean going not only against my father but against myself as well."

"Thank you! Thank you very much!" he exclaimed, lighthearted and irresponsible, with the loud assured laughter that good actors are able to command. He stirred the melted ice cream in the saucer and sighed inconsolably: "Poor neglected ices, poor ices!"

"I have to be going," Lisa said.

"Wait a little, perhaps Vera Nikandrovna will come back. Why are you in such a hurry, Lisa?"

"I must go. Thank you for your promise. Good-by."

She gave him her hand and then hastily freed it, almost tearing it away.

For the third time she was leaving, escaping from Tsvetukhin. Out in the yard the heat scorched her. Burning, motionless, heavy with a presentiment of coming change, the relentless heat was stifling her.

CHAPTER

· 25 ·

THE FURNITURE had long since been restored, the bookcase and couch were crated, the whole suite had to be sent off to St. Petersburg, and still Pastukhov could not stir. He had to finish a new play. The Moscow theater, with the aid of the telegraph, warned him, now kindly, now despairingly, even threateningly, not to take so long over the job, and he himself was afraid that it would be nearly autumn before he finished. But two or three of his characters still failed to guess how to extricate themselves from the game forced upon them by their author, and so he was dispiritedly trying to fit some of his acquaintances on them in an attempt to unravel the awkward tangle.

He realized that he had stayed too long in this town of gingham, retired generals, and flour kings. But he knew, too, that once he had moved his father's study suite out of the house, there would be no more reason for him to come back here under the roof that had sheltered him in childhood.

Seated at the desk which still smelled faintly of polish, in front of the open window, screened by a limp, faintly breathing muslin curtain, he analyzed the scents that had reached him from the neighboring garden, as he had sat here earlier, scribbling on paper and turning the leaves of books. He remembered the cloying sweetness of the white acacia, an old tree that every spring tormented a whole block of the town

with its intoxicating fragrance. The honeyed, earthy
breath of the peonies, great bunches of which migrated
to his desk and window sill from the cool flower beds.
The brown vinegary-cinnamon smell of the metiolas,
reminding one in the evenings of the open doors of the
better-class grocers. The delicately virginal aroma of
mignonette, like the distant breath of mowing scarcely
begun. All this had come and gone, and now that the
sun was low, the heavy narcotic smell of tobacco flowers, titillating the nostrils with the shamelessness of
spirits, burst in at the window.

Yes, before it gave way to the first chilly evenings,
August tormented the earth with its fruitful languor,
and all living things hastened to gather while they
might at that time of inexhaustible abundance, a store
of delight for the future.

Pastukhov's nostrils dilated as he inhaled the sultry
perfume of the gardens and thought of how he would
go away as soon as the season of scentless flowers,
dahlias and asters, would be well begun; and whether
he should graft some naïve characteristics of Tsvetukhin's onto a person in the play; and that although
Balzac wrote poorly, he understood like no one else
the nature of art, which is in the quality of the effect
of the artist's work and not in the quality of the
making of the work itself; and he was also thinking
that imagination is, of course, a god, but like every
other divinity it is arbitrary, though it rests on the
foundations of actual experience; that there exists a
brother of imagination that represents a much higher
gift of the mind—and this is foresight, possessed only
by analytical characters. Imagination sees things in a
circle, everything is accessible to it without selection,
and therefore it can foresee nothing; foresight passes
straight from cause to effect, and the future for it is
only the consequence of the present. As he scrutinized
with his mind's eye the thronging medley of people
out of real life, out of the unfinished play, out of the
book lying open on the table, Pastukhov mused—perhaps among our contemporaries who lack imagination
there are prophets who see clearly even now the future
of man, of nations and the whole earth. One may picture to oneself in the imagination any form of the
future, but foresight alone has the gift of determining

the form that will inevitably materialize. Yet, though imagination is helpless compared to foresight, it is sweeter. Imagination scents all the fragrances of the world, logic—only the strongest.

So Pastukhov sat and dreamed, writing his play or turning the pages of Balzac. And everything taken together was enjoyment. This was how he had once pictured his maturer years—in a similar fluency of fleshly sensations and the free impact of thoughts. It might be that someday the town from which he was so soon to depart, the town of flour merchants, would become a town of universities, and he—a member of the Academy by that time—would return to recall the love language of the acacias, mignonette, and tobacco flowers at eventide, and once more thoughts would crowd in upon him in a whirl, as they did now, thoughts of the hopes of youth, of Moscow students' rounds of the cabbies' pull-ups, of the first throbbing of the heart in the wings of the theater, of the gratification of vanity after the public had called for the author, of everything at once—except death. No, no, Pastukhov was not going to think of death. Could death exist in art?

Pastukhov rubbed his hot face with his palms as though washing away uninvited care, and then wrote down in a little red book the places he had underlined in Balzac, where the author seemed to echo his own convictions. "The aim of art does not lie in imitating nature but in expressing it. You are not a mere wretched copyist but a poet! . . . Otherwise the sculptor might accomplish his work by making a plaster cast of a woman." "Superfluous knowledge, like ignorance, leads to negation. . . ."

Suddenly he began to ponder on superfluous knowledge. Need one really know how art was produced? Did Balzac know this? Was it not the secret of his triumph that he had breathed life into his two thousand personages without comprehending the laws by which he created them? Was it, after all, vain to struggle in search of the laws of art? They did not exist; they were embodied in action. If art was effective, then it was legitimate. If it was dead to perception, then what law could animate it?

This absorbing duologue with himself was interrupted in a very strange manner: the shadow of a head slid across the window curtain. A very tall man must have passed through the yard, for the window was high. Alert, Pastukhov heard the jingle of spurs; then the doorbell gave a disapproving jangle. He went to open the door.

From the doorstep a swarthy gendarme, smelling of burned sealing wax as though melting in the heat, scrutinized him. At every curve or bend in his towering form, powerful bones demanded an outlet. He saluted, inquired who occupied the house, and handed Pastukhov a notice which he fished out with a hook-like finger from his cuff.

The headquarters of the Gendarme Police Force required the presence of Alexander Vladimirovich Pastukhov, gentleman, as a witness today. He blinked at his somber visitant and voiced in a tactful tone his natural doubts.

"Isn't there some mistake about this, my lad?"

It appeared there was no mistake.

"But what business am I wanted for?"

To that the gendarme vouchsafed no reply.

"There's surely some mistake about it, my boy; today's Sunday, a holiday, the offices are all closed."

"Not at all," the messenger replied stoutly. "Them as sent for you are open."

"So what do you propose to do? . . . Take me through the streets?" Pastukhov went on, covering his discomfiture with a sneer.

"Not at all. Kindly sign this receipt and come yourself."

Alexander Pastukhov signed and, left alone, sat down cautiously, as though on a forbidden spot, on the old humped chest in the hall. His face was distorted with fastidious disgust. The smell of burnt sealing wax still hung about the place. He jumped up, went to the washbasin, cleared his throat, and spat. Then turning to the door, which had not yet been locked after the gendarme, he spat at it.

"Damn you, you stinking singed devil!"

He put on his blue jacket, looked in the glass, and changed the dark blue for a light buff—a color with more refinement and independence in it. Then he filled his cigarette case, but suddenly threw it down on the table and got out an unopened tin all in coats-of-arms, medals, and monograms; it held foreign cigarettes. He picked up his cane, went to the door, spat again, and turned back into the room. In front of the mirror he tipped a scent bottle several times, pressing the neck against the lapels of his jacket. Then his glance fell on his little notebook, and he read the last entry: "Superfluous knowledge leads, like ignorance, to negation."

"It's all very well for you, you Balzacs!" he said aloud, and swept the book into the drawer.

Tearing off a quarter-sheet of paper, he wrote in a large, dashing hand: "Dear Egor, if I should suddenly disappear altogether, damn it, you must know that I was sent for. . . ." His hand paused a moment, then added in a heavier writing: "by the secret police." He left the note in the middle of the table, made a gesture of despair at his manuscript staring up at him with its various corners turned down, its blots and drawings, and, feeling a tickling in his throat, went out.

He walked down the street proudly, with graceful bearing, swinging his cane. No one would have thought to look at him that he saw nothing of what was going on around him, and was only struggling with the haunting idea: supposing I do disappear! Alexander Pastukhov would suddenly drop out of existence!—and never be heard of again. Well, perhaps he might not disappear from the face of the earth, but neither did the prisoners of Chillon or the Bastille—they had not moved to other planets. The earth had become a curse to them, for they had been fettered to it. But who ever heard of them again? Did our own Houses of the Dead, as Dostoevsky called them, yield up their secrets more willingly than Chillon? Alexander Pastukhov knew only too well the kingdom in which he lived. Alexander Pastukhov would be done for. Here he was marching down the street, swinging his cane jauntily, while his heart reiterated: you're done for, you're done for! Here he was taking the gutter at a bound, while the voice in his ears repeated: whether you jump or you don't—you're done for just the same. . . .

"Good Lord!—when all's said and done, this is sheer nonsense!" he muttered indignantly, yet at the same moment the objection started up of itself: "That's just it, that's the worst of it—that you'll be done for, all because of a piece of sheer nonsense!"

It was an exhausting skirmish with an immobile enemy of superior strength, and, worn out with it, he reached at last the house to which he had been called. He hesitated at the door, experiencing the feeling that some have at Epiphany, when, according to ancient custom, a dip in the ice hole in the river is taken. The parallel flashed through his mind, but he thought he could have plunged with pleasure into the ice hole— where at least there were peasants on the bank to pull you out with their long belts; here—no one would throw a straw to a drowning man.

He pushed open the door with as much displeased determination as though he had expected to find a be-medaled doorman waiting to throw it open for him. He was led at once through a corridor smelling strongly of burnt sealing wax to the Lieutenant-Colonel's study. Pastukhov, elegant, pleasant, hesitated on the threshold with an inquiring smile, looking around for a place to leave his hat and stick.

"This way, please," Polotentsev said, hurrying forward. "You must excuse me for troubling you on a Sunday, but as you know . . . er . . ."

"I quite understand, there must be some reason for it . . ." Pastukhov said graciously and rather condescendingly.

"Exactly. Exactly. It's very urgent. I'm very glad to make your acquaintance, though in official circumstances. In others you're rather inaccessible."

"Yes, we're recluses, you see."

Two officials in starched white jackets got up from their places at the desk and nodded stiffly. Polotentsev introduced them as the Assistant Prosecutor and an official from the law courts. The name Oznobishin pleased Pastukhov, and he blinked at the young man who was eyeing him with curiosity.

"They happen to be interested in the case, too," the Lieutenant-Colonel explained; then, turning to the Assistant Prosecutor, he added: "We won't be in your way, I hope?"

"Oh, no, on the contrary," the Assistant Prosecutor said significantly, and the official shook his head.

"Do you care to smoke?" Polotentsev asked.

Pastukhov was about to reach for a cigarette, then he gently put aside the Lieutenant-Colonel's hand, and slowly drew from his pocket his own box of cigarettes. Slitting the label that fastened the lid with his nail, he said:

"Try one of mine. The best in the world. A friend of mine from the Ministry of Justice" (here he glanced at the Assistant Prosecutor and the law-court official) "brought them to me the last time he was abroad. Egyptian tobacco, Belgian monopoly. Please do try them."

Polotentsev took a cigarette. The two officials refused, bowing slightly in acknowledgment. The official was obviously imitating everything the Assistant Prosecutor was doing.

As they smoked their fragrant tobacco, Polotentsev talked.

"You've been staying here with us for quite a time, haven't you? Oh, yes, we know all about it. You're writing, eh? What are you going to give us next, I wonder. . . . Ah, a new play! You won't tell us what it's about? No? But it's something enjoyable and lively? Ah, it's hard to say. Yes, of course, before the time. . . . The creative process. A kind of mystery. And you probably find, as it has been said: 'And through the magic crystal he was unable to discern clearly as yet the shape of his novel.' We remember this from our early days. . . ."

Pastukhov caught the glance Oznobishin shot him and said with a delightful smile: "Very apt, very true."

"It's Pushkin's, could it be anything else?"

"The idea is undoubtedly Pushkin's," Pastukhov affirmed.

"Ah, those aren't the words!" the Lieutenant-Colonel exclaimed, apparently delighted with his own perspicacity. "I understand, oh, how well I understand what words mean to the poet. The thought expressed is a . . . But you must excuse us. It's hard to remember everything exactly from school days. Sometimes I would be glad to refresh my memory about one thing and another, and go over it all again, but where would I get the chance? Look at this!"

He indicated ruefully the pile of various colored folders before him and behind him.

"On the other hand, as fate will have it, we are not

engaged so much with form, not with formalistics, with correspondence or envelopes. You shouldn't think that."

"Oh, I don't think anything of the kind," Pastukhov said gaily. "I've just remembered an anecdote about an official who was promoted to the fifth rank. An acquaintance who congratulated him said: 'I envy you, Excellency, imagine what a splendid uniform will envelope you!' And the other retorted: 'It isn't the envelope that matters—but what's inside it.' "

There was dead silence, then they fidgeted, and Oznobishin volunteered in a low voice: "You mean inside it in the sense of pay?"

"Yes, as you very aptly remark—in the sense of pay," Pastukhov replied with a sigh as though he was committed to it.

Then Polotentsev gave a delighted laugh, and repeated the pun.

"And now, if you will permit me, let's get on to the substance," Pastukhov said, joining in the laughter. "I don't want to take up your time. . . ."

"Oh, yes," Polotentsev agreed, still unable to control his laughter, "there's just one question that obliged us to trouble you. . . . Do you mind telling us—what was it that took place between you and this Parabukin?"

"With Parabukin?" Pastukhov repeated in a puzzled tone. "Who's Parabukin? Oh, you mean that tramp or whoever he was—injured on the wharf?"

"That's the fellow! Only you went to the common lodginghouse to see him long before that, didn't you?"

"Good Lord!" Pastukhov exclaimed with an easy gesture of vexation, dismissing the whole thing as a joke. "Why, that was all Egor's nonsense! You know —Tsvetukhin!"

"Yes, I understand, I understand perfectly—the idea was to study types, to search for material that might come in useful for future masterpieces. It must have been no less interesting to you than to the actor. But just imagine, leaflets of a very radical"—here Polotentsev raised his forefinger high above his bald head —"a very radical trend, you know, were distributed among persons of this type on the riverbanks."

"And you want to pin the leaflets on to me, is that it?" Pastukhov asked simply.

"Pin the leaflets on to you?" the Lieutenant-Colonel

laughed again. "You have a funny way of putting things! What sort of an idea have you of our, so to speak, uniform envelopes?"

"I'm not interested in envelopes," Pastukhov replied with a polite laugh, falling into his tone. "It's what's inside the envelope that matters."

"Yes, I see," Polotentsev said, still indulging his sense of humor. "You think that everything's done as easily as winking here, don't you? Allow me to tell you you're wrong. We aren't going to pin a single line on you, and haven't pinned any yet—we only want you to throw some light on the affair."

"On what exactly?"

"Well, for instance, can you confirm the fact that when you invited Parabukin to your acquaintance's house—to the actor who is Tsvetukhin's friend—on an occasion when Ragozin was also present, the revolutionary leaflets were handed over to Parabukin?"

Pastukhov slowly mopped his face with his handkerchief: it felt swollen and very large all of a sudden. Then he said somberly: "I'll tell you this much, Lieutenant-Colonel: you're asking me the kind of questions that for all I know may decide the fate of others and my own, too. So I am going to ask you to use official language and interrogate me . . . in the way prescribed by law."

"Tut, tut, it seems you're a regular formalist, after all!" Polotentsev protested in a disappointed tone.

"And furthermore, to avoid misunderstandings," Pastukhov continued obstinately, almost dully, "I may as well tell you that I'm hearing Ragozin's name for the first time in my life from you, and I also want to tell you that Mefody did hand something to Parabukin, and that was—a glass of vodka, forty degrees, which he drank to his health."

"Now why are you getting angry, Alexander Vladimirovich?" the Lieutenant-Colonel said in an almost offended tone. "As a matter of fact, you've answered the question. And nothing else is required of you, I can assure you."

He turned to the officials. The Assistant Prosecutor had not uttered a word, but sat there, straight and stiff like a sharpened piece of chalk, as though fearful of wrinkling his snow-white jacket. Then Oznobishin's kangaroo-like body bent forward to the Lieutenant-Colonel, and very cautiously, but with a gloating sparkle in his sharp blue eyes, he said:

"I am not really asking any question, Lieutenant-Colonel, but if you kindly allow me to remind you of it—evidence was given to meetings that took place between Mr. Pastukhov and Kirill Izvekov."

The rather effeminate fingers trembled slightly, and to disguise it, he chafed his wrists, as though it was not a hot day in high summer. The Assistant Prosecutor watched out of the corner of his eye in silence.

"May I consider this question as addressed to me?" Pastukhov demanded, glancing from Oznobishin to the Lieutenant-Colonel. "I have met Izvekov and I have even heard that he has been arrested. But the meetings with him were very brief, I could hardly call him even an acquaintance, and I was astonished to hear of his arrest because he is still only a boy."

"Yes, indeed, how very . . ." and Polotentsev drew in his breath with a pained look. "You know Parabukin, and you've met this boy—a bad boy—I must say he is. . . . How very complicated this mix-up turns out to be. . . . No, not for you, but for the case. And for us, too, I would say. And, believe me, least of all I wanted to trouble you. But . . . you intend staying some time in your old home, don't you?"

"No, I'm going away soon to St. Petersburg."

"You don't say so! St. Petersburg? Well, you must excuse us for breaking up your Sunday. Just sign this form, will you, please, and that will be all for the present."

Polotentsev drew out by its corner an oblong form from his writing case and passed it across the desk. Pastukhov skimmed the printed contents and looked up sharply: it was an undertaking not to leave the town without permission.

"Sign here below," the Lieutenant-Colonel said, half rising and pointing delicately with the long white nail of his little finger. "Where it says—name, father's Christian name, rank in society . . . and what else?"

Pastukhov looked at him, his reddened eyelids blinking. "So you actually do suspect me of being mixed up in an affair I know nothing about?" he asked quietly.

"Oh, really, Alexander Vladimirovich! This is all

purely a matter of form, it simply has to be done for the sake of routine. Until we can unravel this tangled skein."

"But I can protest, can't I? To whom must I address my application? To you, perhaps?"

With this he turned to the Assistant Prosecutor, who, without altering his pose in the slightest, opened his mouth a second, and brought his vocal cords into action.

"In all matters concerning the mode of restraint, applications must be addressed to His Excellency the Prosecutor of Law Courts," he chanted in a voice unexpectedly tuneful.

Pastukhov signed the paper, then got up and bowed with a touch of condescension. It suggested that he had thought he was dealing with gentlemen and had found himself mistaken.

"I may go now, I suppose? It has been a rare pleasure to meet you," he said, showing his dull, sound teeth in a lifeless grin.

He still heard the Lieutenant-Colonel make the motions of getting up from his place at the desk to go and see him out, saying in a patronizingly playful tone: "And all the time I feel sure that you are taking mental notes of us and one of these days you'll show us up in some comedy of yours."

But Pastukhov left the room in silence, hastened down the corridor holding a handkerchief to his nose to keep out the burnt sealing-wax smell, and rushed out into the street.

Someone was to blame for what had happened, but who he could not say with any degree of certainty. He was overcome by a feeling of dejection, and fury wrestled with melancholy in his heart.

The dreary, heat-stricken town choked him like a heavy yoke. Everything around him was petty, despairing. The little gardens with the neglected, dusty-gray brooms of acacias, the sweet Williams in the trampled flower beds that smelled of the ink of postmarks, the hot cobblestones, and the mean jangle of streetcar bells—heavens, how hopeless it all was! Women in their Sunday clothes, with babies in their arms and trains of them clinging to their skirts, waddled slowly along the streets, lingering before the vendors of sunflower seeds or crossing themselves in front of the empty porches of the churches. For how many more Sundays was he doomed to see the same wretched processions? The weatherworn signboard "Katyk and Co.: Cigarettes" on the corner house; beneath it cab horses with pointed straw hats with slits for the ears, pestered by flies, weary, sun-dazed cabbies on the steps of their vehicles, heaps of fresh horse manure, and the policeman with two fingers thrust into the breast of his soiled uniform. Oh, this motionless vacuum! Was it any easier to stand than the Bastille?—and in what way?

He could hardly drag himself home.

As he entered the yard, he saw a woman standing on the steps of the house, pulling the bell in a rather hesitating manner.

"There's no one at home," he told her curtly.

She glanced around and then hastened down the steps, a rather short woman with squarish, masculine shoulders, wearing a Shantung dress with huge buttons, and hatless.

"You don't remember me?" she asked in some agitation but with that steady outward leisureliness that teachers cultivate.

He had a good memory for faces, and besides, too much of the woman's nature had been inherited by her son, Kirill, for Pastukhov to fail to recognize her, but still he gave the face with its pockmarks on the brow an attentive scrutiny, turned away, stared with narrowed eyes in an apparent effort of memory, and shook his head—no, he did not remember her.

"I am Kirill Izvekov's mother. You remember, he introduced us at the fairground last Easter?"

"Please forgive me," he said as though failing to seize upon anything in his elusive memories. "What brings you here to me?"

"But you know Kirill, don't you?"

"Kirill?"

"Yes, the Technical School boy, rather short, dark, and just getting a mustache. Kirill—"

"With a mustache," Pastukhov repeated, turning away again.

"I wouldn't have ventured to trouble you if it hadn't been for your great friend Tsvetukhin. I've come straight from him. He gave me great hopes of you. But you don't seem to remember Kirill," Vera Nikandrovna added in a meek, frightened way.

"Perhaps you'll explain—briefly?"

"Of course. I must ask you to listen to what I have to say: my son was arrested on a quite . . . Well, to cut a long story short, they accidentally found some leaflets in his room. I am trying to get him out on bail, but my request alone will have no effect, as you may suppose. If you cared to . . . If you found it possible to support me . . . as you are so well known—"

"Just a moment," Pastukhov interrupted her, "this is Tsvetukhin's idea, is it? I mean about me?"

"Oh, yes, he said that he would help me with pleasure, too, only that you had far more influence than he has, and he is undoubtedly right."

"What an inventor!" Pastukhov exclaimed admiringly, laughing suddenly in spite of his bad mood, and wiping his perspiring face. "A real inventor! Devil take him and his inventions . . . pardon me!"

He became suddenly serious and pompous.

"You see . . . I remember your son, of course."

"Do you? Oh, thank you, I was sure you would!" Vera Nikandrovna exclaimed, flushing.

"One moment. I do remember him, but that's nothing. I only know that he was a boy. But what kind of a boy? . . . Perhaps he was bad? . . . How do I know? You must excuse me. And that isn't the point. I can't be of any use to your son for the simple reason that I myself am involved in a political affair. And, possibly, on the same charge as your own son. That inventor Tsvetukhin knows nothing about this. And I must ask you to forget it. We're standing here talking, and for all I know, we may be watched. Well, good-by." He shook hands, surprised to find her bony fingers so cold, her face drained of color.

She lowered her eyes and said in an apologetic tone: "Please forgive me," and went toward the gate. But before she had taken very few steps, she turned and asked: "If you are accused of the same thing as Kirill, then perhaps you can tell me what the whole unfortunate case is about? For my ear alone . . . as his mother."

He went up to her and in a totally different voice,

full of resignation and sorrow, said: "If your son is as ignorant of it as I am, I may congratulate you." He felt an impulse to kiss her hand, but only pressed her cold fingers once more.

When he was back in the house again, he strove to understand what he had wanted to convey in his last sentence, but his thoughts were too scattered. He washed and changed his jacket. His glance fell on the note he had left on the table; he tore it up into narrow strips and put a match to them. The flame spurted and fell, furrowed with glowing pink the edge of the paper, which first charred and then turned to blue ashes. Pastukhov puffed on them and they dissolved in the air.

Devil only knew what all this was! He had just been enjoying a reverie at the same desk. He had been praising fantasy. Oh, yes, he could imagine at will an innocent man, persecuted by blind law. But could he ever imagine that the next minute he himself would be subjected to persecution? Was Kirill Izvekov in any better position? Was he perhaps of that species of person capable of foreseeing the future? Could that boy have known even then that the way to the barricades led through prison? And how very far wrong his own imagination had been when he had pictured Kirill as a philistine, a draftsman at railway offices, when it seemed the boy had been dreaming of remaking the world! A bad boy? Perhaps all his, Pastukhov's conceptions of people, were wrong, as wrong as his judgment of Kirill. Perhaps Pastukhov was, after all, a dull-witted, self-opinionated fool with no ability whatsoever. Perhaps Pastukhov was mistaken in his friend Tsvetukhin, too.

Suddenly feeling the need for friendly sympathy, Pastukhov realized that he must tell the whole story to Tsvetukhin.

Twilight was falling, the heat was abating, the refreshing scent of tobacco flowers pervaded parts of the boulevard, and the couples were starting for their stroll in the Limes. The yard of the hotel was watered from a rusty-looking hose which was dragged across asphalted paths, black with water. There was a pleasant smell of moist, warm earth and watered lawns.

In the alley which Tsvetukhin's windows faced, Pastukhov heard a violin. Thin and fine and innocent came the strains of Neruda's cradlesong. Glancing at the open window, Pastukhov saw Tsvetukhin standing with his back to the window facing the dark room. He was swaying slightly as he drew the bow across the strings with an effort. He played like a beginner with the stress on the middle of the bow and with but a poor legato.

"A wooden bow on a leather fiddle—you know what kind of music that makes?" said Pastukhov at the window.

Tsvetukhin broke off his playing at once, slipped the fiddle into its case, and, hiding his embarrassment, called out loudly: "Oh, come along in, do! I've been waiting all day for you."

They sat down on the couch without lighting the lamp, so that only the pale glimmer of face and hands was visible, and Tsvetukhin asked at once if Izvekova had been to see Pastukhov and what he had promised her.

"What was I supposed to promise her?"

"I gave Lisa my word that you and I would help Kirill," Tsvetukhin told him.

"Who is Lisa? That nice-looking young thing? Your admirer? Really, you're the limit, Egor. As long as you only invent paper airplanes and scrape a fiddle it doesn't matter a hang. But when it comes to doing favors for your feminine admirers! It's contrary to the nature of the actor and the admirers: you're born to receive and they to give."

"I'm not joking, Alexander."

"I can assure you, my dear fellow, that I'm very far from joking myself."

"But it isn't my admirer who needs help—it's a very fine young fellow. And it's within your power to help him. In fact, it's your duty as a citizen, if you like to put it that way. And then—it's in keeping with the tradition. . . ."

"Aha, so you've hit on that, have you, at last? The tradition of the Russian social conscience, eh? Leo Tolstoy and the famine. Korolenko at the Multan trial. Is that it? You want me to show a chivalrous spirit? Why? For the sake of self-respect? So that I would be able to respect myself? No? So that others would respect me? Yes? But the point is that in the

first place I fall a long way short of Korolenko, let
alone Tolstoy. You think I don't understand this? And,
in the second place, this isn't 1905. The time has gone
by, my boy. My chivalrous intentions, my capacity
for sacrifice, or, if you like it better, my heroic qualities
would hardly be noticed by the local paper. Think of
it: Pastukhov—the social conscience! About as effective as a fly buzzing! You swipe at it and send it into
a saucer with flycatcher stuff on it, and that's all."

"That's a bit farfetched, isn't it?" Tsvetukhin said
in surprise. "And were you a hero in 1905?"

"Heroes weren't needed then: your Kirill could have
distributed revolutionary leaflets in the streets as easily
as advertisements."

"But look here! A man may help for other reasons,
not merely as a gesture or for the sake of pleasing
himself."

"What do you want from me? That I should go
around the dungeons consoling people in their grief
and sorrow?"

"But the whole thing is much simpler than that.
Neither consolation nor heroism is required of you—
all you have to do is go to the Prosecutor, nothing
more."

"What for?"

"To help."

"Help whom?"

"Whom! Kirill, of course."

"My dear chap, I'd better try and help myself
first of all, let alone Kirill," Pastukhov said. He got
up heavily and, closing the window tightly, took up
his position with his back to it and asked: "You
haven't been invited to the secret police yet, then?"

"What are you trying to say? Are you going out of
your mind?"

"This is what I'm trying to say. . . ." Pastukhov sat
down again, laid his hand on Tsvetukhin's knee and
held it there until he had told all that had happened
to him.

The twilight was so thick now that their faces were
scarcely distinguishable, and the objects in the room
merged into something mysterious and black that
seemed to absorb every word and waited tensely,
ready to join in the conversation at any moment. In

the yard a bough with little leaves hung motionless, picked out of darkness by the light of a neighboring window and poised in the air, seemingly unattached to any tree. Snatches of music played by the brass band came from the Limes, the echo of hoofs on asphalt sounded on the roof, emphasizing the silence.

"Yes," said Tsvetukhin heavily, after a long silence. "If I didn't feel you close to me like this, I'd think it was something I was listening to in a dream."

"Somebody's been spreading rumors about us, Egor," Pastukhov said.

"But who is it? Who could it be?"

"We don't know what that tramp Parabukin has been saying about us, we don't know how that bad boy is behaving, and we don't know who Ragozin is. We know nothing. We're just silly little pawns, Egor."

"Don't say that. I'm sure everything will be cleared up. You and I will clear it up, Alexander. And then they'll come to their senses."

"Who will? Who are they?"

"Well, they . . . those who were tormenting you today."

"No. I can't imagine that they will come to their senses. That's as unnatural as"—Pastukhov searched for a word—"as a headache to a woodpecker."

"What are you intending to do?"

"I intend to lie down on this couch and have a nap. Give me that cushion. . . . I'm so worn out, my dear fellow, that I'd like to resign myself to my fate, like a woman."

The roof was echoing the approaching clatter of hoofs, and suddenly, out of the darkness that enveloped the town, came the cabby's warning shout, distinct and startling: "Hey, look out!"

And, as though in response, the band in the Limes struck up a military march.

plicity and straightforwardness appealed to him and he
began to confide his troubles to him.

"Sorrow is an adornment of man," the bell ringer
consoled him. "And our life here below is so arranged
that the bad and the good, the profits and the losses,
always balance, and sometimes, like sisters, go arm in
arm. Now, what would you say to a story like this? I
was bad with my stomach trouble in those days. It was
in Kazan, and I was in the clinic there. They cut me
open, made some experimental conduits for the passage of food, and, I can tell you, they thought I'd never
get over it. The students said to me, looks like a bad
case of 'perish-tonight-is.' And it was true, I nearly
did perish that night. My life was hanging by a thread.
But the doctors found that the experiments at making
conduits in and out of me had come off very well.
And sure enough, I stood it till now. It wasn't about
myself I was going to tell you, though. That time it so
happened that my neighbor in the ward, like you there
might be, was a weak, sickly looking man, who kept
complaining that they didn't bring the specialist to see
him. I tried to quiet him. I said to him: 'Your conduits
are just natural ones, all they should be, and you
aren't of any curiosity to a big specialist. Rest yourself,'
I said, 'and you'll get your health and strength back
and they'll discharge you.' And he got mad with me:
'We'll see yet,' he said, 'which of us is the bigger
curiosity—you or me. And what do you think! He got
what he wanted. As soon as the specialist had examined him, he was taken into a separate ward and
given a bath and shave and haircut. They gave him
two pillows and a warm blanket to cover him, and he
had proper food. The stuff they put into that fellow,
brother! He had cold food and hot food, meat and
Lord knows what. I happened to meet him in the corridor once—he didn't even want to look at me. I
could see he'd got as sleek and well-fed as a choir-
master. I was afraid to go up to him. And then we
heard all about it: the professor, you see, had found
out his heart was on the right side. Well, that fellow
was in clover from that minute: they gave him clothes
and boots for nothing, soap as well, and tobacco, as
much sugar as he wanted in his tea, and actually paid
him money in the bargain. Now, what would you say

to that? And in return for all that he only had to
let the medical students listen to his heart and tap him
here and there every morning—that was his job from
then on. He did well, I can tell you. Then they started
to take him about from one town to another—from
Kazan to Moscow, and from there to Kharkov, listening and tapping him wherever he went. He was like a
gentleman by that time, he would not even turn around
for them, the students had to move around him. I heard
afterward that somewhere abroad they paid a big
price for him: they hadn't another such as him and
naturally they coveted him—they didn't want to lag
behind. There you are, a man who was a destitute
orphan, as you might say, and look where he got to!
And I'm looking at you and thinking: who knows,
when all's said and done, which of us is the greatest
curiosity for the medical profession? And as for the
turn our life may take—you won't find anything about
that in the Lives of the Saints."

"You've got the gift of the gab, I'll grant you that,"
Parabukin chuckled. But after each of the stories he
heard, he lay for hours thinking and wondering if he
might expect a turn in his life, the dreadful muddle
of which he contemplated with a sober and discerning
eye now on his sickbed.

One morning, while the plates were clattering in
every corner, the patients in Parabukin's ward were
called out for examination and he was left alone. This
was all done in haste and caused some excitement
because it upset the hospital routine well known to
everyone. A few minutes later the glass door of the
ward was curtained with a sheet, and a chair was
substituted for the wooden stool at Parabukin's bedside. Another minute passed and a strange doctor, whom
Parabukin had never seen, came in. His head was
shaven; he wore gold-rimmed glasses; the clean white
hospital coat thrown over his shoulders was obviously
not his size. He was accompanied by a huge, heavily
mustached man, who paused in the doorway and
carefully covered all the chinks with the sheet.

As the doctor sat down by the cot, the white coat
slipped from his shoulders, and Parabukin saw the
gendarme's uniform.

Parabukin knew the ranks in the gendarme police

from the days when he had worked on the railway.
Lieutenant-Colonels traveled first class—they were the
tiptop people. They behaved like the princes of their
own exclusive domain within the railway kingdom isolated from the greater world. Despising and fearing
them, the railway officials, great and small, missed no
opportunity of demonstrating the superiority of their
profession over those ogres of the railway stations.
Train conductors turned their backs on noncommissioned gendarme officers, section superintendents pretended not to notice majors, railway directors and
general managers responded coldly and reluctantly to
gendarme colonels' greetings.

Face to face with Polotentsev, newly arisen out of a
doctor's white coat, Parabukin immediately reverted to
his old position as ticket collector on the express. It
was exactly as though he had slid back the door of a
first-class carriage and discovered the formidable oc-
cupant. He was quite prepared to hear a stern repri-
mand for the long-forgotten faults that had brought
him from the railway to the rooming house.

He raised himself a little, staring dumbstruck at
the Lieutenant-Colonel. Parabukin had lost a lot of
flesh these days, and his shock of hair and beard had
grown.

"Keep lying down," Polotentsev ordered. "In consideration of your illness I have come in person to take
down your evidence."

The things Parabukin subsequently heard astonished
him even more than the gendarme's sudden appearance.
The Lieutenant-Colonel was not in the least interested,
he found, in his past and his career on the railway. He
wanted to know the reason why Tsvetukhin and
Pastukhov had visited Tikhon Parabukin at the rooming house and the purpose for which they had then
gone to Mefody's home.

Hardly had the interrogation commenced, than the
recollection of the strange visitors' inexplicable appearance at Easter assumed brilliant colors in Tikhon's
eyes. It was perfectly clear to him now that the
visitors had not come for nothing, in any case not with
the intentions they announced. They had pretended
they were looking for people who were notable in the
rooming house and at the wharves, and Tikhon re-

membered that Pastukhov had called them "lions."
(A sudden light broke on Tikhon: "So these were the
kind of lions you wanted!") This was the root of the
matter, and since Parabukin had nothing to hide, he
immediately made up his mind to hide at all costs this
intriguing conversation about the lions. Was he, an old
railwayman, going to do a contemptible gendarme a
good turn!

"I can't remember a thing about it, Your Honor,"
he repeated. "I'd had a drop of vodka."

"Yes, but you weren't dead drunk, were you? You
were still wide awake?"

"That's true, I was still wide awake. But I was in the
middle of one of what I call my drinking cycles."

"But still—they were trying to persuade you to do
something?"

"Quite right, they were. They were talking me
into selling them my clothes for stage costumes. Olga
Ivanovna, that's my wife, took them a lot of rags to
the theater. She's a rag woman."

"Perhaps they gave you money?"

"Money? No, I can't remember that they did."

"And how did you happen to be in Mefody's house?"

"Excuse me mentioning it, but I went to get something to put me right after the booze. When I'm in the
middle of one of these cycles of mine I sometimes
even beg in the street. So I went to them and they took
pity on me."

"Didn't they demand anything in return?"

"Yes, they did."

"Well, go on, what was it?"

"They gave me a glass of vodka and they demanded
that I should clear out."

"So that's the sort you are," Polotentsev said contemptuously. "Now answer me these questions, without that drunken beating about the bush that you're
so fond of: when you had that accident when you
were hurt on the wharf, how did it happen that
Tsvetukhin was on the spot with you? And why did
he take you to the hospital? What did he do all that
for? What had you done for him?"

"I was unconscious, so I can't tell you."

"You were in another of those cycles of yours, I
suppose?"

"No, I can't say I was. By that time the cycle had, with the help of God, come to an end. But the terrible injury I got to my ribs knocked me out and I can't say I've a clear memory of anything."

"Either you're about the slyest fellow I've ever seen," Polotentsev concluded angrily, getting to his feet and pulling the doctor's white coat over his shoulders, "or you're just a filthy scoundrel!"

"Quite right," Tikhon agreed, assuming an expression of complete idiocy, so that his emaciated, bearded face looked uncommonly wild.

"Now look here," the Lieutenant-Colonel said as he was going out. "When you're better, and there's anything you need, or you fancy a drink, drop in on me at the office. And remember what I asked you about. And find out down at the wharves who was giving out leaflets there. I won't forget you, you may be sure. Understand what I mean?"

"Damn your eyes!" Parabukin thought to himself with triumph when the officer had gone. He felt in an excellent humor. The consciousness that he had fooled that gendarme tickled him immensely. His opinion of himself blossomed out suddenly with youthful, stirring vigor: there must be something in him, after all, if a big pot, nearly a general, such as the whole station platform used to make way for, had to come and see him, Parabukin. His Excellency the Lietuenant-Colonel wouldn't be likely to bother his head coming here about some trifle or other! Tikhon Parabukin was a different matter! Tikhon Parabukin was acquainted with Mr. Pastukhov and Mr. Tsvetukhin. And these gentlemen were no doubt marked out for particular notice by someone still higher up and that was why the gendarmes were after them. Now, very likely the turning point in Tikhon's fortunes would come, his own bright star would rise and shed its light on the new path that lay before him.

He was longing to share his hopes and conjectures with his neighbors in the ward. But they came back in a bad humor to their cots. The bell ringer lay down with his back to his neighbor, huddling up as though in pain, and when Parabukin spoke to him, did not answer.

"Listen, blockhead," Parabukin said, "what are you turning your big ugly mug away from me for? You'll repent it. I've had that stroke of luck you were telling me about a while ago. My heart turns out to be on the right side. D'you hear?"

Without turning around, the bell ringer asked: "Was that a heart doctor came around?"

"Exactly. A heart specialist. A professor," and Parabukin burst out laughing.

"You wait, they'll start washing you in the bath yet," his neighbor retorted spitefully, sending the whole ward into fits of laughing and coughing.

Highly offended, Tikhon turned to the wall. He was certain now that had it been a laughing matter, he would not have been curtained off from curious eyes: the sheets still hung over the door. . . .

That day Annochka brought him some milk jelly, prepared by her mother, and he was more delighted to see his little daughter than ever before. She perched on the edge of the iron cot and he stroked her thin hand with his big knotty fingers, which had now grown so white in idleness, and asked her how her mother and Pavlik and the rooming house were getting on.

"Your mother has a hard time of it with you all," he said bitterly. "I haven't lived the right kind of life, my girl."

"What's the right kind of life like?" Annochka asked. "Mama says that if you didn't take any drink . . ."

"I'm not gong to drink any more," Parabukin informed her with a rueful sigh, after thinking a moment. "The state of my health won't let me drink from now on." He drew the child a little closer to him and smiled. "How would you like it if your father was to be a famous man?"

"What do you mean?" Annochka asked. "Like the actors?"

"Actors, indeed! I mean so as everybody would hear about me."

"Where? Down on the riverside?"

"The riverside? They know me well enough there as it is. I don't care a hang for the riverside."

"Where else, then?" said Annochka, staring out of the window. "Anyhow, you won't ever be like those actors. They're rich."

"That's what you think! Many of them can't afford a

ticket, they walk the tracks, but when I was on the railway, I used to travel on cushions with springs."

"Then maybe you'll go back to work on the railway?"

"You're only a little girl," Parabukin said thoughtfully, "you can't understand."

They sat in silence, then Tikhon took a spoon and moved the pan of milk jelly nearer to Annochka.

"Here, have some of this."

She shook her head and moved further off. He took a spoonful of the stiff jelly and held it out to her.

"Eat it, I'm telling you."

She licked it off the spoon, swallowed it, closed her eyes with satisfaction and moved a little further off.

"I won't eat it. It's for you," she said. "It's sweet." Suddenly she went closer to her father and asked him: "What was it the general came to worry you about?"

"Who's been gabbing to you?"

"The nurse told me. I was waiting in the passage there till they let me come in to you, and she told me."

"Tell your mother how famous I am: generals come to see me now," he said, laughing, pleased with his joke.

Then she whispered in fright: "He wasn't asking you about Kirill, was he? You didn't tell him anything? Kirill's a good boy."

"Your defender," Tikhon said drily, with a condescending nod. "Don't worry, I won't tell on him. Why should I?"

They took leave of each other, as they did each time she came to the hospital, comforted and at peace, and he was left alone with his thoughts—confused, excited, unfamiliar to him. . . .

Before he was quite recovered, he left the hospital one bright summer's day. Everything seemed new and gentle to him—the houses with their few occupants and the shutters closed from the sun, the hot breeze that every now and then raised a low muslin veil of dust from the road. That was the way he had felt long ago in his childhood—with a kind of wonder at each trifle, and rather weak, as though he had been hungry a long time.

By the spirits' shop at the crossroads he saw two ragged men. One was drinking from a bottle of vodka, the other was eyeing it to see how much remained.

"Watch out, or he'll give you short measure," Parabukin remarked cuttingly as he passed.

They took no notice of him. He passed them, trying to reckon how long it was since he had had a drink. It turned out it was over seven weeks. He glanced back. The other man was drinking now, his head tilted back, the silvery stream pouring down his throat. Tikhon stood stock-still. "The cursed bed!" crossed his mind. He felt a sickening emptiness in the loins; a drop of something wouldn't come amiss. He fingered the silver coin in his pocket: once when Olga Ivanovna had forgotten to bring sugar to the hospital, she had given him some money. He went into the spirits shop; his knees trembled when he inhaled the fumes of the place. He bought a dram, went out, knocked the cork out, and, emptying the bottle down his throat, started homeward. But after he had passed two or three houses, he decided to give back the bottle, returned, and, instead of getting the money for it, asked for another dram, casually, as though it was for someone else. Thrusting it into his pocket, he started out again with a lively, springy gait, thinking of how he would soon be sitting in his own corner again, having his tea, and talking over with the wife his new plans for the life that was now to take an entirely different turn. But when he was only a short distance from the rooming house he realized that if he went in with the bottle, Olga Ivanovna might take it away from him. He turned into the gateway of a stone building and drank the vodka leisurely, enjoying the feverish languor that spread through his body. The houses in the street changed places, tantalizingly, and he muttered approvingly in his beard: "There's life in old Parabukin yet!"

When he went in he found Olga Ivanovna sitting with Pavlik in her lap. She gave her husband only one brief glance of alarm and closed her eyes at once.

"So you aren't glad to see me back again?" he asked in a hurt voice. "Don't think because I'm weak I'm going to live on you. I'll find new work. We'll manage to live."

"Better for you never to have left the hospital. You've gone back to your old ways: you can hardly stand on your feet," Olga Ivanovna sobbed, hiding her face in the infant.

"Now there you are! That's life for you," Tikhon exclaimed, suddenly remembering his neighbor in the ward. "You don't believe in me, that's it. But I'm going to change everything, you'll see."

He groped for the bottle in his pocket; there was money, too. Then he turned and went out. Olga Ivanovna wanted to block the way; she shrieked in a cracked voice: "Tisha!" but he ran between the bunks, and the curtain billowed helplessly behind him.

Returning to his haunts on the riverside, he went on a regular booze. There, in his old lair under the warehouse, lying on the matting and sacks, he found the understanding and feeling that he had missed; the men of his old gang took pity on their former ganger, some saying that anyhow, he wasn't long for this world, others comforting him with the idea that every sickness can be cured by vodka.

Bloated, half naked, he roamed the riverside, was seen occasionally on the wharves and loading stages, and once he dropped in at the rooming house with a present for Annochka of two small poppy-seed cakes no bigger than a finger, in his palm. He was in a mild and peaceful mood but was rambling, mostly about some actors with whom he was supposed to be in league and who were in his hands. Suddenly he would try to convince the first man he met that his noble nature would not allow him to die to no purpose; another time he would threaten that he would demand a high price for his hide; finally, he ran away from home, wandered God knew where until the restless, fiery spirit of depression brought him to Pastukhov.

It so happened that Tsvetukhin was at his friend Pastukhov's and they were sitting in the twilight, in conversation, that leisurely, inwardly wary conversation that arises between people of similar experience while they are waiting for the evening to draw in. By this time Tsvetukhin had also been interrogated in the secret police, and his future looked ruined and unattractive to him. His ignorance of the case that was swallowing him up as in a stream of water sucked in by a monstrous dull fish goaded him all the time to puzzle over those who were to blame for the occurrence, and the aimlessness of the search annoyed and exasperated him. His state of mind was approaching Pastukhov's and this, too, annoyed him.

Hearing a knock on the door, Pastukhov went to open it, and recoiled: Parabukin was frightful to look at; the bloated skin was a dull brownish color, the beard and mustache resembled growths of rotten bark, the faded shirt which had lost its color, was rent in strips from neck to hem and through the rents the pale, hairy chest showed. He was barefoot, and his tread when he staggered into the room was inaudible, as though he was supported by air.

"Who are you? Go away," Pastukhov said, stepping back in alarm.

Parabukin advanced, still apparently treading on air, bowing and scraping meaninglessly.

"Go away, I'm telling you! You're drunk!" Pastukhov repeated, raising his voice to hearten himself.

"Tsvetukhin. Mr. Actor. Very glad to . . ." Tikhon said with tolerable distinctness, scrutinizing Egor Pavlovich and advancing on him. "A chance to thank you. For your sympathy. For your f-f-el-low f-feeling. Very glad indeed. 'Thank you, I never expected it'— that's what they say. But I expected it. Just such a noble act as this. The helping hand. A man of your opinions couldn't do otherwise. A fighter for truth and the people. I understand."

"What on earth are you prating about?" Tsvetukhin broke in.

Tikhon was about to take a seat, but Pastukhov pushed back the armchair.

"You have to clear out, do you hear me?" he said very distinctly, blocking the way to the table, toward which Tikhon was moving.

"You've no business here. Go away."

"There's no point in your hiding your secret thoughts," said Tikhon, sobering down. "I understand everything perfectly. And it'll go to my grave with me—don't you worry. The gentleman actor felt for suffering Parabukin. And I'm grateful. He took me to the hospital for treatment because he had the understanding to appreciate me. That's quite right. Tikhon Parabukin is that very 'lion' you needed once."

"We don't need anything," Pastukhov said with rising irritation.

"You're different," Tikhon said, turning to him, "Perhaps you have your own purpose to serve, like your deceased parent in his time. You want to show that you have nothing to do with this. You're a miserly man. An economical person. But Mr. Actor —he has a soul, he's nobility itself."

"But what is it you want? Something to sober you down, is that it?" Tsvetukhin asked. Parabukin bowed, touched the floor boards with his finger tips; suddenly his knees bent under him and he sat down on the floor.

"This is the very devil!" Pastukhov exclaimed.

"If I'm not good enough for an armchair, I can sit on the floor," Tikhon said with a smirk. "At present I'm a person of low appearance, but only at present! That's just it. And when you permit me to be of service once more in your sacred cause, then I'll take my rightful place. And then you won't believe that the very Parabukin before you once sat on your floor."

"Look here, it's time to put an end to this," Pastukhov insisted nervously. "We've understood everything. Say what you want. And that's the end, the end!"

"On the contrary, excuse me: I came to ask how I could be of service."

"We don't need anything from you. Get up, that's quite enough."

"You don't want anything? Nothing at all? Oh no, excuse me. I can quite understand, of course, you want to test me first to see if you can trust me with a secret or not. You can!" Parabukin shouted, flinging up his arms and shaking them above his head. "Into these hands you may entrust your dearest testament and Parabukin will take it locked in his breast, into the silence of the grave. I'll never give you away. I don't want to live for nothing, sirs. I want to serve the sacred cause. Believe and trust Parabukin! He's the very man you're looking for, I'll do everything, I'm ready for anything. Trust me."

"Now look here, will you be sensible and tell us what you want?" Tsvetukhin asked again.

"Mr. Actor! And you . . . Mr. Alexander Pastukhov! I declare to you as solemnly as though I was swearing on the Bible" (he shook his uplifted hand again), "as solemnly as before the life-giving cross, that I devote myself, jointly with you, to the service of the revolution!"

"Sheer madness! The ravings of a drunkard!" Tsvetukhin said excitedly, starting to pace up and down the room.

"You don't trust me? You don't believe the vow and the word of honor of a Parabukin? Parabukin shielded you from the gendarmes. He took your secret upon himself—the secret of how you came to the rooming house to recruit people for underground work. Not a word did I give away, but kept it nobly to myself."

Pastukhov seized Tikhon by the shoulder, shook him and dragged him up. "I can see plainly, my lad, that you're nothing more or less than a provocateur," he said, "Get up and get out before I call the police."

"Don't dare to touch my person!" Parabukin shouted, springing to his feet and advancing challengingly on Pastukhov.

Tsvetukhin threw himself between them. Tikhon made to push him aside, but found both his wrists seized unexpectedly; Tsvetukhin squeezed them with steadily increasing force. His features looked suddenly sharper and harder, lost their mobility, as he stared fixedly at Tikhon. The man tried to wrench his arms loose, and stepped back, but Tsvetukhin would not let go and took a longer stride toward him, spreading out his arms, his whole body almost touching Tikhon's, and steadily pressing his fingers into the wrists.

"Let go! Take your claws out of me. Aye!" Tikhon groaned. "The bed has drained all my strength out of me."

He kept retreating more and more helplessly until at last Tsvetukhin gave him a shove and got him outside the door.

Pastukhov was standing motionless, watching the unexpected scene with his avid but level-headed concentration. He saw his friend shut the door, and wring and chafe his hands, then raise his head as though irresistibly drawn by something on the molding of the ceiling. Probably he was living over again the moment he had known so long in his fantasies, maybe in his

dreams: now he was face to face with the villain who
had raised his hand against him, and he was seizing that
hand in a merciless grip, forcing the villain to his
knees, and going on his way, free and majestic. He
could raise his head still higher because he had removed the villain not only from his own path, but
from that of the friend who was looking at him with
such gratitude and love . . . no, he wasn't!—with such
disdain and derision, yes, that was it, actually
derision!

Pastukhov was laughing almost inaudibly. Then his
laughter grew louder and louder until it became a
peal and then a roar, and the roar broke off suddenly.
There was a minute's silence.

"You're a poseur, Tsvetukhin," he said.

"I don't know. Suppose I am. Still, you couldn't
throw that monster out and I did."

Ignoring the answer as though he had not heard it,
Pastukhov said: "I told you, didn't I?—that idol of
yours that you think so much about would one day
take us by the throat? We have to pay for your pose,
your everlasting straining for originality and effect.
What the devil took you to that damned rooming
house, anyway?"

"I didn't force you to go, Alexander."

"Perhaps not. But it's all through you that everything started. All because of you I'm caged up in this
godforsaken place and I can't move. All because of
you I may be banned to Lord knows where."

"Look here, Alexander, this is a nasty thing to say.
It's offensive."

"I don't care, you can take offense if you want to,
and go to the devil!" Pastukhov retorted, angrily
breaking a match that would not light.

"Well, I'm going, Alexander," said Tsvetukhin in a
husky voice.

"Yes, do. By all means."

"And I won't come back."

"Very glad, I'm sure. At least there's a chance that
the ragtag and bobtail and the rest of your lovely
favorites will forget the way to my house."

Pastukhov sat down in the armchair facing the
window and threw one leg over the other. He did not
turn his head while Tsvetukhin, controlling his move-

ments with an effort, found his cape, hat, and stick
and passed through the door. Then Pastukhov flung
the box of matches into a corner, jumped up and
darted hither and thither about the room, giving vent
to explosive exclamations, growling, and spitting viciously, losing all of a sudden his habitual picturelike
appearance.

When Tsvetukhin went out into the street, he saw
Parabukin stretched out on the sidewalk with his back
to the fence, in that comfortably relaxed pose in
which one may lie on a couch, with one's legs crossed
and an arm under the head, gazing pensively at
nothing. He seemed to be weeping. In the softened
evening light the bloated brownish cheeks shone with
moisture. Perhaps he was grieving that the chance of
changing his life was gone forever, that the heart in
that long-suffering breast was on the left side, like that
of all ordinary mortals, and therefore there was nothing in him to arouse the curiosity of a cold and decrepit
world. Who could tell? From a distance his vague,
moist face with its mane of hair looked almost handsome.

Tsvetukhin gave him a brief glance, swung his
cape lightly around him, and crossed the street.

CHAPTER

· 27 ·

AT LONG LAST Vera Nikandrovna was informed when to come for an answer to her petition. Lisa was determined to go with her.

The Prosecutor's reception room was being repainted; the entrance was through the yard, and the people waited in a corridor furnished with bare wooden couches. At the beginning of office hours there were no visitors. Painters passed by, whistling, with their buckets and brushes, and a caretaker followed, grumbling about the dirty footprints they left on the floor.

Vera Nikandrovna was intending to go into the office when she encountered Oznobishin. He recognized her as a frequent visitor, said he would tell the Assistant Prosecutor that she was waiting, and invited her to sit down.

"Are you together?" he said, pausing a moment and addressing himself to Lisa.

"Yes, she has come with me," Izvekova replied.

"In connection with the same case?"

"No, we just happened to be going in the same direction, so we dropped in here together."

"Excuse me, but you're . . . er . . . Meshkova, aren't you? I saw you at Commencement, didn't I?"

"Yes," said Lisa.

"Now I'll show you up!" Oznobishin's calculating glance said. "True, you're not to blame for anything and deserve all sympathy," the sympathetic lines about

the mouth said. "But what a satisfaction to gloat over
the fact that all you tried to hide has already been
found out," the furtive, derisive smile objected.
"There's no getting away from it now, you're in for it
but don't be frightened, I won't touch you," the look of
goodwill and good nature consoled and encouraged.

"Did you want to know something?" Lisa asked,
embarrassed by the silent play of expression on this
unfamiliar face.

"I only wanted to know if your business was the
same as Mrs. Izvekova's," Oznobishin said slyly, as,
rubbing his small, effeminate hands, he went into the
office

"What a curious person," Lisa said. "He must know
everything about Kirill, mustn't he? Why didn't you
ask him?"

"I spoke to him once and all he said was: 'To
answer questions of this kind is within the jurisdiction
of the Assistant Prosecutor.' Ah, Lisa," Izvekova
sighed, pressing her shoulder gently against the girl's,
as though seeking support, "it means all my life to
me and for them it's only a case, one in a hundred."

A peal of laughter came from around a turn in the
corridor. Two young officials were strolling toward
the exit. One, plump-faced and freshly shaven, was
talking to his lean colleague, hanging on his arm and
pausing at every step.

"And then what do you think our sprightly little
barrister does? He asks permission to speak and then,
as bold as brass, he says: 'As far as concerns the
articles to which reference was made by the Prosecutor,
he ought to have turned his attention to the explanation of the Senate Commission re—Number 1215, May
10, 1899, which puts an entirely different complexion
on the case.' He sits down. The court adjourns. The
Prosecutor rushes off to the library and—can you
imagine it?—he doesn't find either the number or anything like it, nor even that particular date in May
in the Senate decisions. Off he goes to the barristers'
room, beside himself with rage, as you may suppose,
and declares that the counsel for the defense has
deliberately led the court astray, since no such explanation by the Senate as the barrister referred to exists.
Whereupon His Impudence the barrister replies

coolly: "Well, of course, I may have been mistaken.
But you ought to have pointed this out to the court
while it was sitting. Now it's too late: your temperament can no longer have any influence on the case!'
How do you like that, eh?"

Once more the high falsetto laughter rang through
the corridor, and the lean man finally dragged his
stout companion on his arm to the door.

As soon as the echo of the laughter had died away,
a prisoner appeared around the turning with a clanking
of fetters. He was escorted by a guard. They chose a
place almost opposite, but somewhat to the side, of the
bench on which Lisa and Izvekova were seated and sat
down quietly, with an air of people accustomed to
waiting patiently for long stretches of time.

The prisoner was a tall man with a narrow, handsome face and an intelligent but constrained expression in the eyes, and no light or movement in the dull
pupils. His small, well-cut mouth, which looked as
though it might have been drawn from a picture, was
compressed within brackets of bitter wrinkles, and the
shade of the ill-shaven beard made the cheeks blue. He
sat with his knees apart, the narrow chain hanging
down between his legs from under the rough jacket,
forking toward the ankles. Some links of it touched the
floor. The guard beside him was stumpy. A long
revolver hung at his hip. On the shiny greased surface
of the black holster every part of it, from the
trigger and drum to the huge sight, could be discerned.
As he sat down, the guard shifted his revolver from
the hip to the thigh, so that the holster reached the
knee. He rubbed his straw-yellow eyebrows with his
fists and cleared his throat threateningly. Both the
men sat looking at the women.

Lisa was agitated by the fixed stare of the prisoner.
The motionless, magnetizing, and fathomless depths
of his pupils awakened fear and at the same time a kind
of respect. Young and evidently strong, the man was
concentrated on something, but his face seemed to have
renounced forever the expression of the movement of
his thoughts. It was not dead, this face, it had animation,
but it was a frozen animation, like that in a painted
portrait.

With an effort Lisa withdrew her gaze from the

strange young man's eyes. Turning to Vera Nikandrovna, she saw that she, too, was staring fascinated at
the prisoner. Then Lisa, irresistibly and fearfully
drawn, looked again at the prisoner and suddenly
noticed that his mouth had lost something of its
portraitlike regularity, and wore a childishly peevish
expression. She whispered to Vera Nikandrovna: "Do
you think we could do anything for him?"

"You mean give him something?" the elder woman
asked, not understanding.

"Yes, but I haven't anything with me. Have you?"
Vera Nickandrovna opened her reticule. "Only—you
give it to him, I can't," Lisa urged.

In a cautious tone Vera Nikandrovna inquired of
the guard: "Will you allow me to give him something?"

"Charity? Yes, you may give him charity," the
guard assented graciously.

She went up to the prisoner. He held out his hand
and took the money without a word, only drawing his
knees together involuntarily, so that the fetters spoke
for him in their own language.

"How much?" the guard asked.

The prisoner unclenched his fist, and the guard
counted the coins, fingering them, then nodded his
head, allowing the man to put them away.

"You might go and buy a bit of tobacco," the
prisoner said to the guard, moving his lips with reluctance.

The guard pushed back his cap and scratched his
poll, then settled his cap again. "And what if they
send for you in the office?"

"If they manage it by dinnertime, it'll be a wonder."

"That depends," the other said doubtfully.

"D'you think I won't find the door without you or
something?" the prisoner asked after a minute's thought.

"You'll find it, all right. But supposing they ask
where the escort is?"

They talked without looking at each other, eyeing
the women meanwhile. The guard, steadying the revolver with one hand, pulled a tin box out of his
pocket with the other and tapped it with his nail.
Opening it, he placed it on the seat and he and the
prisoner started to roll cigarettes. It seemed the only

thing that existed for them: their movements were so solemn and reverent that they might have been busy at an altar instead of a common tin box that had held acid drops. As they were finishing their smoke, the guard resumed, as though the conversation had never been interrupted. "We'll buy some . . . on the way home."

"Home!" Lisa exclaimed in surprise, partly to Vera Nikandrovna and partly to the guard.

He gave an indulgent chuckle, like a grandfather who has startled a child for fun, and explained graciously: "Back to prison, young lady."

Vera Nikandrovna, pressing her hands to her breast as she always did when she was excited, and leaning forward, half rising from the couch, asked: "You'll excuse me, I only want to ask. . . . Would you mind telling me. . . What does it mean when. . . . You see, I have a son who is under arrest temporarily. And up till now they allowed me to bring him his linen. And now they've forbidden it all of a sudden. You wouldn't care to tell me . . . why they should do so?"

"That all depends . . ." the guard said.

The prisoner glanced down at him and asked: "Is he . . . . a political prisoner or a criminal, your son?"

"Oh, no, of course he isn't a criminal!" Vera Nikandrovna protested in alarm.

The prisoner looked at her and his face was still as handsome, only with a touch of malice in the immobility of the regular features. "I don't know about political prisoners," he said, "but with us they stop taking in linen and the like from outside when prisoners are starting out for penal servitude or they've been put in the punishment cell."

"Right!" the guard said in confirmation.

"Good Heavens!" burst from Vera Nikandrovna's lips. Lisa looked at her in alarm.

Some ladies came in from the yard, then several prisoners were led through the corridor, and the building echoed to the tramp of heavy boots and there was a stifling smell of much-worn cloth. The people were swallowed up by the rooms, the turnings in the corridors, the labyrinth of the rambling old house. New people came to take the place of those who had vanished, the vast unwieldy machine was consuming instead of fuel a steadily increasing flow of petitioners, prisoners, accused, witnesses, and plaintiffs.

When the traffic was at its height, the figure of Pastukhov emerged as though from the midst of it. Here, as everywhere he went, his air of careless ease and self-assertion, his carriage, attracted attention. Everyone in the corridor was watching him, and he would probably have noticed no one, had Vera Nikandrovna not started up from the bench as he passed.

"How do you do, Alexander Vladimirovich," she said in the pleading, agitated tone that was becoming habitual with her lately. "Would you be so kind as to tell me, if you know it, whether you were troubled in connection with the same case as Kirill, or something quite different?"

Pastukhov's cheeks twitched and creased in his usual impenetrable plaster smile and he glanced at Lisa. At the same moment he shook hands perfunctorily with Izvekova and muttered indistinctly: "You see . . . it's quite impossible to make out what's going on. My own impression is that it's a Chinese puzzle. They keep bowing and asking me not to worry, but I can't for the life of me understand what all this pettifogging means. The fact is that they seem to associate me with some case, but what exactly it's all about—I really couldn't tell you."

He kept looking at Lisa, who had got up from her seat like a schoolgirl.

"I believe we've met before, haven't we?" he said in a half-enquiring tone, bowing and scraping his feet. "It's really so dark here. . . . You must excuse me . . . but are you waiting to see the Assistant Prosecutor, too?"

"Yes, I expect to be called in just now," Vera Nikandrovna replied. "We've been here a long time."

He realized at once that if they went in before him, his situation would be still further complicated by the fact of his being second, and it would be easier to give him a refusal. His cheeks lifted a little. "I hope you won't mind if I ask you to let me go in before you. I have a frightful headache. As a matter of fact, I didn't sleep all night."

Vera Nikandrovna agreed without a moment's hesitation, even hastily, and he went briskly into the office.

He was not there very long. He came out a changed man: all his picturesqueness had faded; he moved dully, wearily. As he sat down by Izvekova, puffing and sighing, he said: "They asked me to wait. To wait—that's what the politeness of officials amounts to!"

Scrutinizing the prisoner with his weary but insatiable look, he stuck his thumb under his lower lip and observed to Lisa with a sly chuckle: "That's the way they do—they put you in iron fetters and off you march into penal servitude. And you can't do anything about it! This is the very devil!"

"What exactly are you applying to the Prosecutor about?" Vera Nikandrovna asked.

"I want him to cancel the order for me not to leave the town. I can't budge from the place, I'm stuck. It's monstrous! I asked to see the Prosecutor, and they told me it was against the rules. And what are the rules? Write an application, they said, the Prosecutor will consider it. I'm telling you it's no better than China here!"

"You know, you're quite right!" Vera Nikandrovna agreed eagerly, ready to confide the whole story of her repeated visits to the place, when at that moment her name was called.

Oznobishin conducted her to the Assistant Prosecutor's office. Now she knew that room, the windows with the linen blinds, the impressive desk in the middle, the three armchairs at a distance from them, and the official who looked like an indispensable part of the furniture. Rising slightly in his chair, he pointed to an armchair and sat down again without bending. Not the slightest crease or wrinkle was visible on his white starched jacket. As soon as his visitor had seated herself he informed her, grinding out words that had been selected once and for all: "His Excellency the Prosecutor of the Court has taken a decision concerning your request: it is refused in view of the absence of grounds for mitigation of the conditions of detention."

He glanced at Izvekova. She turned slightly pale but was silent.

"Have you any questions to ask?"

"Is this final?"

"You applied for your son to be released over your signature as surety, indicating ill-health as a reason. No grounds were found for this. Your son is in good health."

"Is this final?" Vera Nikandrovna repeated in a low voice.

"That is—what do you mean by final? He is well at present. Should he fall ill, a reason will arise, evidently."

"I want to know—is there really no more hope?"

"He will be in custody until the end of the inquiry and the verdict of the court."

"But what am I to do now?" she asked with helpless simplicity.

"You can apply for him to be let out on bail."

"Can I?" she asked in a tremor of agitation. "But how—would you be so kind as to tell me how that is to be done?"

"Send in a petition to His Excellency."

"No, what I really wanted to say, was—I must provide the money, is that it?"

"Yes."

"I understand. But I want to know how much. How much money would be needed?"

"The amount of money required will be determined only if and when His Excellency considers it possible to mitigate the conditions of detention."

"But I must know what it is. How much would it take? A few hundred or perhaps even a thousand rubles?"

"I can only refer to precedents, without stating anything definite beforehand. Several thousand. It is rarely more than ten in practice."

"But," Vera Nikandrovna's mouth widened in a childlike smile and the lines on her brow twitched, "where could I get a sum like that? I haven't anything like it."

The Assistant Prosecutor got up again. "You must excuse me: the question is a purely personal matter, concerning you alone, and so I . . ." He spread his hands in a gesture, suggesting that all this was outside his sphere, and bowed his head.

"Thank you, oh, thank you," Vera Nikandrovna said with a catch in her breath as she minced hurriedly out of the room.

Lisa was waiting for her at the very door of the office. They passed the prisoner and his guard, who no longer took any notice of the strangers' eyes watching them. Pastukhov had vanished; the wooden couch was occupied by a new lot of people.

It was very bright in the yard. Puffs of cloud detached from the flocks floated in the sky. Their startling white was repeated down below on earth in barrels and hods, smeared with whitewash, and a huge square case with turquoise lime ready mixed. The painters, whitened from head to foot and exuding clouds of chalk, were engaged in their cooking. Near at hand stood low piles of trimmed boards. As soon as Vera Nikandrovna and Lisa reached the piles, they sat down on them as though they had previously agreed upon it.

In their silence, which was unbroken by a sound, there was the fear, poignantly guessed at by each in the other, of admitting that a decisive and possibly irrevocable change had taken place in the affair about which they had come here. They were tormented by their silence and still kept speechless, not knowing how best to spare each other at such a moment. The white dust settled thinly on them, they swallowed it, but it did not occur to them to move aside, to leave this yard and go further away from this house, which drew them as a magnet. They looked at the dispassionate façade with the straight lines of its windows, with equal spaces of wall in between, but they were hardly in a state to say where they were looking, any more than they were in a state to understand why they were sitting in the dust.

"Hey, young ladies, mind your hats!" shouted a cheery painter with great enjoyment as he emptied a sack of lime into the big box and leaped back from the rising cloud of thick white dust.

In the tone of one suddenly awakened, Lisa asked: "Has anything happened?"

"No, nothing," Vera Nikandrovna promptly replied. "On the contrary. Quite the contrary. I was told that he is perfectly well. Thank goodness for that."

"And what about your application? Will they release him?"

"Kirill? No. At least, they will, of course, only not on the terms I had thought of. On bail—I have to make a deposit."

"What kind of a deposit?"

"I can see you don't understand. I have to deposit a sum of money—that is, I have to give it or subscribe it —however you like to put it. Then they will release him, you understand?"

"You mean they'll release him for money?"

"Yes, that's it. If I deposit this money, it'll be returned later. When he has been cleared."

"Then why should you have to deposit money if it has to be given back anyhow, afterward?"

"It won't be given back unless, only in case, I mean ... when he's cleared. Why can't you understand? It's bail, you see?"

"Yes, I understand," said Lisa, rather frightened and hurt now. "I can understand: it's just for the time being, temporarily."

"Yes, that's right, for the time being."

"How much have they agreed to release him for?"

"Oh, but they haven't agreed yet," Vera Nikandrovna snapped, then suddenly threw her arms around the girl and pressed her face to the young cheek. "There! Forgive me, my love, forgive me. You see, it's just a kind of ... a matter of form."

"Yes, that's what I meant. I understand that it's a matter of form," Lisa repeated in a still more injured tone, at the same time deeply agitated and feeling the smarting tears in her eyes.

Almost at once they began to talk with more concentration and soberness than usual.

"A petition will have to be written," Izvekova said, "and the thing is—where is money to be found?"

"Now let's think."

"Yes. I have a few things. Quite good things. I could pawn them. And perhaps sell something. There are our engagement rings."

"I can give a ring, too. I have one with an aqua-

marine. I never wear it anyhow and they wouldn't
know about it at home," Lisa said hastily. "And afterward it could be got out of pawn again."

"Of course," Izvekova agreed. "But still this all
amounts to very little."

"How much would we need?"

"Oh, ever so much. Good heavens! What am I talking about?" Vera Nikandrovna exclaimed in sudden,
overwhelming despair. She sat leaning forward, with
her elbows resting on her knees, and seized her head in
her shaking hands. "But I need thousands! Many thousands! Where, where on earth am I to get it, my God?"

"Oh, you mustn't get upset like this," Lisa said in a
weak voice, "let's think about it calmly."

"Ah, my dear, what is there to think about? Only a
rich man could pay such a sum. A man like your
father, or someone richer, perhaps. Now, if your
father had taken a different attitude to poor Kirill, if
he had raised no objection to your marriage, he might
have helped. He would have done that, wouldn't he?
He isn't your enemy, after all."

"Very likely," Lisa said, in a vague way, as though
answering herself. "I never told you—you must forgive
me for that—but Father is planning a very different
future for me, according to his own ideas."

"Marriage?" Vera Nikandrovna asked, straightening
herself and tucking her hair away under her hat.

Lisa nodded her head ruefully.

"And what does your mother say? You don't mean
she agrees?"

"She doesn't. But then . . . you don't know my
father."

"But he knows that you and Kirill love each other!"
Vera Nikandrovna protested with a flash of jealousy.
"How can he coerce you into a marriage with any-
one?"

"He always coerces people, including himself."

It seemed to Vera Nikandrovna that the girl she
knew so well and who was so dear to her, the girl who
had only just been seated beside her, had suddenly
vanished. In this numb and somehow faded creature
she discerned an obstinate struggle against overwhelming odds for a decision that eluded her. If Lisa
had been asked what issue she was fighting for so

secretly, she could not have defined it. She only knew that she was striving toward a decision, but she was unable to believe that she would take it and that it would materialize in her agreeing to marry a man whom she did not want to marry. She was more inclined to the opinion that she would take a contrary decision—disobey her father and refuse to marry, but since she had already turned down the suggestion to disobey, it was hard for her to decide anything.

"Who is this man?" Vera Nikandrovna demanded heatedly, looking into Lisa's face with a sympathy that was almost agony.

"A man called Shubnikov."

"That rich man?"

"Yes."

"The rich Shubnikov?" Izvekova repeated incredulously.

"The very same," Lisa told her, and a spark of mischief, a hint of a mocking smile, lit up her face for a second. "He's crazy about me." She fell silent in sudden dreadful embarrassment, alert, slowly following the train of thought that had come upon her unawares.

Then Vera Nikandrovna recoiled and rose quickly to her feet. She seized the girl's hands and tugged at them as though striving to rouse a heavy sleeper. She spoke sternly, as she might have if she was admonishing a pupil who had behaved badly. "What were you thinking of? Answer me. Tell me what you're thinking of just now. Say something. Could I have been mistaken in you? You don't say anything. . . . So it's true? . . ."

Without releasing the girl's hands, she sat down again.

"It's this way, my dear, dear girl," Izvekova said very tenderly, "my silly girl . . . my noble little girl. If you could think for a moment that the same desperate idea came into my sick unfortunate head as into yours, I give you my word—nothing of the kind ever happened. I swear to you. I swear on Kirill's life. . . ."

She waited a moment, then stroked the girl's hands and patted them.

"If you are going to get married simply because your father orders you to, that'll be terrible. It will

be a foolish and a dreadful thing to do. But if you
have something else in mind . . . If you're going to
marry so as to help Kirill . . . Because I know that's
what you were thinking just now. . . . If you are going
to do it for the sake of that unfortunate bail, that's out
of the question anyhow, it will be unprincipled and
shameless. I wouldn't take the money . . . I certainly
wouldn't take any money from you. That's out of the
question. God bless you, silly child!"

Lisa turned abruptly away from her. For a long
while they sat without speaking. Then Vera Nikandrovna said in the tone of a mother: "Tidy your hair.
Look, there's Pastukhov."

Alexander Pastukhov was quite close, walking toward the gate with his usual independent careless bearing. He nodded familiarly as soon as he noticed them.
As he was passing, he took a step toward them, then
paused and kept at a distance, so that they would not
think he was going to stop.

"I can see plainly we're comrades in distress!" he
said, shaking his head ruefully. "You've been refused.
So have I. Well, well, all hope has vanished!"

He clicked his tongue like a little boy, and gave the
rambling façade of the building a long look of dislike.

"Courts of law," he said very distinctly, with an unpleasant smile. "Quick trial! Well, we'll know in future.
We live and learn."

His cheeks broadened in a forced smile.

"Why are you sitting here in this awful dust? I can
feel it in my nose. I must be going, so excuse me. And
I advise you to try and get a breath of fresh air—in
the Limes, at least. Clear the head of all this rubbish."
He nodded his head in the direction of the house and
raised his panama gracefully.

The street seemed pleasantly colorful to him. He
purposely chose the consoling details and dwelt on
them—for instance, the Chinese doll that nodded its
head in the window of the tea merchant's, the curious
vessels filled with bright-colored liquids in the windows of the chemist's shop, the gay ginghams shown
in the arcade, and the ladies with birds in their enor-
mous hats.

Yet he was frightfully depressed. The play was not
going well: he had lost his taste for it. The season

was wasted. Moscow has ceased its telegraphic assaults, its passion for the play having given way to indifference. It might demand damages next. Pastukhov saw himself doomed to oblivion. A strange, confused dream haunted him, broken several times in the night when he awoke, only to drift into a heavy, unrefreshing slumber: he saw valises cluttering the room and he had to hurry. He kept trying to thrust a case of mathematical instruments into his side pocket, but it would keep slipping out. Beside him stood a student called Karlson, whom he had known long ago, and he was stripped to the waist, plump and rosy, wearing a lace ruff like Pierrot. An actress with inky circles for eyes was sprawling on a couch, smoking a cigarette. Karlson stretched himself out beside her, and her husband, a shy, rather pathetic man in the uniform of a railway engineer, paid no attention to them but was explaining something about a kindergarten to Pastukhov. In the next room children were playing a ring game. There were a great many, and Pastukhov had to do something for them but could not because he was going to be late for the train as it was, and the case of instruments kept sliding out of his pocket. He caught it, pushed it back under his jacket, and it fell out once more. Then the railway engineer handed him someone's comb, and he started to do his hair. There he stood, combing his hair with someone else's comb, passing it through the hair in the wrong direction, so that it fell over his brow, and Pierrot Karlson watched him with colorless, sterilized eyes, and this lasted an interminable time, while Pastukhov kept on being late and hurrying, hurrying, with growing horror at his own helplessness before the increasing number of valises in the room.

Even the memory of this nonsensical dream depressed him, and he felt relief when he suddenly heard Mefody calling his name in the Limes, where he was wandering sadly. Mefody's face brightened with his thick-lipped smile as he walked alongside, telling Pastukhov delightedly that he had not seen him for an age, that a great deal of water had gone under the bridge since their last meeting and so on and so forth. Pastukhov interrupted him with: "You know what, old man—you don't happen to have a dream book, do you?"

"Oho! So it's come to that, has it? It's got under your skin?" Mefody said, laughing. "No, I haven't got a dream book, but I know a wise woman, a fortune-teller, I could take you to her if you like."

"Well, look here, what does it mean if you see a set of mathematical instruments in your dreams? You don't know, I suppose?"

"This is what your dream, being interpreted, means, my boy," said Mefody solemnly. "When you don't touch alcohol for a long time, you begin to see scientific instruments. This is the intellect getting the better of human nature. Yes, it's a bad omen—mathematical instruments."

"I can see myself it is. But an old seminarist like you has no right to laugh at superstition. All seminarists are cynics, as everybody knows. Still, Vladimir Solovyov, the philosopher, carried a nutgall in his pocket all his life because he believed it to be a radical remedy for piles."

"Philosophers are like that."

"But excuse me, he was not a philosopher but an artist, and what an artist. Or take Levitan—you've heard of him? He suffered from dilation of the aorta, and carried clay on his chest, a whole bag of it."

"All right, you've convinced me," Mefody said, bowing his head meekly. "But I don't think it's right to accuse me of cynicism. I really believe that dreaming of instruments is a bad sign. When Tsvetukhin is in the mood for inventing something, he raves about mechanisms."

"Oh, never mind your friend Tsvetukhin," Pastukhov growled contemptuously.

"Ha, you're ashamed of yourself, aren't you?" Mefody said reproachfully. "I can see you are. Imagine quarreling with a friend like that! Such a man! Why, Tsvetukhin's a real genius."

"He isn't a genius, he's just a fool."

"Well, the two often go together. But I can tell you beforehand that when your biographer comes to that passage where you drove a great actor from your house, he will call it a blot on your life."

"I don't give a hang for any biographer." Standing stock-still, Pastukhov burst out angrily: "All right, your genius can come to see me! I don't object. But I'm not the man to go to him first."

"He's proud, he won't come," Mefody protested with a touch of alarm. "It was you who drove him out, he didn't drive you out."

"I have my pride, too."

Pastukhov drew Mefody toward a bench, made him sit down, and sank down heavily on the bench beside him. "The devil himself mixed me up with you and Egor! Now I can't get away, all because of this idiotic promise I gave in writing not to leave the town. I've stopped working. I've let the theater down. Think of it —I've got to sit here and wait. Wait for what, I'm asking you?"

"I can feel for you," Mefody responded peaceably. "But how are we to blame? Egor and I are suffering too. Yesterday Meshkov turned up at my place and gave me a week's notice to quit the cottage in the yard. Why? Because, you see, he wants to pull down all the buildings there so as not to have any more tenants. He says: 'We want to keep clear of trouble.' I tried to talk him round. But he wouldn't hear of it. 'You're a suspect,' says he, 'the police have their eye on you, and that doesn't suit me.' I argued and argued, but I might as well have talked to the wall. He's the owner of the house, when all's said and done."

"Where will you go now?"

"I don't care. I can go to the rooming house if it comes to that."

Pastukhov blinked, sighed, broke off a branch of acacia, and began to pick off the leaves. "When I go away, you can live at my place till the lease runs out," he said graciously. Then, suddenly flaring up again: "But how on earth can I go away?—that's the point. Listen to me, seminarist. You're a clever fellow. Give me a bit of advice: how am I, how are we all to extricate ourselves from the toils? It's driving me into such a state of melancholy that I'm nearly ready to plunge into a love affair."

With an unwearying melancholy he stared at the damsels who had appeared among the flower beds.

Mefody ruminated awhile, and then, his eyes narrowing thoughtfully, he delivered himself of his opinions. "The brain is no earthly use here. Logic won't get us anywhere. What we really need is a touch of the transcendental."

"Such as, for example, a dream book?" said Pastukhov with a laugh.

"Something perfectly silly, anyway. The sillier the better. For instance, when a chicken happens to be a bit elderly, the cook puts a crystal stopper in the pan to soften it."

"You don't say so!" Pastukhov exclaimed in undisguised interest.

"It's a fact. The same kind of stopper helps to soften peas and beans, too."

"That's curious, you know. By Jove, it's a first-rate idea! Funny, I never heard of it before."

"So if we could find the kind of crystal stopper we need, everything would go swimmingly!"

Pastukhov was a new man. He stared at Mefody greedily, with a child's admiration. Yes, he definitely liked this queer fellow with the mark on his nose and a scent apparently as keen as a dog's. Pastukhov burst out laughing. "Come along," he spluttered through uncontrollable laughter. "Let's go and have some fresh Zhiguli beer—they sell it round the corner. Then we'll have a good look for that crystal stopper!"

Throwing an arm around Mefody's shoulders, he raised him from the bench.

pull up, standing more stiffly and solemnly than cannon on the parade ground, and then once more start into animation and move on, reflecting the throngs of idlers on the sidewalks in their polished surfaces.

The leaves were falling, but a warm wind was still blowing, and people were stifled with heat in the Meshkovs' house, where the windows stood wide open. The whole street wanted to peer through those windows, elbow its way to the festive board, penetrate into all the secrets of this wedding, pry into the Shubnikovs' pockets, into Meshkov's coffers, into the very soul of the bride and bridegroom, and the buzz of gossip, tattle and idle talk flew from one side of the street to another, flitted into the yard, oozed out into the kitchen, and, like a draught, burst forth into the street.

Everything became known to insatiable human curiosity; that the marriage very nearly fell through because of the miserliness of Merkuri Avdeyevich, who would not give his daughter a dowry; and that Victor Semyonovich Shubnikov had begged his aunt to sacrifice it because, after all, you had to live with a person and not with a dowry; that Meshkov had undertaken instead of the dowry to bear the cost of the wedding, and now look at the way he was trying to dazzle his rich new kindred; that the bridegroom was crazy about the bride, but she could not sleep at night for grieving. And here, of course, the gossips had to add that according to an old saying they'd get used to each other in time and she would love him, too. And other well-worn sayings in the same vein. And, intermingled with the maxims, how much was paid for the incense, and how much was given to the choir, and who wore what, and who was the first—the bride or the bridegroom?—to set foot on the altar steps, which signified who was going to have the upper hand in married life, and which customs had been neglected, and how weddings used to be celebrated in old times; and had the matchmaker received many silk dress-lengths. And—heavens above!—tongues wag more about a wedding than about any other event in life. It was enough for a showily dressed girl to appear at a window, fanning herself, for the guessing to start on the pavement: who was that beauty? Was she from the bride's or the bridegroom's side? It was enough for a loud voice to carry above the hubbub for people to be all agog, asking: who was that shouting? Was it the man who gave away the bride? Or perhaps the matchmaker? Or maybe the best man?

And what really did take place, what was actually going on in Merkuri Avdeyevich's house, where there was not a corner free of people, where the power was taken out of the host's and hostess's hands by the chefs, cooks, confectioners, and waiters, where the thunder of the music gave way to volleys of cork popping, the deacon's chanting of the prayers for long life, where aromatic fumes titillated the nostrils, and enthusiastic cheers merged in a joyous discord.

Any kind of respectable order had long since been replaced by gay anarchy, and each guest wanted to celebrate after his own fashion.

Nastenka was strenuously trying to turn the merry-making to the old style. After a few sips of plum cordial or any other drink, she would start singing an old folk dance tune. But no one could join in the old tunes, the music broke in every now and then with something quite different, and, waving her handker-chief, she would start a step dance between the chairs, flashing glances from her shiny black eyes, bending now toward the in-laws, now toward the young cou-ple, to whisper compliments in their ears.

Victor Semyonovich's friends, wearing morning coats and high wing collars, proposed toasts and made speeches, and, already past the stage where they could appreciate the elaborate confections of the cooks, called for sour cabbage and pickled apples.

The best man, his face suggesting a bun rather burned around the edges, was wearing sideburns, and his hair was elaborately curled. He thrust out his chest, crackling in a starched shirt front with embossed roses, and strove valiantly to finish his speech despite the uproar.

"Remember our childhood, Vityusha," he shouted, swaying a little and stretching out his arms as though about to save his friend from a fatal step, "and our pranks and the mischief we got into! What words can convey all this! It seems so long ago! And then . . . as the years went by, our friendship grew closer. How touching it all is, when you come to think of it, by God! We watched you make an expert cyclist of yourself. Vitya! Can we ever forget it! Or flying on your roan thoroughbred! What energy, what buoyancy! You were the envy of everybody as you covered the distances, light as the zephyr. And now, look at you, you've outstripped us all on life's race track. You've won by a whole length. But we aren't saying good-by to you, Vitya. We shall meet you again in your married state, as we met in childhood and youth. The new field that has opened before you is not yet sown with flowers. Sow it, my friend, with sweet lilies-of-the-valley and violets. And may you live in joy and for your own delight, and for the delight of your adorable spouse, the ravishingly beautiful Elisaveta Merkuryevna. Permit me to call her by the name you use yourself when you bend your head toward her—your dear Lisa. Lisa, my dear! May you live in unclouded happiness with the man with the heart of gold, met on life's way. Love him as we all love him. On my word of honor, there's no one like him. He's beyond any price . . . he's priceless. . . . We, your comrades to the death, Vityusha, we are calling to you in our own way, we are calling to you, our famous driver, a driver who has no equal: stick it, Vityusha, stick it!"

For the tenth time the guests surrounded the young couple, embracing them, kissing each other, spilling the wine, drowning the sound of their own raucous voices.

The eyes of strangers watched Lisa all day, at home, out-of-doors, and at church. It was becoming natural to her to find everyone looking at her with inquisitive, curious eyes. The same searching eyes of the dressmakers, milliners, hairdressers, bridesmaids, aunts, grandmothers, and Valeria Ivanova, who was limp with agitation, had watched her before the wedding.

Lisa's hair was fluffier than ever. Vivid spots of color rose from cheeks to temples and then flitted back to her chin. For the first time she had put on real jewelry for grownups, a necklace, Vityusha's gift, and a diamond ring. She had been wearing her engagement ring for more than a week now. Besides all these things, she had an ostrich-feather fan, a silver-chain bag which contained a tiny bottle of perfume, and a handkerchief

edged with Venetian lace. She could have had anything she wished for. The one thing she lacked was a
moment of privacy, alone.

What had happened to her resembled in no way the
state of mind of one who had lost a thing of great
value and was searching for it restlessly, hopefully.
No! When she sought a name for her feeling, the only
word that occurred to her was *irrevocability*. The
whole thing was irrevocable. Having once said: let
come what come may, she had, as it were, renounced
the past, and she saw herself as a new, a different Lisa.
A granular opalescent gem glittered on the finger of
that other Lisa, unknown to her; the fan now opened,
now closed on her lap, and beside it appeared a man's
hand, laid heavily on her knee, its warmth penetrating
the thin silk dress. The former Lisa would very likely
have tolerated neither the fan nor the man's hand on
her knee, but to this new Lisa the fan seemed luxurious
and beautiful, its filmy fronds were delicate, and the
man's hand made her turn her head slightly to the left
and look at the man who was called by the unfamiliar
name of husband. The former Lisa would have turned
away abruptly from this black-coated man with the
sharp twists of pale fair mustache at the corners of the
lips and the dashing, fair locks of hair in the middle of
his forehead, while this other Lisa looked into the small
pupils of the humid eyes and smiled condescendingly,
if somewhat sadly. In the midst of the uproar and the
shouts of the guests, he kissed her several times, previously wiping his lips with his starched serviette. She
noticed that his lips were flabby. But she did not pause
to think whether she liked this or not. She simply
could not change anything: everything that was taking
place was unalterable, the past—irrevocable. She
waited, with youth's thirst for happiness, to see what
would happen next.

When the banquet was on the wane and the elderly,
respectable guests had taken their leave, after drinking
a last glass of champagne in the hall and leaving large
silver rubles on the tray for the servants, and while
Vityusha's bosom friends were still noisily drinking the
last of the wine, Lisa slipped out unnoticed to the
gallery.

The distant hills were darkening. Over the ridges

the last farewell bar of light glimmered like tinfoil.
The lower the houses stood on the slopes, the more
effectively they merged into one dim mass. Against its
ashen background three familiar pyramidal poplars
stood out, supporting the sky like funeral columns.
The day wind had not yet dropped; it swept handfuls
of black dead leaves from the poplars, which scattered and disappeared in the darkness. There was no
one near the school, by evening the streets were too
chilly—autumn was advancing apace. Would Lisa see
soon again the whitewashed house, and its three tall
sentinels that once stood guard over her hopes, and
now over the memory of her unhappiness? When
would she stand once more in front of those windows—
the guardians of all her thoughts and expectations?
Or perhaps even now, at this quiet moment, just as
she was in her wedding dress, with leaves of myrtle
in her hair, she should say through those windowpanes her last farewell to all that had been, never to
return here.

She was standing thus, oblivious of the merriment
around the table, her face almost touching the cool
glass. Then she gave a start and recoiled from the
window: Merkuri Avdeyevich, perspiring, mollified,
with a slight unsteadiness in his springy gait, was
coming toward her.

"My little daughter," he began, doing his utmost to
strike a note of gentle warmth and intimacy, and trying not to slur his words, "my only little girl! So you're
flying from the nest! So I'll never hear your chirruping any more? Chirrup, chirrup! Where are
you? ..."

He embraced the girl, fumbling with the voluminous folds of her bridal veil, and laying his rather
ruffled head on her shoulder.

"Do you think it's easy to part with a daughter? You
are sad—but think of what your father and mother
must be feeling. Chirrup, chirrup! Ah, Lisanka! What
have you to say to me? What have you to say to your
father at parting, my little sparrow?"

She raised his head respectfully and put him away.
Straightening her veil and stepping back a pace, she
stared a moment, her brows knitted, at the window.
"Thank you," she said at last in a low voice. "I have

obeyed your will. I have done as you wished. And now
I have a favor to ask of you, Papa. I must ask you . . ."

She paused a moment and pressed her hand on the
window sill.

"I'm asking you to spare me . . ." she said suddenly
in a louder tone. "I'm not leaving home of my own
wish, but of yours. Why do you talk like this . . .
about who feels it more, and who finds it sweeter?
I've flown from the nest, indeed? Let us never speak
of this again. And ask Mama not to cry. It's too cruel.
I can't stand it. Unfortunately . . . it is still to come.
The time of tears is ahead of me."

Sobered now, Merkuri Avdeyevich looked at her as
he rocked backward and forward gently, his fingers
interlaced behind his back.

"It isn't right," he began, and she heard a stifled sob
in his voice. "It isn't right and it isn't praiseworthy to
speak like this to your father. You think your father
has no pity for you and so you'll have no pity for
him. You reproach me with my will. And you've
forgotten that 'not a hair of your head shall fall without the will of Our Heavenly Father.' All that is done
is done by His will alone. You'd forgotten that? And
remember this: follow your mother's example and
live with your husband as she does. She never disobeyed me once in the quarter of a century we've been
togther."

"Oh, if she had only disobeyed just once!" cried
Lisa. "I wouldn't have been all alone today!"

She let her fan fall and stepped on it. Her father
stooped heavily, drew the fan from under her foot in
its white slipper, shook it out, and smoothed the
feathers.

"You're going against all reason," he said, "you ought
to be thankful and happy that God has been good to
you and your parents. If you weren't one of the
Shubnikovs now, you might have been tramping the
long road to penal servitude like—"

He broke off, but Lisa was staring at him in fright.
"What do you know about him? Tell me, tell me . . .
If you do, I give you my word I'll never mention him
to you again!"

"I know nothing about him. I only thank the Lord
that He saved you from misfortune. And the fact that

your thoughts are following him when you're wedded to another man is a great sin. Remember, we are sent into this life to do our duty."

"Ah, who knows what we're sent into this life for!" she cried passionately once more, pressing her hands to her brow. At that moment Vityusha's voice was heard.

"Lisanka! Lisa! It's time for us to be going, come and say good-by!" He was hurrying out to her, his coat flying open. "I've been looking for you all over the house! Oh, you're upset? What's the matter?"

"No, she isn't a bit upset, why should she be?" Merkuri Avdeyevich assured him, his face brightening with a delighted smile. "I'm speeding her on her future way. May you live in peace and friendship, my dear children. And now . . . let us go and say good-by."

He linked the arms of the young couple affectionately.

They all assembled in the drawing room, forming a semicircle with Lisa and Vityusha in the middle. They kissed the icon of the Holy Virgin known as "Assuage My Grief" and crossed themselves. Valeria Ivanovna embraced her daughter and wept. Words failed her; she expressed herself in tears alone. Silently, with burning eyes, Lisa released herself from her embrace. The best man with the sideburns took up the icon with a look of exaltation and moved rather unsteadily toward the door ahead of the newlywedded couple. The guests followed.

For the third time that day the cream-colored coach with the generalized monogram on the door received Lisa into its springy plush bosom. Vityusha sat down beside her and put his arm around her waist. On the way they laughed at the best man, who sat opposite, holding the icon on his knees. Lulled by the jogging of the coach, he began to nod and finally dozed off. Vityusha had to prop him up with his free hand in the chest, his stiff, bent shirt front emitting a hollow sound like a drum.

Lisa's new home welcomed her with two richly laden tables; one was spread with wines and sweets, and on the other the Shubnikovs had arranged the wedding presents, a jumble of sterling silver, German silver and bronze, in which the practical mind of Daria

Antonovna with her spoons, dishes, sauceboats, knives, and forks hobnobbed with Vityusha's frivolity. He had bought a lot of silly little ornamental stands, pendants, goblets, and figurines. The aunt was the experienced skipper fitting out the vessel for a long voyage, the nephew—a passenger on a pleasure trip.

In general he took life from its lighter, pleasanter side, like most of those who inherit it ready-made, built by the toil of their predecessors. He did not care much for the circumspection of old age, nor did he value established customs if they afforded no pleasure. He thought more of modern customs. When all was said and done, the old folks had no movies, they didn't know what a gramophone was, they did not believe that a man could fly. Once their wedding was over, they shut themselves up in their rooms and never went anywhere. But Vityusha, being a thoroughly modern person, resolved to go for a honeymoon at all costs. He meant to go to the Crimea for the height of the season, or to St. Petersburg, the city of wonders, where there were competitions at the skating rink in the summer entertainment hall, and where, from the islands, you could watch the sun sinking into the sea. He drew up a program of ways of passing the time for a whole week before the journey, memorizing the entertainment advertisements in all the newspapers. In short, he belonged to people who knew how to live.

It was the correct thing to begin by being seen at the city theater. It so happened that *Hamlet* was staged there the day after the wedding. Vityusha had started to read it twice as a schoolboy but had fallen asleep over it at the same place—soon after the disappearance of the Ghost. But he thought it would not look well if they went to Everybody's Art Theatre, though there was a play running under a very respectable sort of foreign title, *Gaudeamus*. You could not say as much for the Ochkin Theatre, where they played *Old Times* and even *The Woman Convict*. It would seem queer, certainly, if they were seen straight after their marriage at *The Woman Convict!* As far as Lisa was concerned, the question simply did not arise: it appeared that, to Vityusha's astonishment, she adored Shake-

speare. He could not believe that anyone could like
such boring things. He admitted, however, that the
Ghost scene did stick in the memory. As for the rest
of his program, in his eyes, it was beyond discussion.
The Aeroclub was arranging at the racecourse positively the last flight of the aviator Vasilyev—no matter what the weather. "Special band provided by the
Aeroclub." The French circus was featuring a decisive
match between four pairs of wrestlers. The noted
singer of Russian songs, the idol of the public, Nadezhda
Vasilyevna Plevitskaya, was to give a recital in the
School of Music. Lisa made no objection to the aerial
flight, the wrestlers, or Plevitskaya—she was ready to
go anywhere, apparently, as long as she could see her
Shakespeare.

The entire program of entertainment presented itself
to her in all its obligatory splendor when, early in
the morning, she went out for the first time from
her husband's bedroom into the dining room.

She sat down in an armchair. Vityusha was still
asleep. His breathing was audible through the open
doorway. It reminded her of the sucking of a pipe
of tobacco, punctuated with faint gurgles. The light
was still soft, the curtains kept it out, and it distributed
sparse flecks on the silver and bronze of the wedding
presents. Lisa's weary glance shifted from the slim,
naked electro-plated statuettes of women to the rough-
haired setter, the horse's head, the swallows draping
their long "coattails" over the china vases. She had no
desire to go up and make a closer examination of
this zoo, perched on ash trays, writing cases, and
goblets. She seemed to have been looking at these
things a long time and would soon be tired of them,
as one gets tired of too much leisure. The whole room
seemed very familiar to her, and Lisa thought to herself that now, no matter where she went—to watch
the airplane flight, the play, or simply out-of-doors,
going through with the program of entertainment,
she would always have to return to her dogs and horse's
head, and electro-plated women with attenuated bodies.
This was her future. It was all marked out, predestined,
inevitable. Her path, the only path she could take,
was that of resignation.

She closed her eyes so as not to see the table

laid out with wedding presents. It suddenly cheered
her that she was alone, that no one was bothering her
or touching her. Wrapping her dressing gown more
tightly about her, she curled up in the armchair,
found herself gradually nodding, and in another minute fell fast asleep.

That evening the carriage stood ready at the gate.
Victor Semyonovich, having wearied Lisa by his ex-
quisitely courteous attentions, became rather more
solemn and serious when the time came to get ready
for the theater. He spared no pains over dressing. The
mirror reflected in turn a collection of neckties, which
were tied in bows, and butterflies of various kinds.
He walked through the rooms wearing his mustache
mask and bearing a faint resemblance to a lop-eared
rabbit. As he tried on waistcoats, he asked Lisa's opinion. "You don't think this is too bright?"

He made her change three dresses before he decided
at last on one that harmonized with his suit—a silk the
color of spring lettuce went wonderfully with his
coffee-colored cutaway. Taking her arm and bending
his head down to hers, he posed prayerfully before the
glasses.

"We ought to have our photos taken like this,"
he said. "What a couple! I'm very happy."

At the theater they occupied the center box known
as the governor's. They were surrounded by friends
dressed in the height of the fashion. The heavy folds
of red velvet drapery festooned each side of the box
crowned by the city arms—three sturgeons argent
on a ground azure. The people turned and stared and
whispered. Had Victor Semyonovich been older, he
might have passed for the governor—so important was
his bearing.

The theater lay in full view of Lisa. She could
easily count the rows of seats and find the place where
she had sat the last time she was at the theater—
with Kirill. The white coiled hair of two elderly ladies
glimmered there now. Lisa looked around at the boxes,
raised her head to see the upper circle, scrutinized the
curtain, which was familiar in every pictorial detail,
but still her gaze kept returning to the gray coiffures.
It seemed to her that the air was full of a shimmering
sleepy haze, and in that haze she was aware of herself

as a memory. At some infinitely distant time she had
been there, where the gray-haired ladies were sitting
now. She herself, against her own wish, was holding
herself like those ladies, very straight and stiff, supported by the rigid corset, and wearing a high coil
of hair around her brow. Perhaps she was as gray
as they were? In any case, she was not Lisa. She was
Madame Shubnikova, the wife of a noted draper in
the town. She was sitting in the governor's box. The
theater was whispering about her. The past had
slipped into oblivion.

Then suddenly, as though a frail ladder had given
way under her weight, she fell headlong in a dream—
and was Lisa again.

Once more there was no one between her and the
stage: the play was enacted for her alone, and no one
could see how the tide of the tragedy sucked her in
and carried her away. Before her stood Tsvetukhin,
whom she alone knew—no one else and none better.
And once more he was that strange, ineffaceable vision—with the cloak thrown over his shoulder, the im-
palpably light hand on the sword hilt, the heaven-
born creature who had stood by the window in the
beam of sunlight, warning Lisa to "beware of the
theater!" Each note, each tone of the velvety, unctuous
voice flowed into her as into a blissfully waiting reser-
voir, and she no longer understood who was enchanting her—the Prince of Denmark or Egor Pavlovich
Tsvetukhin.

Vityusha bothered her with his conversation. He
could not keep his impressions to himself, and the
shorter Lisa's answers became, the more insistent his
whispers. In the interval he tried to entertain her with
talk about his program of travel and was offended
when that met with no success. During the scene of
the Actors and the King and Queen he munched chocolate, rustling the paper wrappings, until Lisa stilled
the energetic movements of his fingers with a cold,
unloving hand. Then he turned his attention to the
Actors and watched them with affected gravity, having decided to show Lisa that his own attitude to
Shakespeare was profound enough and that he had
only entertained her with his remarks for her own sake,
so that she wouldn't feel bored. All things consid-

ered, a practical man could learn something from an
author like Shakespeare, after all.

> *Hamlet:* Do you see yonder cloud? that's al-
> most in shape of a camel?
> *Polonius:* By th'mass, and 'tis like a camel, in-
> deed.
> *Hamlet:* Methinks it is like a weasel.
> *Polonius:* It is backt like a weasel.
> *Hamlet:* Or like a whale?
> *Polonius:* Very like a whale.

"There's a smart chap for you!" Vityusha whispered
admiringly.

"Who?" Lisa asked with a swift glance.

"This old fellow."

"You mean Polonius?"

"That's right. He beats the lot for brains."

Lisa remarked that she felt dizzy. Vityusha jumped
up, but she made him sit down again, and went out
of the box.

In the deserted, strangely quiet foyer with its
dimmed lights she sat down on a couch. Almost at
once an obsequious usher came up to her and inquired
if she was Mrs. Shubnikova.

"Shubnikova?" she repeated with as much bewilderment as though she had never heard the name in her
life.

"The actor Tsvetukhin asked me to give you this
note."

She unfolded the note, tearing it in her haste, but for
some time she could not make out the sloping hand-
writing. Only after examining closely the signature
"Yours, Tsvetukhin," she adjusted her eye to the letters
rushing in pursuit of each other and deciphered the
note word by word.

"I heard you were in the theater and I hasten to
congratulate you on an event that became known in
the town yesterday. My most sincere wishes for your
happiness, and congratulations. On this great occasion I dedicate my acting to you. I am glad that you
are present and am terribly anxious to know what you
will say."

What could she say? Except that she had run out in

the middle of a scene because her husband hindered her from looking at the stage? Or that if Hamlet had continued his cat-and-mouse game and she, and not Polonius, had been the mouse, she would have agreed, just as that base Polonius did, with everything Hamlet said because she could not have resisted his charm? Oh, no, she would say something quite different! She might say that she did not believe in his congratulations, and did not want to think him insincere, when he had warned her against this marriage. And further she might say that this evening in the box had become her farewell to the Lisa who had regarded the theater as the wonder of another world, a dream, a cherished wish, and that nevermore would she see Tsvetukhin as of old.

She sat holding the open letter in her lap, in her rich evening dress, with jewels on her fingers and at her breast, with her hair arranged high in some subtle way over a frame, as though she were a figure at an exhibition. No one disturbed her thinking. Occasionally a stifled voice came through the door and an apparent response came timidly from the cloakroom, or—more boldly—from the refreshment bar. Then everything was quiet again.

Suddenly Vityusha came out of the box. "You're not feeling well, I can see that," he said anxiously. "Let's go home."

He bent over her, put out his hands toward her, then paused, staring down at the note. "A letter?"

"Yes. Congratulations," Lisa replied folding it in its creases.

"Who's it from?"

"From Tsvetukhin."

"The actor? Do you know him?"

"Yes, slightly."

He took the note from her fingers and tried to read it. "Did you make it out?"

"Yes."

"What's all this rigmarole, anyway? Read it for me, please."

She read everything except the conclusion. He took it back again and examined it.

"He signs himself 'Yours, Tsvetukhin'—why?"

"What do you mean?"

"Why—'Yours'?" He folded the letter neatly and put it away in his waistcoat pocket. "Was there anything between you?" he asked.

"I don't understand you."

"What is there to understand?" he retorted, bridling. "Well, to cut a long story short, there must be no more of this. Correspondence and all the rest of it. And in general. He's got a reputation, I can tell you. And you're a married woman now."

Vityusha pulled down his coat with dignity and fingered his tie. "Once more, I suggest we ought to go home. What's the use of wearing ourselves out for Hamlet? After all, we're not here for Hamlet."

"Very well. Only please bring me some water first," Lisa asked him, leaning back on the couch.

He coughed, raising his finger tips to his lips, said "At your service" very politely, and, having quite recovered his poise, set off for the refreshment room.

On seeing the usher, he changed his mind and, smoothing his mustache, said commandingly: "Here, my man, bring a glass of water, will you!"

· 29 ·

In the dull windy days of late autumn Pastukhov hardly ever went out. He unearthed somewhere the cook who had worked for many years for his father and, with the satisfaction natural to an old and lazy bachelor, surrounded by books, and struggling with the characters of his ill-starred play, he devoured the artless productions of the only Russian cuisine she knew, based mainly on noodles, millet, and potatoes. He introduced variety by making coffee and mulled wine for himself. Now, as never before, he hearkened to the moods of solitude, tinted in the half-tones of an elusive pale color scheme, like the *fin de siècle* French pictures that he was so fond of contemplating and that awakened in him a curious, wistful love of life.

It was in this subdued, slightly sentimental frame of mind that he once went out for a stroll shortly before twilight. The pavements, dry from the night frosts, were still covered with the summer's dust and it whirled and eddied in yellow cones, soaring over the houses and veiling the distant prospect in an unattractive haze. Pastukhov kept wiping his eyes, and, finding the main street deserted, was about to turn homeward when he noticed a little knot of people around the window of the local newspaper office. He did not read papers very often and now he thought he would see what was going on.

The passers-by pressed closer to the glass to read the open pages of the latest issue. Over the motionless heads Pastukhov could see the framed advertisements of familiar shops, theater announcements, pictures of the new members of the town council. A very stout, pock-marked tradesman stood out among them, a man who always attracted notice in the street by his stolid look of a born city father, which had really accounted for his election. There was nothing interesting in the paper, though the readers pressed their faces against the panes in an effort to make out the print in the last of the failing light.

Suddenly the window lamps went on, and in a column illuminated by the yellow light, in headlines no larger than the rest, Pastukhov read: "Disappearance of Leo Tolstoy." His glance took in the opening sentences: "Startling news has come by wire of the sudden disappearance from home of Russia's great writer. . . ." Pastukhov rubbed his eyes harder. A lot of dust had got into them, the eyelids smarted with the grit, tears kept gathering—"it seems that he was oppressed by having to live at variance with his own teaching, a fact which had been pointed out to him unceremoniously enough by many. Tolstoy's sensitive soul could not but suffer in these circumstances. . . ."

"What on earth is this?" Pastukhov demanded, leaning heavily against someone's back, his glance skimming the lines that dazzled him. "From our own correspondent . . . The Count's destination is unknown. The first searches have proved fruitless. Countess Sophia Andreyevna attempted suicide. . . . He ordered the carriage and . . . Evening telegrams: the whole Tolstoy family assembled just after midnight. . . . The state of anxiety that the family, and particularly Sophia Andreyevna, has been thrown into is beyond description. . . ."

His neighbor jerked a shoulder away from under his pressure, and, yielding to the gesture, Pastukhov moved away. Involuntarily he turned in the direction he had been going before the newspaper had diverted his attention. Still, he had a sense of acting under compulsion; he felt he ought to act differently, because now he was thinking no more of the things that had occupied his mind a minute ago. He turned abruptly and went back to the group at the window, elbowing his way roughly to the glass.

". . . A landowner in the Odoyevsky district saw Tolstoy in a train on the Ryazan railway between Gorbachevo and Belevo on the way to Optina Monastery in Kaluga gubernia."

"But look here," Pastukhov exclaimed excitedly to no one in particular, "what's the date? This is an old paper."

"Yesterday's. No paper today," a respectable-looking man replied, making way for him.

"They must know by now what's happened."

"You mean—to Tolstoy?" the other said.

"Yes, of course. What does all this mean?" Pastukhov addressed everyone at once as he turned away from the window.

The faces he saw were very different: each answered him silently, after its own fashion; one was that of a very tall, clean-shaven man, with a shiny, wrinkled face resembling a lay clerk, then a neat old man with a squint, in a new hat; beside him a beardless youth, staring ferociously; two schoolboys and, between them, a belligerent-looking worker with a flaming shock of hair that had not known a pair of scissors for a long time, and finally, that respectable-looking man, suggestive of a worthy bank employee, who had made way for Pastukhov. Answering him with sly, sharp, covert, derisive, or sympathetic glances full of life, these people waited to hear some real conversation.

"If you've ever noticed it, you know, of course, that an animal, such as a cat, when it feels the approach of death, leaves its home to look for a spot where it can die in peace and quietness," the squint-eyed old man said in a detached, didactic tone.

"What's the cat got to do with it?" Pastukhov interrupted him.

The two schoolboys laughed, and the tall, shiny-faced man looked down at them in a superior fashion.

"It's got this to do with it," the old man proceeded patiently, "that man, a higher creature, perhaps, the highest in the realm of nature, wants to die quietly, far from vanity and idleness."

"I don't know about that," Pastukhov said thoughtfully.

His habitual avid curiosity for the outer world seemed to have left him suddenly, supplanted by an insistent question, the only one that he was asking himself and that he still could not express with sufficient precision.

"What is there to talk about anyway?" the ferocious man said with a scornful toss of his head. "The old man's in his dotage and they've been talking of nothing else for two days now."

"Smarty!" the fiery-headed man remarked with challenging curtness.

"I consider," the respectable-looking man began, touching Pastukhov's sleeve with his finger tips, "Leo Tolstoy has gone and retired from the likes of you and me, for good."

"It isn't Leo, it's Lev," one of the high-school boys corrected him.

"But why from me?" Pastukhov demanded in a displeased tone.

"Well, not from you personally, but from us in general," the other explained, looking around sorrowfully at the group.

"So would I, myself," said the ferocious youth, turning abruptly, and strode across the road.

"You ought to be kicked out, then I bet you'd go quick enough," the fiery-haired man called after him.

Pastukhov elbowed his way somewhat discourteously through the crowd. Seeing the words "Editorial offices" whitening on a door, he pushed it open and, running up the stairs two and three steps at a time, reached the second floor.

At a desk in this room, bent over a pile of moist galleys, stood the proofreader, a fair, curly-haired young man with pince-nez on a tightly twisted cord. He held a foul pipe between his teeth and wore an old seminarist's coat, from beneath which his bandy legs were visible.

"I'm Pastukhov," Alexander Vladimirovich said, taking off his hat.

The proofreader took the pipe out of his mouth, brushed the pince-nez off his nose, and gulped down some of the cold, black tea. Having thus overcome his emotion, he inquired how he could be of service to Pastukhov.

"What's the latest about Tolstoy? Has he been found?"

"Yes, he's ill. He got off the train at Astapovo."

"Where is that?"

"It's on our line. Not very far from here."

"Any details known?"

"They've gone to press. We'll get the proofs in a minute. All Russia is writing about nothing but Tolstoy. Would you like to read this in the meantime? It's all going into tomorrow's issue."

Picking out several galleys, he laid them on the round table inside the balustrade that divided the room. Pastukhov went over to the table.

First of all he saw three portraits of Tolstoy—prints shining with smooth black redolent of kerosene and a chemist's shop. They were pictures familiar from childhood, from school anthologies, from the colored covers of kopek editions, from thick illustrations in large, unwieldy volumes. In one of them Tolstoy looked particularly lifelike to Pastukhov—the big head of the old man with the vast beard swept sideways as though by the wind, the clear, piercing glance under the shaggy eyebrows, and the tangle of sparse hair on the temples. The old man was thinking and looked rather angry. The lines on the lofty brow were striking, as though a wooden plow had been driven with heavy labor over a big field, making furrow after furrow. The hoary hair was as fresh as foam of the sea, and in that foam shone serenely the face of the earth—Man.

Pastukhov caught his breath. Suddenly the understanding overwhelmed him that he had been born and grown up with this Man, lived with him, day in, day out, thinking of him no more than he thought of the air. A terrified wonder seized him, like the amazement of a child who has suddenly lost his father, under whose protection he lived simply and thoughtlessly. He kept staring at the head of the old man. Thoughts flitted strangely through his mind. For some reason he recalled his childhood best of all and a wrong done to him by grownups and not understood. . . . Then he began to think that it was time to change his way of living, begin it all over again—and start from a rare clearness. And after that he thought it ought to start with escape, with a dash for freedom, like a fresh start made by a convict escaping from prison. Then he told himself that it was all nonsense and he concentrated his attention on the proofs.

The editorial, entitled "The Great Conscience," opened with the words: "The great soul of the great man could endure no longer this ordinary life, this falsehood of time in which it had to throb and struggle." Pastukhov could not concentrate—his glance picked out bits of the text here and there. "The conventionality and artificiality of what is called civilized society, that had fenced itself off by a kind of Great Wall of China from the people . . ."

He moved away one galley and took up another. "He has gone, do not try and search for him," the next article declared. "He has gone! He took with him a small valise of his favorite books, put on his working-man's blouse and peasant's boots, and went away. . . . He has retired into seclusion now, to be able not only to live freely but also . . . who knows?—perhaps to die freely. If he has never been able till now to arrange life as he wanted, has he not the right to insist that he may be allowed to die as he wishes? Did he perhaps wish for a peasant's funeral—in a rough, unpainted coffin borne on a country sleigh or a cart? . . ."

"What the devil is all this?" Pastukhov exclaimed, throwing the proofs aside. "They're worrying about his right to die! But who gave them the right to bury a man alive?"

There was no one in the room. He drew the strips of paper toward him again and began to read. "Not only great people but the most ordinary, when they sense the approach of death, often seek solitude. They turn their faces to the wall away from their families, from their friends, and beg them to leave them in peace. . . . Do not search for him! He himself asks you not to search for him but to leave him alone. Is it not our sacred duty to carry out the wishes of one who has departed from us on his last journey, from which there is no return? Tolstoy had a reason for saying that he would not come back. He has gone, but we should not try to find his tracks. Have no fear!

He will not die, he will not perish! Leave him in peace
now, and he will live forever!"

At that moment the proofreader came in with fresh
galleys.

"Look here," Pastukhov said impulsively, "can you
understand anything! I can't. Is Tolstoy alive or not?"

"Yes. He's alive."

"Then why are they saying the burial service over
him? This sounds like a funeral dirge!"

The proofreader put on his glasses, swept them off
again, and sucked at his pipe, which had gone out.
"Yes, of course," he replied, narrowing his eyes with
the shyness of the shortsighted and swaying slightly.
"Of course, it is a bit contradictory."

"A bit? Let us hope it is only a bit!"

"You know, it's the voice of the people. To their
mind he must have heard the call of death. And as
for the contradiction—what is to be done about it?
I read everything twice or three times over and I wonder. They exhort everyone to leave him in peace,
not to search for him, not to touch him, not to bother
him, to respect his wishes—all in one voice, and here,
look at this." He held out the proofs.

With his curiosity suddenly flaring up, Pastukhov
read the telegrams that gave the details of Tolstoy's
flight from home, the search for him on the trains
and stations, in the monasteries, accounts given by eye-
witness and relatives, rumors, gossip, theories. As
he read on, he wanted to know more, to get a wider
view, as though penetration into that distant, enigmatic,
palpitating destiny could appease some fervent need
of his own. As he read on, his bewilderment over the
events increased and became more and more tormenting.

He wiped his cold, damp brow.

Now he could see plainly in the dark night the
squat, whitewashed cowshed to which the snorting
horses were led out of the stables and hastily put between the shafts. The furtive, startled light of the
lantern, flickering in the gust. The valise stowed away
roughly into the cart. And the little old man at a distance, in the waterproof cloak with the hood, from
under which glimpses of the matted foam-white beard
could be seen. "Hurry, hurry!" the old man urged,
peering into the darkness, where, behind the wall of

the dense park, moaning in the wind, loomed the old house, now deserted and neglected forever. Quick, quick! they may catch up and not let him go, keep him back with tears, lamenting, and wailing. Hurry!

"But why? Why?" Pastukhov asked himself aloud.

And hereupon, as though in answer, his eye picked out of the columns of text the sobering, bitter sentence: "It is always like that in life, by the way: when we do the most abominable things, people think it most natural, but when we do what we ought to do, everyone is astounded and cannot swallow it."

He rose and went to the exit.

"Excuse me a moment . . . I mentioned you in the office," the proofreader said in a worried tone, leaving his high desk. "They are very anxious for you to drop in—"

"Afterward, afterward!" Pastukhov called back, running faster.

He hurried through the streets—he did not know where. First he descended the causeway, then turned back toward the hillside, and finally went down almost as far as the water's edge. Darkness enveloped the river. The faint light of the buoys seemed to be dying from weakness. The wharf lights shone weakly. The surge of the waves seemed lost in admiration of its own power. A fine drizzle was falling.

Pastukhov stood in the chilly, penetrating darkness on the edge of some high slippery planks, his dripping hat pulled well down on his head, his hands thrust deep into his pockets. He was conscious of utter loneliness, not subdued by those delicate shades that give it a wistful sweetness, but in the rough, ruthless tone of the all-enveloping gloom. He was already convinced that the departure of a man who had unexpectedly become the crest of his consciousness was a departure into death. And as all really important events in this world are irrevocable, this event, too, was obviously beyond repair.

The rain drove him homeward. Hanging his wet clothes on the backs of chairs, he got into bed, tucked the covers warmly about him, and fell into a suffocating, unpleasant sleep.

Next morning he went to the editorial offices again. The paper was full of the things he had read the previous evening. The living man stared, still more angrily than before, it seemed, from the portraits reproduced. His expression, to Pastukhov's mind, had the wisdom of a peasant. Under the mustache there was a hint of craftiness mingled with reproach and a mocking superiority over the vanity of existence.

The editor, who bore a striking resemblance to the martyr Saint Nicholas, with an oval beard, and a white tonsurelike ring of hair around his bald crown, had not slept for three nights, and the whites of his eyes were shot with rusty red. Blinking and snuffling, he spread the latest telegrams before Pastukhov.

The globe's center of gravity had shifted. It gravitated now toward a small railway station, the name of which became in the course of a single day Tolstoy's second name. No one was to have known where the old man, driven by some high impulse, had gone, and yet the whole world knew where he was. No one was to have known the intentions of his soul, and yet the whole world was aware of his secret purpose. No one was to have concerned himself with the state of his health, and yet the whole world was watching his temperature, the wheezing in his chest, his digestion, and his pulse. Everyone realized that it was the moment to move aside and keep silence, and yet they all crowded around, pushed their way in, created a crush, and talked and talked and talked. No one had the strength of mind to withstand it—they rushed out into the giant bazaar of the world, open to the four winds of Heaven.

The telegraph brought article after article from the papers of the capitals. All of them began and ended with the words: "He has gone." "Gone, gone, gone!" —the papers repeated as though until then everybody had been happy and peaceful simply because Tolstoy had not stirred from his Yasnaya Polyana, and had lost this peace and happiness as soon as he had gone. . . . "Gone from the world, as, in his declining days, the legendary prophet Moses went, and as Buddha, who imparted his teaching to millions, went away. . . ."

"Whom did Buddha go away from?" Pastukhov asked.

"From his spouse Yasudhara," the editor replied. He was waiting for Pastukhov to finish reading, and as soon as he had run through the telegrams, he asked him, speaking of himself in the plural, after the immemorial custom of editors: "We want you to write something for us about his departure."

"But I have no ideas on the subject. Nothing—except confusion and dismay."

"Then write about confusion and dismay."

"Why?" Pastukhov demanded in unaffected surprise.

"It's highly necessary. Not to mention your reputation. You're a native of these parts."

"That hardly releases me from the obligation to write only when I have something to say."

"It will be sufficient for you to say what you feel. The appearance of your name in the papers will be a sign that the press sympathizes with you. After all, the whole town knows you're mixed up in a political affair."

"Mixed up in a political affair?" Pastukhov showed still greater surprise.

"No need to hide it. There are no secrets from us," the editor said insinuatingly, while his countenance assumed the expression of all-comprehending grief suitable to an ancient icon.

"Very well," Pastukhov agreed with a mischievous smile. "I'll try. But I'm going to write about life, not death. I'm going to write of the living Tolstoy."

"That'll be splendid!" sighed the editor, dozing with weariness.

The nearer Pastukhov got to home, the deeper became the nervous excitement that had entered into him. He felt an influx of strength in his soul, sweeping it on to larger deeds: his feeling was going to merge with the feeling of the world, his voice would be heard in the general mourning—no, no!—in the general hosanna! He would write—yes, he was going to write about the unbounded heart of the world, the heart of Russia!

He cut himself some sheets of paper and sat down. He wanted to say that the heart of Russia could not release beyond its bounds a man who belonged to it like the very secret of life, without which there was no heart. The man wanted to retire into obscurity, but this intention was contrary to nature, inasmuch as a part cannot leave the whole. Nature itself had risen against the rebellion and held back what belonged to it. The man was brought to a halt at the place where he had always been and always would be—the heart of Russia. The winds that blew in Astapovo were the same that blew at Yasnaya Polyana. All around lay the same peasant Rūs, the lands of Penza and Tambov, the lands of Voronezh and Saratov, of Tula and Ryazan. It was they who had borne this man and they were going to keep him in their bosom forever.

Pastukhov read over the scribbled pages. It occurred to him that a grave should receive a man in the place where he had lived, and that he, Pastukhov, was reverently digging his grave with others like him. He crossed out what he had written and paced up and down the room.

Another thought occurred to him, and once again he settled down to work. Culture, he imagined, was a closed chain of impelled movement. He borrowed this formula from mechanics, which beautifully defines the conception of mechanism. The whole life of thinking mankind unfolded itself before him like an endless system of cogwheels. He remembered that while Pushkin was writing *The Captain's Daughter*, young Herzen was already going into banishment. Herzen's future had caught the movement of a wheel soon to be stilled. What a multitude of cogs had touched Tolstoy's wheel! Who would carry on its movement? Had not Pastukhov felt in himself a fraction of the powers with which this great life endowed people?

He crossed out these lines, too, smiling as he did so: to introduce himself, however remotely, into meditations on Tolstoy appeared petty to him. He decided to make some coffee. Opening the sideboard, he inhaled the bitter, delicately spicy, burnt aroma of the coffee beans and felt refreshed. He had a scent as keen as a fly's, and smells revived him like contact with the joyous essence of existence. He ground the coffee in the mill, gripping it between his knees and listening to the crisp crackle of the cogwheels as though it was music. He rinsed out the coffeepot and lit the spirit lamp. While the water was coming to a boil, he had a smoke. His thoughts jostled each other as if seeking an outlet, some kind of a door. The doors stood ajar, but opened into empty rooms. He thought to himself that Tolstoy would have enjoyed some strong coffee just now and they were probably giving him thin

oatmeal gruel; one of the telegrams said he had had
some oatmeal. Pastukhov put in the coffee and brought
it to a boil. He sipped a cup of it, scalding hot. His
head grew clearer, he asked himself the question: what
was the chief thing in Tolstoy?—and answered at once:
the chief thing was love.

He ran quickly over to the table and poured out
another cup of coffee.

He described the Tree of the Poor, known to all
Russia. The boughs of the old tree spread over the
open space in front of the house at Yasnaya Polyana.
There was a bell attached to it. Everyone who needed
help or wanted to hear a kind word had only to come
to the tree, strike the bell, and wait on the bench in the
shade for someone to come out of the house. Under
the Tree of the Poor there was a place for all who
believed that men were brothers. Perhaps only few
of the weary had tasted complete repose under its
canopy. But each lived in the knowledge that at the
darkest moments of depression, despair, and need he
might turn his steps toward this shelter, and raise his
hand to the bell and call for aid. In the hour of death
of him who had set the bench under the Tree and
hung up the bell, the last hope of the desperate would
vanish, the shelter of the poor would be no more. The
tree would wither, the bell would be stilled. Russia,
where will you turn then for a word of love?

Pastukhov ceased writing and fell into that state of
trance when thought is numb. Then he flung the paper
to the floor with a despairing gesture. No! He wanted
to write in a lofty style and it turned out mawkish.
He kept thinking, against his will, of death, only death,
and no matter what he began to write about, death
watched him with hollow eyes. He straightened his
back, went over to the bed, sat down on it, then laid
his head on the pillow and slept all day till midnight.

The next day he went to the editorial office to confess that he was a failure. He thought out an excuse:
he was only a playwright, an artist, he knew his own
line; newspaper stuff was beyond him. But the sleepy
editor was not in the least put out by all this.

"It doesn't matter," he said. "We decided to ask you
to go to Astapovo as our correspondent. It would, of

course, be a very good thing for us, and rather tempting for you, too, I fancy."

"Oh, that goes without saying! But it's impossible, for the reason you yourself mentioned last night—I'm mixed up in a political case and I am bound over not to leave." Pastukhov said this proudly and even a little solemnly.

"Never mind," the editor consoled him with a look of understanding intended to convey that he was well used to literary men's attempts to put up their price. "We may be able to help you. Won't you sit down, please, and write an application to the Prosecutor, and it would be better to take it there at once. And meanwhile I'll try to get in touch with the Prosecutor by telephone."

Controlling his agitation, Pastukhov began to draw up the application. He sensed from afar the breath of freedom. Plans for putting an end to the abominable misunderstanding and getting out of this boring provincial town flashed through his mind. His correspondence from Astapovo would attract widespread attention, and the papers of the capital would immediately insist on his transference to St. Petersburg. Or, still better, he would fall ill at Astapovo, and the illness would necessitate treatment in Moscow clinics. Or, he could go simply, without any permission, from Astapovo to St. Petersburg and lodge a complaint there about the conduct of the secret police to the Minister for Home Affairs. In short, Astapovo seemed a gift of the gods, that same crystal stopper that had been needed to bring to a boil the pot Pastukhov was watching.

The world looked more cheery to his eyes as he was strolling to the law offices. The bare trees in the Limes tossed a boisterous welcome to him, encouraging his diffident hopes. The people were hurrying through the streets, glad that the whistling wind was driving the gray clouds over the roofs. Schoolgirls turned to look at Pastukhov as a figure of local renown, and he fancied they were whispering: "Look, that's Pastukhov! He's going to Astapovo! Have you read what he wrote about Tolstoy?" Yes, indeed, it was a long time since he had enjoyed such a heartening, such a resounding day.

At the very entrance Pastukhov encountered Oznobishin. Dressed in black—his autumn clothes—he very courteously raised his cap and very circumspectly slackened his pace, as if giving the impression that he was ready to stop. Pastukhov greeted him.

"Were you going to visit us?" Oznobishin's tone was almost delighted.

"Yes, with an application to the Prosecutor. I have to leave for Astapovo without delay."

"We know that already. They rang up the Assistant Prosecutor from the editorial office and he promised to report the matter to His Excellency tonight."

"Tonight? But you can see yourself that every minute is precious. Tolstoy may—"

"Is his condition really hopeless?"

"We have very alarming news," Pastukhov said importantly.

"Yes," sighed the other sympathetically, "a great sorrow for the world."

"I can see you take it to heart," Pastukhov went on in a grateful tone. "May I ask you to do everything you can to help me to go?"

"May I have your application? I'll hand it to the Assistant Prosecutor myself. No need for you to trouble yourself."

Pastukhov made a swift movement toward Oznobishin and, taking him by the arm, spoke as though he had been intimate with him for years, and yielded to an impulse to confide the idea that had crossed his mind.

"I'll tell you my plan. Astapovo is on our railway. Express trains are leaving for Astapovo one after another. The management will do everything to oblige. Our press must have authentic details of all that is taking place by the deathbed of the great man. The honor of the town is at stake. We'll be ahead of the capitals. If I get permission to leave in an hour's time, I'll catch the express and be in Astapovo tonight." Blinking, he stared at Oznobishin.

"Unfortunately, it's impossible to lay the matter before His Excellency until tonight," Oznobishin said.

"Good Lord!" Pastukhov exclaimed. "But this is Tolstoy—think of it!"

"I quite understand, but . . . but . . . His Excellency . . ." Oznobishin excused himself with a smile.

"What an unwieldy machine your law courts must be," Pastukhov boomed, thrusting out scornful lips.

"The courts of law are not a machine," Oznobishin retorted half jokingly, freeing his arm, nevertheless, from Pastukhov's, "and not so very unwieldy, when all's said and done."

"Oh, it's not for me to listen to such talk! And it's not for you—what is your patronymic?—Anatoli Mikhailovich, to indulge in it."

"Why not, Alexander Vladimirovich?" the other rejoined, not in the least abashed by the reproach, but on the contrary, with a certain playfulness.

"Surely it isn't necessary to ask that? That stupid affair is dragging on for I don't know how many months, and you still keep me tied up like a yard dog," Pastukhov complained.

"Oh, really, you know," Oznobishin protested, embarrassed. "I can assure you things are coming to an end."

"I don't believe it."

"I have no right to speak of the state of affairs in a definite way, but the final decision is a matter of days now."

"I don't believe it, I don't believe it!" Pastukhov repeated, waving him away.

Then Oznobishin himself took Pastukhov by the arm in a confidential manner and, leading him away from the doorway in which they were standing, said in a lower tone: "This is between ourselves. Strictly between ourselves. The case is being held up all because one of the accused is missing. You know who it is, don't you?"

"How should I know? What have I to do with missing people of any kind?"

"Ragozin, perhaps the chief personage in the case, has not yet been found," Oznobishin said softly, casting an attentive side glance at Pastukhov and slowing down. "You can't sentence a missing person in a case like this, and therefore the investigations were more protracted than usual. Only—"

"Oh, for God's sake!—what do I want with all this talk? Forgive me!" Pastukhov exclaimed, almost

weeping with exasperation. "All I want is one thing—
to be released from my bond."

"Very soon now," Oznobishin whispered with something like brotherly sympathy.

Pastukhov halted, gave the man a long penetrating
look, and, gripping his feminine hand, shook it so hard
that Oznobishin winced.

After handing him the application and securing once
more his promise to obtain an answer from the Prosecutor that same night, Pastukhov went for a walk,
taking pleasure in the bracing wind, the animation of
the passers-by, the busy tinkle of the streetcar bells,
and the brisk clop-clop of the horses' hoofs.

He had dinner in a restaurant, made some coffee at
home, packed his bag, shaking out the suits carefully,
thinking over how he would dress at Astapovo should
mourning prove necessary—and what shirt he would
put on when he went to talk over his play with the
theater management in Moscow. As dusk was falling,
he went out to the newspaper office, but, on learning
that the Prosecutor's answer was not expected until
about eleven, wandered about the town, feeling un-
settled.

He dropped in at the movies. The usual pianist was
improvising to the emotional and dramatic moments,
and the screen bobbed and trembled under the explosive and irresistible chords. Henny Porten, a large,
luxurious blonde with the prominent, beseeching eyes
of a Brünnhilde, went through incredible suffering on
the screen. The light quivered, and its beams were
frequently crossed by a huge autumn bluebottle.
"Santa Lucia, Santa Lucia," the piano wailed while
Henny Porten sobbed.

It was quiet in the street; it seemed that the night
was lying in wait for a fresh wind to come from
somewhere far across the Volga and take the place of
the daytime wind that had died.

A few lights shone out in the windows of the houses.
The banging of the wicket gates ceased, and Pastukhov
passed through whole blocks of the town without
meeting a soul.

As he crossed the threshold of the editor's office just
after midnight, he could scarcely control his agitation.

The editor raised his head from the desk and said, without waiting for questions:

"Nothing doing, my dear chap. The Prosecutor has turned down your application."

Pastukhov sank slowly into an armchair.

"But it makes no difference now, unfortunately. We have received word that Tolstoy . . ." He half rose to his feet and bowed his head as he concluded: "is dead."

Pastukhov felt that he should stand up, too, but he could not; he only leaned heavily forward.

"Didn't you know?" the editor asked. "The news has gone all around the town, our telephone never stops ringing, we're only waiting for corroboration from the telegraph agency."

Pastukhov said nothing. Everything around him looked superfluous and somehow fictitious: the neat proofs on the desk, the thick red pencil, the big peaked shade of the lamp, and—in the shadow—the lifeless gleam of the editor's bald head with its tonsure of untidy gray-white hair.

"Everything has to come to an end in this world," the editor mumbled wearily.

Pastukhov held out his hand in farewell.

He wondered at the silence that reigned in every corner. But as he was passing through the narrow corridor, he heard the startled ringing of the telephone and dashed down the stairs like a man set free.

· 30 ·

When he reached the hotel, Pastukhov knocked at the door of Tsvetukhin's room. No one answered. But he kept on knocking. He had to talk, and he could talk to one person only, one who could hearken to his dismay and respond like a friend.

Pastukhov turned his back to the door and kicked it hard. He heard the key jump out of the hole and its ring of metal as it fell on the floor. The door was suddenly thrown open, and he saw Tsvetukhin in his night clothes, barefoot, his chest exposed. They were silent a moment; then slowly and gently Tsvetukhin took him by the hand and drew him into the room.

"You should have come long ago," he said in a delighted tone. "It was all so damned silly."

"It certainly was," Pastukhov rejoined, feeling instant relief and speaking as simply as though nothing had ever happened between them.

They kissed three times after the old custom, and clapped each other heartily on the back.

"What do you think of the news, eh? Tolstoy, eh?" Tsvetukhin said.

"You know all about it, too?"

"Yes, of course."

They did not let go of each other as they stood in the middle of the small room, with the clothing hung on the chairs and the two tumbled beds. Pastukhov could feel through Tsvetukhin's thin clothing the hot, yielding, deeply divided back, and gave it another fond and hearty slap.

At the same moment they heard a loud, sibilant whisper. "Heavens above! Holy Mother of God! Isn't this grand!"

"Mefody? Come in, you ass!" Tsvetukhin said smiling as he glanced over Pastukhov's shoulder at the half-open door.

Mefody plunged noisily into the room. "My dear fellows!" he burbled, gesticulating wildly and hopping from one to the other in his delight. "Here we are again, eh! That's the way! That's what I call sense! It does my heart good to see you! At last you're together. Lord, now lettest thou thy! . . . Let's have a celebration! Come on, let's make a night of it! What about it, Egor? What about it, Alexander Vladimirovich? Let's celebrate the triumph of human reason over the hardening of the heart. Let's wash away with wine the deadly sins of enmity and malice!"

"I can see you've been at the washing business already," Pastukhov remarked.

"A foretaste, in anticipation of the joys to come!" Mefody gabbled, shaking and clutching and pushing his companions about, starting back a step or two to see them better, only to throw himself on them again.

"Well, all right, then, do the ordering, devil take you!" Tsvetukhin gave his permission with evident pleasure.

Mefody pushed the bell with all his might, then poked his head out of the door and bawled into the corridor: "Deniska! Deniska!"

"What are you doing? Want to wake the whole place?" Tsvetukhin rebuked him. "Go down to the bar yourself and see about it."

Fifteen minutes later, assisted by the clumsy Deniska, Mefody, in a state of blissful self-forgetfulness, and with the quiet exaltation of one performing a ritual, was laying the table, rattling the crockery. They all waited in silence until the bottles took their central position among plates of varicolored viands arranged like flower beds around the pedestal of a monument.

"Now, in the fear of God and with faith, let us begin," Mefody whispered.

The room had been tidied, Tsvetukhin had dressed, everything had acquired a respectable look, and so, with due consideration and even respect for each other, the comrades took their places at the table.

"Well," said Pastukhov rather sadly, " so it is a wake, after all?"

"Yes, when you come to think of it," Mefody said, startled. "What are we to do about that? What shall we say?"

"We'll start like this," Pastukhov answered, pouring out the vodka.

Eating leisurely, with their eyes downcast studying the plates, they sighed, one after the other, and Tsvetukhin said half questioningly:

"We drink to the repose of his soul, is that it?"

They had another drink and started on the cold jellied fish with lemon.

"The deceased didn't approve of it," Mefody remarked, flipping the decanter with his hard nail and shaking his head regretfully. "This was the only flaw in his otherwise useful activity. It can be overlooked and forgiven. But what matins he gave the priests!"

"Yes, he certainly gave it to you hot," Pastukhov remarked.

"Us? What do you mean?" Mefody exclaimed, taking offense. "We've shaken the dust of the priesthood off our feet. We are Protestants. By our break with the seminary we contributed to the great work of the great Protestant."

"You have indeed contributed to the great work," Pastukhov repeated mockingly, pushing his empty glass toward Mefody. "Fill it up, rhetorician, fill it up."

They clinked glasses cheerfully, and Pastukhov, looking much brighter, but with his head bowed, said very quietly: "I can see plainly where this is going to lead" (he jerked his head in the direction of the bottles). "So, before we get quite drunk, I want to tell you about the one who will never come back again." He paused. "I've been wondering all the time—why this flight? Why did he go at nighttime with the lantern, the torch, through the darkness? Was he escaping from his spouse Yasudhara? What nonsense! Was it not from the present time, in which everything was against him? Was it not the time that ejected and discarded him as something entirely foreign to its essence? After all, he had not gone alone. He had taken our past with him. Was it only the nineteenth century? No, it was more than the nineteenth century. More, let us say, than humanism. He took into the grave with him not only the Encyclopedists, let us say. Perhaps all that was best in the Christian era found its expression for the last time in him alone and vanished with him forever. There will be none like him. In memoriam—and—nothing more."

Pastukhov thrust his fingers through his hair and said nothing for a few moments.

"Who will come to take his place? That's an enigma. But his weapons will no longer serve. His fight will be continued in a new guise, in different battles. And very likely we, my friends, will come to the conclusion at the end of our lives that just as the era ending with him lasted for centuries, so the other era following it will last centuries, too."

He gave Tsvetukhin a swift glance.

"Have I dug deep enough?" he asked ironically.

"Good heavens, old man—go deeper, by all means. You don't know how I adore this kind of thing!" Mefody implored.

"That'll do," Tsvetukhin stopped Mefody and laid his hand on Pastukhov's shoulder. "It's fine, Alexander, do go on."

"No, that's all I have to say," Pastukhov said wearily. "I'm not a prophet, I don't want to foretell the future. I shall say only one thing. He has left us a rule, as plain as a word. Here is the earth. Here is man on earth. And here is a task: a life good for man must be built up on earth."

"And if we have any respect for ourselves," Tsvetukhin continued his friend's speech, "We have no right to think of anything but this rule. If we are going to learn of life—we are going to achieve something. As he learned. As he created for the sake of life and not for the sake of flourishes. If not, then we shall remain, like our art, mere flourishes!"

"So that's what you're getting at, is it? Back to your pet subject again," Pastukhov pounced on him, blinking. "But it's true, undoubtedly true. After him—there can be no joking either in life or in art. It would be a disgrace."

"It is a disgrace—it is a disgrace!" Mefody exclaimed, tearfully. "Now we're off! Good lads! Let's get on a bit further! No good just marking time!"

They drank in unison, and their heads seemed to have been waiting for that glass, as for the last cleaving blow. Now freed of all toils and ties, they roamed at will through some wonderful planless city where the streets interlaced, intertwined like a ball of yarn a kitten has tangled. Here everything was mixed up—tears, censure, and joy, the French Revolution and the written promise not to leave the town, the government that opined that excommunication should be lifted from Tolstoy, the Holy Synod, which resolved not to permit this, the rights of man and citizen, Mefody's crystal stopper, the poet Alexander Blok's verses, Kirill in prison, daybreak seen through the window, a herring's tail in a wine glass, kisses, curses, empty bottles, Tolstoy's teaching of nonresistance to evil—until all these turned into a blurred mess, and sleep overcame them.

The host gave up his own bed to Pastukhov, while he and Mefody took the other, and they knew nothing of the cold, cheerless day awaking, how it came to life, reached its climax, wore on to its decline.

When they awoke, they felt the necessity to pull themselves together and dispatched Mefody, who suffered more than anyone, for vodka. But he had only just gone out when he ran back again, calling out hoarsely —he had lost his voice overnight—"He's alive! He's alive!"

He waved a big sheet of paper over the beds.

"Get up! Get up! He's thought better of it! He's put it off!" The three men, with tousled hair and shirts open at the neck, huddled close to read the newspaper, almost tearing it in their eagerness. The stop-press news was headed in bold type:

"We hasten to contradict the information published last night of Leo Tolstoy's death—Leo Tolstoy is alive."

They did not look at each other. Mefody was sub-

dued. They stood motionless, reading with difficulty
the telegrams strung in columns—the jumble of in-
consistencies asserting things that no one believed,
and denying those that everyone was convinced of.
Pastukhov pinned the news sheet to the wall. Tsvetukhin opened the window. They got dressed and
straightened up the room.

"Still, I can't think he'll last long now. Just a brief
delay," Pastukhov said.

"Who can tell?" Mefody ventured. "He's a very
sturdy old man. He's stood the test of time, the old
fellow has. He may get over it yet."

"Don't gab so much," Tsvetukhin rebuked him
gloomily. "Do your own job."

"I understand you: and what a blessed occasion for
it!" Mefody said delightedly as he disappeared through
the doorway. "This very minute!"

He came back as promptly as though he had simply
spun round on one foot. They seated themselves at
the table again. As easily as children slide down into a
gulley, they tumbled into a noisy confusion out of
which they had just been dragged by drunken sleep.

For two days running they seemed to themselves
to be now infinitely happy, now miserable. They could
not, even had they wished, remember the order in
which the beer house, the theater, the mulled wine, the
sturgeon soup in the tavern, the night spent at Pastukhov's house, the awakening in Tsvetukhin's room,
the pancakes fried in sunflower seed oil, eaten in Guzzlers' Row in the Upper Bazaar place, had followed
each other. The world turned into a swing, now
soaring to the sky, now rocking, like a cradle. Then
suddenly, out of somewhere, a street conversation,
given by anxiety and pain, would break in:

"Well, is he still alive?"

"Good heavens, no! He's been dead these two days."

"You don't say so? Why, that was contradicted, I
read it myself."

"So they were in too much of a hurry, eh?"

"Yes, well if he has to go, better to go quickly. He's
had enough pain in his time."

Then, like something on a page over which ink had
been spilled, telegrams written in the post office and

sent to Moscow and St. Petersburg emerged inde-
cipherably in the memory. The telegrams were torn up,
rewritten, unexpectedly repeating the Astapovo telegrams, and then the post office merged with the newspaper office, from which, once more, with striking
clearness, the memory bore out the freshly printed
lines: "Later in the evening the temperature was 36.6,
the pulse 110, breathing 36. The patient ate little."

And now, after dull tossing and turning in a fog,
Pastukhov saw himself in the morning in the street,
as an unexpected gift—after a refreshing sleep, and
feeling like a man who has come to a new place and is
delighted to find himself alone. No one hung on his
arms, talked nonsense in his ear, or tried to kiss him.
He was his own master and kept silence with pleasure.
The sense of desired sobriety consisted of pleasant
trifles: he was shaven, had changed his clothes, his
hands smelled of soap, his sight distinguished one object from another as though everything around him was
cut and faceted.

He could see from a distance the crowd around the
window of the newspaper office, but he did not quicken
his steps; he went toward it in a reserved, quiet manner. Two artillerymen, smelling of Eau de Cologne,
moved away from the crowd, and a very young ensign
turned a radiant face toward his comrade and said:

"And still, he wept and said: 'It is the peasants—the
peasants who know how to die!'"

"You think he was afraid? He fought at Sevasto-
pol."

"Still, he envied them."

"It's harder for the old to die—they know too much."

Pastukhov saw behind the glass, high over the heads
of the crowd, a long supplementary column in a broad
mourning frame. The old man's living image was looking down at the people. Pastukhov noted that his hair
curled like a child's at the temples, and he slowly
read the words he was fully expecting to see: "6:50 a.m.
(from our own correspondent)—At 6:05 a.m. Leo
Nikolayevich Tolstoy passed away quietly."

Then he skimmed the headings: "A Dangerous Condition," "His Last Moments," and then again: "Today
at 6:05 a.m. . . ." and the signatures of five doctors.

After this he read spasmodically: ". . . The correspondents rushed off to the telegraph, reluctant to believe in the inevitable end. . . . We correspondents feel the last moments of this great man, heart and soul. . . . Mourn, Russia, and be proud! . . . Very slowly, in single file, the correspondents paced around the house where the sufferer lay. . . ." But he could not read to the end and returned again to the lines: "Today at 6:05 a.m . . ."

Moving away at last, he decided it was time he went home. He started at the easy, poised stride with which he usually set out on long walks. It seemed to him that he was still enjoying the sense of sobriety. He still saw each object with the same startling, clear-cut sharpness of outline. It was a week now since he had thought of Tolstoy's death that everyone was awaiting, and he had been sure that he had already grown accustomed to it and it could no longer startle him. That he thought only in snatches somewhat surprised him. His thoughts kept returning to the same incoherent phrases: "fled . . . from his spouse Yasudhara" and "very slowly, in single file, the correspondents paced." He tried to drive out the trifling, senseless phrases, and to think coherently but could not manage it.

The house was damp and smelled like a lodging-house of drunken people. He opened the windows and the flue. He soiled his hands with the soot, washed them thoroughly, and, with the towel over his shoulder, went up to the table.

The scattered sheets of manuscript reminded him that he had tried to read his play to his far-from-sober friends, and that Mefody had roared that he was a genius. He carefully put the sheets together. A sentence took shape in his mind, and he did not know whether it belonged to him or had occurred in one of the articles he had been reading this week: "If the inhabitants of other planets were to ask our world: 'Who are you?' —mankind might answer with pride, pointing to Tolstoy: 'We are he!' "

Very calmly, with the conviction and consciousness of doing right, Pastukhov tore his manuscript to bits, and the scraps of paper flew about the floor. With a grimace of contempt and pain he turned away from the table, went over to the bed, stood motionless for a moment, and suddenly slumped down. Burying his face in the towel, he burst out crying and sobbed as he had done as a child—in the same room—when his father punished him cruelly and unjustly.

CHAPTER

· 31 ·

MERKURI AVDEYEVICH was climbing the steps of the lodginghouse, surveying the rickety staircase meanwhile with reforming scrutiny. The caretaker, a veteran of the war with Turkey, followed close behind his employer. Meshkov would point with his silver-knobbed stick at a rotting board, a nail sticking out, a broken baluster, and turn around each time to the soldier without speaking, obliging him to look in the direction his stick pointed. Disconcerted, the old soldier shook his head ruefully. At last they reached the bunks where the tenants, shivering with cold, were getting through the business of the morning, preparatory to sallying out into the town in quest of the day's precarious earnings.

In the corner by the Parabukins' curtain, an elderly, bristly carpenter was sharpening his gouge on a whetstone.

"You'd do well to take your ax and go mend the stairs," Meshkov remarked to him. "Anyone might break his neck coming up those stairs to you."

"What business is it of mine? It's your house, you repair it," the carpenter retorted coolly, without pausing in his work.

"You think you're still living in the village, I suppose? It's not my road—so it doesn't matter whether it's passable or not, eh? The stairs—it's for common use, isn't it?"

"Aye, and when it comes to collecting the money, it's yours, I expect, but when it comes to repairs, then you talk of common use. You think you're Tolstoy, do you? All for the common good, and the rest of it."

His neighbors in the bunks laughed. Parabukin popped his head through a slit in the curtain; his features were fined down by emaciation and there was a swollen bruise of very recent date under one eye.

"You know a lot about Tolstoy, I'm sure," Meshkov said, rather taken aback by this retort.

"We know all right," Parabukin put in, having cleared his throat. "You aren't the only one who reads the papers."

"And what are you doing here?—delivering Sunday lectures?" Meshkov demanded. "Maybe you're preaching Tolstoy's ideas here? How many times have I told you to get out of that corner? Are you waiting for the constable to come and evict you?"

He turned to the caretaker.

"Why don't you see to things? You were told this corner had to be cleared."

"That's right, Merkuri Avdeyevich, I'm at him to get out day in, day out, I tell you, but all he says is: 'Where am I to go?—with the winter setting in and all, and me with young children?' He's as stubborn as a mule, honest to God he is!"

"I'm giving you fair warning, Tikhon. Don't get me angry, look out for another place to live while there's time," Meshkov said. "I don't care for suspicious characters: the police have their eye on you, and do you think I'm going to keep you here? Stirring up the folks hereabouts with your talk of Tolstoy?"

"Tolstoy's got your back up, has he? I daresay you're glad he's gone to his Maker."

"God can't have any use for him."

"A heretic, eh?" Parabukin sneered with a chuckle.

"Who are you to set yourself up as a judge?"

"And who's to judge, if not us? He listened to our judgment."

"How do you make that out? He was against drunkenness, and you're a drunkard. Look at that countenance of yours, swollen and bruised again—it'd make anyone sick to look at it."

"He was against drunkenness—that's true, of course. But he never went against conscience."

Merkuri Avdeyevich cleared his throat, and his brows drew down over his eyes as he demanded sternly: "What do you have to say about conscience?"

At that moment the curtains parted, and Olga Ivanovna appeared from behind her husband's back. Hastily tucking her pink flowered bodice, which matched the curtain, into the waistband of her skirt, she interposed in her usual garrulous manner: "Quite true, Tisha, as true as you're standing there! He had a conscience! He never did the poor any harm, Count Tolstoy didn't, all his life he helped them. He wouldn't turn a mother and her little children out into the frost, he would have pity on them."

"Why didn't you go to him for sympathy, then? Maybe, he'd have left you something. And you never started to think about him until after he was dead. It's a bit late to try to dally with him now. Your Count won't be able to help you from the grave."

"You're gloating over the heretic's death!" Parabukin repeated with ironic superiority, towering over Merkuri Avdeyevich and taking the offended Olga Ivanovna under his wing.

"You're talking a lot of nonsense," Meshkov interrupted him sternly. "It's unbecoming in a Christian to rejoice in anyone's death. I'm sorry for it, I'm not glad. I'm sorry that the old man died unrepentant, understand? He didn't cleanse himself before the holy church, but died in pride and impiety—an apostate!"

"Aha, so that's it? The impious wretch! Anathema! The brigand! Well, not a bit of it! He's cleaner than you are! Cleaner than your Coenobites, with their candles and their incense. All the Coenobites know is how to destroy every word of justice."

"They don't destroy the word, you babbler, they preserve it. The word that is God Himself. That's too hard a nut for you to crack."

"There are lots of nuts I can crack, Merkuri Avdeyevich. Only I can't crack them when people knock my teeth out. But maybe when it comes to thinking, well, I daresay I understand as much as you do."

"I'm not trying to knock your teeth out. It wasn't I who gave you that bruise, was it?"

"I'd like to see you do it! You're a cautious old fellow, you know who'll take a blow and who'll give it back."

"You're threatening me? You dare to threaten me before witnesses?"   .

Meshkov glanced around him. The rooming house tenants had gathered around, waiting to see where the argument would lead. Their greedy smiles had a touch of childish curiosity, as though they were standing before a cage where a mischievous boy was teasing an angry but amusing bird.

"What's that? Inciting the people against the landlord?" Meshkov said to the caretaker, and buttoned up his coat tightly in a businesslike way, as though he had decided to go somewhere for protection.

"Can't you hold your tongue, instead of letting it run away with you, you windbag?" the soldier said to Parabukin.

Olga Ivanovna threw herself forward to shield her husband. "Don't say any more, Tisha, don't say any more. We're poor folks, poor helpless people, nobody will have pity on us. You should be ashamed, Merkuri Avdeyevich—here's a sick, unhappy man, what has he done to you?"

"He's sore over Tolstoy," Tikhon said with a sneer again.

"Oh, leave Tolstoy alone!" Meshkov raised his voice. He had been shamed a little by Olga Ivanovna, but he still felt very irritable. "And don't dare to mention his name in vain. He was endowed with rare gifts, and you're no better than riffraff."

"Oh, now you're singing another tune. Rare gifts. It appears you've nothing against his gifts, you'd gladly have grabbed them and added them to your own domain. But the trouble is the apostate business. The pelt's a good one, see, it wouldn't have been a bad idea at all to enter it on the credit side, but he's a freethinker, he broke away, he disobeyed the Church, his sins won't let him into Paradise. It's different with me, he was neither kith nor kin of mine, and his mind is far above me, but still I can sing his praises. Because he called men to the truth. Whether he called them according to the rules or against them, it's all one to me. People looked up to him regardless of whether they agreed with him or not. And even you, Merkuri Avdeyevich, you're looking up to him though you abuse him. He stirs human feelings in you, too. . . ."

Putting his arms around Olga Ivanovna's shoulders, Parabukin pushed her gently away from him and took a step forward. He spoke in a quiet, melancholy voice, as though ashamed of his anger, and addressing his fellow tenants alone, avoiding Meshkov, who was staring somewhere over the heads of the people.

"Don't you start picking on me for that black eye: anybody can get into a fight. And I'm not boozing at present and that's when I understand that I'm a good-for-nothing. Olga Ivanovna is right. It's a pity I don't work any longer on the railway. I'd have been on that line and stopped at Astapovo Station—the times I've been there in my lifetime!—and I'd have stood at the window of that house where he died. I would have stood there, thinking; here am I, one of those good-for-nothings you turned your eyes upon, Leo! Aye, what's the use of talking! The general manager of the railway sent a wreath subscribed to by the railwaymen for his grave. If Tikhon Parabukin had been working on the railway now, there would have been a leaf or at least a blade of grass in that wreath from him. And now, as it happens, I'm out of it. Aye, Parabukin!"

"Those words might gladden his heart more than the wreath if he could hear them," Meshkov said, conciliated. "What does he want with a wreath?"

"What does he want with a wreath?" Tikhon mimicked. "You wouldn't want him to have it. You'd have driven an aspen stake into his back, as if he was the evil one."

Merkuri Avdeyevich started back, his trembling fingers touching the hand of the soldier, seeking support, gasping noisily for breath. He did not raise his voice but croaked with an effort, as though lifting a weight from the earth:

"Well, Tikhon, blame yourself for it now. I was going to take pity on your little ones, but you would put Beelzebub himself out of all patience. Gather your rubbish together and get out! I won't have even the smell of you here! I'm going straight to the police station. You'll sing a different tune there! They won't stand your dallying with the Count there!"

Parting the crowd of people glowering at him, he passed between the bunks, thumping his stick threateningly on the floor.

"You can go and good riddance!" Olga Ivanovna called after him. "We never expected anything good of you!"

Her prominent eyes dimmed, the corner of the mouth turned down and twitched, her broad brow flushed in red patches. An impulse of irresistible energy seized her small body—she rushed over to the box that served Annochka as a bed, lifted the lid, and started flinging out various articles of clothing and rags, talking without stopping:

"There must be some kind folks in the world still. Someone'll take pity on my poor little mites. We won't freeze. Annochka, dress Pavlik. Here are his stockings. No, the white pair looks better. And dress yourself. Here, take this. Put on this blouse. Never mind. We won't die. Here, take this tape to tie around your stockings. Pull them up higher. We've managed to live to this day, we'll manage to live a bit longer, I daresay. Take this belt and fasten it around Pavlik."

So she went on, seizing first one thing, then another, holding them up and looking at them against herself or Annochka, striving for a beauty known to her alone out of a combination of pitiful, cast-off rags.

Parabukin stood silent by the curtain. His face was petrified; he watched his wife with stunned fear. Suddenly catching sight of his expression, Olga Ivanovna broke off in the middle of what she was saying, darted up to him, and pressed her cheek to the chest that was still broad and deep.

"Never fear, Tisha," she said, seizing his hands and squeezing them hard. "There's nothing to be afraid of! I've thought it all over. And I've talked to the right people about it. Let's all go together. And now you get dressed."

She handed him a clean Russian shirt with embroidered neckband that she had saved in the trunk against a rainy day, and he, meekly enough, changed his shirt and put on a wadded jacket, very faded and rusty-looking, the product of his wife's indefatigable labor.

Olga Ivanovna, having shaken out and dusted and perched on the crown of her head a crumpled pale-blue felt hat with a canary yellow wing, tucked the elastic under her knot of hair with trembling fingers, and taking Pavlik in her arms, went ahead. She was closely followed by Annochka, who trotted along with short, stiff, anxious steps, and Parabukin. The rooming house watched them go with gravity, realizing that the woman's absurd holiday finery had been dragged out to the light of day as the last desperate weapon of indigence against the world's harshness. It was only after taking some vitally important decision that Olga Ivanovna could turn to her happy and forgotten past as resource. Not a word was said as the Parabukins passed between the bunks. And only when their footsteps had died away on the stairs, the carpenter sighed as he laid his planes, gouges, and drills away in his toolbox: "M-yes, he's in for it now, the old man is."

The Parabukins went up the causeway and turned the corner. Before they reached the school gate, Olga Ivanovna set Pavlik on the ground, pulled down his clothes, smoothed the fair curls resembling his father's which escaped from under the homemade cap, and took him by the hand. He had learned to walk. He toddled, held on to his mother, managing his foot rather like a scoop.

When they came level with the wicket, the Parabukins did not enter the yard, but after making two or three slow and uncertain steps, paused by the big gate which stood open.

Outside Vera Nikandrovna's home a carter was finishing loading the dray with furniture and bundles. The inevitable peak of all such loads, the samovar, shone already between the legs of an upturned chair. The carter was throwing a rope over the load and drawing it tight, having slipped one end through the slats of the side, and stood bracing his foot against the wheel. Vera Nikandrovna came out of the house carrying two lamps. There could be no doubt about it: she was moving.

Olga Ivanovna glanced at her husband in alarm. He

had guessed her intentions and understood that they were now completely shattered, but he said nothing. She darted forward, dragging the dawdling Pavlik after her.

"My dear!" she cried, nodding an excited greeting to Vera Nikandrovna. "We were just coming to see you!"

She pushed Pavlik before her, as though confident that he, in his homemade cap and tape belt, tottering on those uncertain legs that had not yet straightened, would provide an exhaustive explanation of all that had taken place.

"We were coming to see you. I hope you'll excuse us, I'm sure I would never have dared to do such a thing, only once, in the course of conversation, you remember?—you said that if anybody ever threw us out of the rooming house, you would give us shelter somewhere. So that's how things have turned out, dear Vera Nikandrovna. Meshkov has thrown us out in the street, unfortunate people that we are, just like this."

Her hand moved from Pavlik to Annochka, then to her husband, and she pulled down and straightened the children's frocks and then straightened her own hat, which had slipped sideways.

"But you see," Izvekova said, in some embarrassment, glancing down at the lamps, which she was pressing rather awkwardly to her sides.

"Yes. What's all this? Where are you going?" Olga Ivanovna asked, trying to pretend that she did not understand.

"Well, I've been thrown out, too, in a manner of speaking."

"Who on earth dared to do such a thing?"

"Oh, indeed!" Vera Nikandrovna said with a smile. "It's all so simple. The High Commisssioner of Education gave orders for my transference to another school. I'm moving to Soldatskaya Settlement, outside the town."

"Good heavens! How can such a thing happen?"

"Why shouldn't it happen? My son's in prison and I am not considered a trustworthy person any longer."

She said it with unprotesting bitterness and with such conviction that Olga Ivanovna stretched out her arms involuntarily to her and glanced around at her husband as though appealing to him for sympathy.

"Tisha! We would have helped Vera Nikandrovna to move to her new home, wouldn't we, if we weren't in the same fix ourselves. We're thrown out in the street, right out in the street."

"Well, what about it, if we are on the street?" Parabukin said contemptuously. "Nothing new, is it?"

"But the children—the little children!" Olga Ivanovna cried imploringly.

"Oh, don't trouble about me, thank you for offering to help me, I'll manage, I daresay," Vera Nikandrovna was saying, apologetically and at the same time consolingly.

"We'll manage, never fear—it isn't the first time," the carter called out suddenly, giving a jerk to the reins lying slack on the horse's mane. "Now we're off, ma'am!"

At that moment Annochka darted up to Vera Nikandrovna and, seizing a lamp by its foot, gabbled in her mother's loquacious, eager manner: "I'll carry that, let me, please let me! I'll see you there, I'll go with you. Let me have it, please, do!"

She tugged and tugged at the lamp trying to drag it away, while Vera Nikandrovna clutched it closer to her, looking at the girl with her eyes aglow. Stooping, she kissed Annochka on her brow and whispered tenderly: "Never mind that. Let go. You stay with Mama. Will you, like a good girl? And you'll come and see me some other time." Then, turning quickly to Olga Ivanovna, she said: "You must forgive me for not being able to help you this time. I'll have but one room in the place I'm going to. But if you like, Annochka can come to stay with me. I'd have her with pleasure."

"Oh, no, thank you, we couldn't think of troubling you!" Olga Ivanovna exclaimed, wiping away the tears with her knuckles. "We don't want to be a burden to you. Why should we? And besides, Annochka is the only help I have—what would I do without her? But if you'll allow us, we might stay in here, in the empty house, maybe? Just till we find a corner? What do you think of it? Only for a day or two while it's empty, eh?"

"But I'm afraid it isn't empty: the new schoolmaster is moving in today."

Oh, goodness me! It seems as if everything is . . .
well, really . . . Well, what do you think?" Olga
Ivanovna demanded with a fresh burst of energy,
"what do you think if we were to go to Meshkov's
daughter with our troubles?"

"To Shubnikova? Yes, why not? She's a kind-
hearted person. Yes, I think you should go."

"Well, if you've finished chatting, ma'am?" the carter
urged them again, taking the bridle and starting to
turn the rattling, clanking dray.

"That's the idea! That's just what I'm going to do!
Why didn't it occur to me straightaway, I wonder?"
Olga Ivanovna went on, hardly pausing. "Tisha, here,
you carry Pavlik. Come along, Annochka. You know
Lisa, don't you? Well, then, let's go. She's a lady
now—married and rich and happy. Lisaveta Merku-
lovna she's called now. She'll help us. Come along,
quick."

They all moved off behind the cart and passed
through the yard to the fussy Olga Ivanovna's unbroken flow of chatter. While the carter was closing
the creaking gates, the schoolmistress and the Parabukins
said farewell to each other, with many good wishes.
Then the family trailed away in the other direction
with Olga Ivanovna at the head of the procession,
and Annochka, turning, winked at Izvekova, as to a
very special friend of her own age, while Pavlik
stared attentively at the horse over his father's broad
shoulder.

Vera Nikandrovna was reminded of the day when
she and Kirill had watched the curious procession of the
Parabukins cross the yard, the first time she had made
the acquaintance of that odd family, and she felt very
sad. She glanced at the school. The three stark poplars
bowed before the wind, and their dry boughs creaked.
Within the walls of the house a shrill bell rang and
the sound came through the open panes in the windows and was followed by a chorus of high-pitched
voices of schoolboys. The lesson was over.

For more than twenty years now Vera Nikandrovna had been living in that house, and that same
shrill bell, those high-pitched boisterous shouts had
become a part of her life. Here began the way she
had gone with her freedom, her love, and her sorrow.

Here Kirill had been born, and while she had lain in
the throes of childbirth, the same bell had clanged
through the house, and she had tried to count the
lessons—the first, second and third, and when the
fourth and last lesson had started the child had come
into the world and his first cry had mingled with the
cheerful shouts of the boys racing downstairs because
they had been allowed to go home. Vera Nikandrovna's
husband had come over to the bedside, knelt down,
and kissed her brow, damp with cold sweat. Here,
in the attic, in the beating and whirring of doves'
wings, the boy Kirill had amused himself, and here,
when he grew older, he used to bring some favorite
book with him and sit by the dormer window, calling
it his country seat. Here, in this house, he had spent his
last day of freedom and from here had been taken
away into the unknown.

All that long and poignantly memorable path was
ended now, like a trail that, lost in the undergrowth of
the bank, leads to a slough. All that remained of the
past was piled on the dray, and Vera Nikandrovna
was following it.

The dray rattled over the cobbles, the carter, plod-
ding beside it, twirled the ends of the reins in the air
and from time to time pushed the back of a chair
farther under the rope. The streets stretched before
them, deserted and silent at first, then busier, with
clattering droshkies and noisy streetcars, and then again
came quieter, silent streets. The melancholy gray expanse of the river with its stark inhospitable sands
came in sight. The pavements came to an end, and
the wheels rolled soundlessly along the dusty ruts
between the ridges of frozen mud. Vera Nikandrovna
trudged alongside the dray, clutching the lamps, which
smelled of kerosene, close to her like something precious, and keeping her eyes on the linchpin, smeared
with tar, of the back wheel. She felt neither weariness
nor desire to reach her destination soon, nor even
reminiscences—they seemed to have been left behind
with the white house, the fence and the three bare
poplars, tossing in the wind.

Izvekova's new quarters were in a small cottage
with two windows, in a long row of houses in an
immense waste. Behind it lay the sidings of a freight

depot and the smoke-grimed buildings of the round-house and workshops. The piercing whistles of the engines and the long-drawn-out moans of the sirens now and again swept over the wasteland and over the roofs of the houses, or were carried in the direction of the hills and melted into their silence. The night was full of the angry puffing of the steam, the ring of hammers on iron, the spasmodic grating of the buffers between the cars, seeming to pass from carriage to carriage the warning words: steady there, steady there, steady there. All these sounds were new and distracting to the ear.

Vera Nikandrovna had not yet settled into her new home, had not yet grown accustomed to fetching pails of water from the pump at the corner, locking the door, bolting the shutters, lighting the smoky little stove that had its moods—when one night late someone knocked at her window.

From the time that Kirill had been taken away, she had waited constantly for some unexpected ter-rifying or joyful visit that would put an end to the wearying melancholy and bring about a complete change in her destiny. At times it seemed immaterial whether this would mean a change for the worse, a still greater misfortune than the one she was en-during, or whether it would mean relief and peace. But the expectancy was feverish, painful, morbid: it had undermined her strength and was becoming more and more unendurable.

The tap at the window in that little, lonely, and still alien house alarmed her. She wrapped herself in her shawl but did not go out or light the lamp; keeping close to the wall, she waited for the signal to be repeated. It was a windy night; the gusts sighed and whistled in a thin flutelike note in the cracks of the walls and window frames. A locomotive emitted a dreary hoot and shunted against a train of empty, hol-low carriages. It was a long train, and the alarmed sound of the buffers—steady there, steady there—drifted far away into the distance. The tap at the window was repeated. It sounded more insistent, yet at the same time there was something uncertain and tactful about it. Vera Nikandrovna ventured into the lean-to. It was not so quiet there; the piping of the wind in the crannies was bolder and livelier. She held her breath and listened. Then three steps rang out on the hard ground: someone had left the window and was at the door; it groaned under the blows of a heavy fist.

"Who is there?" she demanded, her breath catching in her throat.

"Does the schoolmistress Izvekova live here?" a man's low voice asked.

"But who is it?" she repeated, still unable to control the catch in her throat.

"Don't be so frightened, I am not going to harm you," the voice replied with such warmth and serenity that she felt relief, gaining control of herself at once.

"What do you want?"

"I have a message here about a certain business."

"Tell me who the message is from and what is it about."

"I don't know," the voice replied in a lower tone, adding questioningly: "But if you're Izvekova herself, then the business concerns your son."

"I'll just light the lamp," she cried loudly.

But instead of going into the room for the lamp, she struck up the heavy latch with both hands, putting all her strength into it, and opened the door.

The figure that emerged from the pitch darkness and stepped into the lean-to seemed extraordinarily tall to her. Bending his head, the man took a step forward and peered about him, apparently adjusting himself to the narrow space.

"Where's the message? Give it to me!" Vera Nikandrovna demanded in a whisper, as though startled by the noise the lifting of the latch had made and forgetting her recent dread of the newcomer.

"I'll have to get a light," he said, "my wallet is a very deep one, I can't feel for the note in the dark."

"You aren't deceiving me?"

"What would be the sense of deceiving you now?— the door's open."

The stranger spoke mockingly but so kindly that though she saw neither his face nor his eyes, and did not know whether he held something in his hands or not, she understood instantly, from his manner of speaking alone, that this was an old man, and she trusted him. She groped for the matches a long time on the hearth, and the stove, and in the kitchen drawer. After waiting patiently awhile, the visitor clapped his hands to his pockets to feel for a box, found one, and asked her:

"Where's your lamp?"

In the flare of the match she caught a glimpse of a lean face on which the folds of wrinkled skin hung loose, of a wedge-shaped white beard, and narrowed eyes. The thick belted jacket he wore shone with black patches of engine oil that had eaten into the material, which in consequence looked as stiff as bark. Taking off a cap as oily as the jacket, he laid it down on the wooden stool and leaned against the door post, his gray head reaching to the lintel.

"So you're Izvekova herself, are you?"

"Well, what do you think? Would I have let you in if I were anyone else?"

"I mean—maybe there might be someone else living here?"

"No, I'm alone."

"I see. So you'll be Vera Nikandrovna?"

"Look here, are you joking or what?"

"Hardly. At nighttime I wouldn't be likely to come for fun. I'm asking just to make certain."

"But I'm telling you—I'm Vera Nikandrovna, Kirill's mother, if it's Kirill Izvekov's mother you're looking for. The letter's from him, is it? Give it here, do!" She spoke in an almost commanding tone, holding out her hands and advancing on the old man.

One corner of the shawl slipped from her shoulders to the floor, exposing the embroidered nightgown, with the long, dark, hastily plaited hair hanging over it.

The old man's eyebrows rose understandingly and then drew together. He removed his cap from the stool to the table, sat down, and said with the goodnatured slyness of a grandfather: "As to who the letter's from, you'll read that for yourself. We'll get it out of the wallet in two ticks."

Gripping the edge of the stool, he stretched one leg stiffly, trod hard on the back of the dusty heel with the other foot to loosen it, pulled off the vamp with his hands, and slowly drew off the boot top. Then he drew out the inner sole and shook it lightly, nodding ruefully as though dissatisfied with its worn appearance. Again he thrust his hand into the boot and started to scrape something out of the toe.

"Good heavens, what a time you take!" Vera Nikandrovna exclaimed impatiently.

"That's the proper way," he agreed peaceably enough. "The better it's hidden, the easier it's found, you know."

At long last he drew out a paper rolled to the shape of the toe and handed it to Izvekova.

She unrolled it, turned up the lamp flame, and, standing close to it, deciphered the small but carefully written epistle.

"Dear Vera Nikandrovna,

"The writer is your son's friend. It's true, I'm much older than Kirill, but he called me his comrade and I call him mine. I am writing to comfort you in your anxiety about him. The affair has not ended so badly for him after all, but on the contrary, he's got off lighter than we might have expected. You may not know, but you will hear very soon that Kirill was sentenced to three years' banishment to Olonetsk gubernia. It isn't a very bad place, really, though it is in the North. He won't be alone there. There are some decent folks there and they will help him. I can promise you that during the initial period Kirill will be supported both as regards food and lodging. Money, too. Money may be sent to him as soon as he has a definite address. He will write to you himself. And books are to be had there, so he need not waste his time. There are educated people in those parts, too, so he will rather advance in knowledge than otherwise. Vera Nikandrovna, I want to tell you that Kirill has received word that you are well. I cannot promise definitely, but there may be a chance of sending him a letter. So you should get one ready, only a short one, though. And I must tell you, too, that you need have no doubts about your son. He is very young, but he could be an example for many a one far older than he is. The term will soon pass and Kirill will be such a support to you as perhaps you never expected him to be. Do not regret that he has laid such a trial upon your shoulders; the trials will stand him in good stead, for he is a strong man. I will say in closing this letter that though he has gone out for things that are big, he will never regret it, for he has aimed at something within his powers. And now good-by and best wishes. So get that reply ready. Destroy this letter as soon as you have read it."

Vera Nikandrovna gathered her shawl around her and turned toward the old man. He had put on his boot again and was sitting with his cap on his knees. His attentive, steady, and rather condescending gaze expressed satisfaction. The woman tried to discern in that gaze all that the stranger might know, and she understood that he was cut out for this kind of thing—to disguise with a good-humored gibe, and the sly glance of the quizzically narrowed eyes, all that might be known to him. Yet she could not help but ask the question that seemed the most vital at the moment.

"Who is this letter from?"

"Doesn't it say?" the old man exclaimed in feigned surprise, shaking his head regretfully. "There you are now!"

"You're not supposed to tell, is that it? But you know who sent you, don't you?"

"Who would send me? I've got legs and I can walk, can't I? Nobody's likely to go into the ins and outs, the why and the wherefore."

"Well, but just tell me this one thing—may I write a reply to this man? Just a few lines? And you'll send it to him?"

"Why bother to write, my dear Vera Nikandrovna? I've a good memory still, I can repeat whatever you want me to say, word for word."

"But I only wanted to write a line or two to thank him," she persisted gently.

"All right, then," he agreed in the kind tone he had used at first. "Only I can't wait very long. . . ."

"I won't be a minute!"

She ran into the other room and returned at once, tearing a leaf out of an exercise book on the way. She did not sit down, but leaning close to the lamp, she began to write in pencil, and the shawl slid slowly down from her shoulders as before.

"You did not want me to know from whom I re-

ceived the bitter news of my son. But I can see that
you are his friend and so you are mine, too. Thank
you, my dear friend, for the help you have promised
my boy and for your sympathy in my sorrow. I, too,
believe that he will bear his suffering with the dignity
that I think is characteristic of him. But so many dangers await him on the way, so many dangers and
torments! Help him, since you have taught him to call
you comrade and since you call him by that name!
And above all things, do not turn away from him when
things go wrong, when others may turn away from
him, should he prove weak or timid at an hour of
weariness, despair, or cheap temptation, if such an
hour should come. I can promise you that he will never
hear from me a word of bitterness and never know
of a single tear I shed. For now I know from you
that he himself chose the way he is going, and I want
to be a staff to him and not a stone dragging him
down. We will help him to this larger life if he
feels his powers equal to it. Once more—I send you my
sincere thanks, my unknown friend and comrade. If
you write to him before I do, tell him I send him a
mother's blessing."

She rolled up the letter carefully as the other had
been rolled and went close to the old man. With the
solemnity of one who has just finished an elevated
work, and the glance of one who looked deep into
men's hearts, she scrutinized his face.

"Here," she said softly, "give this to . . ." She paused,
and then pulling herself together, concluded: "Give
it to Ragozin."

The old man pulled his cap down on his head, got
to his feet, and thrust his fingers into his belt. "Give
it to him yourself, my dear, since you know more
than me about it," he retorted.

"Oh, no, I don't know any more than you," she said,
smiling, "I've only heard there was such a person, and
so I thought it was he who sent me the letter."

"Well, I can tell you there's nothing in those foolish thoughts of yours. And anyhow, it's time I was going."

He stood there, his hands still thrust into his belt,
while she stood holding out the letter.

"You'd better do what he tells in the letter," he said sternly.

"Who? He?" she asked.

"Yes, what did he tell you to do?" The old man strode up to the table and picked up the letter.

"What do you want? You mustn't! That's mine—it was sent to me!" Vera Nikandrovna protested, her voice rising almost to a scream. "Give it back to me!"

The shawl slipped down to her feet, her hair was shaken loose, she stretched out her arms, trying to wrench the letter away from the old man. But he pushed her masterfully out of the way, and, going up to the stove, threw the letter on the hearth and got the matches out of his pocket.

"You've read it, haven't you?" he demanded roughly, and answered himself: "So you have. You've memorized it? You did. Then that'll do. Do what you were told to do—before my eyes. Do you understand?"

He struck a match, set the letter alight, and waited calmly while the flame, soaring eagerly, sank and went out. He took the handful of ashes and rubbed it between his palms.

"Give me that note of yours," he growled in a milder tone.

She handed it to him and unexpectedly, her flushed face brightening with gratitude, she said: "Wait a minute."

She opened the cupboard and got out a bottle of dark-green sparkling glass. She broke her nail in trying to get the cork out and started to look for the corkscrew.

"Don't fuss about so much," the guest said in a fatherly tone.

His gnarled brown fingers caught the cork like pincers and drew it out with ease. Vera Nikandrovna filled a glass with the thick, blackish-brown liquor.

The old man took off his cap again. "And what about you?" he said.

She poured out a small glass for herself. He wiped a sticky drop that was trickling down the side of the bottle with his finger, licked it, then raised his glass, and with a suggestion of a wink of his small, quizzical eye, asked:

"To your son's health, eh?"

"You know him, do you?"

He drained his glass, smacked his lips, and shook his head. "It's cherry, isn't it?"

"No, plum. So you know my Kirill?"

Still keeping his eyelids tightly closed with satisfaction, he croaked: "It's got a sting to it!—it's like real Communion wine, honest!" Then, opening his eyes a crack, he winked again. "Your son, you say?" He wiped his lips, gathering his beard in his fist and straightening it with one movement. "He takes after you in looks. . . ."

"Yes, you're right! He's very like me!" she agreed eagerly. "Where did you see him? When?"

Happy, excited, and impatient, she waited for him to tell her, but instead he frowned, thrust the letter neatly into his boot, got up with a businesslike air, and held out his hand.

"Thanks for the treat. It's time for me to be going."

Stooping rather awkwardly, he went into the lobby, and there she hesitated to repeat her question. He vanished into the darkness whence he had emerged, still more suddenly and mutely than he had appeared.

Vera Nikandrovna did not lie down to sleep that night. She sat on the edge of her bed until daybreak ruled lines of light on the chinks of the shutters. Then she went outside.

It was a raw November morning, with whitish clouds hanging low, and various kinds of ragged, sluggish smoke rising from the station to meet them. They rivaled each other in dull tints—gray-blue, golden-rusty over the tracks, fiery red and purplish-black over the roundhouse, with milky strands of steam twining in them like ribbons in braided hair, outsoaring each other on the way to the sky, where they merged in a canopy of soot.

Vera Nikandrovna stood there for a long time, watching the unfamiliar struggle of smokes that threatened to overwhelm the world. The smell of coal, oil, overheated lubricants, and paints rolled in waves over the great dusty stretch of wasteland from time to time. The iron knocking, clanking, and grating multiplied and spread.

But the morning light surged in like the tide irresistibly, and it seemed to her that she was inseparable now from the insignificant little house where she had seen the dawn break this morning and which was to be her home for a long, long time.

She went to open the shutters.

CHAPTER

· 32 ·

Soon after her wedding, a lucky day, like a lost card turned up from a rejected pack, fell to Lisa's lot. It had been decided to alter the original program of entertainments and go for a cruise on a yacht.

Vitenka was at the helm, and two of his bosom friends were taking turns at the sails. Lisa settled down in the bows. A lateral wind was blowing, and they were tacking first to windward and then to leeward, describing a wide curve, from sands to shore, then back to the sands, and Lisa cried out at the turns when the yacht rolled. She was not alarmed; she was thrilled, and it amused the yachtsmen and they laughed. The yacht was painted white, set off with light blue, and bore the name of *Petal*. It suited the vessel, which glided easily over the bottle-green waters, the sail looking like the curled edge of a white petal.

When they emerged in mid-channel, the huge Green Isle spread before them, deep in reeds and undergrowth that had taken on autumn coloring. The willows' silver was growing sparser and almost all drowned in pale lemon, darkened in places with tobacco, delicately merging with the Naples-yellow of the sands.

The keel hissed as it drove into the yielding sand of the shore, and the crackling and swishing of the willow branches seemed to fill the space between river, earth, and blue sky.

The party went ashore, the fine sand filling their shoes. They spread a sail on the ground and set out their plates and glasses on it. Vitenka tried his tenor in a song. It was the voice of an unsophisticated singer, fond of listening to himself. It rose very high and dropped suddenly like burning straw that has gone out. Lisa craned her neck in astonishment at discovering in her husband this unknown and impressive gift. After they had drunk some wine, they attempted to sing in chorus, but it appeared they did not know any of the songs properly. The best effect was achieved in the students' songs, for though they did not remember them very well, they repeated them with great gusto:

> *"From dusk to late dawn*
> *Soon's the lights are turned on,*
> *The students are out on a spree.*
>
> *While Harlampy the Saint*
> *With his head in gold paint*
> *Looks on at the great jamboree.*
>
> *From the church he would run.*
> *And join in the fun*
> *Were it not for his age and the joss.*
>
> *When he's tempted too sore,*
> *The Saint waits no more,*
> *And nimbly slides down the cross."*

From that point on it did not go so well, though everyone knew that the old man had descended from his lofty site, enjoyed himself with the students, and then had been expelled from the company of saints by the implacable council of the other world.

Talking of the carefree student days, both Vitenka and Lisa—particularly Lisa—grew rather sad. Judging by the tales you heard, how quaint those cabbies' pull-ups in Moscow must be at night, where one joins the drivers in eating fried eggs and grated turnip radish! How pleasant to sit in a boulevard, turning the leaves of a syllabus of lectures and sometimes dozing off on a friend's shoulder! How entertaining it must be to move from one lodging to another with a few belongings in a laundry basket, a pillow, and a bundle of books! How poetic those outings to Sparrow Hills, from where you could see the hundreds of gas lamps lit in the streets and the fireworks on holidays! What fun to take examinations for somebody else, fooling some absent-minded professor, and to go to evening parties in turn in the same students' uniform!

"It's a pity, though, when these students get mixed up in politics and spoil the good time they're having," Vitenka said.

"That's it," his friend agreed, "they start collecting money for convicts and exiles, get hold of some weapons or other, and stir up trouble of all sorts. There's a spot here, on this island, where they used to come and practice shooting. Do you want me to show it to you?"

"If it isn't very far."

"It's over where those big trees are."

They decided to go and look. The supple willows parted easily, and the strangers passed through one by one, the branches closing behind each, so that it seemed a monster snake was creeping through the underground, opening and closing the coils of its body. A man would be as hard to find here as a needle in a haystack, and it was no wonder the Green Isle was the haunt of all who sought a quiet retreat—fishermen, lovers, secret underground workers, suicides, fowlers, and fugitives. Nature gave shelter to all alike, chastizing passions with mosquitoes and midges, gratifying them with the landscape, bathing, and pleasant, carefree rest on the warm beach. In the hues of its dress the island was equal to the townsman's most exquisite dream, and now in the autumn the lake, the backwaters, the willow copses, the groves, and the solitary trees were symbolic of deep relief and sweetness after long pain, like that of a mother when her travail is over.

They reached a clearing fringed by white willows and alders and towering among them a poplar with pale trunk and crooked shoulder. The scene was now set for the winter stage—the dry, crumpled grass on the earth looked seared, the trees were bare, the sky showed vividly through the dark network of branches.

The big trunk of a popular was excoriated for a space, the height of a man's belt to his head, the bark was peeled off, and the white wood riddled with bullets that had gone deep. Vitenka dug one out with his knife, and the friends argued as to what kind of a firearm it had come from.

"A Browning, of course," Vitenka's friend said. "It must be, because the underground people don't use anything but Browning revolvers now. I know for a fact."

"But how can you tell when the shot was fired?"

"Well, the bullet hasn't had time to rust yet, and it's near the surface, too. Old bullets lie deep, you see, and the new are near the surface. What do you think? The whole trunk is full of lead, through and through. The tree is dead."

He pulled at a big gnarled branch that broke with a crunching noise.

"See, it snaps like a twig. Who knows—maybe Perovskaya herself fired at this tree. She used to come here to meetings."

"And who is she?" Vitenka asked.

"The less you know, the better for you! Our boys who were sent to prison in the summer knew too much. They used to come here last spring with their revolvers. I was fishing at the time and I saw them."

Lisa was listening, absorbed, and looked at the tree so attentively, it seemed that she wanted to impress on her memory every splinter of its trunk, with the bark like a loofah, every scorched pit where the bullet had left its trace.

Vitenka went up to her and suddenly pinched her leg hard, twice. She gave a start and a little cry escaped her.

"What's up?" he demanded in astonishment. "Did anyone bite you!"

She could say nothing—his face expressed only innocent concern. Then he added, with peevish boredom: "Oh, come on, let's go home, we've had enough outing for one day."

They tried to talk him into staying a while longer, but he was stubborn: he complained of a headache, very likely from the sun, and assured them that he was going to be ill.

On the way back he refused to steer or handle the sails. He sat down in the bows, in Lisa's place, and uttered only one word when the helmsman let go the wheel as they were tacking and the vessel narrowly missed taking in some water. "You fool!"

When they reached the Yacht Club, and they had a moment alone, Lisa asked her husband what was the matter with him, but he pretended not to notice her, and said nothing. She followed him with a sense of undergoing punishment for something. He took a cab and they drove home in silence.

He retired into his room, locked himself in, and remained silent until the evening, when Daria Antonovna came home. Then he complained to her, through the closed door, of feeling very ill. Lisa had to listen to the aunt's reproaches. How could she pay so little attention to her young husband? Perhaps he needed a cold bandage on the head, or a hot-water bottle to his feet, or perhaps the doctor should be sent for. Standing outside the door, painted to imitate oak, Daria Antonovna, with her head on one side the better to hear his answers, carried on her interrogation.

"Did you take your temperature?"

No, it appeared that Vitenka had not thought of the thermometer.

"But how can you manage without the thermometer?"

It seemed he could manage.

"Are you perspiring?"

No, there was no sign of perspiration.

"Perhaps you've caught a chill and you're shivering?"

No, he wasn't shivering, either.

"Well, if it's only your head that's bad, maybe you ought to take a powder?"

But Vitenka was not inclined to take anything. He wanted to give himself wholly to suffering, since he had been driven to that state.

"You've been driven to it, you say?" Daria Antonovna exclaimed in horror, turning accusing eyes on Lisa. "But here's Lisa standing at the door, suffering too. So perhaps you'd better let her in and suffer together: it would be easier, I should think, eh?"

But this ruse evoked no response from Vitenka.

Late that night, as Lisa was dozing off, he appeared at her bedside in his dressing gown and bedroom slippers. Even his mustache had lost its spruceness and drooped; his face looked slack and bloated, as though he had overslept. "Perhaps he has really been asleep the whole evening," Lisa thought. But no, Vitenka's manner was not that of a person just awakened: he was breathing like an athlete after a long run.

"You think I'm an idiot, but I can tell you, you're very much mistaken!" he panted hotly.

"Tell me what has changed you all of a sudden!" Lisa cried, sincerely upset. "What's on your mind?"

"You want to know what's on my mind? I'll tell you. I would have told you in any case. I'm not one of the deep sort that keep everything to themselves, I'm outspoken and straightforward. And you shouldn't be secretive, either, it's like a knife in my heart, do you hear?"

He bent over the bed.

"Who were you thinking of on the island when you were standing by that tree? Who was it? When we were looking at that bullet—who was in your thoughts?"

"I? . . . Who? . . ." Lisa repeated, raising herself on her elbows, and recoiling slightly. "I wasn't thinking of anybody."

"You're lying!" he said, moving after her, so that she felt his breath coming closer.

"I never tell lies."

"You're telling one now! You don't want to admit you were thinking of your Izvekov? I know all about it—about what went on between you and Izvekov! You are silent now, eh? I was told everything—about the whole affair from beginning to end!"

He still hung over her, and became almost unrecognizable to Lisa. It was almost as though he had turned into an infant, and again, he had something decrepit about his face, his suddenly aging mouth trembled— he was so hurt. Then he straightened himself, as though satisfied and triumphant that he had made the necessary impression, and in the voice of a judge pronouncing the verdict he announced: "If you think we're going on a honeymoon, you're mistaken. There isn't going to be one."

"I'm not forcing you."

"What right have you to force me, anyhow?"

"All right, then, I'm not asking you for one."

"Aha! You've taken offense! So I guessed right! If I had been mistaken about Izvekov, you wouldn't have taken offense. Remember this, I can read through your mind."

A low sob escaped him, and, with his shoulders drooping and the long belt with its red pompons trailing behind him, he went out of the bedroom.

Lisa was struck by the effective domestic scene, enacted almost with professional skill, but still she felt sorry for Vitenka, and at first was ready to make up the difference somehow as soon as possible. He seemed very young, much younger than she herself. He needed some strong influence, as a spoiled child needed it, and Lisa was wondering where to begin her efforts to correct his character. Her feeling for him was not, of course, without some reserve, and therefore she felt something like guilt and almost guessed that he must feel disappointed in her. Perhaps for this reason she pitied him. He had looked for passion in her, and she, too, had dreamed of expending her tenderness, but as yet she was afraid to acknowledge that she could give it fully only to somebody else. It was becoming clear to her that if she wanted to have it out with her husband, she would have to touch on the main question, and the main question was the thing that she was obliged to hide. And so she suppressed the impulse to make up the quarrel. After all, one of them would have to apologize. For her to do it would be to admit that he was in the right. And such an admission would turn the conversation to the main thing that she was concealing. She resolved to wait until he made the first advance, for in that case she would remain in the right, and indeed she was right, for excepting the main thing the guilt was his, with his roughness, slyness, and childish mischievousness. As is usually the case with young couples, she was still convinced that it was out of the question to live together in disagreement, and never suspected that squabbles, and differences, and insults rarely prevented people from jogging along in the family wagon to the grave. So she made the first step toward the training of her husband: she waited for his repentance.

Victor Semyonovich, however, was in no hurry to repair the shaken married bliss. His was a nature that found it extraordinarily easy to replace what it had lost by new acquisitions. The first week of their marriage, as Lisa saw for herself, he exchanged one amusement for another in a twinkling. Now he found collecting old coins absorbing: even to the extent of going around the churches and exchanging the various small coins in the taper boxes. He formed an acquaintance with church wardens and encouraged beggars who came to offer him old copper coins at a profit. Sacks of coins, green with age, stood in his room, and he would dive into them, fumbling for some specimen dating back to the conquest of the Crimea, which was mentioned in the catalogue. He threw over numismatics when he came upon a stamp album in his desk, and his old fondness for stamp collecting was resuscitated. Now the beggars who had been his visitors gave place to schoolboys, and day by day the pursuit of old Zemstvo postage stamps and the exchange of the Transvaal for Colombia or Siam for Canada went on.

"My agents, the schoolboys, are quite educated people," he would say. "There's no doubt about it, stamps do broaden one's horizon."

He devoted all his spare time to his hobbies, and since it was within his power to spare as much time as he liked, he was constantly absorbed in them.

He had a telephone installed and used to ring up and ask the telephone operator the time.

"Exchange? Good morning, miss. Shubnikov speaking. What time is it, please?"

It was the fashion then to ring up the exchange instead of looking at your watch. And one had to watch the clock, as, besides new crazes, there were many regular pastimes: billiards, the barbers', his horse, and his friends.

For this reason it was soon clear to Lisa that the whole burden of the quarrel was to be borne by her. Vitenka never had a minute to spare, and was never bored, while she was idle from morning till night. Moreover, Vitenka was an adept in the art of silence. He could hum through his nose one of Vyaltseva's favorite songs, gazing dreamily meanwhile at the samovar tap and oblivious to the most persistent questions. He had the look of a man who has renounced the world for the sake of a poetic inner life that affords him unmeasured bliss, and this mask of a pensive, slightly crazy creature under a vow of silence gave him the advantage over those around him. Naturally, Lisa tried to keep silence, too. But the weapon was as unwieldy in her feminine hands as a rapier in a child's. She would take it up, only to cast it aside, then turn to it again to struggle for victory, thus affording her opponent a chance to enjoy the spectacle of her weakness.

The end of the quarrel was effected, not by Vitenka's repentance, but by his unexpected magnanimity. One morning he presented himself before Lisa as though nothing had ever happened: he was pleasant, courteous, considerate to the point of gallantry, as if he had slept over the incident and now was incapable of believing for a moment that any disagreement could divide a happy pair like him and Lisa.

Once more a program of entertainment was drawn up; Vitenka no longer pretended that his attention was engaged in more serious matters. He was very fond of the music halls and in this respect did not differ from merchants, ancient and modern, so many of whom had gone to the dogs for the sake of the music-hall actresses from Ochkin's Winter Gardens. Ochkin's orgies were notorious from Nizhni Novgorod to Astrakhan, and gay sparks came from all parts to drink a half-dozen bottles of champagne in good company and carouse with pretty girls in a fashion to be remembered until their dying day.

Lisa had heard of this music hall, but as a forbidden place, and she remembered that when the girls at school had uttered the word "Ochkin," they had exchanged significant glances and then lowered their eyes. But she was a grown-up lady now, and it was permissible for her to visit all places of public amusement in the company of her husband. So one day, smartly dressed and accompanied by their friends, the Shubnikovs went out to hear the singers.

In Ochkin's Winter Gardens tall palm trees with fronds of a dead lacquered sheen shaded the fountain, and red lamps were reflected in its basin. Fat sterlet with black backs hung motionless—their sharp jaws pointed toward the cascading waters, or glided slowly in a circle, with languidly stirring fins. Along the narrow avenues moved plump German women, languid as the fish, in décolleté dresses of heavy silk with large brooches and fans on long gilt chains. Their white arms showed below the shoulder three vaccination marks like the stars on brandy bottles, and paste diamonds glittered in their high rolled hair. They gathered up their trains, made two or three steps, then let them trail along the asphalt path. Paper lanterns glowed among the oleanders. Couples were talking in the grottos of porous stone covered with ivy and furnished with couches. The string band was playing a medley from *La Traviata*.

Lisa discovered for the first time all that the human glance may mean: the eyes here outdid the tongue in their serpentine sinuosity of expression. They beamed, sparkled, clouded, melted, disclosed fathomless depths, shot fire and darted lightning, dashed icy water over you, lifted you to heights you had never known, pleaded and refused, gave and took, drew, promised, filled with prayers and impatience, tormented pitilessly, were ready for anything, and rejected everything. Oh, yes, those eyes were far richer than pitiful human speech—they could lend innumerable shades of meaning to each thought, and a simple "yes" could be seen expressed in any tone or color, from a heavenly blue to a muddy gray, from jet-black to brown, from ashen-gray to raven's-wing indigo, and each of these colored assents shone after its own fashion in the eyes of men and women, and each "yes" held its own "no," each contained a doubt, a "but," while calling and rebuffing, reveling in its implicit power.

This wordless language of glances excited Lisa so much that when she took her place at a small table in the large restaurant, her eyes, without answering anyone's, spoke too, spoke of embarrassment, of curiosity, of shame, of satisfaction, of childish bewilderment and sudden feminine comprehension. Vitenka was transformed. He was obviously in his element, like a fish that has been kept for a long time in a bucket and then has been suddenly released into a rushing

torrent of water. He carefully tracked down his favorite dishes on the menu, and, lighting on his prey
with predatory glee, had it noted each time on the
maître d'hôtel's order list.

Supper was served and the entertainment began. Lisa
was facing the stage. A Chinese juggled with spears
and swords; a conjurer transformed doves into ribbons, water into smoke; an acrobat turned somersaults
on a trapeze. Then a singer appeared in the prosce-
nium, a fair-haired woman in a black dress that
clothed her so completely that it seemed she was
afraid to expose even the merest portion of skin: her
collar was boned and reached to the ears, her train
coiled about her insteps, long black kid gloves covered her arms above the elbows. Clasping her hands,
she pressed her wrists to her breast and strove vainly
and yearningly to unclasp them, and it seemed impossible, and her yearning grew stronger and stronger
as she looked around the tables with eyes full of tears,
and sang in a mournful contralto:

> "*I hear the winds of autumn moan,*
> *The faded leaves are driven in a whirl.* . . ."

The next turn was a singer of very different temperament who dashed out to the footlights to the
tinkling of the piano. She wore no dress at all, and
what little she had on seemed to encumber her and
never gave her a moment's peace, and she kept trying
to shed the little gauze belt she was wearing in lieu
of a skirt and flung up her legs so high that her slippers
seemed to be always in front of her face, while she
explained her impatience by stormy cries of:

> "*Oh, I'm just mad about China!*
> *Could anything be finer?*"

There was loud applause from all the tables and
demands that she should sing "The Fireman." She
ran off, ran on again, and sang "Chanticleer." This
made the tables still more rabid in their demands for
"The Fireman." After disappearing behind the scene
three times, she finally gratified the desire of the public.

Her performance of "China" and "Chanticleer" could not bear comparison with the ecstasy that "The Fireman" aroused in her. She bubbled, and boiled, and twisted, revealing to the audience the depths of her passion for the extinguisher of fires.

Vitenka clapped as loudly as any of the members of the audience and overturned a glass of champagne in his excitement. "That's the real stuff!" he exclaimed, wiping off the splashes with his serviette.

But, glancing at his wife, he discovered that she did not share his enthusiasm. Lisa's cheeks burned, her brows were knit, her gaze fixed on her plate.

"Didn't you like it?" he asked disappointedly. "That was a regular cabaret girl."

"I see you have to twist your neck," Lisa replied. "Let's change places."

"What for? You won't be able to see as well from here."

"I prefer to sit with my back to the stage."

They changed places and Vitenka explained to his friends: "She's only a child yet."

They all laughed and made fun of her, begging her to turn around whenever a new girl came on.

"Go on, have a look," Vitenka coaxed—he was rather tipsy by this time. "Look at this one, she's quite modest."

"Prim enough to go to church with, almost," a friend chimed in.

"There isn't even a knee showing," another explained obligingly.

Suddenly Vitenka noticed a curious change in Lisa's eyes, as though they were slowly altering from their usual greenish-blue to dark, and dilating. He fidgeted a little, sat up alert, and at a distant table, amid the unfamiliar faces, caught sight of Tsvetukhin's sleek, raven's-wing hair. Glancing back at Lisa, he saw that she was hastily tidying her fluffy hair. He fancied he saw her fingers trembling. Bending toward her, he said in a low voice: "So that's why you wanted to change places, is it?"

She had hardly time to raise her eyebrows when he kicked her ankle hard under the table, and she winced from the pain. Then he clinked glasses with his friend and, raising his high, exclaimed: "Friends, let's drink to saintly women! To those who can't stand frivolous entertainments!"

They had hardly time to drain their glasses, when Tsvetukhin and Pastukhov appeared at their table. Both men were in evening dress, with white asters in their buttonholes, and smoking extraordinarily long cigarettes. After they had shaken hands with Lisa, they bowed to the company.

"Allow me to introduce you to my husband, Victor Semyonovich," Lisa said rather uncertainly, in a low tone.

Vitenka and then his friends stood up stiffly and bowed.

"We wanted to suggest," Pastukhov said simply, "that we should join forces. You're having such a good time together that Egor and I became envious. Come and join us at our table or we'll come here, just as you like—I think there's a better view from here."

"No," said Vitenka, "this is the first time my wife has been to Ochkin's and she's sorry she came. She can't bear the music-hall style of things. She prefers the theater," and he cast a glance at Tsvetukhin.

"Quite right, too," Pastukhov rejoined seriously. "Let's go into the question at more length over a bottle of Depré."

"You're a sportsman, aren't you?" Tsvetukhin said, smiling at Shubnikov. "The wrestling is to start just now."

"My wife can't look at women who aren't fully dressed, much less men. She wants to go home." Vitenka made an impressive bow.

"What a pity," Tsvetukhin remarked to Lisa. "We were hoping to have a chat with you. Do stay a while."

"No, she doesn't want to stay on any account."

"I can see that the husband's will is law," Tsvetukhin said, smiling again.

"Quite right, law it is!" Vitenka said, scraping his feet ceremoniously as he stood waiting; then, addressing his friends: "Please pay the bill and I'll settle with you afterward. Come, let's go, Lisa."

He showed her out with a theatrical gesture. She

said good-by and passed between the tables, followed by Vitenka, the picture of courtliness and consideration.

Once more he buttoned himself up closely, as it were and retired into himself. But when he got home, he shed the cloak of inaccessibility and taciturnity so quickly that the buttons flew off and scattered in all directions: Victor Semyonovich Shubnikov had emerged in his natural state once more.

He dropped into the first armchair that happened handy, uttered womanish shrieks, and burst into sobs. His hands and legs trembled, his head shook, he tossed from side to side, now falling on his knees, and beating his face against the upholstered seat so hard that the springs hummed.

Lisa stared at her husband with callous dislike, and then the horrid thought struck her that he might be an epileptic. She ran for some water and offered him a glass, but he dashed it aside, splashing the water about, and uttered still more piercing screams. Gradually he roused the whole household, and his aunt came running in from her part of the house. They managed to get Vitenka to bed, where he continued to toss on his pillows and feather beds until he was exhausted. By the time the doctor came, he was lying motionless and looked like a corpse. His aunt was weeping quietly. The doctor was full of sympathy for her, but prescribed the simplest treatment: a weak solution of laudanum in case of a repetition of the fits, and at the same time—perfect quiet, ordinary diet, and baths of a temperature of twenty-nine degrees Celsius.

It was this temperature of twenty-nine degrees Celsius (neither thirty nor twenty-eight) that impressed Daria Antonovna particularly: it was evident that the illness was no joke, and since Vitenka had never ailed anything like this before his marriage and his illness grew worse whenever Lisa appeared, the reason for it obviously lay in his unhappy marriage.

"Well, my dear, there is no point in walking up and down the rooms with your arms folded," Daria Antonovna said one morning to Lisa. "Goodness knows when Vitenka will be well again, and business doesn't stand still. You'd better go and sit at the cash desk in the shop at the bazaar. I can't be everywhere at once."

And though Vitenka had done next to nothing for the business, they demanded as much from Lisa as if he had toiled in the sweat of his brow, and so she spent a great deal of her time in the drapery shop near her father's store, where but a short while ago she had first met her husband.

WHEN SHE HEARD the word "bazaar," Lisa remembered
the fear she had felt in childhood of the beggar who
frequented the Peshka Market. He used to sit on the
ground, baring his teeth like a horse trying to rid himself of an uncomfortable bit, and every inch of his
face twitched, rivaling the head, shoulders, and the
body in dreadful shaking. Lisa's mother had told her
that the man had St. Vitus's dance, and that she must
always give him a couple of coppers. And every time
she threw the coins into the painted wooden saucer
resting by his feet, she ran away and plunged into the
thick of the crowd, so as not to see that awful face
dancing before her. For this reason she always avoided
the bazaar and kept as far as possible from it.

True, there was one pleasant corner of Peshka—the
remains of an old arcade where the birdcatchers traded.
Inside and out, on its old peeling, dilapidated walls,
hung many cages and snares, inhabited by hundreds of
goldfinches, blue-tits, bullfinches, and crossbills, and
from a distance the medley of bird notes sounded like
a musical box with broken needles. Among the bird-
sellers there was one old man whom she liked particularly—he looked like a pilgrim. He was training the
young nightingales that he kept in low cages, covered with thick canvas. Lisa paused by the old man and
looked at his deeply tanned face, the broad nose,
the shaggy, curly, grizzled beard and whiskers, the

narrow slits of eyes, and it used to give her a thrill of surprise when two pinpoints of light suddenly appeared in those slits, and the twittering and trilling, the whistling and velvety flow of song issued from his hairy mouth. At Annunciation she would come here to free the blue-tits, holding in her palms the fluffy little warm bodies, then letting them go, and watch how they darted like arrows, described two or three festoons in the air, then settled on the gable of the arcade, preening and spreading the wings long unaccustomed to flight. Often she saw herself in dreams taking flight with a strange lightness and swiftness, as some unearthly body, and then alighting on the iron roof of the arcade.

The Upper Bazaar was harsh, grasping, ferociously desperate, and violent. It was swarming with cardsharps and thimbleriggers. There were drunken brawls, thieves were caught and beaten to death, police whistles shrilled from end to end of it. All around, there were people eating, gobbling, guzzling. The marketwomen rolled the sausages in their greased palms to make them shine, fried pancakes and the like in sunflower seed oil, and piled them up in towers and mountains. Crafty peasants presented peep shows, seating their spectators under a black canopy where it was stuffy and smelled of kerosene lamps. Country folks who had come up to see the sights moved in aimless droves among the booths and stalls, clutching their purses tightly. The Tatars haggled till they were blue in the face over prices, old crones swore and vowed by the holy name, the blind chanted nasally their prayer for alms, and pious old men, festooned from head to foot with strings of onions, piped thinly: "Hey, goodwives, onions, onions, onions!"

For hours on end Lisa would watch the seething bazaar crowd from the shop window.

It so happened that one dull, cold midday she saw a tall, powerful rough, with a shock of light curly hair, carrying a child in his arms and pushing his way through the knot of people to a sharp who was playing a kind of blind hookey. The game consisted in the sharp's flinging on a mat bars of chocolate with pictures of beauties on the wrappers. The bars lay picture downward, and the point was to turn one up like a playing card. If the gambler happened to pick it up by

the beauty's head, he won the bar; if he turned it by
the feet, he paid the price of the chocolate. Everything was perfectly square and above board: the
sharp holding the bar with the tips of his fingers
showed everyone plainly where the head and feet were,
then he flung down the bar, which, having described
an arc and made an imperceptible flourish, fell on
the mat. Practically everyone who tried his hand at
it was tricked and lost. But the sharp's assistant, who
worked with him on the quiet, won bar after bar
as the public looked on, and this roused the gambling
instinct in the simpletons.

When the big man with the baby pushed through
the onlookers, a little girl with fair hair like his own
ran up behind him and tugged at his coat.

Through the open lattice Lisa could hear her insistent
voice.

"Papa, listen, Papa! Don't play, don't play. Come
away!"

The man turned and said: "I'll win something for
you and your brother, wait a minute," and on he
went, elbowing aside the idlers.

A moment later he turned around with a wry and
rather guilty smile lighting his hollow-cheeked face.
"I've lost this time. But wait, I'll have another go."

Hardly had he reached the sharp, when a little
woman with a canary feather in her hat ran up and
clung like the little girl to his coattail.

"Bother you!" he said, pushing their hands away,
"let Pavlik have a try. Pavlik's lucky. Now pull,
Pavlik!"

He set the child down on the ground, and bending,
pushed him forward, to the encouraging remarks
of the bystanders.

At that moment the woman with the little girl, who
had been whispering anxiously together, turned so
that they were seen in profile from the window, and
Lisa recognized Olga Ivanovna and Annochka. She
tapped on the glass to attract their attention, but they
could not hear, for the man exclaimed triumphantly:
"He's won! Pavlik's luck is in today!"

"That's fine, thank goodness for it, I'm sure, and
let that be enough for us, and come along," Olga
Ivanovna started in her garrulous way.

"Look, wait just a minute," the man protested good-humoredly. "It's only quits so far: I lost once and won once. Now let Pavlik have another go: he'll win, he's lucky, he is!"

"No, he's won once, and that's enough."

"Stop gabbing, I'm saying. Let Pavlik win some chocolate for himself. If he does, then it's a sign that your lady will help us."

The people willingly moved aside to let him pass with the child, and he pushed him gently to the front. The sharp flung the chocolate again with a flourish, and the bystanders surrounded the child, admonishing his father: "Don't push him! Don't touch him, let him pull it himself! See, take it, little one, win a bar for yourself."

Little Pavlik made a grab at the chocolate and bore it straight to his mouth, when many hands were stretched out at once and took it away from him to see which corner he had picked it up by. He set up a roar.

"He's lost!" the man exclaimed, shaking his head.

"We'll have no luck with your lady. But let's have another go."

He trust his hand into his pocket for money. But Olga Ivanovna picked up the crying baby, handed him to Annochka, and clung to her husband's arm.

"Come now, let's go!"

Lisa was longing to interfere, to buy Pavlik some little present and caress him, so she ran out from behind the counter. But at that moment the whole Parabukin family trooped slowly into the shop.

Olga Ivanovna held out her hand to Lisa, with repeated nods of astonishing vivacity, her hat bobbing on its slack elastic.

"I hope you'll excuse us, dear Elisaveta Merkuryevna, for bringing the whole family to see you at once. This is my husband. You know our Annochka, don't you? And this is Pavlik, the baby. What are you about, Annochka? Shake hands nicely. Put the baby down on his feet and wipe his nose properly. You see, Elisaveta Merkuryevna, we made so bold as to go and see you at home, but we were told that your husband is ailing and laid up, and you're taking his place in the shop. So we've come here to see you, excuse us, for goodness' sake. What ails your husband? So young and all! Pavlik, stop picking your nose, will you, and stop crying this minute or that old man behind the counter over there will run away with you. Yes, of course, he'll be all right, he'll get well, won't he? And you—you're just the same young thing that you were. As if you'd never got married at all. That's right, isn't it, Tisha?—I always told you what a lovely girl Lisaveta Merkuryevna was, didn't I?"

"You'd better tell her what you want of her," Parabukin said, "don't waste her time."

He paused by the door post, shading his injured eye with his hand in embarrassment, and holding Annochka's elbow with the other. She held Pavlik by the hand. In front of the group unconsciously arranged like steps of stairs stood Olga Ivanovna, facing the bewildered and motionless Lisa.

"I'm sure I don't know how to begin," Olga Ivanovna began breathlessly, and her eyes searched Lisa's face, wondering what she was thinking, and flitted to and fro, dilated to their fullest sickly large extent.

"You know, we're tenants of your father's, we live in the common lodginghouse. And all of a sudden, for no reason that we know of, and how it happened we don't even know—your father took a dislike to Tisha, my husband—there he is with us. Well, it went from bad to worse and the long and the short of it is—he ordered us out of the place. You don't believe it? We didn't believe it at first either, we couldn't! And now we have to believe it whether we want to or not, because Merkuri Avdeyevich is threatening us with the police and won't hear a word about our being stranded with little children and with no means of support, and Tisha, my husband, in bad health, too, ever since he got crippled at work—look at him, you can see he's no good for heavy work any more. And now our only hope is in your kind heart, dear Lisaveta Merkuryevna."

"Well, I can see . . ." Lisa said with indecision in her voice, glancing around involuntarily at the clerks, who were watching the scene curiously. "Of course, I'll do whatever I can. . . ."

"She has a heart of gold!" Olga Ivanovna exclaimed, clasping her hands in admiration. "And then you're so rich now! Surely you'll find some little room in your house—just a corner, no matter how humble. We don't ask for much, really we don't! We've been used to cramped quarters for so long. Please try to put us somewhere!"

"I can't say yet . . . I don't know how my husband . . . what my aunt could do about it, that is, about rooms." Lisa said. "I think perhaps I ought to speak to my father first."

"Oh, no, what use would that be? He won't want us at any price."

"Still, if I try to persuade him. . . ."

"My dear, my dear, you're the soul of goodness, I can see. But he'll never agree! He's terribly angry with us. He wouldn't hear of it! And where are we to go with little children? If it wasn't for them, do you think Tisha and I would be going about begging people to take us in? We used to live in a very decent way at one time. Tisha was on work that was far from rough, I can tell you. . . . Perhaps you'd find work for him and take him on at your place?"

"Oh, never mind that," Parabukin growled.

Lisa glanced at him, and then, with tormenting and timid sympathy, at the children. Annochka caught the glance and, craning forward, with the same hurried volubility as her mother, pleaded:

"It's all true. It's all true. Tell your father he shouldn't touch us. Please do. It's not that I'm afraid. I can live in the streets and Papa also can live in the streets. But poor Pavlik—he's so little, he's awfully cold."

Lisa darted toward her and threw her arms around her.

"Oh, heavens!" Olga Ivanovna burst out with a sob, and was about to throw herself into Lisa's embrace, when the shop door opened suddenly, almost crushing Parbukin against the jamb, and Victor Semyonovich Shubnikov strode into the shop, casting a searching glance at each person in turn.

"Who's that you're embracing?" he asked Lisa. "Relatives of yours, are they?"

There was dead silence for a moment; no one stirred.

"Who are these people who come after you? What do these meetings in the shop mean?"

"You must excuse us," Olga Ivanovna said, pulling

herself together. She bowed to him, straightened her hat, and took an almost unnoticeable step backward, thus expressing the height of tact. "We came to see your wife because we used to know her as a girl. We were asking her, and she's been kind enough to promise, to help us in our trouble about rooms."

"She shouldn't promise what she can't carry out without my consent," Victor Semyonovich said, glaring at Olga Ivanovna as though she was his personal enemy.

"We were just thinking—I hope you'll excuse us— that maybe if your wife asked you to help us . . . you see, she knows me and my little girl Annochka. But as you're not feeling at all well. . . ."

"I'm in excellent health, and wish you the same," Victor Semyonovich said curtly. "And it isn't the thing to go traipsing around the shops, begging and cadging."

"Their request concerned my father," Lisa said.

"Then why did they come hanging around my place?"

Olga Ivanovna held out her arms impulsively to Lisa. "I'm imploring you—don't refuse! Don't go back on your kind intentions."

"Don't worry, I'll do as I promised," Lisa replied rather coldly, but her voice shook and this alarmed the other woman.

Suddenly, stooping toward Pavlik and gathering him to her, she planted him before Lisa and fell on her knees. The tears streamed down her cheeks as freely as a child's. Pushing Pavlik gently before her, she crept to Lisa's feet with a strangled cry. "The little ones, pity the little ones, you have a heart of gold! Don't change your mind! Help me, dear, help me! Don't think better of it!"

Both Lisa and Annochka darted toward her and tried to raise her, but she struggled in their hands and fell. The knot of hair was shaken loose and fell about her neck; her hat hung on it by the elastic. She buried her face in her hands, outspread on the floor, and her whole body shook as she gasped out incoherent scraps of words and phrases.

Parabukin detached himself from the door post, which seemed to have held him fast all this time.

Raising Olga Ivanovna easily to her feet, he turned her toward him and laid her shaking head gently against his breast. Annochka picked up the hat from the floor and clung to her mother, pressing her cheek against the woman's back and looking at Victor Semyonovich with unwavering sternness.

"It's time to end the show—this isn't the stage," Shubnikov said, turning away and going behind the counter.

"We're going—keep your hair on," Parabukin retorted in a muffled tone.

"If you don't, you'll be made to," Victor Semyonovich raised his voice, and his face flushed as though with some crimson solution other than blood.

"Go on, insult us a bit more, you haven't done enough yet!" Parabukin said scornfully. "The more anyone insults me, the less afraid I am. You can't frighten me. Annochka, you take Pavlik. We've done enough begging from fine ladies and bowing down to them. We'll manage to keep alive without them, I daresay."

He opened the door and, still holding Olga Ivanovna clasped to his breast, led her out gently into the street and the crowd.

Slowly and painfully Lisa passed her hands over her temples. There was desolation in her eyes as she stared at her husband, who was sitting, turning the leaves of the account book at the cash desk.

"This is all unthinkably heartless," Lisa said after a long pause.

"You've got rather too much heart, haven't you . . . for other people," he said without looking up from the book.

"You haven't any at all."

"I have when it's needed."

"I think it's always needed," she said, and, suddenly raising her head, she added almost inaudibly: "goodby!" and walked out with a stiff, unfamiliar tread.

She almost ran through the market, bareheaded, in her rich light-colored dress. People stared after her, and the cries of the vendors, the calls, and the haggling now barred her way, now sped her on as she darted through the crowd.

When she reached her father's shop, she stopped to take breath.

Merkuri Avdeyevich greeted her with a smile, then, noticing something, looked her over from top to toe anxiously.

"So, you've come around—you found time to drop in on your father, my dear neighbor?" he said gently, though his face remained grave. "That's nice. But why didn't you put anything on—a cold day like this?"

"I've come home," Lisa replied, sinking heavily onto a chair. "And I'll never go back there again."

Merkuri Avdeyevich leaned over the counter to look at her and turned to stone. Everything around seemed to turn to stone at the same moment—the shop assistants, and boys, and all the paints and varnishes arranged and exhibited and sorted on the shelves.

CHAPTER

· 34 ·

THE Society for the Aid of Children's Homes and Educational Institutions under the patronage of the dowager Empress Maria was arranging a literary gathering in the Gentlemen's Club, and it was to be followed by a ball and a lottery. The wives of the law-court officials drove about the town, collecting from the wealthier citizens prizes for the lottery and inviting prominent people to take part in the affair. It fell to the lot of the Assistant Prosecutor's lady to visit the Shubnikovs. She was accompanied by Oznobishin. Daria Antonovna received them. The richly dressed visitor in her autumn hat with the black ostrich feather spoke to her with kindly benevolence. Oznobishin lent his respectful support. She expressed a desire to speak to the young Mrs. Shubnikova ("Elisaveta Merkuryevna," Oznobishin prompted) to ask her to help in getting up the lottery, but it appeared that she was not at all well and could not come down to the drawing room. Oznobishin inquired with a show of deep sympathy whether Elisaveta Merkuryevna was seriously indisposed, and said that the Society was particularly anxious to see her at the lottery wheel the evening of the affair. Daria Antonovna promised to convey the wishes of the guests to the young couple, then the lady and Oznobishin took their departure, well pleased with their visit.

The unexpected visit of so notable a personage was

the reason for a new deliberation together of the aunt and her nephew to consider the method of procedure before the news of Lisa's scandalous desertion should have spread. It was decided that the aunt would go to Merkuri Avdeyevich to ask him to admonish his daughter as a father, after which Vitenka could make his peace with Lisa and bring her home. Of course, it would mean a certain sacrifice of self-esteem, but that would have suffered still more if the story had become known to others besides the shop assistants who had witnessed it. The scandal had to be nipped in the bud. It would be no joke if it went around the town that Shubnikov's wife had run away from him before they had been married two months.

This was the fourth day that Lisa was spending in the room that had been hers as a girl. A new, queer feeling haunted her. She could not believe any longer in her former life, which drifted smoothly on toward the unknown future that called to her whimsically in vague dreams, or in the idle, thoughtless moments of leisure. She could not turn back and become one with that girl who had once tidied the books, straightening the rows of gilded backs with the ruler. Nothing had changed in the slightest, from the china inkstand with the chip off on the sparrow's tail to the cords for fastening the open window lattice, but the feeling of it all was different, as though someone, some incomprehensible person was standing between the past and the present and hindering the grown-up Lisa from joining hands with little Lisa. And only the mother convinced her with every word, every casual touch, that the indivisible life of the one and same Lisa was going on, growing and filling with sorrow and yearning for happiness.

Valeria Ivanovna's lot was that of all mothers who give their daughters in marriage, with defenseless submissiveness to the requirements of the circumstances, simply because marriage is inevitable, and a union which promises good provision for married life is better than one which promises indigence. She repeated the experience of this lot, too, in that having married off her daughter simply because it was out of the question not to marry her off, and having made her thoroughly unhappy, she then began to grieve with her in her grief and took her side in her dislike of the young husband. She was trying to make up for the wrong she had done by supporting or nursing in Lisa an enmity to the existence that the girl would never have known if her mother had not permitted it. She railed with the daughter against the disaster that she herself had prepared for her by her own passivity, and wept over her disaster.

At the bottom of her heart Lisa had been deeply shocked that her mother had delivered her to her fate without the slightest attempt at resistance. But she became reconciled with her mother and her old love for her returned with still greater force as soon as she realized that by her desertion of her husband she had freed not only herself but her mother as well. For Valeria Ivanovna, horrified for an instant by the flight, was delighted by it next moment as if she had found a child whom she had feared was lost beyond all hope of recovery.

Once more, just as it had been all their lives, they talked and talked all the evenings far into the night, and sat with their arms around each other morning and evening, sometimes weeping softly, and again, with feminine calculation and patience, going over the smallest emotional experiences of their two months' parting and estrangement, when they thought there would be no more of the tender confidence between them that had made them as one.

All their talk turned on the one thing, that it was impossible to live with Victor Semyonovich, and since Lisa had left him, it would be an irreparable mistake to go back to him. If Lisa's flight from her husband had encountered no hindrances, the mother and daughter would have settled the question at once and there would have been no particular need to sit side by side on the bed with their arms around each other talking and weeping for hours. But the husband had the law on his side, and he might use it. It was not certain, either, what decision Merkuri Avdeyevich would come to as regards his daughter: he might deny her his home since she had scorned her husband's. But the principal uncertainty lay in the thing they mentioned least of all, but that was constantly in their minds. They brooded over it with feminine anxiety, understanding each other at a glance, exchanging question and answer in silence, expressing themselves through subtle changes of mood. And when the thing that Lisa suggested became a certainty, they both saw that the separation from her husband which had been practically decided upon came up against an insuperable obstacle: on the fourth day of her stay in her old room Lisa told her mother that she was to become a mother.

That morning broke wintrily, reluctantly, and very gray. The flowers on the window sills and the branchy philodendron looked ashen. There was a smell of damp clay from the stoves that were just lit. The cat curled up on the couch and buried his nose in his hind paws.

Throwing on a light, fluffy shawl, Lisa went out on the gallery for a breath of air. For the first time since the wedding she gazed through the small latticed panes. The hills looked rather dismal and as though sprinkled with ashes. The yards of the houses huddled closer and seemed smaller in the vague, thick, shimmering light. The school had lost its whiteness; its outlines became dim, and the once stately poplars had a mean, shabby look.

It was very quiet, and everything had retreated into the distance. Lisa grew quiet, too. No longer looking out through the window, she pressed the tips of her fingers against the framework. A wasp, orange and black like a campaign ribbon, lay on its back, dead. Cobwebs hung like gray pencil marks between the hinges and the frame. The windows had not been opened for a long time now. Autumn was at an end.

Suddenly Lisa gave a start: her father entered the gallery. He was coming straight toward her with his curious, springy gait.

Since his daughter had returned home, Merkuri Avdeyevich had retired into himself. He seemed unable to free himself from the stunned state he had fallen into when he heard from Lisa that she had left her husband. He talked neither to her nor to Valeria Ivanovna, and this foreshadowed some particularly awful and lengthy sermon. He was preparing himself for what lay before him, studying the teaching of St. Theophane the Hermit, whose works he collected

on his bookshelves and regarded as a true source of
spiritual guidance. Merkuri Avdeyevich had composed
in his head a whole lecture, consisting of a preamble,
main argument, and inference, and only when he felt
perfectly ready for it, with all his spiritual forces
mustered, did he resolve to face the task, so as to be
done with it, once and for all.

The preamble was to consist of a condemnation of
frivolous thoughts, idle musing, and in general all
manner of daydreaming and errant thought. The argument concerned the rise of need in soul and body;
out of the first—sometimes fortuitous—gratification of
a need, comes the desire, always for some definite
object; gradually, the desired objects increase in number, so that in time man's needs are obscured by his
desires. What, then, is the soul to do with these desires?
—Merkuri Avdeyevich intended to ask at this point.
The soul had to choose: to which of the desired
objects was it to give preference? This was to be
followed by the decision: what was to be done with
the object chosen, or how was it to be used? This
in turn was succeeded by the selection of the means
and mode of carrying out the desire. Finally, in its
own time and in its own place, came the consummation of the act itself. It was Merkuri Avdeyevich's
intention to devote the final part of the talk to a
transition from general principles of a soul-saving nature to the substance of Lisa's existence. And then it
would become clear that Lisa had selected the most
desired object when she had given preference to Victor
Semyonovich Shubnikov above all others. The resolution to make use of the chosen object had been taken
when Lisa consented to unite her life with Victor
Semyonovich's. Following the resolution, the mode
of carrying it out had been found—the wedding had
taken place. And thereafter, the act itself had found
its consummation in its own time and place.

How, then, had it come about that after so correct
a procedure such an event could take place? It could
not be but the outcome of the breaking down of the
spirit. At this point Merkuri Avdeyevich meant to
intervene to restore the lost balance, and direct his
daughter's steps on the path of righteousness.

Thus, fully armed, Merkuri Avdeyevich went in
search of his daughter to have the matter out with

her. He was somewhat surprised to find her at the same window, and in almost the same pose, as he had seen her on the evening of her wedding day. He looked upon it as a bad omen.

"As obstinate as ever?" he asked, going up to her.

"About what?"

"About staring in the forbidden direction, as you were before."

He jerked his head in the direction of the window. Lisa did not answer.

"Are you not neglecting your duty to your husband for the sake of foolish, senseless dreams?"

Lisa smiled calmly and said in unusually level tones, as though the doubts that had tormented her had long since found assuagement: "Ah, don't worry yourself, Father. You want to convince me that I should go back to my husband? I've made up my mind about it. I'm going back today."

He was taken aback by her words. He had prepared for such a high hurdle that the run he had made for nothing almost knocked him off his feet. He turned away and pressed his palms to his face to control his agitation. Then, glancing sharply from under his raised shaggy brows that had lost their glowering look, he put up a hand to stroke her hair.

When he touched her brow and made the sign of the cross over it swiftly, she held his hand lightly.

"I want to ask you to have pity on those unfortunate Parabukins. You refused to let them stay in that corner of the lodginghouse: leave them alone, they have little children."

Merkuri Avdeyevich gave a sniff, and then chuckled.

"The Lord endowed you with sense in big things, but left you very foolish in little things. Imagine bothering your head about people like that. Still, let them stay there, since you want it. Surely I'm not as heartless as all that, am I? But you listen to me and don't meddle in their business. They're common people, they wouldn't understand it. And that tramp— he's an unruly grumbler. Pity's like poison to him."

He embraced his daughter.

"Let them stay there, then," he repeated, "let them be."

Lisa's decision took a weight off his mind, and to tell the truth, the whole household livened up at once, as though peace had been sent down from heaven. They were now expecting Victor Semyonovich to come for his wife and started to bustle about, preparing to receive him, as though to make up for some act of which they all felt ashamed.

Lisa ran to let the Parabukins know the news. With the same light, fluffy shawl thrown over her head, and in her old school dress that had grown rather tight for her, she hurried along the pavements with their broken bricks, and as she went, she looked at each familiar house and fence, the ruts and ditches under the gates, the benches by the fenced-in front gardens, and only half believed that the earth bore her so readily.

The first person she saw outside the rooming house was Annochka, who took the flight of stone steps at two jumps, swinging an empty bottle with a string around the neck. Lisa called to her. She hesitated a moment, then, recognizing Lisa, ran up to her.

"Now you look just the same as you used to," she said, her slow gaze taking in Lisa's old school dress and surprised at her discovery.

"Is Mama at home?" Lisa asked.

"No, she's gone to Peshka Market. Papa's laid up, sick. And Mama told me to run out to the store for sunflower seed oil."

She swung the bottle, and, with another glance at Lisa and then at herself, she straightened the drooping revers of the old jacket she was wearing and boasted: "This is Mama's jacket I'm wearing. It's only a bit too big for me, isn't it? She'll alter it for me."

"I came to see her," Lisa said, "but now there's no need, as I've seen you. Tell Mama that you can all stay on here."

"Can we?"

"Yes."

"What do you mean?"

"The way you used to live before."

"Before? Before what?"

"Tell Mama that no one will touch you, and you can go on living here in this house. Understand?"

"Yes, I understand. And . . . Papa?"

"Yes, the whole family. Understand? And you and your little brother."

"No, that's not what I wanted to ask. I understand I can tell Mama, but can I tell Papa, too?"

"Oh, what a girl! Well, of course you can!"

Crouching a little, with one foot planted firmly on the step, Annochka persisted. "Then I may tell him now, may I?"

"Yes, of course you can. Run along! Good-by!"

Annochka, as though released by a spring, bounded up the steps and darted up the stairs to the big room.

Lisa stood, undecided. At first she meant to make herself go back home the way she had come, but then she said aloud, with a little shrug: "What difference does it make?" In any case she would be going home, no matter which way she went, in any case she would be returning to her husband today—everything was settled for good, and nothing would be changed if she passed by the house that drew her, she imagined, only like a part of the past and nothing more.

She turned the corner and climbed the causeway. The nearer she came to the school, the slower she walked. Not because it was hard to go—no, but because she wanted to take as long as she could in passing the brick walls, the low, barred windows. She almost stopped sometimes, and even touched the walls of the building, feeling the rough cold limewash against her palm. A new and hitherto unexperienced inner silence made her feelings more poignant; she felt neither grieved nor hurt that everything around her responded with indifferent silence.

On reaching the gate, she was about to glance into the schoolyard when she heard nimble footsteps running after her: Annochka had overtaken her with the lightness and swiftness natural to the child.

"You went away!" she cried, bounding up to Lisa.

She was panting, her face was radiant, but there was a look of bewilderment and a touch of alarm in her large, dewy eyes.

"You went away," she repeated, changing the empty bottle on the string from one hand to another. "And I forgot to say—thank you."

"Oh, nonsense! Why, I could see that you meant to thank me," Lisa said, smiling. "Fancy running all this way after me! I suppose your father sent you?"

"No, I came myself. I thought when Mama came

home, the first thing she would ask me would be: 'Did you say thank you?' So I ran after you as fast as I could. You're not angry with me, are you?"

"No, not a bit, everything's all right," Lisa said with a sigh, laying her hand on Annochka's shoulder. "Everything's all right."

She peeped in through the open gate. The yard was deserted; the door of Izvekova's old home was closed. "Have you seen Vera Nikandrovna lately?"

"She doesn't live here any more," Annochka replied cheerfully, "she's in another school, a long, long way off. That time we came to see you, we had just been here—she was moving, and the carter had come for her things."

Lisa stepped back and leaned against the gate post. "A long way off? Do you know where?"

"No. I'll ask Mama, though, she knows."

Lisa waited a little. "And . . . have you heard anything about Kirill?"

"No. Do you want me to find out? I'll run to Vera Nikandrovna's and then come back and tell you everything. Shall I?"

"Yes, I do, I'd like it very much!" Lisa said quickly, taking Annochka by the hand and drawing her toward her. "Run and find out, will you? Say you will."

"Yes, of course, as soon as Mama lets me go."

"That's right. That'll be a very good thing," Lisa muttered, drawing Annochka after her, then stopping all of a sudden, "but why am I dragging you after me? You have to go to the grocer's, run along!"

They said good-by and Lisa set out homeward at a brisk pace, walking on air, excited by the unexpected revival of vague expectations. The silence of the streets was no longer indifferent, and had given place to the conspiracy she had belonged to of old.

At home she was met by Vitenka, who had come for her. He hurried forward to greet her in a delighted, festive mood: everything had been done without any effort on his part and better than he could have hoped.

"I knew it, I knew it," he kept saying, drawing Lisa into the room, where her autumn coat, hat, and gloves that he had brought were laid out ready. Lisa had gone out just in her dress!

"Oh, my dear sweet Lisa!" he exclaimed, kissing her and looking at her closely as though they had been parted for ages. "You know, I've had my photograph taken! It came out wonderfully. I've found a most fascinating frame for it and I've put it on your dressing table. At first I was going to write on it—you know what? No, I won't tell you! I'll write whatever you want, you can dictate it. And then you'll have yours taken, too, and write whatever I dictate on it, do you agree? I used to sit for hours, looking at your photo, you know, the one Nastenka got for me long ago—taken when you were still at school. Ah, Lisa!"

While she was changing her dress, he sat down near her, twisting his interlaced fingers lightly and speaking in a repentant tone.

"Oh, of course I'm a faddy, unbalanced sort of fellow. My aunt often reproaches me—'It's all because you're so badly brought up, Vityusha,' she says. I tell her: 'Why blame me? You gave and I took.' But you know, Lisa, I'm telling you the truth when I say that I'm going to make myself all over again, and we shall never—I swear to you!—never fall out again. I'm a man, aren't I? I'll take myself in hand and that's all there is to it."

He would not stay to breakfast on any account, no matter how pressing they were; on the contrary, he insisted that they should all come that evening to Daria Antonovna's, where the reconciliation was to be celebrated. He purposely sent back the carriage so as to be able to walk home with his wife and he chose the busiest streets so that everyone could see how happy they were.

They strolled along arm in arm in arm at a leisurely pace, pausing before the shopwindows to look at the photographs, the postage stamps, the new winter hats, and even the galoshes made by a famous rubber company.

"You know the latest news?" Vitenka said, delighted that the passers-by turned to look at them, "the Prosecutor's wife has been to our house to invite you to a party that's going to be held—a big affair in the Gentlemen's Club. We'll go, won't we?"

"Oh, yes, all right!"

"You'll have a chic dress made for it. We'll have to show 'em. They're going to put you at the lottery wheel. It'll be fun, don't you think?"

"Oh, yes," was Lisa's invariable answer to everything he said.

She was quietly absorbed, and her unusual eventemperedness gave Vitenka no peace: he kept trying to rouse her.

When they came home, he led her through the rooms and they chose the things they might spare as prizes for the lottery. He pulled out a table for the things into the middle of the drawing room, while he himself went to his aunt's rooms to see to the preparations for the evening party to which the Meshkovs were invited.

For a long time Lisa stared with a kind of languid weariness at the ornaments and bric-a-brac, taking them from their usual places and setting them on the table. They were things she did not care about, reflecting a taste that had been forced upon her by a ready-made home, built up by strangers' hands. Yet they already held a remembrance of something endured; they were involuntarily a part of her mental experience within these walls, and, touching them, Lisa seemed to be saying things she could have said to none but herself. And when she saw the table, cluttered up with ash trays, goblets, vases, and the like, with those silver-plated sinuous women and bronze setters, and birds with their dead open beaks, she remembered very clearly her first morning and her resignation to all that had passed. Then, too, she had sat in the armchair beside the table of wedding presents that had apparently been arranged anew on purpose.

But gradually a strange smile illumined her face, pensive and at the same time thoughtless, happily vacant and carefree—it was as though Lisa had retired from the life around her, freed herself from it for the sake of the shadowy visions she saw ahead.

This was the state in which Vitenka found her when he returned, excited by the preparations.

"Why so sad?" he asked anxiously. "Maybe you don't want to part with all these knick-knacks? They're not worth bothering your head about. I'll buy you better things. We'll go and buy them together, shall we? And this stuff can all go to the lottery. But you haven't picked out very many things for the lottery. I'll add a few more. They must know what the Shubnikovs are like: don't grudge them anything."

"I don't grudge them," Lisa said very softly.

"Then what is it?"

"I want to tell you something. . . ."

"Well, what is it?" he urged.

"I'm going to have a baby."

Vitenka said nothing. He gave a little start, straightened himself, coughed, and twisted the ends of his mustache.

"*We* are going to have a baby," he corrected her in a new, impressive tone. "It's yours and mine. Shubnikov is going to have a son, another Shubnikov!"

He darted forward, opened his arms, and, picking Lisa up out of the armchair, he laughed with glee as he raised her high, almost tossing her in the air.

CHAPTER

· 35 ·

LIEUTENANT-COLONEL POLOTENTSEV was informed that evening by telephone that the prisoner Ksenia Afanasyevna Ragozina was dying after childbirth in the prison hospital, and was asked if he had any orders.

"Is she conscious?" Polotentsev demanded, and, receiving an answer in the affirmative, said he would be there shortly.

He had been intending to go to the charity ball, his dress suit, linen, cuff links, and so on were laid out on chairs, and he had not quite finished manicuring his nails when the telephone rang. He was a zealous worker, and since he had been unsuccessful so far in the Ragozin case, he could not afford to miss a chance of interrogating Ragozin's wife once more, especially at a moment like this, when the prisoner was at the point of death. He sent for a droshky.

The person from whom the most information might be obtained was less vulnerable than the rest: Ksenia Afanasyevna's pregnancy had protected her to a certain extent from the zeal with which these interrogations were usually carried on, though she had been sent to the dark and cold isolation cell twice for her obstinate refusal to give evidence. She herself was accused of being an accomplice, the evidence of this being the type cases in the kitchen and the press in the cellar, in which the proclamations must have been printed before her eyes. But she did not name a single under-

ground worker and said nothing that could set them
on the trail of her husband, who had gone into hiding
and could not be tried until found. Intimidation had no
effect, the attempt to bribe her by lightening the prison
regime met with no success, and in the end Polotentsev
thought it best to leave her to the natural course
of things—that is, to privation, hunger, and suspense.

Her travail began in the cell, where she was left
unattended, and it was only toward morning that she
was carried to the hospital on a stretcher. She had lost
so much blood that the midwife who had taken
the matter in hand until the doctor came considered
it hopeless to try to save the mother.

But the infant born into the world was healthy. It
was a boy with a red, marble-veined skin, a darkish,
matted, brown tuft of hair below the crown of his
head, a wide mouth, clenched fists, and purplish knees
drawn up tight against the stomach. He kept his eyes
closed; his ears were flattened against his head, the
lobes as white as though powdered. He did not cry
very loudly: his mouth twisted a little in wrinkles like
an old man's. He was washed, his eyes and nose
smeared with some medicine that made him cry louder,
his navel was bandaged, and then he was borne away
in his washbasin to the adjoining room.

Ksenia Afanasyevna was very weak indeed, but still,
when she had been examined by the doctor and he was
giving orders for her to be placed in a. separate room,
she asked for the baby to be given to her. The child,
swaddled in a rusty, smoky-looking napkin, was
brought in and laid beside his mother so that it would
be convenient for her to give him the breast. But the
milk would not come, and the baby wailed and
sucked in vain. At last he unglued his eyelids, perhaps
from hunger, and in the milky white slits the mother
caught a glimpse of his vague, senseless little eyes.

"They're brown!" she gasped in a happy, exhausted
whisper.

Pyotr Ragozin had brown eyes.

The baby was taken away from her, and she was
told that a foster mother had been found for him. By
midday a peasant woman from the common cell of the
criminals' jail was found who agreed to feed the child.
The hospital nurse tied an oblong tally around his

ankle with a tape. On one side the tally was marked in ink "Ragozin," on the other—"Christened in the prison church . . . named——" A space was left for the name and date.

The child was wrapped in a gray wadded prison jacket, and the nurse, accompanied by a guard summoned for the purpose, carried him across the yard to the women's section. The first diffident prickly snowflakes besprinkled the gray jacket with damp spots, and, moved by womanly compassion, the nurse carefully covered the place where the child's head was. The escort trudged heavily ahead of her, holding his sword against his side. At the entrance the guard who unbolted the grating laughed and said loudly: "Breeding and multiplying, aren't we?"

At the far side another guard, opening the grating into the corridor, heard the echo of his laugh and chuckled grimly.

On the bunk nearest the window a big woman, with the neck of her rough shirt open, was feeding an infant. The nurse laid the bundle down beside her and threw back the jacket that covered the baby she had brought.

"Here's a foster child for you, take pity on him and care for him."

The other women got up slowly from the bunks and drew closer, forming a semicircle around the mother. She took her own child from the breast, laid him on the pillow, and picked up the newcomer in her arms.

"Looks lighter than yours," said one of the women.

The prisoner put the moist nipple into the pitiful open mouth, but the baby only wailed and made helpless sucking noises with his lips. She pressed his lips around the nipple with her hard fingers. His tiny chin twitched convulsively and he began to snuffle.

"Now he's taken to it!" the nurse said approvingly.

"Is his mother still alive?" the prisoner asked, patting her own baby with her free hand—he was lying a little behind her and had started to cry.

"Yes, she's still alive."

They all watched in silence the new tenant of the cell learning to suck the breast. He must have begun to like it, for he thrust out from the big napkin the foot with the tally tied around it and wriggled it a little.

Two or three sighs were heard. A young prisoner wiped her face with her sleeve and moved aside.

"I've no diapers for the baby," the foster mother complained.

"Well, when the mother dies, you can have her clothes and make some for the baby," one of the women consoled her.

"You'll see about it, won't you?" the foster mother asked the nurse.

"Yes, I'll see you get them," the nurse promised, and, as she was going out, added: "God bless you. . . ."

The only thing that could be said of Ksenia Afanas-yevna now was that she was barely alive. When Polo-tentsev entered the ward, he was afraid at first he come too late.

By the light of the wretched lamp that hung behind the head of the bed, Ksenia's rounded forehead, sharp nose, and cheekbones looked the transparent yellow of limeflower honey. The shadows lay dark and motion-less on the eye sockets, and the raised upper lip, the slender hollow neck glimmered through the shade. The mouth was open, exposing the thin line of teeth, and these and the loose tangled hair spread over the pillow made the head look very small, like a child's.

Polotentsev sat down by the bed, leaning forward and propping his chin with his hand. He watched her as a doctor watches a patient fighting for her life. He would have felt her pulse, very likely, only that she kept her hands under the blanket. Soon he came to the conclusion that she was not asleep—she must have noticed when he came in.

"Water," came from her audibly enough.

He took the drinking pot from the table and held the spout to her lips. She swallowed a mouthful of water and opened her eyes, and he sensed that she saw him.

"Do you recognize me?" he asked.

She made no reply.

"How do you feel?"

"All right," she said, and her eyelids closed again.

"But still you are in a rather dangerous state of health at present and you have a little son. You ought to think of him."

Her breathing became louder, she stretched out a

hand palm upward, and as it fell helplessly on the blanket, it resembled a long canoe cast up on the shore.

"Who is to take care of the child when you are gone? Only the father. And he doesn't even know he has a son. How is he to find out?"

Ksenia Afanasyevna tried to raise herself.

"No, lie still. You understand what I'm saying, don't you?" Polotentsev asked.

He moved nearer. She was looking at him now with eyes that held all her failing strength; the flaming pupils were fixed in her big slanting eyes.

"I can see you understand what I'm talking about. Your husband won't thank you if the child dies. Tell me, who could send word to Ragozin that a son is born to him?"

He took her hand and shook it lightly.

"Speak! Before it's too late! Who can tell Ragozin about his son? Speak, I'm telling you!"

She drew away her hand and raised her head a fraction from the pillow but could not hold it up. Polotentsev bent over and put his ear close to her face. He could hear her teeth chattering with the fever. She whispered suddenly, every word perfectly clear:

"You want to drive him to his death, as you've done with me."

He recoiled. "You're crazy! We're talking about the baby. You lost the first, do you want to lose this one, too?"

"You'll torment the boy to death, as well as me," she gasped, making a last effort.

He got up and demanded indignantly: "For the last time: who is to be told about the baby born in prison?

She turned her face to the wall. He pushed back the chair, took a step or so away, then, after a moment's thought, asked so that the whole ward could hear him: "What are your last wishes? I am going."

The fever shook her so that the blanket jerked on her body. Turning suddenly, she moaned: "Christen him Pyotr!"

Polotentsev raised his shoulders with an angry jerk. "So you want to leave us a second Pyotr Petrovich, do you? No, we aren't going to have any legacies of that kind—the child's going to be plain prison Ivan!"

He pranced about a few moments more, then tramped angrily out.

"The devil's in them!" he said to the prison superintendent, who saw him out to the gate. "Those people seem to be devoid of any feeling whatsoever!"

He drove home and changed his clothes unhurriedly. Wearing boots with silver spurs, and a black dress coat to his knees, he was just throwing on his gray winter cape with its beaver collar when he was called to the telephone again. He went back into the room without taking off his coat. The prison office informed him that, according to the doctor's report, Ksenia Afanasyevna Ragozina had just died.

"Very well!" said Polotentsev, and set out for the ball.

CHAPTER

· 36 ·

THE AFFAIR BEGAN rather late—the literary part was still
going on. Half of the big lobby was occupied by an
exhibition of the things that were to be prizes in the
lottery. The ladies engaged in charity work were still
busy, putting the finishing touches to the shelves and
tablets. By the lottery wheels stood little girls with
ringlets and pale blue frocks—with their round faces
they looked like Murillo's cherubs: they were to draw
the tickets. From time to time the ladies would give
a touch to the little girls' hair ribbons and frocks. In
the middle of the exhibition there was a picture in a
gilt frame of the biggest prize—a Kholmogor cow. The
bouquet of chrysanthemums that reared itself just
under her head was to be presented to the fortunate
winner. Everything around shone and sparkled: the
samovars, inkstands, embroidered Tatar slippers, bottles of champagne, gramophone horns, alarm clocks,
mandolins, and mincing machines. Every taste was
catered for, and neither an admirer of Nadson's sentimental verse nor a connoisseur of cactuses would be
likely to complain that he had been forgotten.

Pavilions were ranged around the lottery; in the
monstrous jaws of a tiger a beauty attired as a circus
lion tamer was selling punch, and in a gaily patched
tent another beauty, plump, well-nourished, and wearing a gypsy costume, was sitting with a parrot that
picked out of a box open gummed slips of paper with

fortunes told on them. The tent bore the legend:
"No magic will speak when it has naught in its beak!"

When the ladies had come to the conclusion that
everything was perfectly ready, they partly opened
the door into the concert hall and stood listening.

Lisa was standing in front of them all, so that she
could get a good view of the stage.

Egor Pavlovich Tsvetukhin, in evening dress, was
reciting the monologue "To be or not to be," and
the audience was listening with respectful attention,
as though all those officials, officers, merchants' wives
in low-cut dresses, and young society girls had assembled here especially for the purpose of settling
once and forever the eternal question of life and death
which the actor was presenting to them. Tsvetukhin
delivered the monologue very simply, but the simplicity had finish, and was therefore perfectly theatrical—every word and gesture suggested: see how charming, how fascinatingly simple and unaffected I can
be! There was a grateful burst of applause—his fame
was unquestionable and no one would attempt to deny
it.

But when he had gone and a little table and an
armchair were brought in, and Alexander Pastukhov
appeared before the public, the general feeling that
stirred the crowd was the lively, wondering curiosity
with which an unknown but perfectly self-assured
performer is greeted. "You see," Pastukhov seemed
to be saying as he settled himself comfortably and
with careless ease in the armchair, "I have no intention of trying to make an impression on you, but
since you made up your mind to invite me, I have
here an excerpt from a comedy that really isn't bad
at all, just a trifle, of course, and I'll read it to you,
as I might read it to friends of an evening in the
country cottage, over a glass of wine—well, anyway,
here it is." Without the slightest effort for effect, but
simply as though he was doing it for his own bene-
fit, he began to read from his notes, never thinking
for a moment that anyone might hinder him, or that
his voice might not carry, or that his manner might
displease someone, but with the natural assurance that
he was doing exactly what everyone had been impatiently expecting him to do. And he was listened

to, at first with a faint smile, then with titters, and finally with a hearty laughter they were no longer able to suppress, and controlled only by fear that they might miss something still more amusing and curious. And when Pastukhov had finished and came out on the stage to acknowledge the encores, he laughed too, gaily and rather condescendingly, suggesting by his magnificently gracious appearance that —good heavens!—he hadn't doubted for a moment that it would all be frightfully funny and irresistible, though, of course, it was just sheer nonsense, and he wasn't intending to let them see all he could do! So let them laugh if they liked, of course, but they must surely understand themselves that it was really not worth all the fuss!

The literary part concluded with his triumph. The audience broke up and gradually drifted out of the hall, while the strains of "Toreador" announced the commencement of the lottery. The seals were removed from the lottery tickets, the cherubs in pale blue dipped into them with their dimpled hands, pulled out rolled papers, the ladies set to work to find the prizes on the shelves and, with enchanting smiles, present them to the winners.

The young people made way for Tsvetukhin and Pastukhov. Mefody was with them, attired in an old-fashioned evening suit from the costumery of the theater, comfortable-looking garments that fitted like a sack. He was flattered and pleased that a modicum of the attention due to his famous friends, a kind of reflected glory, was accorded to him. All three came up to the wheel at which Lisa was seated. Cracking jokes, like the rest of the people, about the prize cow, which they declared should have been offered as a prize in the form of ice cream or ripe old cheese, they started to buy tickets. Mefody won a bunch of toothpicks and declared that now he only needed a beefsteak, which meant returning to the old cow. Tsvetukhin drew five blanks. He sighed:

"Of course, I've seen for a long time that I've fallen out of favor. And you never even told me whether you liked me as Hamlet or not. Well, God is your judge. But at least I was better than that insufferable idol of the mob—Pastukhov, eh?"

"Don't be cross," Lisa said, smiling, "Though the two are incomparable, Alexander Pastukhov beat your Hamlet!"

"Avaunt!" Pastukhov said grandly, stepping in front of Egor. "Your star is waning. I'm to the fore today. Will you be so kind" (he showed all his strong even teeth in a smile) "as to drawn ten tickets for me with your own hand?"

With the utmost gravity all four unrolled the tickets Lisa had drawn until at last the winning number came out.

"Good heavens, what can it be? I don't think I can bear it!" Pastukhov gabbled, pressing his hand to his heart.

It took some time to find it, and Lisa went searching among the labels for the winning number, while the friends followed her movements, prompting her and guessing impatiently: "It's a saucepan! An umbrella! A sewing machine!" and then they all gasped: "A decanter!"

Lisa was lifting down a commodious-looking decanter of excellent cut glass with a rich, engraved design thrown into relief on its gleaming pomegranate-crimson planes. Pastukhov accepted it from her with the reverence of a devotee, gazing at it admiringly, and said with profound meaning:

"It's a pity, you know, it's one of those nasty tricks that fortune plays: this thing should belong, by reason of his special services in honor of Bacchus, to our incomparable friend!"

He presented the decanter to Mefody with a low bow.

"Wait!" Mefody stopped him with emotion and real alarm. "Don't tempt Providence! See!"

He drew the stopper out of the decanter and held it before Pastukhov's eyes. "Don't you understand, you madman, what this signifies?"

Pastukhov stared at the stopper, clapped his hand to his mouth in fright, and shook his head. "What a fright you gave me! I understand. Yes, of course I understand!" He took out the stopper, put it in his pocket solemnly, and then, handing the decanter to Mefody, said: "You may carry this!"

"Bah! this symbolism!" Tsvetukhin jeered.

"Black magic!" Pastukhov declared in a sinister tone, making a few hypnotic passes at Tsvetukhin and Lisa.

They all laughed, but the people were thronging around the lottery, so that the friends had to move out of the way, and Lisa left the wheel in order to hear what Tsvetukhin was saying.

"I'm bankrupt! You'll have to make up for my losses by letting me have the first waltz."

She assured him that she had already promised it to someone, obviously afraid that she would not be believed. He looked at her with admiration—her excitement pleased him, her youth still throbbed in her, only just blossoming into beautiful womanhood.

"Oh, very well, I'll take your word for it! But if you're engaged for the waltz, perhaps you'll let me have some leftover dance, will you? Promise me."

"A leftover, yes!" she promised.

Mefody broke in on their raillery: he drew Tsvetukhin aside by the tail of his coat and murmured excitedly: "Come along, quick, we're going to be introduced to the Prosecutor!"

Proud of his acquaintance now, Oznobishin was leading Pastukhov up to the Prosecutor's wife, who was gushing all over him, assuring him she had never heard such a fine recital or suspected they had an author of such amusing and perfectly sweet comedies in their town. Pastukhov listened with his head slightly bowed, and his smile of triumphant and convinced perfection.

"You simply charmed everybody and I must thank you on behalf of our Society! Thank you very much indeed!"

"Yes, indeed, delighted, thank you," the Prosecutor said, shaking hands with Pastukhov. "You illumined our dull club like the alpha of a constellation, one might say. Isn't it a sin for you, living here as you do, to have hidden your talents, your gifts from us, like this?"

"Well, but you see, Excellency," Pastukhov replied with the easy charm of an old acquaintance, "I never thought I would be of interest to you in that capacity."

"Oh, come now, do you really think that we never take a book in our hands, or drop into the theater,

or interest ourselves in the . . . well, what we may
call the phenomena—"

"Not at all," Pastukhov hastened to explain, "I simply thought that your interest in certain fictitious and
suspected characteristics of mine hindered you from
seeing anything else in me."

"Suspected! But we've always suspected you of—
talent!"

"Still, the noble institution over which you pre-
side would not permit me to demonstrate it to you
personally, would it?"

"Oh, they wouldn't let you see me? Yes, of course,
I see now," the Prosecutor replied, as though the
whole thing had suddenly come back to him. "You're
talking about all that affair? Now you're forcing me
to lay my cards on the table! Allow me to tell you
we purposely prevented you from going anywhere
else before you had delighted us with your brilliant
public appearance here!"

Pastukhov passed his hand lightly over his face,
brushing away, it seemed, its rather mischievous expression and then, with a hearty laugh, was transformed into the life and soul of the party, one of
those gay young sparks.

"Just imagine," the Prosecutor's lady was saying,
interrupting the conversation between her husband
and Pastukhov, "your friend has won a decanter without a stopper!"

Mefody and Tsvetukhin were waiting in indecision to see what success Pastukhov might achieve,
when, with a confident smile, and assurance in every
movement, he drew the stopper out of his pocket
and shook it before the eyes of their excellencies.

"I hid the stopper. You can't rely on actors, they're
dreamers and frightfully absent-minded. And I need
the stopper for checking an experiment of the utmost
scientific importance."

"So you're interested in science, too?" the lady inquired.

"Are you fond of peas, Excellency?" Pastukhov
asked.

"Peas?" the Prosecutor repeated, obviously shocked,
but with perfect politeness. His curiosity was aroused.

"The French eat pea soup to sober down. As a

remedy, of course. You never heard of it? I advise you to try it. And while the peas are cooking, you have to put a crystal stopper in the pot to make them soften sooner. I got this from a great epicure and I am confiding it to you."

"Dear me, how very interesting!" said the Prosecutor's wife, laughing heartily and evidently struck by this rare joke: no one had ever suggested before in her presence that the Prosecutor might need to be sobered down after a spree.

Twiddling the stopper in his fingers, Pastukhov moved a little closer to the Prosecutor and said, almost confidentially: "So, Excellency, now that the subtle plan has been carried out and I have been kept here until this evening, I may hope that you have no further use for me in the town?"

"No further use? But we've only just got to know you!" the Prosecutor protested, yielding to an impulse of irresistible hospitality and almost embracing Pastukhov. "The real necessity for keeping you here has arisen in good earnest only now. We can't possibly let you go until you have found time to honor us with your company in a narrower circle."

"Yes, exactly—in a narrow, intimate circle," the lady chimed in, "you must promise us now, at once."

It looked as though everything was going swimmingly—they all smiled pleasantly and bowed, but Pastukhov would not let the crystal stopper out of his hand—he made up his mind to go straight for his goal, unhindered by considerations of conventionalities.

"Still, Excellency, a bird in the hand, you know, is worth—"

"But why a bird?" the Prosecutor demanded, his eyebrows lifting.

"Ah, why a bird, indeed?" Pastukhov said, "I feel more like a cockroach in a matchbox."

"A bird? A cockroach! After the furor you created here? Oh, you must be simply spoiled. And then . . . if you are referring again to that—"

"That's exactly what I am referring to again, Excellency," Pastukhov persisted.

"Oh, you mean that little affair—but good heavens! I'll see to it tomorrow and then . . . by all means . . . soar into the sky like any bird, a clear-eyed falcon,

if you like, and fly off wherever you want to. . . .
My dear Oznobishin, do tell them tomorrow to send
me that case . . . you remember, that misunderstanding
about Mr. Pastukhov."

"And Tsvetukhin," Pastukhov put in.

"Yes, and Mr. Tsvetukhin. Very well. And . . .
er . . . just a moment! . . . Do I see a bald head over
there by the lottery? It looks like the Lieutenant-
Colonel. Ask him to come over here, will you, if you
don't mind?"

"There you are!" Pastukhov sighed with immense
relief. "Now I'm ready not only to read on the stage
but dress up as a Spanish beauty, if you like, and do
a dance with castanets."

"That's just what we're going to make you do!"
the Prosecutor rejoined, laughing as he bowed and
followed his lady.

Pastukhov stood motionless, his nostrils quivering,
like a man in the thick of the battle smoke after a
victorious campaign, his parted lips set hard as though
he had the prey in his teeth. His two friends contemplated him with awe and admiration.

"Was I right?" Mefody demanded eagerly.

"You're a prophet!" Pastukhov conceded magnanimously, putting the stopper in the decanter very solemnly. "The soup is ready. I don't need this any
longer." He took the two by the arms. "Left shoulder
forward—to the bar, double quick!"

Not that there was any possible chance of speedy
advance: one could merely wriggle one's way through
the noisy swarms of people. Those who had been
lucky in the lottery were going "to sprinkle" their
winnings, and those who had not were going to drown
their sorrows, while those who had not taken part
in it at all were going to spend their money without
tempting fate.

Victor Semyonovich Shubnikov was of the number who preferred certainty to luck. With his boon
companions he remained seated at a table in the bar-
room practically the whole time the entertainment
was going on, and he had no intention of moving.
He only wanted to look at Lisa—and see how she
suited her new role among society women. So, having
made his way out of the refreshment bar at last, he

stood at a distance from the lottery, keeping well behind the people and watching his wife. Yes, he had every right to say that he was truly happy: Lisa's dress was richer than any of the others, her jewelry was incomparably more brilliant, her coiffure—far higher than the others, perhaps the highest of any at the ball. The throng was thickest around her lottery wheel, she smiled more enchantingly than the rest, she moved with a lighter, more gliding grace, the things she touched seemed to gain in value from her touch—yes, she was worthy of the name of Shubnikov!

Vitenka went up to her. His face was all smiles. "I can see you'll soon have made your market, eh?"

"Working in the shop seems to have come in handy," she replied gaily. "I see you've already had a few."

"Only among friends—a few of our fellows. We're waiting for you."

"I can't. You see what's going on here," she said, and, in the same lighthearted tone, added carelessly: "I've been asked for a dance—by Tsvetukhin. You don't mind, do you?"

The straightforwardness of it appealed to him—his feelings melted in a flow of general benevolence, and he took his wife's success for his own.

"You only have to ask me, I'll always allow you!"

She said nothing, only moved about still more briskly as she picked out and compared the winning tickets with the labels on the things. There was really quite a lot to do.

Vitenka returned to the refreshment bar, feeling like an enchanted suitor. On the way he had his fortune told by the gypsy. The parrot pulled out of the drawer a useful maxim that harmonized with his own convictions: "Persevere and you will soon obtain what you want. Remember that you are envied."

He saw Tsvetukhin and Pastukhov looking for a vacant place. As they passed, Shubnikov bowed to Tsvetukhin and proposed that they should join him at his table.

"You must have thought me very unsociable at Ochkin's that time. It was only that I was in a very bad mood. Don't you think this has been an awfully pleasant sort of evening? My wife tells me you are going to dance with her."

"She probably promised the waltz to you?" Tsvetu-khin asked.

"I'll let you have it, if you like," Vitenka declared magnanimously.

He wanted to speak to Pastukhov but was astounded and disconcerted to find that the author did not appear to have noticed him, as though Victor Semyo-novich's person was part of the electric fittings and nothing more. This was so obvious that Tsvetukhin was as startled as Vitenka, and tried to smooth over the awkwardness; he even twitched his friend's sleeve, but it was all to no use, and Vitenka moved away.

Alexander Pastukhov was staring with a concentra-tion unusual even in him at the corner where Polo-tentsev's bald head gleamed and his spectacles glittered. The Lieutenant-Colonel was talking to the Prosecutor. Pastukhov was watching every change of expression that flitted over His Excellency's face, the shades and variations in his gestures; it was as though he were reading the Prosecutor's thoughts from a distance, and, to tell the truth, he could hardly have learned more from this brief and significant conversation if he had been standing beside them listening.

"Lord bless you!" the Prosecutor was saying with an encouraging smile, "you have nearly worn our local devotees of the muses to shadows! What do you think of those two for talent, eh? Our pride and glory, eh?"

"No doubt, Excellency," the Lieutenant-Colonel agreed, "still, it seems to me that they serve not only the muses, but some pernicious trend."

"Seems!" the Prosecutor repeated. "That's hardly sufficient, you must admit. There is no real case, I am informed. No, let us release them and give them a chance to repent."

"The whole point is, Excellency, that they are not in the least inclined to repent."

"Well, and supposing they have nothing to repent, what then?"

"Everyone has something it would do him no harm to repent of."

"Something!" the Prosecutor repeated, this time with a hint of impatience.

"And then, after all, it's very good for them, Your Excellency."

"I don't suppose it does them any harm. And perhaps in all justice you are right, but according to the law you are not. Get the material ready, I am going to wind up the case."

"The whole case is winding itself up as it is, Excellency, by degrees: Ragozin's wife died this evening."

"Of illness?" the Prosecutor asked sharply.

"Childbirth."

"And what about it?"

"She did not deny that her husband was the head of the group."

"Was there anything else she did not happen to deny?" the Prosecutor persisted inquisitively, scrutinizing the Lieutenant-Colonel's glasses with alertness.

"She did not deny what to all intents and purposes there was no sense in denying," Polotentsev replied cryptically, rubbing his mathematical bump.

"Humph, well, I see my partners are waiting for me," the Prosecutor said finally. "Forgive me if I've kept you away from amusing yourself. But it was all because of those two. What talent, eh? Did you win anything in the lottery? No luck? Oh, don't say that! Why, you're always in luck. Well, I hope you'll win the cow—go ahead!"

He drifted away, heading for the cardroom, and Polotentsev went toward the exit, passing close by Pastukhov without greeting him; in the first place, it was not his custom to regard people he met in the execution of his duties as acquaintances, and in the second place, there was always the risk that a gendarme's bow might not be acknowledged.

Pastukhov, smoking a cigarette tensely, let the Lieutenant-Colonel pass. Then his massive shoulders, chest, and belly jerked and shook with silent laughter. He threw an arm around Tsvetukhin, who was beaming with satisfaction and lighthearted enjoyment and led led him up to the table at which Mefody had seated himself. They ordered the Burgundy to be slightly warmed, and poured it into their new decanter. As they sat chatting of this and that, they returned by different routes to the thing that engrossed their attention at the moment: after the Prosecutor's conversation with the Lieutenant-Colonel, interpreted by

Pastukhov to their advantage, their recent troubles
turned into a curious anecdote, and all that remained
was to drink to it.

The dances had already begun; the voices of the
brass band sighed sonorously through the room. Tsvetukhin was trying to get away, but the decanter was a
large one, the wine made them heavy, the friends
proposed toast after toast until at last Pastukhov
pronounced as though it were the remission of sins:

"Here's to the health of the one who gave us this
talisman. To poor Lisa"—he looked quizzically at
Tsvetukhin—"To Poor Lisa and Erastes!" *

Egor Pavlovich drank it standing, accepted his new
christening very well, and, trying to look the sly se-
ducer, went away.

He was just in that state when the first tipsiness,
winding skyward, completes its first loop and
wherein everything from that point begins to look
ethereal and accessible. He wanted to be more lithe,
more graceful in his gait, to look more passionate, to
wear a brighter smile, and find a more colorful idiom
in which to express himself. It gave him enjoyment to
push through the throng, rubbing shoulders with
others, apologizing with exquisite courtesy, and excusing others graciously.

Lisa seemed enchanting to him and raised him to
another level at once, where the tipsiness made a second
curl, not daring as yet, but still quite bold. He escorted
her as though it was not for the first time, making way
for her among the richly dressed throng, into the
brilliantly lit hall, through the smart black-and-white
rows of people, making her submit, as he submitted
himself, to the command of the musical entertainment.

The leftover dance he did not fail to remind her of
turned out to be a quadrille. They turned away from
each other, faced each other again, whirled around,
and turned away again; the changing figures parted
them to reunite them for a flash, then they glanced into
each other's eyes, attempted to say something, had to
break off, and wondered what to say when they met
and waltzed again. All these things were repeated
endlessly, becoming better and better, though the

* Lisa and Erastes were the characters in a sentimental
tale *Poor Lisa* by Nikolai Karamzin (1766–1826).

rhythm did not alter at all, only the breath came quicker and one wanted to go on and on. And though they were only one couple in a long train of couples like themselves, they felt as though they were the only dancers and that the band was thundering for them alone.

The words they exchanged left but a fleeting impression on Lisa, passing with the lightness of a transparent dragonfly poised for an instant on a reed before taking off, only to return again for a brief halt. All that remained was the movement, the air cleft for an instant, the flash of light—no more.

Then suddenly Tsvetukhin's flow of words began to interfere with the empty flight of thought, to halt and drag it back. The band seemed to break up into individual instruments, the chandeliers into isolated lamps—the dance claimed closer attention.

"You were saying?" Lisa asked at the last turn.

They turned away from each other again, did a couple more steps, looking into each other's eyes, and, as she laid her hand on his shoulder, he repeated clearly: "You ran away from your husband already?"

Fortunately, the turns came one after another, the third and the fourth, and again she had to turn her back to Tsvetukhin and so had a moment to think.

"Who told you that?"

"I just fancied that you would be sure to run away." What a difficult dance this was, how awkwardly all the silly parts were tied together and how soon one got tired!

"Would you like me to run away?"

"I would like you to be happy."

Someone bumped into Lisa at this moment, she lost a beat, the set behind her closed in, someone stepped on her dress, and she took Tsvetukhin by the arm.

"I'm tired."

He led her off the dance floor, and they went back to the lottery, still with her arm in his. He was heated from the dance, his face was moist and shone, he breathed quickly, and often pressed his folded handkerchief to his chin, temples, and neck.

"I have to go back to work now," she smiled, pointing to the revolving lottery wheel.

"Are you happy?" he asked persistently.

"Yes, of course," she replied stiffly, then, glancing at

him with the directness of one prepared to sell her life dear, repeated: "Yes, of course, I'm happy, perfectly happy. And you oughtn't to ask me about it."

She bowed and turned away, so that she did not see how dumbfounded he looked for a moment, holding his handkerchief in his hand in mid-air.

She spent a good hour after that at the wheel, reading the tickets and labels, mixing up the numbers, making mistakes in handing over the prizes, until one of the ladies remarked with amused sympathy that she must be overtired and ought to have a rest.

She went to the refreshment bar. Vitenka's and Tsvetukhin's parties had joined forces, setting two tables together. They were laughing uproariously over Pastukhov's stories. He looked more massive in his chair, and by his eyes, which were closing with tipsiness, it was apparent that he was pleasantly amused by this far from exacting and hilarious society. They all rose and offered their places to Lisa.

"What people, oh, what people!" Vitenka gushed. "It wouldn't matter if you heard some of the stories. Honestly, they're all quite decent."

"Perfectly sterile!" Mefody, who had drunk more than any of them, assured her.

But Lisa did not want to stay. She did not feel well. Her head was going round, and Vitenka was suddenly overcome with sympathy and nodded heartily and meaningly, giving her to understand that he had been struck by a very important thought.

He pulled out of his pocket a bundle of securities coupons and announced that he was going to pay for everybody. But he found that he was past counting aright. The friends offered to help him and muddled it up too. Pastukhov took the coupons away from them all, crushed them into a bundle, and handed them to Lisa.

She made a serious attempt to count them, but got into a muddle at once because some were worth rubles and a few kopeks, others less than a ruble, and the chief thing was that Tsvetukhin kept his glowing black eyes on her. She admitted, rather pettishly at last, that she found it bothersome—all these percentages and so on. Then Tsvetukhin said:

"Mark my words: you'll never make a good merchant's wife if you don't like counting money."

"Aye!" Vitenka cried, gathering up the coupons and stuffing them back into his pocket. "And why should a rich woman count? Anyone will be glad to count for her! Waiter! Tell the manager to send the bill home to me tomorrow. I'm Shubnikov!"

He offered his arm to Lisa.

"My wife's taking me home tonight. I'm agreeable. Perfectly agreeable."

He walked away rather unsteadily, whispering all the time: "I understood you at once: little Shubnikov wants to go bye-bye, that's it, isn't it? Did I guess right? Our little fellow wants to go to sleep, eh?"

Out in the frost he sagged and grew sloppier, his lisping grew thick and inarticulate, and at home, before he got half of his clothes off, he fell fast asleep, snoring loudly.

LISA COULD NOT fall asleep for a long time that night. The clubrooms kept reappearing very strangely in her mind's eye. Each view that opened before her remained fixed, and she could distinguish in the flood of light the faces, the women's evening gowns, the floral decorations and the prizes she had distributed in the lottery and which the lucky winners had to carry around with them, a grotesque burden, all the evening. But every time Tsvetukhin's dark, glistening face arose before her eyes, she strove to forget him and pass on to some other memory and linger over it, so that the dark face would not return for some time. In the exhausting confusion that this struggle bred it seemed to Lisa she would never fall asleep but would lie tormented all night by insomnia, trying to fight through a thicket of scenes and things that hindered her from obtaining rest. She fled from them, but her flight was too feeble. She wanted to flee on horseback, and even saw horses on which she might ride away. They were all very different, and among them was Victor Semyonovich's pacer. Lisa thought of mounting this one, when suddenly a black horse caparisoned with a big blue net dashed in from somewhere. Lisa had just time to make a grab at the net, and found herself in the carriage. The horse was racing through the dark, deserted streets, through the gloom, and the hoofs rang in the silence of the town. A wind was blowing, Lisa shivered, she was wearing nothing but a lacy nightgown and a boudoir cap all in lace and bows. In pitch darkness the carriage suddenly drew up before an immense black door, and here someone on either side of her took her by the arms and helped her to alight. She opened a heavy door and found that she was in the theater. On she moved between the rows of seats toward the stage. Only a single dusty yellow lamp infinitely high, on the chandelier, faintly illumined the silent auditorium. Barefoot, Lisa moved noiselessly, with painful slowness, in her lace-trimmed nightgown and cap, like the old Countess before her death in Pushkin's *Queen of Spades*, which she had seen at the opera house. She crossed the deep pit of the orchestra by the narrow board that spanned it and stepped over the footlights. The curtain had gone up. Suddenly a myriad of lights blazed out at her feet, dazzling her. She began to measure the stage by paces. The boards were rough and full of splinters, and a cold wind blew through the cracks. The stage was twenty paces long, seventeen deep. It might have been deeper, but something dark hindered her from going further and she did not know what lay beyond that obscurity. She turned back. The cold wind was still blowing up from the floor, and her long nightgown flapped about her ankles. She began to count the lamps, but they glowed still brighter, her eyes pricked, she pressed her hands hard to her face, and at that moment a piercing voice called out desperately from somewhere at her back, from the darkness, and she awoke.

She was trembling with fright, but she had a strange and very clear feeling that she had learned something extraordinarily new in her dream and had herself become renewed. Vitenka was snoring peacefully. Lisa passed her hand over her body, she was perspiring, her collarbones were damp. She took off her nightgown and hung it on the armchair, put on her dressing gown, and went over to the window.

A layer of fine dry snow covered the street already busy, for it was morning. The black wheel tracks showed on the snow, like rails. The snow-powdered roofs were spotlessly white and the houses seemed to have risen. The sky was an even gray. The smoke from the chimneys curled across it in blue globes that swelled, faded to a lighter blue, and merged with the sky. There were no sleighs out yet.

Lisa repeated to herself a line from Pushkin's *Eugene Onegin:* "Awaking early, Tatyana saw the snow making the courtyard and the rooftree white," and then went into the dining room.

Almost at the same moment the opposite door opened. The old servant beckoned to Lisa mysteriously, with significant movements of the eyebrows, and tiptoed toward her.

"There's a little girl here to see you. It's you she's asking for."

"Where? In the kitchen?"

"Yes. She says you told her to come. You're waiting for her, she says."

Lisa cast a swift backward glance into the bedroom, and with a trustfulness that was new to her, whispered to the old woman to be on guard.

Running into the kitchen, she found Annochka there, leaning against the door post. She was still wearing her mother's jacket, which had not yet been altered for her, and had an old woollen shawl around her head.

"Hello, so you're here?" Lisa said softly. "Well, what news?"

"I went to Vera Nikandrovna's yesterday."

"Did you? And what did she say?"

"She was glad."

"Glad to see you, you mean?"

"No, glad that you'd told me to go and see her."

"I see. So what did she say?"

"She has only a little place to live in now—about as big as from here to the stove."

"Didn't she tell you anything?"

"Yes, of course she did. We sat talking all the afternoon. She teaches girls now, she hasn't got boys any more."

"And did you talk about—what I asked you to find out?"

"Yes, we talked about that, too. She kept asking me a lot of questions about us and I told her everything —about Papa and Mama going to see you at the shop and then how you—"

"No, I don't mean that. I mean about Kirill."

"Yes, and about him, too."

"But what?—what did she tell you?"

"She sent you a letter."

"She sent me a letter?" Lisa's voice dropped to a whisper, but she could not control her eagerness.

She was standing very close to Annochka now, and her eyes missed no movement of the child's. Unbuttoning her jacket and pausing with her hand on the front of it, she looked up at Lisa with a bright, impish smile.

"When Vera Nikandrovna saw that my lining was ripped a bit, she hid the letter inside it and then stitched it up herself."

She picked at the lining, slipped her finger inside, ripped the seam, and pulled out a small envelope with a purple edge. It bore the one word "Lisa," but the word explained everything: it was from Kirill.

"Wait a moment . . . or, no, go away, you'd better go," Lisa said, breathing quickly and shutting the door with her foot. "Come later on, will you?"

"Any time or some special time?" Annochka asked, disappointed, but not taking offense.

"Whenever you like, it doesn't matter, but perhaps you'd better wait," Lisa babbled, no longer able to think of what she was saying, moving over to the window and slitting the edges of the envelope with her fingernail.

The small sheet of notepaper was closely covered in a hand that was fairly large and easy to read. It seemed to Lisa that she could not grasp the meaning of all the words and only read the beginning and the end of the sentences, yet she did not miss a word and understood much more than was expressed in the letter. She strove greedily to catch the sense that lay behind this bit of paper, and that was the chief thing.

Kirill wrote that now at last he could write letters to his mother and to her, he had been waiting so long for this day and had written letters to her so often in his head that now the memory of them hindered him from recalling what he had wanted to say, so perhaps he would not be able to set down what was most important. Since he had last seen her, so much unexpectedly altered in him that he himself was not quite sure in whose behalf he was writing, the Kirill she had known, or the Kirill as he knew himself now.

Lisa caught her breath at this point and forced herself to read more slowly.

"I live a different life now, not in the least like the life I used to lead. It seems as though my school had never really existed, but was only a dream. I am living in a village such as you would never see on our Volga; there are only eleven houses in it. The nearest village is seven hours' walk from here through the wood. There are fewer people than there were in our class at school, but they are very unusual. I have begun to learn how people live, and you know, Lisa, I see I was just a child in those days. You wouldn't know me now perhaps.

"I am lodging at an old woman's house, she has grandchildren. Of an evening she sings: 'Oh, I hide gold, I hide it away.' I asked her about it once and found out she had had never seen any gold in her life. Even a silver engagement ring is rare in these parts, they all wear brass. It has already started snowing. The great long Russian winter has begun. I suppose the cold hasn't set in at home yet. My old woman here tells fairytales such as we never heard. I suppose one couldn't live without stories.

"I am writing things that are of no consequence, but then I think you will be better able to judge of the place where I shall stay for a long time. All this endless time we won't be able to see each other and though it will be terribly hard for me, I have made up my mind to it and I know I can bear it. But this is what I have decided to write to you about at once. Dearest Lisa! Time will drag on and all this may become unbearable to you. So I want you to know that I will understand if you don't care to wait until my time is up—three years. I am telling you this honestly, because I have thought it all out. I give you my word I won't take offense. Your freedom and independence are dearer to me than all else.

"And another thing—I want you to write to me and please don't be angry with me if I am mistaken. Was I right in guessing that you were attracted by Tsvetukhin? If it is so, I can't have anything against it, and if not, I'll be even happier than before and I will still hope that we shall be together someday. I have been thinking all this over.

"This is all I shall say about you at present. You should write more to me about yourself. I want to know everything, I have written a great deal about myself to my mother and asked her to read the letters to you if you would like to hear them.

"And still another thing. On the journey someone bought me dried apples instead of tobacco—I don't smoke—at a station. They were wrapped in a bit of newspaper. That was how I found out that Tolstoy was dead. Write to me and tell me how you took his death and how people in general took it. I have thought a lot about it and I came to the conclusion that he is among my Great Men. I remember our conversation, and in general I remember everything, everything about you! I have sent Mother a list of the books I need. Write to me. Kirill."

The hand that held the letter dropped. The color flooded Lisa's face; the darkened wet eyes glowed; she stared before her unwinkingly.

"Should I go?" Annochka asked in a scared tone.

Lisa made no answer. Life was centered for her now at the depth she had never suspected in herself and she imagined that she needed nothing but that tumultuous soul that shook her very life.

But when the old servant peeped anxiously into the kitchen, Lisa hastily hid the letter in her bosom, and asked in a whisper: "Is he awake?"

"I don't know, but it seems to me Victor Semyonovich is stiller now," the old woman whispered behind the door.

It was then that Lisa with a start noticed Annochka and waved her away with both hands.

"What are you waiting for? Run along now, and come to see me some other time."

"Shall I tell Vera Nikandrovna anything or will you tell her yourself?" Annochka asked, hunching her shoulders up to her ears and showing with all her might that she fully understood the secret she was let into.

"I'll tell her myself! Everything myself!" Lisa replied, waving her away and hurrying out of the kitchen.

She stole softly to the bedroom door and listened. Vitenka was snoring but on a lower scale. Lisa opened one half of the double door. The room was in semi-darkness. Her husband lay sprawled out on his back.

The white lacy nightgown lay over an armchair. "Just like the dead Queen of Spades," Lisa thought, recalling her dream, but when it came back to her, she found she could not but evoke the impressions and details with which she had fallen asleep that night and once again she saw Tsvetukhin's dark face, his burning eyes, and felt an overpowering desire to reread that place in the letter where Kirill spoke of him.

Sitting down by the window, she went over the whole letter, reading scraps here and there, trying to analyze it with a mind that was still in a turmoil. She tried to answer herself as collectedly as she could: was she to blame, ought she to blame herself?—but for a long time she could form no adequate reply or understand what she was asking herself. She stared through the window at the snow, and tangled phrases recurred in disorder, expressing better than all her questions the life of the soul that had overwhelmed her at her first reading of the letter: the great long Russian winter. . . . "Awaking early, Tatyana saw the snow making the courtyard and the rooftree white." . . . I will still hope that we shall be together someday . . . he is among my Great Men . . . you will never make a merchant's wife . . . still . . . still—the Queen of Spades!

"Good heavens, how am I to blame!" Lisa whispered, laying her cheek helplessly on the window still, like a child.

Little by little she got a hold on her thoughts and realized with an aching bitterness that by doing her duty, first by her father, then by her husband, fearing to trangress the duty inculcated from childhood and impressed on her, she had gone against her duty to herself, a duty unknown to anyone but infinitely bigger and more important than all. And although Kirill, very nobly and as courageously as he could, had released her from her duty, she felt she was the transgressor of love, because her love had never ceased to live in her, now as well as in the past.

She was conscious of a burning anxiety to soften this sentence over herself and knew that it would be softened, or perhaps even collapse, before a new and higher duty, never before experienced—now that she was expecting a child, but she found this no relief;

CHAPTER

. 38 .

WHEN THE FIRST SLEIGHS were out, Alexander Pastukhov departed from his native town. His luggage had been sent on to St. Petersburg beforehand, so he was traveling light, with a couple of suitcases.

The driver drove his sleigh in fine style, the sound of the horse's hooves and the plop of the clots of snow on the sleigh front could be heard. The wind, stinging like drifting sand, whipped the color into Pastukhov's full cheeks. He wore a high beaver cap, but his coat was open at the throat; he looked about him in relief—the sense of freedom animated him with its vitality and novelty. As he was driven up the long street that stretched like a white ribbon to the station, he kept looking at both sides, at the houses—practically all familiar—and he was saying a last mental farewell to them with a happy smile, rather stiff and cracked from the wind. "Well, that's that, I'm finished with the old ancestral home," he thought to himself, "good-by forever, or, at any rate, till better times!" Yet, involuntarily, he kept finding something elusively pleasant in the past, and delighted though he was at going away, he felt a pang of regret that the past was gone, never to return.

As he drove by the jail, he turned away and stared at the other side of the street until the seemingly endless prison wall was left behind. He sometimes wondered at this peculiar trait in himself—this careful protection of himself from unpleasant impressions: his eyes did not like to look at distressing things.

The university was half covered with scaffolding, veiled with long streamers of snow. Outside the barracks the soldiers, in their shirt sleeves, were briskly clearing the snow off the pavements. In front of the railway station the cabbies drove noiselessly away from the entrance and drew up in a line, their horses more distinct in color now against the snow.

Pastukhov did not call a porter, but, carrying his bags, went slowly toward the first-class waiting room. There were not many people here; officers were drinking strong tea at a long table with palms on it, a merchant was eating scalding hot cabbage soup, ladies in long cloaks were carrying on excited conversations with porters, a large family had settled down around an open basket, and a nurse, breaking up a spiced cake, was distributing it among the children. They were all in winter clothes, and the warmth, permeated with the smell of food and cigarettes, deepened the atmosphere of wintertime.

Tsvetukhin and Mefody came forward to meet Pastukhov, shaking their heads reproachfully as much as to say: there you are, deserting us, you traitor, and we have to stay here and envy you your happiness! They relieved him of the valises and sat down at a small table adjoining an imposing bar, flanked and embellished by large decorative plants. They looked at each other and smiled, each thinking of himself and of what the other might be thinking of him. Then Pastukhov rubbed his hand over his face, chilled with the frost, and said in a pleased tone:

"Nice weather, isn't it? Well, what about a farewell drink?" Tsvetukhin looked up at the clock over the bar.

"There are forty minutes yet."

They ordered Nezhinsk rowanberry vodka and meat pies, then lit their cigarettes.

A gendarme in a long greatcoat passed with a clink of spurs, leaving behind a smell of coarse cloth and kerosene. Pastukhov snorted, made the sign of the cross just above his stomach, and muttered: "Oh, Lord, deliver us!"

The three laughed and took up the glasses that had been filled by the waiter.

"In cases like this," said Pastukhov after a drink, "it is pleasant to look back and, as one may say, draw lessons from the past. You are such splendid fellows! I am deeply grieved that we have to part. I've lived with you long enough for a man to be born into the world. We've gone together to the very brink of the abyss and have not plunged down into it. We've learned, we may say, that miracles do happen. But do we understand ourselves better than we did before the miracle?—that's the question."

"It isn't enough to understand," Mefody said.

"Wisely remarked," Pastukhov said approvingly. "It isn't enough to understand, but still one must understand. Sometimes, in these months, I have felt the waft of the dark wings over my neck. I have asked myself: why should people want to push me headlong into the pit? And I could find only one word in answer: accident. Then the trouble blew over. The wings of the family guardian angel were spread over my defenseless back as in my childhood. I ask myself: why should I have been spared? And again I answer: accident. And now I sit looking at us three and thinking that some mysterious chemical compounds are working within us. When some combine, as in your case at least, Egor, you get your flying kites or your violin. Were others to combine, you would have started to distribute leaflets on the riverside. It's all sheer accident."

"Maybe I'm an actor by accident too?" Egor Pavlovich asked gloomily.

"Yes, indeed!" Mefody said in a hurt tone.

"That's not the point—that you're an actor, I'm a playwright, and he's a chorister."

"Why a chorister all of a sudden?" Mefody demanded, offended.

"Well, not a chorister, then, but a student of theology—it doesn't matter. The point is—why are we all singing our respective tunes in our goaty baritones?"

"Well?" Mefody prompted crossly.

"That's just it—why? Never mind pretending you're wounded in your best feelings. Fill the glasses."

They drank and, munching their pies, sat looking at each other in silence, realizing that no difference could estrange them at this moment.

"We all have days," Pastukhov went on, "when we

cast about from morning till evening for something to do. You start writing verses, you drop in on a friend, you trifle with a girl. And before you know where you are, it's time to go to bed. Sometimes I'm afraid that old age will creep on you like this. And somewhere, hard by, someone is forging our future for us, and, through the wild untrodden woods, torn and bleeding, pushes on toward the goal."

He paused, glanced out of the window, and added: "I mean some good-for-nothing boy."

"Conscience has the claws of a beast," Tsvetukhin smiled. He, too, looked out of the window.

A light snow was falling, such as is sometimes seen on a quiet windless day, when the first flakes seem pensive, wondering whether to fall or not, all but pause in the limpid air, hang imponderable for a moment, then fall uncertainly to earth, yielding place to others as capricious and delicate.

"I've been thinking about that," Tsvetukhin said slowly, "and it seemed to me that we took those absurd accusations as hardly as we did because—you know why? If we had not been accused by mistake but deservedly, for actually having been mixed up in something, then we would have found it easier, don't you think?"

"How true that is!" the faithful Mefody exclaimed.

"The mistake was, perhaps, that we were not doing the things we were accused of."

Pastukhov treated Egor to a penetrating scrutiny, then suddenly burst out laughing. "Playing a part again? And rather overdoing it! And in general, I must say, I somehow don't like you. Tolstoy must have been talking about you when he said that a man who had been tried in a court of law had a particularly noble countenance."

They all laughed, filled their glasses, and Pastukhov raised his higher than before.

"Our lives are much too mental, my friends. I want to drink to our participation in life, less through our minds and more with our bodies!"

Mefody was the first to drain his glass to this, but, after a grunt or two, asked with an air of profound significance: "In what sense, exactly, do you mean that?

"In the sense, my dear theologian, that we are all

just idlers, understand? Loafers. Far nobler would it
have been if we had spent those months in the company
of good women. I can see by your Lenten face, Egor,
that a lofty and beautiful creature is what you most
lack."

"What makes you think I lack one?" Tsvetukhin
asked with a queer earnestness.

"Exactly," Mefody supported him. "Why make these
rash surmises?"

Pastukhov set aside the glass he had not yet finished.
He fancied he saw something lost and bewildered in
Tsvetukhin's expression, as though he was scared to
the point of superstition.

"Has anything happened?"

"It certainly has," Mefody assented with a sigh.

"Agnia Lvovna has turned up again," Tsvetukhin
said quickly, with an awkward, almost shamefaced
smile.

"Why have you kept so quiet about it?" Pastukhov
exclaimed, jumping up and then sitting down heavily.
"But it seems impossible!"

"We didn't want to spoil everything and put you in
a bad humor," Tsvetukhin admitted reluctantly, turning away to the window again.

"And why should it be impossible?" Mefody continued in the same tone. "You have to know the
character actress Agnia Perevoshchikova. She turned
up with her suitcases, her hatboxes, a smoked fish,
a jar of honey, and some faded flowers, dumped them
all down in a heap, burst into tears, kissed him, and
—there she was, hanging up her old playbills on the
wall, trying her contralto, demanding that Egor should
fix her up at the theater and driving me out of the
room. All complete—like the first act of a farce."

"To hell with it!" Tsvetukhin interrupted in a low
tone and raised his hand as though about to thump
the table. But he paused, picked up the bottle with
an attentive look, and then glanced at Pastukhov
with eyes that suddenly softened. "This is a long story,
and hardly suitable for a railway station. Alexander,
say what the last toast is to be—and that's the end.
The second bell's gone."

"Yes, the second bell," Pastukhov said slowly; it
seemed he was trying to understand what the words

meant, but failed. "Well, let's drink to the woman we are looking for and not the woman who is looking for us!"

"A cruel toast," Mefody remarked. "You are depriving the woman you drink to of the great pleasure of looking for us!"

Hastily paying their bills, they made their way out of the refreshment room in the midst of the sudden general bustle and went on to the platform. When the luggage was placed in the carriage, and they had seen that everything was right for the journey, they all three left the carriage again.

Under the roof of the platform, snowflakes were flying, sprinkling the anxious faces with their ephemeral traces. The last mail truck was rushed past with the usual shouts of "way please!" Gendarmes appeared on the scene and stationed themselves at either end.

"We didn't have very long together at the station," Mefody remarked.

"We didn't even drink to art," Egor added mournfully.

"Art, art!" Pastukhov mocked, "you can never settle everything in art, just as you can never say everything in love. Art without misunderstandings is like a banquet where nobody gets tipsy."

"Be sure and write that down, make a note of it in your little red book," Mefody exclaimed.

"It often seems to me that this notebook of mine is full of pointless information. And now I have come to believe that the chief thing is to have an aim in life."

"And I don't seem to believe in anything any more," Tsvetukhin said, in the same apologetic tone. "I don't think I even believe that the earth revolves around the sun."

"Yes, Agnia Lvovna has been a hard blow," Mefody said, nodding his head sympathetically. "But somehow, my dear Egor, when all's said and done, it's of no great importance whether a man believes that the earth revolves or not. It has no effect either on the earth or the man."

Pastukhov leaned over and gave Mefody a hearty kiss. "Socrates!" he gasped right into the broken bridge of the nose.

"A fool talks sense oftener than a wise man talks foolishness," Mefody returned, obviously flattered. "That's why the wise are so much more boring than the fools. More monotonous, anyway."

Pastukhov embraced Tsvetukhin. "Now you see, Egor, you'd better not try to be too clever. Don't fret."

He had just time to kiss both his friends again, and quite happy, jump onto the step of the train. They all took off their hats.

"Take care of each other, my lads," Pastukhov called out from the train.

"We're inseparable!" Mefody shouted back. "We've got the same saint's day—Egor and Mefody!"

"Don't forget us!" Tsvetukhin shouted, raising both hands.

"See you don't forget me either, fellows!" and Pastukhov waved his heavy fur cap.

Mefody mopped his face with his handkerchief and put on his hat. The engine was enveloping carriage after carriage in a shaggy white fur coat of steam, and Pastukhov was swallowed up in it. Mefody took Egor's cap from his hand, put it on his snow-sprinkled dark head, turned him gently around, and led him away.

They hired a cab and drove to the theater. Mefody kept his arm protectingly around Egor. Every now and again he would cough anxiously, trying to read in his friend's glance the faintest trace of a change in his mood. But Tsvetukhin's thoughts were running on one thing.

"It was interesting . . . what Pastukhov said about art," Mefody ventured at last.

Egor Tsvetukhin did not answer.

They were driving through shabby side streets, startling flocks of sparrows and daws from the roadway. Dogs dashed out from the wicket gates, raced after the sleigh, barking without any particular fury but more from enjoyment of a pleasant duty promptly performed and ran back briskly and cheerfully. The frame houses, illumined by the sun, took on a varied coloring against the snow and first seemed to run to meet the sleigh, then swiftly glided past, as though recoiling in fright from the whistling speed of the horse.

"What did you say?" Tsvetukhin asked suddenly.

"I? . . . That . . . er . . ." Mefody was taken aback for a moment. "I was talking about Pastukhov. He was right about art, wasn't he?"

But Tsvetukhin, his chin buried in his collar, had fallen into a reverie again. It was only when they were within sight of Theatre Square that he roused himself at last and said, as though continuing the conversation: "That's an old theory of Alexander's. Once he was explaining something to me about the belfry of Ivan the Great and a matchbox. Of course, he said, you can't get on without a box of matches, whereas Ivan the Great is no earthly use to anyone: you can't light the stove or your pipe with it. Yet anyone in the world who would look at Ivan the Great would say at once that this was Moscow, this was Russia. And he would rattle the matchbox once to see if there was anything in it, and if there wasn't, he would throw it away."

He unfastened the fur sleigh rug, alighted from the vehicle, and, as they went up the steps to the theater, he concluded in a decided tone: "We're going to build our belfry." Then he sighed. "It's a pity Alexander has gone away just now. He would have been the greatest help to me."

"What about me?" Mefody pounced on him. "The both of us? Don't you think we two could manage your trouble?"

Tsvetukhin squeezed his elbow. "Thanks, mate."

With their arms around each other's shoulders, they went behind the scenes.

Rehearsals were going on—a new actress was playing in an adaptation of *Anna Karenina*. The stage manager, a new man, was nervous and querulous. He had evidently resolved to take the bull by the horns and often raised his voice in displeasure. The curtain was up; the auditorium, chilled by the first frosts, yawned darkly before them. Its emptiness looked watchful and mysterious. The rehearsal was not going smoothly; the cast kept repeating and making a mess of their cues.

Suddenly the producer turned sharply toward the auditorium and called out: "Who is there?"

They all listened, peering into the darkness.

"Didn't I say there mustn't be anyone in the theater!" he shouted again, then listened.

"You must have just imagined it," the tragedian said languidly.

"You think I'm drunk? I tell you I distinctly heard a cough out there."

There was dead silence and immediately a stifled cough came from the row of seats.

"I won't allow anyone to make fun of me during work," the manager yelled, rushing off the stage.

At the same time several of the actors, the younger or livelier element, appeared in various parts of the auditorium and moved among the rows of seats.

"There! There!" a hollow voice exclaimed.

"Nonsense! There isn't a soul here!"

"Look, someone's hiding over there!"

"Yes, there he is, look in the fourth row!"

"No, in the fifth! Under the chair, can't you see?"

"Turn on the lights! Turn on the lights!"

They could all make out now a white patch in the middle of the row and, delighted at the unexpected diversion in rehearsals, formed a noisy, excited ring.

"Aha-a!" a sepulchral bass boomed.

"Aha-a!" was echoed in various voices.

"Aha-a! You're caught!" came in a formidable chorus.

Then loud laughter soared in the echoing heights, and the crowd swept the victim toward the exit.

"You're caught!" the gay crowd chanted and yelled, highly amused as, encircling the victim solidly, they tumbled through the narrow door leading to the stage.

"I see nothing amusing at all," the stage manager protested, trying to push through the ring and see whom they had caught. "What's the matter? Who is this?"

The actors fell silent at once and made way, and the manager saw a little girl, who covered her face with her small hands. Her short flaxen pigtail stuck out, her frock only reached to her knees, and one of her red woollen stockings had slid down.

"Who is this?" the shocked stage manager demanded.

"Why, it's Annochka!" an old actress exclaimed, affectionately.

"This is our Annochka!" the actors chimed in chorus. "It's our errand girl! The volunteer messenger, Annochka!"

"It doesn't matter who it is," the stage manager snapped. "Nobody gave you the right to upset the theater arrangements. The theater isn't child's play, you know. Remember that." He clapped his hands and turned away. "Now, ladies and gentlemen!"

"Well, this has brightened us up!" the tragedian drawled approvingly as he came on to the stage with the rest.

Tsvetukhin went up to Annochka. She was still standing there, motionless, unable to take her hands away from her face. Her shoulders twitched from time to time.

"You're surely not crying, are you?" Egor Tsvetukhin asked, stooping and putting his arms around the sharp, quivering shoulders. "Why, you naughty little girl, this isn't a bit like you! What are you crying for, tell me?"

He led her away and, sitting down on the iron steps of the staircase, set her between his knees. "Whatever is the matter, eh?"

He took her hands and parted them gently. Her face was almost indistinguishable now from the flaxen hair: even her lips were white, as though she had been plunged into chill waters.

"Well, what's the matter, tell me?"

"I got a fright," she murmured inaudibly.

He smiled, looking into her large heavy eyes, tear-washed to a deep and shining blue. He stroked and patted her back.

"You little siren!"

"I'm not a siren," she replied promptly.

"Oh, so you remember where you heard that first?"

"Yes, I remember quite well."

"It's a good thing you do," he chuckled, shaking his head. After a moment's pause, he added: "I remember, too."

He stared somewhere away from her, with what seemed a displeased, disapproving glance.

"Look here," he asked, squeezing her more firmly between his knees. "Tell me one thing. Why do you hang around the theater?"

She said nothing.

"Now what's the matter, why can't you open your mouth, tell me?"

But Annochka hung her head again.

"You ought to be going to school instead of scurrying about the theater like a mouse. Well, why don't you say something?"

"Maybe I'll be going to Vera Nikandrovna to live, and she'll teach me," Annochka mumbled, without raising her head.

"And then you won't come here any more? Lost your tongue again? Perhaps I should say it for you, eh? Shall I? All right, I will. Perhaps you come because you want to be an actress when you grow up, is that it? I've guessed it, have I?"

He took her small chin and turned her resisting face up to his.

Annochka's face was suddenly flooded with deep crimson; she looked at him in desperate fright. Then, suddenly leaning toward him as though she was falling, she almost touched his cheek, but recoiled, tore herself from between his knees, and, clearing the paraphernalia that was lying around them, ran away without looking back.

She picked up her shawl and jacket as she ran, threw them around her shoulders anyhow, and dashed out into the street. After she had run around the theater building, she glanced back to assure herself that no one was following her. Then she pulled on the jacket, wrapped the shawl around her head, and pulled up the stocking that had slid down. Reassured, she looked back once more and, as though for the first time, saw the great blue-gray building that she haunted, she knew not why.

The building towered in the middle of a spotless white square, its row of doors, unlike those of any other building, securely locked. A broad balcony supported by iron columns hung over those doors, each column bearing a pair of lamps, bent like an elbow. High over the balcony rose the roofs, first a narrow one, then a wider, and so on—a multitude of roofs of different sizes, some like the peaks of caps, others like belts, and the topmost like a huge umbrella. They were all covered with a level layer of snow, which made the building look as clear-cut as a drawing on smooth, shiny paper. It must have been the largest house Annochka had ever seen.

She trotted straight across the square, across the snow field, raising her knees high as she went and leaving in the snow tracks of her oversize boots, and when she reached the middle of the snowy expanse, she glanced back once more and made up her mind that this was the very largest building of all. She thought for a few moments, and made up her mind that it was the most beautiful, too.

She did not look around any more, and, having crossed the square, went at the pace of grown-up people who are aware that they have urgent matters and obligations weighing on them.

1943-5

KONSTANTIN FEDIN was born in the Russian town of Saratov, on the Volga, in 1892. After training at the Moscow Commercial Institute, he went to Germany for further study. At the outbreak of the First World War he was interned as an enemy alien. In 1918 Fedin went back to Russia, worked in the Commissariat of Education, and served in the political section of the Red Army. He continued to do extensive work as a journalist even after publishing a number of novels. Some of these are: *The Wasteland* (1923), *Cities and Years* (1924), *The Brothers* (1928), and *The Rape of Europe* (1935). *Early Joys*, which is the first volume of a projected trilogy, began to appear serially in 1945. It was awarded the Stalin Prize in 1948. Fedin, who lives in Moscow, is one of the leaders of the Union of Soviet Writers.

THE TEXT of this book was set on the Linotype in Janson, an excellent example of the influential and sturdy Dutch types that prevailed in England prior to the development by William Caslon of his own incomparable designs, which he evolved from these Dutch faces. This book was composed, printed, and bound by The Colonial Press, Clinton, Mass. Paper manufactured by S. D. Warren Co., Boston. Cover design by GEORGE SALTER.

VINTAGE RUSSIAN LIBRARY

V-708	Aksakov, Sergey	YEARS OF CHILDHOOD
V-715	Andreyev, Leonid	THE SEVEN THAT WERE HANGED and Other Stories
V-705	Bauer, Inkeles, and Kluckhohn	HOW THE SOVIET SYSTEM WORKS
V-722	Dostoyevsky, Fyodor	THE BROTHERS KARAMAZOV
V-721	Dostoyevsky, Fyodor	CRIME AND PUNISHMENT
V-709	Fedin, Konstantin	EARLY JOYS
V-707	Fischer, Louis	THE SOVIETS IN WORLD AFFAIRS
V-717	Guerney, B. G. (ed.)	AN ANTHOLOGY OF RUSSIAN LITERATURE
V-716	Kamen, Isai (ed.)	GREAT RUSSIAN SHORT STORIES
V-710	Kohn, Hans	PAN-SLAVISM: Its History and Ideology
V-706	Leonov, Leonid	THE THIEF
V-720	Mirsky, D. S.	A HISTORY OF RUSSIAN LITERATURE
V-703	Mosely, Philip E.	THE KREMLIN AND WORLD POLITICS: Studies in Soviet Policy and Action. A Vintage Original
V-718	Nabokov, Vladimir (trans.)	THE SONG OF IGOR'S CAMPAIGN
V-714	Pushkin, Alexander	THE CAPTAIN'S DAUGHTER and Other Great Stories
V-719	Reed, John	TEN DAYS THAT SHOOK THE WORLD
V-701	Simmons, Ernest J.	LEO TOLSTOY, Volume I
V-702	Simmons, Ernest J.	LEO TOLSTOY, Volume II
V-713	Tolstoy, Leo	THE KREUTZER SONATA
V-711	Turgenev, Ivan	THE VINTAGE TURGENEV Volume I: SMOKE, FATHERS AND SONS, FIRST LOVE
V-712	Turgenev, Ivan	Volume II: ON THE EVE, RUDIN, A QUIET SPOT, DIARY OF A SUPERFLUOUS MAN

V-715 Andreyev, Leonid THE SEVEN THAT WERE HANGED *and Other Stories*

V-158 Auden, W. H., & Isherwood, Christopher TWO PLAYS: *The Dog Beneath the Skin* and *The Ascent of F6*

V-80 Beerbohm, Max SEVEN MEN *and Two Others*

V-93 Bennett, Joan FOUR METAPHYSICAL POETS

V-21 Bowen, Elizabeth THE DEATH OF THE HEART

V-48 Bowen, Elizabeth THE HOUSE IN PARIS

V-79 Bowen, Elizabeth STORIES

V-2 Camus, Albert THE STRANGER

V-28 Cather, Willa FIVE STORIES

V-140 Cerf, Bennett A. (ed.) FAMOUS GHOST STORIES

V-127 Cerf, Bennett A. (ed.) GREAT MODERN SHORT STORIES

V-142 Chaucer, Geoffrey TROILUS AND CRESSIDA

V-146 Clark, Walter Van Tilburg THE OX-BOW INCIDENT

V-155 Conrad, Joseph THREE GREAT TALES: THE NIGGER OF THE NARCISSUS, HEART OF DARKNESS, YOUTH

V-138 Cozzens, James Gould S.S. SAN PEDRO *and* CASTAWAY

V-10 Crane, Stephen STORIES AND TALES

V-722 Dostoyevsky, Fyodor THE BROTHERS KARAMAZOV

V-721 Dostoyevsky, Fyodor CRIME AND PUNISHMENT

V-139 Faulkner, William THE HAMLET

V-5 Faulkner, William THE SOUND AND THE FURY

V-149 Faulkner, William THREE FAMOUS SHORT NOVELS: SPOTTED HORSES, OLD MAN, THE BEAR

V-709 Fedin, Konstantin EARLY JOYS

V-130 Fielding, Henry TOM JONES

V-45 Ford, Ford Madox THE GOOD SOLDIER

V-7 Forster, E. M. HOWARDS END

V-61 Forster, E. M. WHERE ANGELS FEAR TO TREAD

V-8 Gide, André THE IMMORALIST

V-96 Gide, André LAFCADIO'S ADVENTURES

V-27 Gide, André STRAIT IS THE GATE

V-66 Gide, André TWO LEGENDS

V-717 Guerney, B. G. (ed.) AN ANTHOLOGY OF RUSSIAN LITERATURE

V-15 Hawthorne, Nathaniel SHORT STORIES

V-716 Kamen, Isai (ed.) GREAT RUSSIAN STORIES

V-134 Lagerkvist, Pär BARABBAS

V-23	Lawrence, D. H.	THE PLUMED SERPENT
V-71	Lawrence, D. H.	ST. MAWR and THE MAN WHO DIED
V-706	Leonov, Leonid	THE THIEF
V-176	Lowell, Robert	LIFE STUDIES
V-59	Lowry, Malcolm	UNDER THE VOLCANO
V-170	Malamud, Bernard	THE MAGIC BARREL
V-136	Malraux, André	THE ROYAL WAY
V-3	Mann, Thomas	DEATH IN VENICE and Seven Other Stories
V-86	Mann, Thomas	THE TRANSPOSED HEADS
V-36	Mansfield, Katherine	STORIES
V-137	Maugham, W. Somerset	OF HUMAN BONDAGE
V-78	Maxwell, William	THE FOLDED LEAF
V-91	Maxwell, William	THEY CAME LIKE SWALLOWS
V-144	Mitford, Nancy	THE PURSUIT OF LOVE
V-718	Nabokov, Vladimir (trans.)	THE SONG OF IGOR'S CAMPAIGN
V-29	O'Connor, Frank	STORIES
V-49	O'Hara, John	BUTTERFIELD 8
V-18	O'Neill, Eugene	THE ICEMAN COMETH
V-165	O'Neill, Eugene	THREE PLAYS: Desire Under the Elms, Strange Interlude, and Mourning Becomes Electra
V-125	O'Neill, Oates (eds.)	SEVEN FAMOUS GREEK PLAYS
V-714	Pushkin, Alexander	THE CAPTAIN'S DAUGHTER and Other Great Stories
V-24	Ransom, John Crowe	POEMS AND ESSAYS
V-16	Sartre, Jean-Paul	NO EXIT and Three Other Plays
V-85	Stevens, Wallace	POEMS
V-141	Styron, William	THE LONG MARCH
V-63	Svevo, Italo	CONFESSIONS OF ZENO
V-178	Synge, J. M.	COMPLETE PLAYS
V-131	Thackeray, W. M.	VANITY FAIR
V-713	Tolstoy, Leo	THE KREUTZER SONATA
V-154	Tracy, Honor	THE STRAIGHT AND NARROW PATH
V-711	Turgenev, Ivan	THE VINTAGE TURGENEV Volume I: SMOKE, FATHERS AND SONS, FIRST LOVE
V-712	Turgenev, Ivan	Volume II: ON THE EVE, RUDIN, A QUIET SPOT, DIARY OF A SUPERFLUOUS MAN
V-152	Waugh, Evelyn	THE LOVED ONE

VINTAGE HISTORY
EUROPEAN

V-44	Brinton, Crane	THE ANATOMY OF REVOLUTION
V-704	Deutscher, Isaac	STALIN: A Political Biography
V-707	Fischer, Louis	THE SOVIETS IN WORLD AFFAIRS
V-114	Hauser, Arnold	THE SOCIAL HISTORY OF ART (Four Volumes)
V-50	Kelly, Amy	ELEANOR OF AQUITAINE AND THE FOUR KINGS
V-710	Kohn, Hans	PAN-SLAVISM: Its History and Ideology
V-83	Kronenberger, Louis	KINGS AND DESPERATE MEN
V-43	Lefebvre, Georges	THE COMING OF THE FRENCH REVOLUTION
V-92	Mattingly, Garrett	CATHERINE OF ARAGON
V-703	Mosely, Philip E.	THE KREMLIN AND WORLD POLITICS: Studies in Soviet Policy and Action. A Vintage Original
V-719	Reed, John	TEN DAYS THAT SHOOK THE WORLD
V-122	Wilenski, R. H.	MODERN FRENCH PAINTERS, Volume I (1863-1903)
V-123	Wilenski, R. H.	MODERN FRENCH PAINTERS, Volume II (1904-1938)
V-106	Winston, Richard	CHARLEMAGNE: From the Hammer to the Cross

VINTAGE HISTORY AND CRITICISM
OF LITERATURE, MUSIC, AND ART

V-93	Bennett, Joan	FOUR METAPHYSICAL POETS
V-57	Bodkin, Maud	ARCHETYPAL PATTERNS IN POETRY
V-51	Burke, Kenneth	THE PHILOSOPHY OF LITERARY FORM
V-75	Camus, Albert	THE MYTH OF SISYPHUS *and Other Essays*
V-171	Cruttwell, Patrick	THE SHAKESPEAREAN MOMENT
V-4	Einstein, Alfred	A SHORT HISTORY OF MUSIC
V-177	Fuller, Edmund	MAN IN MODERN FICTION
V-13	Gilbert, Stuart	JAMES JOYCE'S "ULYSSES"
V-56	Graves, Robert	THE WHITE GODDESS
V-175	Haggin, Bernard	MUSIC FOR THE MAN WHO ENJOYS HAMLET
V-114	Hauser, Arnold	THE SOCIAL HISTORY OF ART, Volume I
V-115	Hauser, Arnold	THE SOCIAL HISTORY OF ART, Volume II
V-116	Hauser, Arnold	THE SOCIAL HISTORY OF ART, Volume III
V-117	Hauser, Arnold	THE SOCIAL HISTORY OF ART, Volume IV
V-20	Hyman, Stanley Edgar	THE ARMED VISION
V-38	Hyman, Stanley Edgar (ed.)	THE CRITICAL PERFORMANCE
V-41	James, Henry	THE FUTURE OF THE NOVEL
V-12	Jarrell, Randall	POETRY AND THE AGE
V-88	Kerman, Joseph	OPERA AS DRAMA
V-83	Kronenberger, Louis	KINGS AND DESPERATE MEN
V-167	La Rochefoucauld	MAXIMS
V-90	Levin, Harry	THE POWER OF BLACKNESS
V-81	Lowes, John Livingston	THE ROAD TO XANADU
V-55	Mann, Thomas	ESSAYS
V-720	Mirsky, D. S.	A HISTORY OF RUSSIAN LITERATURE
V-77	Mizener, Arthur	THE FAR SIDE OF PARADISE: A *Biography of F. Scott Fitzgerald*
V-47	Murray, Gilbert	THE CLASSICAL TRADITION IN POETRY
V-118	Newman, Ernest	GREAT OPERAS, Volume I
V-119	Newman, Ernest	GREAT OPERAS, Volume II
V-107	Newman, Ernest	WAGNER AS MAN AND ARTIST

V-161	Picasso, Pablo	PICASSO AND THE HUMAN COMEDY
V-24	Ransom, John Crowe	POEMS AND ESSAYS
V-89	Schorer, Mark	WILLIAM BLAKE: *The Politics of Vision*
V-108	Shahn, Ben	THE SHAPE OF CONTENT
V-39	Stravinsky, Igor	THE POETICS OF MUSIC
V-100	Sullivan, J. W. N.	BEETHOVEN: *His Spiritual Development*
V-166	Sze, Mai-Mai	THE WAY OF CHINESE PAINTING
V-162	Tillyard, E. M. W.	THE ELIZABETHAN WORLD PICTURE
V-35	Tindall, William York	FORCES IN MODERN BRITISH LITERATURE
V-82	Toye, Francis	VERDI: *His Life and Works*
V-62	Turnell, Martin	THE NOVEL IN FRANCE
V-122	Wilenski, R. H.	MODERN FRENCH PAINTERS, Volume I (1863-1903)
V-123	Wilenski, R. H.	MODERN FRENCH PAINTERS, Volume II (1904-1938)